I KNEW YOU WOULD CALL

A Marta Goicochea Mystery

By Kate Allen

Other Mysteries by Kate Allen

Tell Me What You Like

Give My Secrets Back

I KNEW YOU WOULD CALL

A Marta Goicochea Mystery
By Kate Allen

NEW VICTORIA PUBLISHERS

Published by New Victoria Publishers Inc., a feminist, literary, and
cultural organization, PO Box 27, Norwich, VT 05055-0027.

Cover photo by Judy M. Sanchez

Printed and Bound in the USA
1 2 3 4 5 6   2000 1999 1998 1997 1996 1995

Library of Congress Cataloging-in-Publication Data

Allen. Kate. 1957—
   I knew you would call / by Kate Allen.
            p.   cm.
      ISBN 0-934678-70-7
      I. Title
   PS3551. L3956K58   1995
   813' .54 -- dc20   95-19140
                                                                 CIP

ONE

"I feel what you're feeling," said Marta Goicochea into the phone, nodding her head as if the woman on the other end of the line could see her. "I can sense that you're really confused about this. You're really feeling lonely—it feels like everyone is attacking you, right?" She was attempting to keep the right amount of sympathy and interest in her voice—half the people who called the Grass Roots Psychics' nine hundred numbers were just looking for a friendly ear and could give a rat's ass about what the cards showed—while simultaneously grimacing at her coworker, Louann, to keep away from the pile of paperback books lying on the Womminsight desk, just out of Marta's own reach. She and Louann both wanted a new Kate Allen mystery that Char, the dyke who worked the night shift, had brought in to exchange, and Marta was damned if she was going to let Louann high-grade the goodies again.

Louann, not at all impressed by Marta's worst scowl, nevertheless clicked her tongue and quit sorting. She picked up a slate from her desk— she was currently speaking on the Hot Woman Talk Line—and, cradling her receiver against her shoulder, wrote on it. "All right, have it, you big baby" with a piece of the colored chalk their boss, Gloria, supplied for communication. She flashed the slate at Marta, holding up the best sci-fi novel in her other hand.

Marta turned away and slapped down two new tarot cards, keeping half an eye in the direction of Louann, who had no honor. The rickety card table on which the Women's Psychic phone sat rocked with her vehemence.

There were three lines served by the Grass Roots Psychic service and each phone reached only as far as the table on which it sat. At first the phones had been on long cords which Louann and Marta and Char could trail over to the refrigerator or bathroom or the ratty old couch, but Gloria, who was Char's girlfriend, and who paid everyone's five dollars an hour paycheck, had shortened them all after Grass Roots Psychics' first week in business. It was not just because of Louann's habit of fixing herself a snack during a session of phone sex—Gloria maintained that chomping in a paying customer's ear killed the mood, though it had never seemed to slow down Louann—it was also because once the phones were moved from their identifying desks it was too easy to mix up the lines. More than one suburban housewife calling to get her cards read on the Women's Psychic line had been driven off by Marta barking, "Dyke Psychics" into the wrong receiver.

"...and I feel like they all the time be telling me what to do, but they don't know how hard it is, or what is in my heart..." a verbal volcano of feeling in the woman on the end of the line, into which Marta needed to break with some delicacy.

"Mmmmm." Practice allowed Marta to draw the sound out so long and loud the reverberation of the line silenced the other woman. "Well, Sherry," she said, hoping, a minute after it was too late to change things, she had used the right name, "We've got some good news and we've got some bad news." Ouch, needed to work on her phrasing. Something a little more cosmic. "We've got the Five of Wands, and of course, that stands for all which is bad in your life right now. It stands for your pain and sorrow. It can even stand for some *enjoyment* of pain and sorrow, and the use of trickery to make you think that something bad for you can be an escape from pain—like the drugs." A telling silence here—time to slide onto the next card before her caller got indignant and suspected she was receiving clandestine drug counseling. "But this is the good news! Right beside him is The Priestess! She represents good! She represents change! She represents powers in you you've forgotten about—the strength to push away the representative of death..."

"Oh, please," said Louann, placing a hand over her own receiver as the woman on the other end worked herself up into an orgasm. "I'm going to be ill."

In the end it was a draining call, but one that gave Marta a good feeling. This meant a combination of things. It meant, if there really was a problem, she felt she had actually given some worthwhile advice. There wasn't always a problem—women called up to chat or because they were bored or because they wanted the cards to validate a choice they had already made. And not all problems were solvable, either. Marta had listened to callers who had described situations of such magnitude there was really nothing to be said besides, "Good luck. You'll need it."

Besides giving the advice, if Marta wanted to feel good about a reading she also had to feel that she had not milked the caller. Grass Roots Psychics and its off-shoots did not charge nearly as high a fee as many 900 numbers, but still, Marta could not come away with a good feeling if she thought she had kept someone poor and desperate on the line too long. There were currently few things that made Marta feel good, so it was important she protect the integrity of her calls.

Louann was still deep into her sex call. There were only two chairs in the room, and Louann, who had snagged the more comfortable early on in the shift, was sitting tilted back with her feet up on the Hot Woman Talk desk. Louann, who always turned herself out so nicely for a night at the bar that you felt you could bounce a quarter off her, acted as if the eight hours she spent every day in the little basement room that Gloria rented for a couple of hundred a month were an extension of her bathroom at home, which was an apartment two flights up. She was currently dressed in a pair of dreadful red sweatpants with half of the crotch ripped out, and a Hothead Paisan t-shirt so old that most of the picture—Hothead and Chicken with a Saturday Night Special—had been worn off. Her straight black hair, short on top, long in the back, which she probably intended on washing later in the bathroom between calls, was crammed up underneath a pink gay-pride cap, worn backwards. She looked as if she had slept in the whole outfit. Louann's mother, whose first language was Korean, would have died of embarrassment if she had seen Louann in this outfit. She was under the impression that Louann was still going to school at DU while she waited for a letter from Julliard.

Louann actually looked worse than Marta, and this was saying a lot, for Marta had been on a personal roll during which she had not showered for over a week. Her heavy, black hair which, washed, hung to her shoulders and caught blue highlights that made the butch girls look after her a second time, was tied up with a ripped red bandanna that did nothing to make things better. The olive skin on her face had that look of neglect a thirty-five year-old woman gets right before breaking out like a fifteen year-old boy, and her jeans, which she had hand-washed in the sink a week before in order to avoid a trip to the laundromat, were best not mentioned.

Still, Louann, who was now clipping her toenails, looked so dreadful that it was actually painful for Marta to listen to her calls while watching her. So she looked instead at the Womminsight desk, which, one boring afternoon after they had just opened, she and Louann had turned into a little lesbian shrine with a can of lavender paint and a glue gun. If they had been men, perhaps there would have been pinup pictures from *Playboy* or *Sports Illustrated.* But, since they were dykes, they had put their own little spin on things. All along the top and sides of the cheap lavender wood were snapshots of old girlfriends chopping wood and petting their cats, glued down between plaster Marys, goddess necklaces, candles, crystals, incense burners and Barbies who had been given buzz cuts. Char, particularly, was a maniac with a glue gun—hardly a week went by that she did not add a bit of tack from the flea market to the lavender desk. Pretty soon there wasn't going to be room for the phone.

The little zing of satisfaction Marta had gotten from the good call had gone, and she looked at her watch despondently. Another hour until she could go home and curl up in her unmade bed. She glanced again at the

Womminsight table. In the middle of the junk glued all around the edges and over the sides, there was a photo of Louann and Char and herself, taken the week they had opened. She had felt like a hot woman then, and it had shown as she stood in the middle with her arms around her coworkers, laughing for the camera. She touched the ends of her dirty hair, wondering when she had last laughed in that way. It was so long ago she couldn't even remember what it had felt like.

"Goddamn!" Louann slammed her phone down. "I hate those girls who want lick fantasies!" Louann was not a private kind of gal, and so Marta knew her own sexual preferences did not include oral sex. She knew, in fact, a little more about Louann's proclivities than she really wanted to know. Still, you couldn't tell that Louann didn't like muff diving while listening to her on the Hot Woman line. Just as Marta had a gift with the cards, Louann had a gift with the ladies. Every woman who paid thirty dollars for a ten minute fantasy hung up feeling that she was the most sexy thing in jeans—or a skirt for that matter—for Louann could talk butch or femme, top or bottom.

Sometimes, in better times, when sex was still desirable rather than a curse, Marta envied her—Louann's gift certainly seemed a more usable talent than her own. Maybe there really were people who could predict winning horses and advise the president and find lost children for the police. But what, really, was the point in being just a little psychic? What was the point in having a little shine that kind of sparked off and on at random? It was a silly gift. It was like having perfect pitch—except for the rare diva, it was nothing more than a party trick. You might argue that it had gotten Marta's job for her, but on the other hand, Louann had gotten hired because she was a good bullshitter, and Char had gotten hired because she was doing the bump with the boss.

Absentmindedly, still wondering about the universe, and gifts, and whether everything that went around really did come around, Marta picked up the receiver of the phone again. "Dyke Psychics," she said, forgetting they were trying to phase out that particular greeting in order to court the yuppie dykes who lived in Wheatridge and Golden. Damn, she had not only not gotten a chance to use the bathroom, she had left her chair at the other table, which meant perching on the desk or crouching on the floor, both uncomfortable. She picked at the edge of a photo—Marta's cousin and best friend Mary Clare posing by her truck —glued to the lavender desk. There had once been photos of Marta's ex, Teri, on the lavender desk, but they had been scraped off one day while Marta was not at work. She did not know if it had been Louann, or Char who had kindly done what she was too weak to do and she did not ask.

"Dyke Psychics," she said again, because there had been no response on the other end. She heard a sound that she had come to dread over her year of working on the line.

A sharp gasp, the sound of a woman trying not to weep.

"The phone didn't even ring," said a woman's voice. Just from the tone, from the way she was choking back tears. Marta knew that this was not what she cared about. Still, she gave her standard answer.

"I knew you would call," she said. It was her best trick, the only one she could do almost every time.

There was a silence that went on for so long that, for a moment, Marta wondered again if she had lost the line. "Are you there?"

"Yes."

A young voice, she thought. She couldn't tell much else through the choked sobs. "It costs just as much when you don't talk. Why don't you tell me what's wrong?"

"I thought you were supposed to be able to tell me." It was a line Marta heard often, but usually it was said in a cocky, prove-yourself-to-me voice. This woman sounded dull and hopeless, as if Marta were the last in a long series of disappointing appeals for help.

"You're depressed," Marta started to say, a statement that Mary Clare, who followed *Star Trek: The Next Generation* with a passionate devotion, would have punctuated with a "Thank-you, Deanna Troi!" In other words, pretty damn obvious, counselor, it didn't take a Betazoid. Which was exactly why Marta was so startled to hear herself say instead, "You're afraid."

"Yes," the woman said in the same dull, lifeless voice, not in the least impressed Marta had guessed, not in the slightest hopeful there would be any out.

"You're alone," said Marta and again there came that lifeless, "Yes." Then there was the sound Marta had long come to recognize as that of the receiver hitting the table, and long, hopeless sobbing. It was not, Marta could tell already, a call which was going to leave her with a zing, but she tried anyway.

"You're afraid," she said again, because more than anything, over and above the despair, this was the emotion leaking through the line. Unasked, she began casting the cards out on the desk. "Are you in danger now? Do you need to go someplace safe? Do you need me to call the police?" As foolish as it seemed, she had gotten calls before from frantic women who had decided to call her first in an emergency, when what they needed to dial was 911. Louann, who could keep an ear on Marta's calls no matter what she was saying to her ten-minute squeeze, tossed her the cellular phone they kept for just such emergencies, and such emergencies only, for Gloria got in a tiff whenever she had to pay the thirty-five cent a minute airtime. If Marta needed to, she could keep the caller on the line until help arrived—again, something she had done before. "Are you in danger right now?" she asked again.

"No," the woman said, gasping it out between dry sobs, and then

5

something that sounded like, "She's not here right now."

"Is it your girlfriend?" asked Marta. "Has she been hurting you?" She reverted to the questions she had learned years ago working on a women's hotline, because frankly she wasn't getting a feel off this call. Or, rather, she was getting way too much of a feel to sort out any one emotion, save the overlying fear. It was as if she had walked into a restaurant and out of the smells of soup and fruit and desert, was trying to pick out the single scent of cinnamon or sage. Most of her calls were that way—either a flat wall of nothing around which she had to maneuver with questions and the cards, or a flood of emotion too jumbled to process quickly. But this woman was sending more even than most—she was at the high end of the bell curve for projecting.

"Because if she's been hurting you, we can find you a safe place to go. I can send somebody to pick you up." Marta's hands fluttered away from the tarot cards she had laid out on the desk and over to the second-hand Roladex she had picked up at the flea market. The women who ran the safe houses in Denver and Littleton and Lakewood and Aurora and all the other suburban communities were used to referrals from her and would, as she promised, drive almost anywhere to pick up a wife or girl-friend who had finally been hit one too many times. For the most part, those kind of calls came from straight women, but there were always a certain number from dykes. 'We're just getting more and more main-stream,' thought Marta bitterly. Aloud, she said, "Should I send someone to get you?"

"No. Don't do that. It's not that. She doesn't hit me." Slowly, the young woman—each time she spoke, Marta edged her age down a notch—was becoming more controlled. "It's not that at all. We can work that out—I know we can." Fear was still the main feel, but as she firmly said these words, Marta also got an uncomfortable, cloying feel in her mouth. The kind of taste you get when your best friend is telling you that things are going to be different with this new girlfriend, this one was going to be the one who really would change, and you both know, not only that she is lying, but that in some part of her mind she knows she is lying. "It's the letters. I got another one today. I can't stand this! I can't stand seeing her and knowing that she's sending me those things!" The fear had edged its way to the top again—whatever the woman was trying to tell her, she really believed that she was in danger.

"Who's sending you—" began Marta, but the woman cut her off.

"I've got to go! I hear my girlfriend pulling up! She'll kill me if she thinks I'm on the phone with another woman—she's so jealous!"

"Wait, wait!" Frantically, Marta cast about for a way to prolong contact. Eighteen months with Teri had made her familiar with jealous girlfriends, and the lengths to which you could go to excuse them. It was because she loved you so much. It was because she just needed some security. It was because other women had cheated on her. It was all a bunch of shit, and even knowing it at the time had made no difference, and would make no difference, either, to the young woman she was trying to keep on the other end of the line. Her eye fell on the business card that she had glued into the phone shrine and surrounded with rhinestones.

"Tomorrow," she said quickly, "Come and see me. At the flea market. The big one, the Mile High. I'll be in space G-77."

There was no reply but for the dial tone. Had she gotten the message? Marta could only hope. She looked at the tarot cards that, face down, she had dealt out onto the table while she had been speaking, and then began to sweep them back into a stack. One fluttered down to the floor, and she picked it up and placed it face up in the center of the table.

The picture was of a skeleton mounted on horseback. The title of the card was "DEATH".

TWO

Gravy, Marta's oldest male cat, was sitting on her back porch, and he began to complain the moment she got out of Louann's truck. The full name of Gravy, a handsome black and white boy whom the vet had pronounced part Maine Coon because of the size of his paws, was Big-Old-Lumpy-Bag-of-Gravy. He had gotten his name by being a master of passive resistance. Trying to push him on or off anything was like trying to push a Ziplock filled with Thanksgiving leftovers. He would envelop her foot while never shifting an inch.

Marta unlocked the downstairs door and Gravy thundered up the two flights of stairs ahead of her, complaining the whole time because he had been locked out the entire day in the cold without food or water. Marta happened to know for a fact that whenever she was out, he spent a good part of his time in the apartment of her sixty year-old lesbian neighbor, Lottie, being fed little treats and groomed with a special brush. Whenever she confronted him with this information, however, he would close his eyes in a pained way, as if she were acting with the poorest of taste by bringing this up. So, for the most part, Marta just accepted his version of reality.

She murmured soothing admissions of guilt and neglect as she sorted through her junk mail. There was nothing worth taking up the stairs, so she tossed the whole stack, free offers and all, into one of the big trash cans on the porch. G-hey!, her across-the-stairs neighbor, who had been called Gail until earlier in the fall, was supposed to put the trash cans out on Fridays this month, but the smell that hit Marta in the face when she lifted the lid told her this had been forgotten. Again. All of them—Marta, G-hey!, Janie and Renee, the rugby players who lived on the second floor and the Queer Nation girls who lived in the basement—were supposed to take turns with the household chores. It was always a relief to everyone when G-hey! went off garbage duty.

At the top of the stairs, Marta could hear the anxious cries of her oldest female cat, Five-Cents. The vet had persuaded Marta to adopt Five-Cents-a-Day over a decade before, when she was the most wretched and neglected of kittens, by predicting that a nickel a day would be the maximum amount ever spent on her. Five-Cents had proven her wrong immediately by refusing to be weaned of the expensive kitten formula she was being bottle fed until she was ten weeks old. being accident prone in her youth (two broken legs and numerous abscesses) and developing. in her old age, a passion for eating anything string-like. An operation so expensive it was embarrassing to discuss had trained Marta to daily check the apartment floor with a devotion usually found only in those engaged in a religious quest, but occasionally something would slip past her, and Five-Cents would happily down a rubber band or piece of Christmas tinsel just for old times' sake. Marta had once supported a car—now she just had an open account at the vet's.

Even more passionate, however, than her love for objects that would lodge in her small intestine, was Five-Cent's adoration of Gravy. She seldom went outside herself anymore, and protested mightily whenever Gravy did. She overwhelmed him with kitty-kisses as he came through the door, simultaneously giving Marta a look of sorry reproach. In the natural order of the cat world, everything was Marta's fault.

Most of the light bulbs in Marta's top floor apartment had been dead for weeks, but just from the hall light, one could see that the apartment was trashed out with a totality that could almost be admired if approached from an archeological point of view. Ah, one could say, picking up the empty boxes of Chinese take-out scattered on the floor, we see that though this civilization had mastered the cultivation of rice, they still had retained the custom of the midden. The absence of string amid the other trash might have been confusing.

Marta had once loved her loft apartment. She had spent weeks decorating when she had first moved in, hanging the walls with bright posters and weavings made by friends. These things were still there, but they had a dingy look, as if their beauty depended on being admired and appreciated, something Marta had not done in months. The plants that she had once cared for like babies were all, except for the cactus, dead and dripping brown leaves.

Near the door sat a beige, touch-tone telephone. The receiver was off, but there was no dial tone. The body of the phone had been painted with permanent markers—it was a perfect little sample of graffiti, though instead of bragging about gang prowess the messages said things like, "Don't call Teri, it only makes you cry!" and "You'll feel humiliated in the morning!" These were overlaid with an emphatic red scrawl in the hand of Mary Clare reading "She was an abusive fuck and dumping her was the best thing you ever did!" This reconstruction of reality was simply a kindness on Mary Clare's part. Teri *had* been so self-centered that she did lean towards the abusive, but everyone knew it was she who had dumped Marta, and Marta's friends further knew Marta would go back to her in a flash given the chance. Not gladly, because she was an intelligent woman who knew damn good and well this was a train she should not ride, but fighting it and in spite of herself, as if Teri were an attack of malaria she had no option but to sweat out. From this point of view, it was lucky that Teri had moved a new girlfriend into her house the very same day she had left Marta the Dear Jane message on her answering machine, for it distracted her from the reunions and breakups with which she had tortured Marta the previous year and a half. Or so Marta, throwing herself down on the couch, told herself and so she repeated to her friends. It helped ground the myth she was trying to be healthy, that she was eating her loneliness like bran muffins and raw vegetables, that she had not had her phone disconnected because she had no will power not to humiliate herself with sobbing calls that Teri wouldn't even pick up.

In reality, however, Marta was tortured by the unbidden images of Teri with another woman, and a twenty-three year-old at that. She had made herself vomit with anguish simply by imagining Teri and the young one—she had taken great care not to know her name—cooking a meal together. Imagining sex could lay her out for a week.

Marta threw herself on the couch without bothering to remove her coat. There was a tentative movement by the door of the one closet. Marta closed her eyes. "There are no kittens here," she droned in a soothing voice. "No kittens at all." She peered out from beneath her lashes without moving her head and was rewarded by the sight of a small black head. "No, no kittens. And if there *were* kittens, no one here would be interested. No one here wants to *pet* or *catch* kittens." She managed to make herself sound horrified by both verbs, as if they were just euphemisms for decapitate.

Assured either by her promise or, more probably, her deathlike pose, a kitten advanced stealthily from the jungle of tennis shoes. Totally coincidentally—for how could you plan something like that with a bunch of strays?—all of Marta's cats had basically the same markings. They were all black with white paws and tuxedo, and looking at them was something like seeing a series of service uniforms from different years. Gravy was a handsome flamboyant dress uniform, and Five-Cents was old and out of date—something from your father's attic. Caught-With-Baloney, whom Marta could see asleep on top of the refrigerator, wore an everyday uniform, and Closet-Kitty was a scruffy, cross-eyed version—the jungle fatigues. With one eye on Marta, a known enemy who had before broken treaties and attempted hideous acts of war such as *picking up*, Closet-Kitty crept beneath the coffee table to the kitchen alcove. Marta caught only the briefest glimpse of black as he dashed across the open space. There was a squawk—he had startled Five-Cents—a hurried crunching— eating under enemy fire—and the rustling that meant he was now hiding

10

back behind the water heater. Closet-Kitty was a feral kitten who had been captured just a little too late for socialization, and this stalking and hiding had gone on for months.

With a sigh—even her cats rejected her—Marta turned on the TV, which was sitting on a metal milk crate not more than ten inches from her face. A grainy black and white picture of Murphy Brown filled the screen. Marta owned a cheap stereo, but music was risky at this stage of the game. Her usual radio station played country western, a genre which Mary Clare, upon finding Marta sobbing in the hall the week before, had pointed out would not even exist were it not for unrequited love. Her personal tapes ran towards John McCutcheon, whose sensitivity could make one cry even when not suffering heartache. The TV was much safer. Murphy Brown did not make you burst into tears and sob until you had to go to bed at seven at night.

Marta knew something needed to be done about her life. She knew that she needed to work out or take antidepressants or go to therapy or get a hobby or goddamn something! But she was as incapable of initiating any of these actions as Closet-Kitty was of suddenly making friends. The only thing she could do was drag herself to work, and then back home again. She thought for a moment of the young woman who had called her, frightened and sobbing, and almost felt a pang of envy. How wonderful it must be to feel an emotion, anything except the dark layer of depression that cloaked her. There were times when she felt almost as if she were feeding off of her callers—as if their fears and joys were the only things which came close to her core. And there were times, like right now, when she just didn't care. Perhaps the woman would contact her at the flea market. Perhaps she would not. Either way, the only thing that matter to Marta now was the grainy little black and white picture playing on the TV, no more than ten inches from her face.

THREE

There were no lights showing in the third floor apartment when Mary Clare Echevarria pulled up in front of Marta's place two hours later. Mary Clare was wearing jeans, which was a given, and a black leather jacket, which was a safe bet on any winter day when the mercury rose above thirty. The one street light—G-hey! and Marta and Janie had been nagging the city people about safer lighting for months, and the Queer Nation girls were threatening an action—shone off the shiny worn patches in both fabrics, and made the seven gold hoops in Mary Clare's right ear sparkle. Mary Clare did not believe in halfway measures. Everything about her was extreme—her jeans were the tightest, her earrings the slickest and her black hair cut the shortest. Mary Clare had attended twelve years of Catholic school, and as early as second grade there had been predictions among the staff that she was going straight to hell when she died. She was now approaching forty, and she had not mellowed a bit. Whatever you were playing, from Trivial Pursuit to soccer, it was a good idea to get Mary Clare on your side right away.

The divided house in which Marta had lived for five years was, like much of Capital Hill, of the Victorian era. It was not one of the charming little single family dwellings with a touch of gingerbread trim that responded so well to a gay man with money. It was a big old white elephant of a house, (even with no birth control and servants it was hard to imagine just one family beneath this roof) and what little grace it might have had in the beginning had been destroyed by poorly conceived additions—laundry rooms and closed-in porches and outside stairs that brought things up to fire code. It was crammed close beside an equally ugly brick building that cut off the sunlight for most of the day. Marta and G-hey!'s apartments were considered primo, because they both had skylights.

Actually, the block as a whole had not made the transition to the nineties well. Denver's Capital Hill was an eclectic mix that often had the power to charm totally. It was delightful to see Gay Pride flags flying in front of renovated Victorians that were backed up against community gardens. People lived in old firehouses and storefronts, painting them up like San Francisco's painted ladies or just letting DeDe LaRue do her stuff. There were occasional pockets where a few stores and restaurants flourished, village style, which encouraged foot traffic and a sense of community.

There were also, however, mixes not as pleasing, and buildings which seemed to be cursed with bad tenants since the day they were erected. Marta's building, though ugly, had been settled with dykes for twenty years. Dykes, of course, were like roaches—once you got them, you could never get rid of them. Any apartment that came up for rent was immediately snatched up by the lovers, exes and friends of the current tenants.

However, all through the summer and fall Marta and her neighbors had been avoiding a crop of skinheads who had sprung up in the new apartments across the street. These apartments were the cheap kind that were flashy for about a month and then dingy until they were torn down. Through some trick of architecture, everything that was said in any apartment with an open door echoed down into the courtyard and out into the street as if it had been shouted through a tin can. As a result, Mary Clare knew more about the skinheads than she did about some of her personal friends. There were always at least six of them sharing an apartment— they were apparently a pack animal. Mary Clare's interest in them was endless.

Mary Clare truly loved people, which was, of course, one of the reasons she was so good at her various counseling jobs. The dykes in the building—except for G-hey! who could be a little too idealistic to live on earth among mortals—had only one line on the skinheads. They were bad crazies. Avoid them. That was it.

It was a good, well supported attitude. The skinheads harassed the dykes when they saw them in front of their building, which wasn't often because of the alley parking behind Marta's building. Everyone was sure that the skinheads were the ones who had broken the windshield of G-hey!'s car, which was ornamented with every queer bumper sticker available locally, and they were equally sure that the skinheads were the ones who had painted the swastika on the front door. The skinheads were a hassle, but not so much of a hassle that anyone was going to move in the middle of winter. Dykes had held the building for twenty years—they could wait out the skinheads. And who could say it was going to be better anywhere else?

Mary Clare, however, could not write the skinheads off so totally as did Marta and her neighbors. She only lived five blocks away, in another renovated Victorian, and she was constantly seeing the skinheads around the neighborhood. They did their laundry where she did and shopped where she did and waited for the bus where she did. Presumably they suffered from lost loves and loneliness and bouts of depression and the stomach flu as she did. So what was it that made them different, that filled them with such hatred? She tended to see them as the carriers of a particular loathsome and vile disease, a kind of modern day leprosy that spread with the ease of a head cold. She felt this would surely devour them in the end, under the most disgusting of circumstances, and there were times when she viewed them almost with a kind of pity.

On this night she was even more interested in skinhead observation than usual. Besides wintering in the building for the first time, the skinheads had done something even more unusual and out of character. Within the last couple of weeks, a girl had moved into the apartment. Girls had been known to stay before, but they had never actually seemed to live there, and they had always seemed to be the property of one, usually the dominant, male. As far as Mary Clare could tell, this girl was no one's squeeze. Perhaps in order to maintain this position, she seemed to have become something of a house drudge. Now, as Mary Clare watched her, she was humping a cardboard box full of laundry up the stairs. It was not her own laundry—Mary Clare thought that the girl had only one pair of jeans, and a light jeans jacket not nearly warm enough for a Denver winter. Her laundry did not fill a box.

Mary Clare stood, holding her groceries, and watched her wrestle the box to the second landing before she walked around back to Marta's door. She had tried to park in the back, but G-hey!'s new girlfriend, Salad, had a big truck and poor parking manners, so Mary Clare was finding herself on the street more and more these days. She didn't mind—she liked to get in a few minutes of skinhead watching. Maybe someday she'd write a paper.

The light on the stairs that led to G-hey! and Marta's apartments popped and went out when Mary Clare flipped the switch. Mary Clare was not surprised, but she was dismayed. Marta was probably upstairs in the dark without even the TV on. At this point even an interest in really junky TV like *Charles in Charge* would be hopefully viewed as a good sign. She barked her shin in the dark and swore loudly. Marta had begun abandoning things—her laundry, bags of kitty litter, groceries, and from the smell of it, trash, halfway up or down the stairs. It was as if getting them in or out of the house sapped what little energy she had.

Mary Clare was cursing full force by the time she finally shoved her way to the top landing. There was a strong school of thought these days, and it was especially strong in the lesbian community, that deemed nothing worse than codependent behavior. This school, Mary Clare knew, would highly disapprove of her almost daily visits to Marta's place. They would cluck over the fact that she brought groceries—which this week included light bulbs—and shoveled out the kitchen and occasionally even bullied Marta into the shower. These people would feel there would be no reason for Marta to ever get better unless she were allowed to hit bottom herself. These people, thought Mary Clare, could go to hell. Again, it was a question of looking at everything in absolute terms of black and white and this was not an ability Mary Clare possessed. Yes, codependency was bad, enabling was bad, but wasn't it also bad to allow Marta to waste away in the dark, grieving over a woman as thoughtless and selfish as Teri?

Marta and Mary Clare had become friends only as adults, but still, they had known each other for almost their entire lives. Marta had helped Mary Clare move more than once, had lent her money during bad times, had taken her keys away from her on nights when she was too drunk to drive, and had kept her, on those same nights, from going home with women who were known to be bad news. She had watched Mary Clare's cats when she went out of town, and comforted her when two of those cats died from feline leukemia, never once suggesting the grief that lasted for months was excessive. Marta had helped her paint several apartments and had accompanied her to court in order to get a restraining order after a particularly volatile love affair (which would never have gotten off the ground had Marta been in town) had gone bad. It was not that Mary Clare had not done these things, or similar things for Marta as well, for she had. The point was—if Marta needed to have a nervous breakdown, Mary Clare could live with the role of caregiver for a couple of months. After all, who knew when she herself might slip off the deep end? She'd want Marta to be looking out for her then.

Of course Mary Clare had her own keys to the apartment, which was good, because lately Marta had taken to just lying there on the couch if G-hey! or Salad knocked.

Sure enough, there she was, with all of the cats except for Closet-Kitty arranged on top of her. She didn't even move her gaze away from the TV screen when Mary Clare came in, but the cats looked at her in an annoyed manner, as if they had been in the middle of a difficult healing ritual, and she had broken their concentration.

"The skinheads have a girl living with them," said Mary Clare, as she put a new bulb in the lamp on the coffee table. This lamp, and the one above the sink, were the only ones she could reach without standing on a step stool or chair, and her codependency did not extend to climbing up on things. Marta was almost six feet tall, and Mary Clare was only five two. Marta could put in her own damn bulbs.

Marta considered this for a long moment. "The cops were over there again the other day," she finally said. Since the skinheads could not be turned down like the TV, one tended to follow their plot line. "Also, they hassled G-hey! yesterday."

"They're just pissed because she looks better with a mohawk than any of them do." Mary Clare spoke lightly, but her blood ran cold at the thought of G-hey!, Marta's twenty-one-year-old neighbor, exchanging words with any of the skinheads. Mary Clare might be interested in their motives and living habits, but she had no delusions about their danger when it came to queers. Watching them was like watching feeding at an animal park —you didn't get out of the car, and you sure as shit didn't try to go in and take the kill. "I thought they pretty much left you alone."

"Pretty much. We use the alley, they use the street. And there's a lot of us. G-hey! was canvassing for the Recall Two campaign—she went over there for signatures." There was a silence, as both of them contemplated this act of idiocy. The problem with G-hey! was that, in her zeal to change the world and break down all barriers of prejudice and hatred, she acted as if those things just didn't exist. It *should* be safe for a young woman to walk along Colfax at eleven o' clock at night—therefore it *was* safe and she did it without a second thought. All people *should* be in support of recalling Amendment Two, the gay-hate bill pushed through by the religious right, calling themselves Coloradans for Family Values, the previous November—therefore all people were. G-hey!'s friends lived in daily fear that she was going to get the shit kicked out of her.

"Well," Mary Clare said finally, unable to think of anything to say about G-hey!'s approach to life that had not already been said by older and wiser women. "Why did the cops come? Another fight?"

"No. They lit a dumpster on fire."

"They did what?" Mary Clare, who had been shoveling fast food containers from the floor into a trash bag she had brought with her, stopped to make sure she had heard this right.

"Oh, yeah, they all got drunk one night"—this particular group of skinheads needed to visit the AA house over on York Street five or six times a week—"and just set it on fire. They were all standing around it when the cops came, like it was a bonfire. They were probably roasting wienies and marshmallows." It was a rather exciting story, but Marta spoke in a disinterested tone, much more focused on the figures on the TV screen.

Mary Clare pursed her lips. This was dismaying news. She wondered if she should pull her fire extinguisher out of her truck and carry it upstairs for Marta, in case the fire thing turned out to be a fad and not an isolated incident. She looked at her and shook her head. No point in it. The way Marta had given up on life, the skinheads could probably set fire to her own building, and she would just lie there on the couch, wondering what was fucking with her reception.

"I got a strange call today," said Marta, and then was silent again, for Jordie Le Forge, the blind head of engineering on the Starship Enterprise, was obviously bonding with a young Borg, and following without sound was a challenge.

"'Run away with me.'" Mary Clare said, supplying the conversation.

"'Let me introduce you to a world of virtual sexual reality and sex toys beyond your imagination.'"

"Data is going to be unhappy," said Marta. "I thought he and Jordie were doing the monogamy thing."

Marta and Mary Clare, who had been raised in a third generation Basque community in Idaho, were a part of that huge group of baby boomer lesbians who had grown up in small western towns and cities in the seventies, and then split for Denver or San Francisco or Portland or Seattle once they had gotten old enough to stick out a thumb. They were some kind of shirttail relations, involving second marriages and the sisters of great-grandmothers. Because they were within ten years of age (Mary Clare was the elder by two years) everyone in their large extended family simply referred to them as cousins. Mary Clare called this the *Reader's Digest Condensed Version of Genealogy*. If the age difference had been over the ten year limit the older of the two would have been deemed the younger's aunt.

It was not a bad system. It enabled the Old World concept of the big family to work smoothly without getting bogged down in distracting blood lines.

They had both grown up being taught there were two main rules concerning family. The first was—family is more important than anyone else. Two was—everyone whom your grandparents force you to call cousin is your family. Like all clans, there were both advantages and problems to the system. Advantages—if one was Basque one could travel all across Idaho and Montana and never have to pay for a hotel room or meal. Likewise, when your mother had to be hospitalized for an operation, you could go to the house of your Aunt Joanie who lived two doors down and hardly realize there had even been a break in routine until bedtime.

The disadvantage, of course, was that you might become involved in supporting, shielding or even lying to the police about some old man who had once produced a child with your father's cousin's grandmother long after she had totally wiped the incident from her memory.

The extended Basque family also produced a finely tuned gossip and spying network, which family members tended to regard as good or evil depending upon their age. Basque teenagers all over not only Boise, but clear out into Nampa and Caldwell complained loudly about lack of privacy. However, mothers worried about drugs, premarital sex and dating Mormon girls blessed the hot line. Marta's friends sometimes complained about the fishbowl aspect of the lesbian community, but frankly, it was amateurish compared to the network of Marta's aunts and cousins. Marta had never once, in three years of high school, cut class, shoplifted, stayed out late to cruise Main when she told her mother there was extra band practice, or spent the night with an unapproved friend, that she had not been busted before she even got home.

So, when Mary Clare Echevarria, who had fled to Denver the moment she had graduated from high school, returned home for her brother Joey's funeral in '76, Marta, who was half-heartedly attending Boise State University while still living in her parents' home, already knew quite a bit about what was happening in her life before she even saw her across the open grave at the old cemetery. She knew, for example, that Mary Clare was going to appear in pants, and that the subject of the pants was so volatile it had threatened to overshadow the more immediate scandal concerning Joey's sobriety at the time of his motorcycle accident. She knew Mary Clare's father, who was, like his twenty-four year-old son, a drunk, had forbidden her to come to the ceremony unless she could show some respect for the dead by dressing like a decent woman and that Mary Clare had told him to fuck off, adding that she didn't want to have her ass uncovered around the evil bastard even if he was dead. A bomb dropped on relatives remaining in Spain could not have caused a bigger furor or more traffic over the phone lines, and like everyone else, Marta covertly divided her attention between Mary Clare, who was not only the sole woman in pants, but further had her dark hair in what was almost a buzz cut, and Joey's younger brother, Jimmy, who had been a passenger on the bike. He had escaped with his life, but his braces had been shoved up into his gums by the force of the impact and his mouth and face were swollen beyond decency, as if he had been dead and rotting for several days himself. The ceremony was closed coffin, and no one whose eyes rested on Jimmy even for a moment could help wondering in what state Joey was lying within. "Shoveled off the sidewalk," was whispered more than once. Like his father and brother, alcohol was Jimmy's drug of choice, but since his mouth was still an open mass of sores from which the doctors would be picking bits of gravel and splinters of steel for weeks, he had opted for getting as high as connections with the best pot dealers in Boise would allow.

No one had been surprised by the accident. The Echevarrias were the traditional black sheep and scapegoats of the family. It had started innocently enough several generations before when one of Mary Clare's great-grandfathers had married a young Mormon girl. It would be hard to say who had been more scandalized by the union—his family, her family, or the local community of German and Swedish stock farmers, who regarded both minority groups with some disdain. The Mormons had settled for ostracism. (It turned out later there had been a certain amount of relief involved in this decision and that the marriage was even referred to once or twice as god working in mysterious ways. Apparently this girl, who was actually still alive and cruising as late as Marta's sophomore year of high school, had a bad reputation for carnal activity, and her family had become resigned to her continuing to live at home for the rest of her life, for no decent young Mormon man would have her.)

The Basque community at that time was made up almost solely of unmarried young men who had been sent by their families to America to either keep them out of local trouble or with hopes they would find a better life far from home and eventually bring their families to join them. At home, in the Spanish Pyrenees, they had been fishermen. In Idaho and Montana, they had been put to work as sheep herders. It was a job where English was not necessary. They were strong Catholic boys, all engaged or married to girls back home to whom they sent most of their paycheck.

When Rubin Echevarria, who had been sent away from his home to avoid talking to a judge about a neighbor's chickens, had first started making eyes at the slutty Mormon girl, his comrades had brought out the big Catholic gun—guilt. What could Rubin be thinking? What would his mother think about him consorting with an infidel! It would put a blot upon the entire family!

But Rubin was eighteen years old, and none of his friends and cousins were speaking to the head with which he was thinking. Though talk of homeland and loyalty to family might have been effective before the elopement, they were frankly poor weapons following the couple's return from Twin Falls (which is where they had to go to find a priest who would perform the ceremony). First of all, anticipating exactly this kind of attack, Rubin had insisted he and his bride not only stay away almost a week, but spend one night together in a hotel as well, so there could be absolutely no question at all of their having shared a bed, thus cutting off the question of annulment. Second, it was almost immediately evident that Rollene, his wife, was pregnant, and that seemed to seal the fate of the marriage. None of the good Catholic men could, in all conscience, bring themselves to urge a man to abandon his pregnant wife.

There was some hope in the beginning that the problem would be solved by the bringing forth of a child who was redheaded or had the blond Swedish mop—anything but the swarthy, Mediterranean Basque look—but that was squelched almost immediately after the ten hour birth. Anyone who had ever seen the nose of Juanito Echevarria next to that of his father would have had to be a liar to question paternity.

Mary Clare's great grandparents had not been bad people—at least individually. They had not been any stupider or more thoughtless or less law abiding—except for that one chicken incident—than any of their relatives. Maybe they would have turned into a model, loving couple had it not been for the fact that everyone they knew so obviously expected the worst of them. Being thought the worst of and treated like outsiders are hard handicaps to fight. Eventually, faced with the prejudices of both families, they had turned into their own stereotypes, and had settled down to produce a dynasty of drunks, fiddlefoots, con artists and laggards.

This had all been in the head of eighteen year-old Marta Goicochea as she watched her cousin Mary Clare across the open grave. She had not been close to Mary Clare as they were growing up. They had overlapped at the Catholic High School, and been to a million family Thanksgivings and Christmases and First Communion parties together, but Mary Clare had been a wild kind of girl with a reputation, and the good girls had shunned her. But as Marta, who had been sneaking up to the second floor of the public library to read from *Sappho Was a Right-On Woman* and *Loving Women* looked at Mary Clare's angry hair cut and the pin on her jacket that said 'Sister', she began to wonder if, possibly, she were not the only one in the world with the strange feelings she had about women. She began to wonder if perhaps they ran in the family. Mary Clare had driven back to Denver after two days of fighting—and Marta went with her.

To a certain extent, this background had colored Mary Clare and Marta's friendship as adults. Mary Clare knew that, even if it were not for the loyalty she felt for Marta, she would still be there throwing out her diseased food. She would not be able to survive the onslaught of commotion that would radiate back to her from her relatives were she to allow Marta to just waste away. Their background also affected some of the things she had been wanting to tell Marta lately—some of the secrets that had been kept for far too many years. As Mary Clare put the cans of soup she had carried up the stairs into Marta's cupboard, she opened her mouth to tell her about her weekend. This was the moment when she was going to say the words.

"I got a weird phone call at work," Marta said again. Repeating herself was something she had begun to do more often as she lost her thread of reality.

"Oh? What was it about?"

"I'm not really sure. She was too upset. But I'll tell you tomorrow— if she meets me." Then, without even turning her head away from the screen, Marta was asleep. The light of the TV flickered eerily over her face.

Mary Clare sighed. The moment for talking had been lost again.

She stayed half an hour longer, long enough to do the worst of the dishes, and to change the boxes of the grateful cats. Then she let herself out the back, locking the door behind her.

FOUR

Mary Clare was late to the flea market the next day, which Marta took to mean she'd had a date and gotten lucky, something that hadn't happened in ages. Marta, who had an arrangement with Louann to use her truck on Saturday mornings, thought about this as she showed her pass to the guard at the gate of the vendors' parking lot. It was only nine, but the flea market was hopping, for the day was already living up to the weatherman's prediction of unseasonably sunny. As Marta wrestled their table, four folding chairs and signs onto a dolly, thinking with a flash of resentment how much easier this job was with two, she was surrounded by a flow of vendors and customers dressed in that odd Denver winter combination of tank-tops and snow boots. The eighty-eight acres of blacktop — the largest flea market in Colorado!—had been plowed, but an inch of icy water from the giant piles of snow stood everywhere. Marta saw the four children belonging to the Korean couple who ran the sock stand next to her regular spot playing King-of-the-Mountain with a bunch of Latino kids on top of one of the snow heaps. She winced when the littlest girl took a thump in the chest that made her fly down the parking lot side, envisioning her crumpled under the tires of some truck loaded with secondhand office supplies, but a moment later she came scrambling up again. Marta turned away before she could predict any new disasters.

She did not begrudge Mary Clare getting lucky. She did not, in fact, begrudge Mary Clare all the hot, fantastic kinky sex she could get. Let her go to a play party a night, let her answer Sapphaphone ads—let her do it all. Just let her not get a girlfriend. She knew it was selfish, but Mary Clare with a girlfriend was fucking worse than useless. Asking to see Mary Clare during affairs usually resulted in a vague put-off, for Mary Clare with a lover was a woman obsessed. Her schedule existed only to accommodate the woman upon whom she was currently fixated. Firm plans with anyone else were out—everything had to be left open in case a few extra moments of passion (or hysterical fighting, depending on the stage of the relationship) could be squeezed in. Even talking on the phone was a problem, for one always sensed Mary Clare's nervousness lest your call cut off the one from *her*. Mary Clare with a lover was, to put it bluntly, a royal pain in the ass whose friends were always in various stages of alienation. Marta needed Mary Clare too badly herself now to give her over to some stranger who would just use her up and throw her away.

The space on the other side of the slot Marta and Mary Clare rented each weekend was usually occupied by a biker couple who sold Harley memorabilia and vulgar hat pins. Abe, the man, saw her trying to dodge the crowd in front of the sock table and came out from behind his counter to help her. He looked out for Marta because he and his girlfriend were good buds with Mary Clare. He liked Mary Clare because she could talk about bikes just like one of the guys. Pamalita, the girlfriend, liked her because she could confide all of her current and past sexual experiences and never worry about Mary Clare lifting an eyebrow or trying to steal her man.

Neither one of them quite knew what to think of Marta, whom they both obviously thought was Mary Clare's main squeeze, and just as obviously thought a little boring for a fine, high-spirited girl like Mary Clare. Still, as long as she didn't bat Mary Clare around, in which case Abe would have been honor bound to flatten her, it was only the code of the road to give her the respect accorded Mary Clare's old lady.

Today Marta was grateful for their misunderstanding, because one of her bungee cords had come loose and she was dragging a corner of the big sign that G-hey! had lettered for them. Experience with last year's winter market had made Marta paint this second sign with hull varnish, as the first one had been horribly warped by continually standing in two inches of water. Still, dragging one corner across the black top was not prolonging its life any.

Mary Clare had written the text of the sign. In two inch, black letters it said: *It costs too damn much to get someone to listen. Do those people with the high-rise offices think that you have to be rich to be stressed out? I have the same skills and training as any Cherry Creek therapist, but I'm a working class woman and believe in being available to other working class people. You're not paying for a fancy office, you're not paying for a nice address. You're just paying for some who will listen—and help.*

It drew customers in like flies. Everybody had ten dollars—the cost of half an hour—at the flea market. Business had been particularly good for Mary Clare since the dyke population had clued in to the flea market and started coming out, particularly for a session at an unbeatable price. Mary Clare was fussy, however, about her clients. If she thought she was being scammed by a guppy who was just bargain hunting she had no qualms whatsoever about doubling her price in a second. She had a sliding scale—it just slide up.

It helped repeat business, of course, that Mary Clare was actually very good. She did, as the sign claimed, have a fair amount of training and had worked in a couple of drug and alcohol places until becoming too burnt out. Now she did the flea market gig and picked up jobs here and there, running groups, teaching classes, and occasionally stocking shelves over at Wild Oats when one of their people was out, just to make ends meet.

In addition to being good with advice, Mary Clare had a skill that Marta envied—she had the air of caring deeply about every single person who could slap down ten dollars. Abandoned lovers toying with the thought of suicide, unwed teenage mothers and men going through mid-life crisis all went away with the feeling that at least one person in the world really gave a shit. If you could have bottled it, you could have sold it.

Marta, shuffling her flea market tarot deck, was too fair not to know this last was actually an unjust thought born of irritation at Mary Clare's lateness and jealousy of her way with people. Acknowledging it did not make her feel any better.

Her flea market deck was a traditional tarot, not the Motherpeace deck she sometimes used at work, though she did have that deck with her in case any dykes came by. The flea market crowd did not appreciate the naked dancing women on the Motherpeace deck—they wanted every-body clothed and familiarly symbolic. A crowned woman could easily be seen as good, a hanged man as bad, but how the hell did you interpret three Amazons prancing around a fire? But don't think for a minute just because people were coming to her as an expert they treated her with deference. Hell, no, they argued with her about her interpretations, wanted to pick up and finger the cards. Which was another reason she didn't use the Motherpeace deck and why she sprayed her main deck with Scotchguard every week after wiping off two days worth of roasted chilies, cotton candy and flea market hot dogs.

She began to lay the cards out on the table in an alluring fan. Mary Clare had been trying to get her to smarten up things with some kind of exotic table cloth, but she had thus far resisted, just as she had stubbornly resisted wardrobe suggestions having to do with long skirts and scarves. She didn't wish to attract a clientele who expected to cross her palm with silver and be told about tall, handsome strangers, even if it might be more profitable.

A child on a Big Wheel raced by, splashing her legs with a fine spray of water. His parents followed far behind, pretending they were not with him. They were obviously aware he was spraying people right and left and just as obviously had made the decision that with the right amount of disassociation no stranger would bother to confront them. Marta, watching him clip an old Latino man while executing a U-turn, decided she was in just foul enough a mood to shoot that hope to shit.

"Hey," she said in a loud voice, "your kid just got me soaking wet." The couple ignored her and continued sauntering along without varying pace. They were obviously old hands at this game. Marta, who had merely been annoyed up to this point, became fired with a fury that was totally out of proportion to the event and screamed, "Hey! You two! Yeah, you in the sleazy red tank top! You're not supposed to have any riding vehicles on the blacktop! You either take that goddamn trike away or I'll call security and have them do it!" All the vendors and most of the customers stopped to watch the scene with interest. A free show at the flea market was always good—it made you feel like you'd gotten your money's worth out of the admission price even if you couldn't find any pants that fit. Obviously Marta was overreacting, but she had the advantage of being on home turf, surrounded, as it were, by her own team members in the form of other regulars who were either leaning over their tables looking menacing or standing and talking rapidly and censoriously in another language, according to sex and culture.

"Fucking dyke," said the father, flicking his eyes sideways towards her for the quickest of seconds. He was, Marta knew from previous experience, merely throwing out the worst insult he could think of.

"Oh, hurt *my* feelings," said Marta scathingly. Those in the know snickered. "Corral the kid, Scooter-trash." This was an insult Abe and Pammie had taught her and she wasn't sure exactly what it inferred, but it seemed to hit home. The woman let out a shriek and turned her way as if to leap over her table.

Unfortunately for the couple, at this moment the child, heady with power at the near toppling of the old man, ran his Big Wheel full speed into the twin stroller of two little girls whose parents were inspecting car parts. There was instant pandemonium. The twins, who couldn't have been more than eighteen months old, shrieked with fear and tried to climb out of their seats, which put them in more actual danger than the collision had. As was the custom among many of the Latino families who frequented the market, they had come straight from church and were dressed in identical dresses of pink dotted Swiss trimmed with lace, now splashed with mud. Their entire family, which turned out to be numerous as well as multi-generational, swarmed to the rescue and began berating the hapless parents in Spanish, backed up by ninety percent of the booth owners. Some, like Marta, were fed up with out-of-control kids, while others were just bored.

The father, who was at least smart enough to realize that if it came to blows the neighborhood was traditional—he was the one who was going to get the shit kicked out of him—decided a hasty retreat was in order. He jerked the child off the trike with one hand and picked up the offending three-wheeler itself with the other. The little boy began to shriek in the long practiced way of a tantrum thrower, gathering huge breaths of air like a diver. The twin girls were shocked into silence by his expertise. They clung to their mother and grandmother and watched with envious eyes.

"Did it ever occur to you," said Mary Clare coming up behind her, "that it's time to get a little professional help?"

"Oh, the gypsy curse to you, too," said Marta crossly as she slammed herself down in her chair.

"Seriously," said Mary Clare. "Don't you think it's a little strange that you have these two totally diametric modes—absolute zombie and insanely angry?" She had switched to Basque, which she often did at the flea market. It was partly a matter of privacy, but mostly because she theorized the exotic language drew customers to Marta. Neither of them could write or read a word of Basque, and as they had learned their vocabulary from talking with their parents and grandparents, their Basque conversations were always sprinkled with a number of English words. The percentage depended on the topic and whether it was something they'd the occasion to discuss with their grandparents whom all the children had called Mooma and Cheecha, from the harder to master Amuma and Aitxite. In these two sentences, for example, Mary Clare had used the English words diametrically, zombie, and had also used a Basque phrase for crazy person that Marta was almost sure was not applied to dramatic actions. They could both curse quite fluently, and Mary Clare could also talk about fencing stolen goods, drugs, and creative ways to turn your car's odometer back before selling.

"Gypsies *are* temperamental," Marta replied with a laugh, using the English for the last word. She tried to put the right note of warning in her voice to tell Mary Clare that was enough of this topic, thank you.

Mary Clare, though obviously getting the warning, decided to ignore it. "This is the third time this week I've seen you so angry over some stupid little thing that you're shaking."

"Come on! You know how these people are with their damn kids—"

"No, you come on! If it's not the kids, it's something else. You almost lost it the other day in the store because they overcharged you ten cents on tofu. (English) You're not angry about kids, or tofu or your job—you're angry about Teri, and you need to get it off your chest."

"You may have noticed," Marta said, "that I did not put down ten dollars to be psychoanalyzed. (English) In fact, I will pay you ten dollars if you will just shut the fuck up and mind your own business."

"You're lucky you have me to care about you and be honest with you," retorted Mary Clare hotly, "because everybody else is just starting to get tired of it." They actually were beginning to draw a little crowd, for Mary Clare, as was her custom, was throwing her all into the argument. Though Marta was dressed in the olive drab and brown colors she had pretty much adopted as a uniform lately, Mary Clare was wearing full leather that included an array of studded bracelets and a harness over her black tank top. The only thing spoiling the outfit were the second hand L.L. Bean boots her leather pants were tucked into. She looked as if she was going to do some serious partying and then go sit in a duck blind.

Mary Clare's ten o'clock—a regular—strolled past, and she got up and followed without saying good-by. After reading *The Great Escape*, Mary Clare had started doing most sessions on foot, walking the boundaries of the market for privacy while talking, just as the prisoners had walked the compound. Mary Clare liked a little drama.

Marta sat in one of the rickety folding chairs. Her hands were shaking as she slapped the cards down. "Fuck other people," she muttered aloud. That was a blow which had hit home. She already knew her friends and coworkers were tired of her depression, and it seemed no more fair than being impatient with a lingering and possibly fatal illness. Did they fucking think she wanted to behave like a zombie? To her horror, she realized she had begun to cry. This was one of her least favorite symptoms, and it had begun to manifest more and more frequently. To date any episode of *The Waltons*, any human interest story in *Reader's Digest,* three-fourths of all current country songs, certain cat food, Kodak and long distance commercials could set her off with absolutely no warning. She was, she thought, blowing her nose on the handkerchief she had become resigned to carrying at all times, like one of those cars which could go from zero to ninety in sixty seconds.

"Hey." The greeting came from a woman standing no more than two feet away. Marta lifted her head crossly.

"Hey what?" she said in an irritable voice, not trying to hide the fact that she was crying, for she had cried so much within the last six months she had finally just resigned herself to it as if it were a tick or a birthmark.

"Hey...," repeated the woman, "...there." She smiled weakly. She was a dyke. If one of Marta's straight friends had asked her to defend this instant conclusion, she might not have been able to break down her reasoning, for things were no longer as clear as they had been when Marta was in her twenties, but she knew she was right. In fact, and here her heart sank a little, she could clearly see through her tears, not only was this woman a dyke, she was a young, cute dyke. Just like Teri's new girlfriend. Fuck. And Marta could tell, just by her stance as she stood pressed up against the table, she expected to be helped. If Marta had owned a gun she would have shot her. She had no trouble understanding these shooting sprees which seemed to be so fashionable now—'Out of work mail carrier shoots twenty-three and self—Police, neighbors are baffled.' Okay, she would think, when she read the paper, I can understand that. She could imagine blasting the dance floor at the women's bar, and Teri and her girlfriend didn't even have to be in the picture. It was enough that all those other women were happy and coupled when she wasn't. They deserved to die for that. The thought of the carnage served as an icon for her pain.

She shook herself out of her fantasy. Mary Clare was right—she did need professional help. "Yes," she said to the young woman with the fashionably spiked hair, "can I help you? Do you want a reading?" The woman hesitated, biting her lip. She was what Marta, feminist trained in the seventies, would call a woman, but her parents would still refer to as a girl. Say twenty-one to twenty-three. Pretty. Femme. The type that in the summer would wear kicky little culottes outfits and short skirts.

"I..." she hesitated again and then lifted her head to look right into Marta's eyes. "I talked to you."

Oh. Okay, now she got it. Now, in fact, it hit her like a little wave— I'm frightened someone wants to hurt me I have nowhere to go. This was the woman for whom she had felt so over the phone. Rather automatically, Marta motioned her back behind the table. It had been much easier to feel sorry for her over the phone, when she had not had to face an image that made her feel old and unattractive.

The young woman hesitated visibly. She was not part of the regular flea market crowd—she did not understand the attitude of communal living which would make her invisible sitting behind the table. At the flea market you could eat or sleep or practically fuck as long as you were in your own space, and everyone's eyes slid politely past. It was what Marta imagined it must have been like to live crammed together in a cliff dwelling or a cave. With a sigh, Marta hoisted herself ungraciously to her feet. She shoved the legal pad on which people could write appointments to the front of the table: Out to walk the fence.

"Don't you—" asked the young woman, tentatively, as Marta took her arm. She looked back over her shoulder.

Marta, interpreting the look correctly, said, "Look. You can have the cards—for which we're both going to have to sit down, or you can have the walk. Which is it going to be?" Then, aware that, as bedside manner this was a little lacking, she added in a less brusque manner, "The cards are a tool. I can do a reading for you after we talk, if you still want me to. But they're only a tool." In fact, she was already getting such a vibration off this woman that she felt like she was clutching a live wire in her hand. "What's your name?" Marta asked, because she couldn't go on thinking of her generically.

"Karen," she said in a dull voice that told Marta she was telling the truth—lying took a bit more animation. She clasped her right hand over a silver bracelet on her left arm and moved it up and down her wrist.

"What's your girlfriend like?" Marta asked, as she moved her around two men who were trying out an electric drill. This was the advantage to calling oneself psychic—it was not necessary to stick to the ordinary rules of conversation. People who might normally be touchy about something as simple as where they worked would spill the most intimate details about personal relationships to her without hesitation.

For the first time the young woman's face lit up, but it was with a peculiar combination of delight and trepidation. Oh shit, thought Marta, and she had to look away, because that was just how she must have looked when she used to talk about Teri. She's so great, but… She really touches my soul when we make love, but she's so angry the rest of the time. She can be sweeter than anyone I know, but she blames me for everything that goes wrong. She makes me feel like Aphrodite, but she doesn't want the real me in sweatpants. She wants the packaging—she wants dresses and high heels and make-up all the time. She controls me with her anger. Marta shook her head like a dog with water in its ear. She was unable to tell which of the raw, hopeless feelings were coming from the girl and which were her own, they were so alike.

But the girl was looking at her expectantly, so she must have spoken.

"So," Marta said brusquely, "you really should leave her, and you know it, but there's no way you're going to do it until it gets really bad, or maybe until she gets another girlfriend and throws you out, so this must be about something else."

Karen lifted her head and started to speak and then cut herself short. Instinctively Marta knew she had been about to voice all the same defenses she herself had made to her friends during the reign of Teri. It wasn't that she was really mean, it was that she had grown up in a really abusive family and she thought screaming and blaming was the only way to disagree. Yes, she did always have to win, but only because she had learned at any early age the one who got the most angry was the one least likely to be hurt. Yes, but…

"They never change," Marta said, and because she was trying to keep from crying it came out hard and rough and Karen turned her head away from her, surely wondering if she had done the right thing in coming to this harpy for help. Marta turned her own head, pretending to be interested in a bootleg lot of Colorado Rockies T-shirts. For a moment she hated this young woman with all the passion she had never been able to summon up to hate Teri's new squeeze. She felt as if her heart had been shot full of holes, like a human sieve. Futilely she tried in her mind to cover first one hole, then another but, unchecked by the attempt, the feelings and memories poured out like a loathsome stigmata. She had hoped—she had wanted—she had thought until the very end, like a child who insists unreasonably on believing in Santa Claus long after the myth has been stripped bare—that her love would change Teri. That if she just loved enough her and forgave her enough and was tender and understanding enough—if she backed her actions up with the money and comforts Teri had never had as a child—one day she would somehow feel safe enough to say, "You're right! This is all childhood stuff! I need to work on this and treat you better!"

Get the fuck away from me! Marta thought, and in her mind she pushed against the woman who was laying raw all her barriers. She felt a familiar hand on her arm. Mary Clare peered into her face with that old combination of concern and exasperation Marta had come to know so well.

"Feed her," she snapped at Karen, whom she identified immediately as both family and client, despite the girl's efforts to press back into the crowd. She slapped a five into Karen's hand, and then she was gone. Like Marta, Mary Clare had realized that some things were just too damn time consuming. Marta couldn't always pretend she wasn't crying, and Mary Clare couldn't stop a ten dollar gig every single time she needed comfort.

Flagging down the snack cart took a minute; exchanging the money for a hot dog and Diet Pepsi took another.

Both of them were calmer by the time Karen spoke again. "It's not that," she said. "I mean, yes, the thing with DJ is hard. And the thing with her daughter is impossible! But that's not what I wanted to show you." She dug in her purse and pulled out a large, manila envelope which she pressed into Marta's hands.

"Someone who hates you sent this," said Marta, answering from instinct, rather than tact. That was why she preferred doing a reading, rather than having something thrust into her hand which could radiate nothing, or send out a jolt of emotion almost too high voltage to hold. "Somebody who hates you," she murmured again, opening the envelope and lifting out the contents. There was no letter, just a mass of clippings cut both from the local paper and slick magazines like *People* and *Time*. She lifted the top story, just a paragraph titled, "Man Shoots Ex-wife and Boyfriend." The hatred covering it seemed to leak, hot and sticky, onto her fingers. She picked up the next story. It was the longest, and she had already read it, for though she did not buy *People*, her doctor did, and she'd had a sinus infection just the week before. The photos showed a blood-stained wall, and an unrepentant first wife standing outside the house where she had shot her husband and his new lover.

"All the same theme?" asked Marta, reluctant to sort down any further. Just holding the pile was giving her a headache.

Karen nodded.

"What'd you say your girlfriend's name was? DJ? DJ's got herself an unhappy ex, huh?" Didn't take a Betazoid.

"Yeah, but..." Karen paused, and for a moment the tide of depression and fear rolled back and she projected a deep bewilderment. "She's nice to me to my face. I don't get... she's even given me some..." she stopped, evidently not wanting to use the word advice. "She's told me some things about DJ..."

'Yeah,' thought Marta. 'Don't make her mad, don't talk to other women' all the classic things one abused woman said to another, because abuse was what she was getting off this kid, even if her girlfriend didn't hit her. It didn't always take a fist to control—she should know.

"How come you're socializing with the ex?" she asked, more interested, really, in the dynamic the woman had with her lover than the clippings she held in her hand. It was true they dripped with rage, but there was something strange and powerless beneath it. She was not afraid that the person who sent the clippings would do anything to harm Karen—she had spent her ability on this one act.

"Oh." Karen was dull again with depression. "The kid. The goddamn kid. She didn't even tell me that she had a kid. She didn't tell me she had a crazy ex-lover…"

"Crazy? How?"

"Oh, she hears voices or sees things or something. We have to see her because of the kid—DJ lets her baby-sit when we go out."

"You moved in with her without knowing she had a child?" Marta kept her head down over the clippings to prevent any note of censure from leaking into her voice. Karen had stuck the business envelopes in which the clippings had been sent into the back of the big envelope. Marta picked one out. The address had been printed on a computer. Of course there was no return.

"It was… I met her at Michigan, and it was…" She held up her hands hopelessly to show all the things she could not express, and Marta understood. It was hearts, and fireworks and explosions of the soul and a set up for failure.

"Where's your family?" Marta asked, still without looking up. Where's your family, and can you afford a one way ticket home? That was what a kid this age needed, not a hostile stepchild, a crazy ex-lover and a girlfriend whose need for control bordered on this side of abusive.

"In Wisconsin. After the festival, she called me and…"

And I came, filled in Marta. Because that's what dykes do, and she'd bet this one didn't have a pot to piss in. Maybe some dead end, minimum wage job that she was kicking into the household money. Not a separate savings account with a nice little nest egg that could go for her own apartment, that was for sure.

"But that's not the problem…" Karen insisted again. "We can work that all out. We just have to want it bad enough. But I just can't take getting any more of these things! I can't stand her being nice to my face and then sending me something so hateful!"

"Have you told DJ?" Marta asked.

"No, I… It's just that she's so jealous…"

That she'd think you had some kind of exchange with the ex to start it off, particularly if she's seen her be nice to her face, thought Marta. She'd been there. Women who were prone to that kind of jealousy and the rage that accompanied it didn't operate according to reason. That was probably also the reason Karen hadn't confronted the ex herself. She didn't want to risk a phone call or private conversation that might set her girlfriend off. The picture of Karen's life was getting uglier and uglier. No friends, no family, no money, just a jealous girlfriend, a crazy ex-lover, and a hostile child for whom this young woman, not much more than a kid herself, was supposed to play mother. What was a kid this young doing in a relationship, anyway? Marta wondered. She should be in college, or hanging out with the other queer kids at Cheeseman park. She shook her head. Another part of the dyke thing. She remembered when she first came out herself—goal one had been to get laid, goal two to get married, preferably to the same person. She'd had no concept of a single lesbian—it had seemed to her an oxymoron. And the idea of women loving each other—why, that had seemed so great she had assumed she would be with her first lover the rest of her life. Why not? They wouldn't have all the shit between them that men and women did, all the struggles for power, the stereotypical roles, the difficulties in communication. Just that pure woman energy until the day they died in one another's arms.

Marta shook her head again. It had taken her close to ten years to realize the falsity of these beliefs, and even then she had gone to Teri the same way she had gone to her first lover, guided by feeling alone. So what was she doing judging this young woman, who at least had the excuse of age and naivete?

"What do you want me to tell you?" she asked, realizing how stupid the question was even as the words left her lips. Karen didn't really want to be told anything, except maybe that she wasn't crazy. She had just reached out, one flailing hand before she was sucked totally under, one little spark of independence not yet quenched. The phone had seemed safe, and maybe DJ worked Saturday morning. Marta was probably the first dyke she had talked to once DJ had taught her the rules of the house. She was way too mired in what she thought was love to follow any advice Marta might give her.

Still, she had to try.

"Do you get along with your family?" she asked, hoping Karen had not burned all bridges when she left.

"Yeah. My mom, at least."

"Give her a call. Ask her to send bus money. Don't tell DJ. Leave when she's at work."

"But this is what..." Karen began, gesturing towards the envelope. Marta handed it back to her.

"Throw them away. If any others come, just throw them away without opening them. Whoever sent these isn't going to hurt you. She doesn't have the ability."

"How much do I owe you?" Karen suddenly turned stiff, as if realizing she had revealed too much. picturing how DJ might respond to this conversation.

"Nothing, if you take my advice." Marta didn't usually give free-bies—she couldn't afford to. But waiving a fee gave her certain powers of manipulation, and she was willing to short herself for the leverage in this one.

"Then I'd better give you some money, Karen said formally. She was still radiating the dreadful depression, but overlaying it was a kind of indignation, and also a kind of sorrow for women like Marta who thought that everything could be solved by running, who didn't realize that true love really could conquer all. Marta had to turn briefly away to shield herself from her idealism.

"Give me twenty dollars, then," she said, sticking out her hand.

Because one of them might as well come out ahead.

FIVE

Mary Clare showed up at work just before Marta went off shift on Monday, carrying a truly dreadful and tacky mug shaped like a headless woman wearing a bikini. "Ah!" said Char, who was waiting for Louann to wrap up her last call, and went to fire up the glue gun.

"Come with me," said Mary Clare to Marta, as she handed the mug over. Marta shrugged. Mary Clare often showed up after work and carried her away to the laundromat or dinner or a movie. Though she would have preferred to lie on her couch with her face ten inches from the TV, she had no real will to resist Mary Clare's attempts at normalization.

Wordlessly, she climbed into the cab of Mary Clare's truck, a little red '75 Ford she kept in mint condition. It had a bumper sticker on the back that said, "Hate is not a family value," another that said, "I saw you naked at Michigan!" and a tiny rainbow flag hanging over the rearview mirror. In better times, she and Marta had driven it to Womminfest and Yosemite and Burgdorf and Michigan, with Holly Near and Sweet Honey popped into the tape deck. Now, they drove in silence, Marta unable to even work up the energy to ask where they were going

"Here we are," said Mary Clare. Marta, who had been looking dully out the window without seeing anything, started and glanced around for identifying landmarks. She had no idea at all where they were.

"Where?"

"Therapy!" said Mary Clare in a perky voice, but just the set of her shoulders said that she was ready to fight on this one.

"Fuck you," said Marta with some heat. "You don't just arrange for someone else to go to therapy!"

"You do if all they do is lie in the dark and watch TV. You do if it's been six months and nothing has changed!"

"Oh, and what comes next? Kidnapping and reprogramming?" Marta was so angry she could feel spittle forming in the corners of her mouth.

"Marta, if I thought there was a reprogrammer in the country who could get you out of this funk, I'd pay five thousand dollars in a flash. But they don't do depression—they just do religious cults. So we're doing this instead. Give it a chance! It's not one on one—it's a group for dykes who are having a hard time recovering from a breakup. A woman in my incest survivors group recommended it."

There was a dead silence. It was not the way Mary Clare had intended to introduce the topic of incest survivors, and she felt a little guilty about having used it as a weapon. Now Marta had to decide whether she wanted to go into the group or sit in the truck and talk about something they had never before talked about in thirty-five years.

She couldn't choose the talk, not blindsided like this, so she chose the group. She huffed out of the truck with a slammed door, but hesitated when she reached the building at which Mary Clare had aimed her. Damn Mary Clare! Damn upward mobility! Twelve, ten years ago neither Mary Clare nor any other dyke she knew would have tried to send her to see a professional. Back then, if a friend was in trouble, hell, not even a friend but any other dyke, you stayed up all night and talked to her about it. There was none of this "go get help, your friends are tired of you" bull-shit. Fuck them! She glanced back over her shoulder to the truck, where Mary Clare was sitting and reading with a flashlight, bundled in an ugly rust colored parka she had gotten for a dollar at the flea market. She ought to march right back over there and demand to be taken home.

As if she had read her mind, Mary Clare cracked the door of the truck and called softly across the parking lot, "Marta, I love you dearly, but if you don't do something to change this situation I am going to hunt you down and shoot you like a mad dog." Angrily Marta hunched her shoulders inside her own flea market jacket, which was at least a flattering color, and pushed the door of the building open.

***

Afterwards, she felt more forgiving. Mary Clare had run over to Wok to You while she had been inside, and they sat in the cab and ate out of cardboard cartons while they talked. They both liked to eat inside a parked car—it felt safe and cozy, yet somehow in contact with what was happening around them.

"Did you like the other women?" asked Mary Clare

Marta chewed slowly, considering. Like and dislike of individuals hadn't really entered the game at this stage. What had appealed to her at this point was—well...

"Have you ever," she asked slowly, "kind of agreed to enter a state of controlled craziness? I mean...okay, take falling in love. I mean, the really out of control kind. The kind where you've only known her a week and she's all you can think about and you've both missed work without calling in. And there's some part of you that's saying 'This is not wise. You don't even know this woman's last name, you can see she has a bad temper, you're being real dumb,' but you just go 'Fuck it.' Because she's acting just as crazy as you are. You're egging each other on. You're like joining forces to celebrate your craziness, and everyone is okay with it, because it's a kind of craziness totally accepted by the lesbian community."

Mary Clare was giving her a look that clearly said she was doubting the wisdom of this.

"No, no," Marta tried to reassure, and then fell silent as she struggled for words. Even with Mary Clare, with whom she discussed everything, it was difficult to explain. "It was like," she finally went on slowly, "everyone in that room was totally stripped down. Do you remember—this was a couple of years ago—that crazy woman who used to hang out at Ms. C's? The one who used to just stand and stare at her ex-lover?"

"Yes," said Mary Clare shortly, with a strong note of horror in her voice. "I do remember. The one who broke into her ex's house? The one who finally had a restraining order filed against her? Didn't she finally end up in jail or something?"

"Yeah, I think. But I used to love to stand next to that woman. I never talked to her, but I got such a rush off her. She put out...well, it was like I just said. Everything was totally stripped down. There was no pretense of civilization on that woman. She was like a pure emotion machine. Being around her was like—oh, I don't know. Experimenting with a drug that could be really dangerous. I mean, I could feel her stuff creeping in and trying to take hold—it was like any minute I was going to be as crazy as she was."

"Marta," Mary Clare said, "this does not sound good. I mean—not to be rude, but I think you've pretty much been in a state of controlled craziness for months and it's nothing to celebrate. Trust me. We're trying to get back to normal here. Let's keep that in mind, okay?"

"You picked the group," answered Marta, with no small amount of malicious satisfaction in her voice. How the hell was she going to explain this to Mary Clare? Yeah, she had been crazy, but it had been something she had been restrained about and ashamed of. She had been so aware of the hiding-their-impatience attitude of her friends—isn't she fucking over that bitch yet? It wasn't at all like the support the lesbian community gave to the crazy-in-love feeling. She had loved the matter of fact yes-we're-crazy-as-can-be aura that had radiated off the other women in the group. Like, "Yes, I work at AT&T, yes I have two cats and square dance on Saturdays, yes, I'm really out of control over this issue right now, oh well, what can I say, guess I'll just go with it."

There was tap on Mary Clare's window, and they both started. Marta spilled a handful of rice into her lap.

"I thought that was you!" The woman who leaned through the window was quite pretty in a washed out kind of way. The washed out impression might have been because she was one of those redheads with pale freckles and almost translucent skin, but Marta, who had watched her cry for almost an hour, thought it was probably more because of stress. This was a woman who had been through a lot lately.

"Marta, you've met my friend Polly, haven't you?"

"In a manner of speaking," said Marta, wiping her hand on her shirt so she could stick it across Mary Clare's chest for a shake. "We cried together."

"Did we ever," laughed Polly. "Between group tonight and survivors' group Friday, I haven't stopped crying for more than fifteen minutes for days. But I'm all cried out now. What about some coffee?"

Marta felt a twinge of nervousness. There were many nuances to be considered when you went out with someone in your therapy group. It was not a question of ethics, like having dinner with your therapist would be. It was a question of boundaries. Did you want all that emotional shit— and particularly from a group as out of control as the one she had just visited—to bleed over into your carefully controlled and compartmented personal life? There were some things that were best shared only with total strangers. That was why people were always spilling their guts to the bartender in movies—they were never going to see him again.

Still, Polly and Mary Clare seemed to be friends, and Mary Clare was looking at her expectantly. Marta shrugged—okay, fine, they'd do coffee.

Polly didn't have a car, so Marta and Mary Clare, who had ridden three-in-the-cab *lots* of times, switched places so Mary Clare was in the middle. There was just too much of Marta to fit on top of a gear shift. They drove over by Delafield's, the gay coffeehouse on Broadway, but they were changing hands *again* and closed for redecoration, so they ended up at the White Spot down on Ninth.

"So how's the government job?" Mary Clare asked Polly, after the waitress had come with the coffee, and had been asked twice for real milk instead of creamer.

"Oh, the government job is good," said Polly. "Just the right amount of challenge. Not much room for advancement, though."

"What do you do?" asked Marta politely. Polly and Mary Clare both laughed.

"I get a disability check that's barely big enough for rent and groceries," Polly explained. "I totally intend to stick Mary Clare with the tab, since I know she's gainfully employed."

"So, what's wrong with you?" It was a graceless question, but the therapy session had stripped away a lot of that polite veneer that coats so many social conversations.

"Oh, I'm nuts," said Polly lightly. It seemed for a moment she was going to leave it there—and Marta was certainly not going to push an answer like that, therapy bonding or no therapy bonding—but then she seemed to change her mind.

"Do you know much about incest survivors?" she asked.

"I've read a little. Mostly what's been available through the mass media. Mary Clare..." Marta stopped, not wanting to go on with the thought, which was that, even though she had known for years about Mary Clare's brother, Mary Clare had never said the word 'incest' aloud to her until three hours ago.

Mary Clare herself jumped into this void. "I haven't talked to Marta a whole lot about my stuff," she said. "Remember, I talked about that last week? My brother tried to fuck her as well, remember, we're cousins?— and she got away. That's been a real hard issue for me this time around. It's made it hard for me to talk to her."

Marta looked at her in amazement, and even opened her mouth, but Polly didn't notice, and went on with her explanation.

"Well, you probably know that a lot of incest survivors totally block out their experience. For a number of reasons. Mostly it's just too hard to admit someone who is supposed to take care of you and protect you is abusing you instead. That's a real crazy-making situation, so instead you just pretend it didn't happen. Only it's more than pretending—it's like you *really* don't know it happened. And so you can't figure out what a lot of your adult behavior problems are all about, because you don't have big chunks of information. For me, it was constantly getting involved with women who were borderline abusive—volatile tempers, the kind who do the whole blow up and then make up with flowers pattern. Intense sex that brought me to tears, followed by mind fucking. See, that felt comfortable, because that was what Daddy did—denied what was happening, fucked with my reality, punished me with anger or coldness if I even thought about questioning what was happening... Even the sex I had with my lovers was similar to the sex I had with my father."

"Oh," said Marta, who did not know what else to say.

"Yeah," said Polly. "Pretty twisted, huh? People who don't know much about survivors tend to assume that sex between a child and adult is always brutal. Or that the child always comes away with a really clear sense that she was violated, she was the victim. But that's not true."

"No?" asked Marta, still at a loss.

"No." Polly shook her head. "My father, for example, was a really gentle rapist. Now, *that's* twisted. He really treated me as if I were a lover. It wasn't just that I was Daddy's favorite little girl, and he brought me presents and took me places and all that. He also had sex with me as if I were an adult—I mean in the sense that there was a lot of foreplay and sexual tension between us. He was really careful not to hurt me in a physical way—I was too young to get very wet, so he always used lube. That kind of thing."

"I'll bet *that* fucked you up," said Mary Clare, who was still gesturing for milk.

"Oh, yeah. In a lot of ways, it would have been much easier if he had been brutal. Then I might not have had so many mixed feelings about what he was doing. You know, like somehow I was an accomplice instead of the victim, because I was turned on when it was happening."

"My brother fucked with my head, too," said Mary Clare. "The first time he raped me—I was older than you, about twelve. He was sixteen. I knew about sex—you couldn't help it in our family. Our parents were the fighting and fucking kind. I'll bet they never had sex once in twenty years where they weren't pissed at each other. For years, when I threatened to go to someone for help—it was just a threat, there was no one to go to— Joey would say, 'Oh, you wanted it, too, you were hot for it, you were hot for it, if you didn't want it why were you dressed that way, why were you in a place where I could get to you?' Fuckhead!" She slammed her fist angrily into the back of the padded booth, and again the diners around them all stopped to stare. "I almost started to believe him. Like you say— some 'truths' are easier to live with than others, and it was a lot easier to believe I was a whore than to believe that my family—and I don't mean just my parents, but the whole fucking clan—wasn't defending me. Because everybody knew."

Marta stared into her coke, cringing and near tears. Because Mary Clare was right, everybody *had* known, even if no one said it out loud. Especially after Joey had tried to corner her in Mooma's barn, and her three brothers had kicked the shit out of him. She had been too embarrassed to talk to her parents about the incident, which she didn't fully understand, but her big brother Rob had spoken with her father, and the unsupervised visits to Mooma's had stopped. She remembered now snippets of worried conversation overheard between her parents, and realized, faced with the dilemma of exposing even more of the family's dirty linen or sacrificing Mary Clare, they had chosen the latter.

"So, anyway," continued Polly blithely, as if they were talking about any old thing, about the boycott or the new airport, "I blocked all this shit for years. Years! I went to high school and I was an honor student, and I went to college and I got a degree and all my friends thought my dad was great. Wasn't it wonderful how close we were!"

"Was he still fucking you?" asked Mary Clare as if it were casual, still trying to flag down the waitress. They had talked about this a lot, Marta realized. How long had Mary Clare been involved with this without telling her?

"No. That stopped when I was about ten—but I was still Daddy's little girl. I was also anorexic and totally destructive about my relationships, but nobody saw anything unusual about that."

"You can never be too thin or too codependent," said Mary Clare.

"So true. And then one day," Polly made a "poofing" motion with her fingers, "I remembered. Like a ton of bricks. Like being hit by a car. I discovered I had a whole different past. Not only was I not the person I thought I was, neither was anyone else in my family. I had been in an incredibly passionate relationship for six years," she kissed the tips of her fingers as if she were saluting a fine wine. "Passion! Fucked up, but still incredibly passionate. Then all of a sudden there was just no way. The thought of sex with anyone at all..." she shuddered, "It was awful! If she even touched me I became a little girl again, I would flash back to my father. It destroyed the relationship—which of course," she said to Marta with a laugh, "is how we met."

"That sounds just dreadful," said Marta, hoping that she couldn't go wrong with compassion.

"Oh, there's more," said Polly. "I left my girlfriend—I was a big girl, I could make it alone. But the whole thing just got worse and worse. I couldn't concentrate at work—I freaked out and cried or thought I was somewhere else. Nothing appreciated by corporate America. And then half the time I was too freaked out and frightened to even *go* to work."

"Post trauma syndrome," said Mary Clare. "I know women who are still being hit by it years later."

"Don't say that," begged Polly. "Please. It's too depressing. At any rate, I haven't been able to work for a while. I got a good doctor, so I qualified for disability. Temporary. I'll have to be re-evaluated next year. That's always fun."

"What do you do?" asked Marta.

"Oh, I go to therapy and walk and work with the Capital Hill AIDS Project as a home visitor—or, at least I did until my ex decided her new girlfriend should get involved with them. I ran into her once on the job, with Lexy, and decided that was not a scenario I needed. I also stick my friends with the check. And I try to remember that AA saying—you know, the one about taking things one day at a time. "

***

"I didn't know you were mad at me about Joey," Marta said later, after they had dropped Polly at her apartment building. She lived not far from Marta, in another funky old Victorian divided into flats.

"Not mad...exactly." The streets were icy, and Mary Clare had chosen to come straight down Colfax because there, at least, the snow pack had been melted down by the traffic. The streets were quiet. The experienced street people kept close tabs on the weather forecast—when a cold snap was predicted they made sure they had a place to shelter. There was always a rash of petty crimes and an increase of public intoxication before the temperature plunged—men who had no homes and who had been turned away from the overcrowded rescue missions knew a couple of nights in jail or de-tox were much preferable to sheltering from the wind and snow of a Colorado storm in a cardboard box. The less experienced huddled wretchedly in the doorway of the McDonald's on Penn and the cathedral across the street, their backs to wind like the cattle the ranchers ran up Gunnison way. "It's more like... I mean, someone saved you. Your brothers beat the shit out of Joey—you know, like you were worth saving. That made me so envious! I never felt like I was worth anything—if I had been, how could it have been allowed to go on for so long? For years, Marta, and everybody knew! I was just a kid, and everybody knew. Your mom and dad knew, and they didn't do anything, because they were afraid that it would come out in the community, and it would be one more reason to be ashamed about being related to the Echevarrias. How could I talk to you about that—how could I tell you there was a real part of me that resented you getting away? That sounds so terrible! But it was like if it had happened to you, too, I would have at least known it wasn't my fault. Because I knew it wasn't your fault. You were so...inusentia."

"I was tonta," said Marta.

"Well, that too. But you weren't a bad girl, like I was. For you to be rescued—it was like God giving me a shot in the gut. Marta is good—she doesn't get raped, you're bad—you do."

"You weren't bad, Mary Clare," said Marta softly.

Mary Clare laughed. "Oh, I was bad. I think I'm still a legend at Bishop Kelly. You know how they used to have that policy of never expelling a child—We don't give up on our Catholic youth? I think they changed that rule after I left. But I didn't deserve to be raped for four years. And I think one reason all the aunts and uncles decided to look the other way was because there was a real part of them that felt that I did. Or, if I didn't exactly deserve it, that at least it wasn't that big a deal. You know—there's Mary Clare, she's a wild kid, she always was, she's going to be fucking boys by the time she's thirteen anyway, everybody's always said so, so what does this matter?"

Marta said nothing. What was there to say? The truth did not become less of a truth because it was ugly and hateful.

"But do you know what your brother Rob did?" asked Mary Clare, breaking carefully so she would not slide into the curb as she turned the corner. "He beat up Joey one other time."

"I didn't know that."

"It was before he left for Vietnam. He freaked. Joey wasn't even doing anything. They were playing football, and he just freaked out—he started pounding on him in the middle of the game. They were out in that field behind Cheecha's and the whole game stopped and all of them—your brothers were all there, and the Mormon cousins, and they just stood around and watched Rob kick the shit out of Joey like it was the best thing they had seen in days. And when Rob was leaving he grabbed my arm and told me that if he ever bothered me again I should come to him."

"So what happened?"

"So Joey was out of commission for about a week, and by the time he was up Rob had shipped out and he figured it was safe to start up again. But the whole thing had taught me a lesson."

"Which was?"

"Sometimes the only thing that can protect you from one man is another man. Which is not something I told the lesbian community when I came out, believe me. We were all too cool, we were learning karate and judo and making knives. But the only weapon I had available to me then was adolescent boys. I never dated a boy who couldn't beat up my brother, and I made sure he knew it." Marta thought back on the string of bikers and rebellious ranch boys Mary Clare had hung with in high school—size certainly had been a factor.

"But didn't they...?" she asked.

"Yeah, but it was a trade off. They were content with a hand job a couple of times a week. It wasn't every fucking night. And I felt as if I had some control—you know, like, goddamn, I was a whore, but at least I was a whore who was getting paid."

SIX

On Wednesday night, they took Louann and G-hey! out two-stepping with them, a social interaction Mary Clare forced upon Marta about once a week. Get Marta cleaned up, get her out with the girls—hey, it killed two birds with one stone. Sometimes Marta felt as if she were Mary Clare's 4-H project.

Louann, who was so duded up one could not envision her even *owning* a ratty bathrobe, made several disparaging comments about going out on Wednesday, which she referred to as "butt-ugly night." But she brightened up once they had arrived and she had hassled the woman at the door about checking her ID. G-hey! pulled Mary Clare onto the floor before she even got her coat off, and Marta figured that was the last they'd see of them until the line dances came on. Which was fine—it was great fun watching G-hey! who besides her red mohawk, sported two nose rings and an eyebrow piercing, dance with Mary Clare in full leather. Marta loved watching the cowgirls get a what's-wrong-with-this-picture? look on their faces.

Marta bellied up to the bar and paid for two beers. She glanced over into the pool room. There was Karen, leaning against the wall. She almost lifted a hand to wave, then stopped herself, warned by the careful way that Karen looked away from her.

Louann, who was the kind of woman who successfully line danced in tight jeans on Saturday night, was scoping out the bar in such high speed that she looked as if she had a tick. Marta waited until after she was through with her first once-over to approach her.

"Roladex," she said, handing her a bottle of beer. Louann, after checking to make sure it was lite, looked smug. She was well known for her ability to pull up information on almost any bar regular.

"Point 'em out," she said in a macho voice, as if someone had asked her, the best gunman in Dodge, to shoot up the new bully in town.

"The woman over by the TV, the one with the red shirt on." The woman had a proprietary arm around Karen, who was still making a big point of not catching Marta's eye. The girlfriend, no doubt, and she didn't know her little love slave was unhappy.

"Honey," said Louann, "are you getting into rough trade? Take it from me—leave this one alone. She doesn't like your type anyway—she likes femmes."

"I don't want to fuck her, I just want the dope on her. Anyway, I can do femme."

"You can't do femme like this gal likes femme. This gal likes lipstick, highheel femme. Look at that pretty little thing with her. You do old hippie femme. You'd have to shave your legs before even talking to this one."

Marta was so stung by this blithe assessment she had to take herself to the bathroom. Louann was on the floor when she returned, and she didn't get a chance to question her again until almost an hour later, when she seized her for a Randy Travis number.

"So tell me more about Ms. Rough Trade," she said, trying to grab Louann's right hand. Mary Clare was such a damn good dancer she never challenged her right to lead, but she and Louann had a power struggle every single time they danced together.

"Mr. Rough Trade," corrected Louann.

"Either way, finish Roladexing," Marta demanded, giving in grudgingly and putting her hand on Louann's shoulder. Louann, whose sense of humor was one of her saving graces, made a computer processing noise and began to speak like a robot.

"Rough trade. Bad news. Bad news. Bad news. Eats nice girls for breakfast. Stay away. Stay away." She whirled Marta disdainfully around a beginning couple who didn't know enough to stick to the middle of the floor and then began to talk in her own voice. "Her name is DJ, she has a kid, and she does something incredibly butch like welding or something." When Louann did a Roladex, she always had all the dirt. "She is very intense—probably why she always gets the girl. Turned it on me a couple of times and I could see how you'd get sucked in—when she's hitting on you she makes you feel like Aphrodite. I'll bet she's a great lover. Of course, she knows it, which is like the world's biggest turn off." Marta had to rest her head on Louann's shoulder to hide a snicker at this, for Louann was known to brag about her own prowess after a couple of beers. "She's with that young thing with the long hair currently, but it doesn't stop her from hitting on other gals. I think she believes in that 'No one talks to you, I do whatever I want' type monogamy. She's always got some sorry little thing hanging on to her with this worried look on her face, like she's done something wrong, and she can't figure out what it is, but she knows she's going to get yelled at when she gets home. This one," she lifted a chin towards Karen, "is a new one. She had this poor old girl-friend for the longest time—skinny little redheaded femme, but she's traded her in for a later model." She stopped abruptly, and for a moment

43

Marta did not know why. Then, with a sinking feeling, she realized Louann had described exactly her relationship with Teri. Doesn't know what she's done wrong, but knows she's going to get yelled at when she gets home. She felt herself flush and pretended to be interested in two punk girls with shaved heads and tattoos who were performing an excellent back turn.

"So," said Louann weakly, as if there had been no pause, "you're not planning on hitting on this woman, are you?" She had only been joking before, but now there was a very real fear underlying the question. She might have, thought Marta bitterly, just as well have come out and said, because you're known for this, Marta. You're known for falling for women who'll treat you badly.

"No," Marta, allowing herself to be twirled. "It was just a professional interest."

SEVEN

The next Monday was payday. Which meant Louann was on edge all day, anticipating not only money but leaving early—without even asking if Marta would cover—so she could cash her check and go buy dope. She was irritable to the housewife clients and so down-and-dirty-mouthed with the women who called on the Hot Woman Talk line that all her calls stretched to epic lengths.

Marta, on the other hand, had reached a stage of apathy she had hitherto been able to achieve only at home in bed with *The Loveboat* on TV. Nothing mattered. Nothing had mattered for six months, but today nothing mattered more than it ever had before. The thought of money was not exciting. It was, if anything, just a further measure of how little anything mattered. There was nothing she wanted to buy with money— not food, or treats, or presents for friends. Part of her check would go for rent, and part to the vet, and she did not care about the rest. She read the cards as if she had been switched to automatic.

"You'd better get a life pretty soon," Louann commented in one of her passes to the bathroom. "You sound like one of those computer fortune tellers. Nobody's going to call back to talk to a machine."

Had she felt better, Marta would have been offended, but nothing mattered.

"Girls, company," called Peter, one of the gay men who ran the deli upstairs. Oh, great, thought Marta sourly. Probably Mary Clare, stopping by to tell her she'd arranged to check her into Denver General or Gloria complaining about the tone of her work.

But it was neither. It was Polly.

"Hi," she said. "I hope you don't mind. Mary Clare said it was all right to stop by if you weren't busy."

"No problem," said Louann hastily. "It's not our busy time." Polly smiled at her, and Louann gave a short smile back, obviously roladexing.

"I wanted to ask you something," Polly said to Marta. "I..." She looked at Louann, who was all but giving Marta a thumbs up, right-on sign. "Can we talk upstairs?"

"Oh, yeah, yeah," said Louann, as if she had been the one asked. Louann, thought Marta grimly, would probably guard the door at this point if she indicated she wanted to have sex on the phone table. Which was just another little indication of what a drag she had been, and how eager all her friends were to embrace any sign of normalcy.

They stepped outside the front door of the deli. It was nice out. The air was a little chilly, but the sun was shining, and people were busy on the streets, carrying groceries, waiting for the bus, walking to work. It was due to storm again soon, so everyone wanted to catch the window of sunshine.

"So," said Marta, after a moment. She wasn't sure why Polly was there. This wasn't a date thing, was it? The thought both heartened and terrified her. She could not possibly date, not now, not ever, no, no, it could never be. Yet, there was a very small part of her which knew, though it could never be, it would be good to be asked.

"So," answered Polly. And then, as if she had read Marta's mind, "This isn't about dating."

"Oh." Marta had not wanted it to be a date, had known she could not handle any other woman asking her out, not now, not ever again. But hearing Polly say it in a rush, as if she were afraid Marta had been interested, and wanted to head that off at the pass made Marta cramp with rejection. It was like being punched once again in the wound Teri had left. She looked at Polly with something close to hate. She had been, if not happy, at least comfortable in her routine of work and watching TV in the dark. Who was Polly to come along and start poking into her feelings again?

"Because I'm way too fucked up," said Polly.

"What?" It took Marta a moment to react from the depth of depression into which she had so eagerly slid.

"That's why it couldn't be a date," explained Polly. "Because I'm way too fucked up sexually and emotionally. I'd jerk any woman I tried to date all over the coals."

"Oh," said Marta.

"But I do like you. I'd like to be friends with you."

They both laughed, because they'd talked about that at group, about how lesbians tended to go right into being lovers, saving friendships for after they'd broken up. Marta explored the idea. Being friends actually sounded okay. It might be nice to have a new friend. She had many dear old friends, but they were all either like Mary Clare and Louann— watching her eagerly for signs of normalcy and emergence, as if she were coming out of a high and prolonged fever, or women whom she had cut off completely in her sorrow, with whom there would have to be some mending of bridges. It might be nice to hang out with someone with whom she had a completely clean slate.

"Hmm," she said, because yes was more of a commitment than she could make at the moment. But it was a friendly hmm. They stood contentedly side by side, watching the customers going in and out of the deli. Marta was pleased to see that about half of the customers were neighborhood people. For the boys' first six months, they had been supported completely by loyal gay friends, some of whom had to drive ten miles during their lunch hour to get a hoagie.

"I wanted to ask you," said Polly, and then stopped. "Mary Clare said," she started again, and then stopped. "Are you really psychic?" she blurted out finally.

Oh. As always when asked this question, Marta hesitated. Finally she said, "Did you take music lessons when you were a little girl?"

"Yes," Polly answered, and you could see her turning the question over in her mind, wondering, was this the proof? Was this a reading of her past?

"No," said Marta, reading her mind in a total non-psychic way. "It was just a guess." Because Polly had been a nice little girl in a middle class white family, and that's what nice little middle class girls did, whether they were Daddy's girlfriend or not. "What did you play?"

"The piano."

"So are you are you a pianist now?" She watched curiously as Polly turned over the question in her mind, knowing the look showing on her face must be similar to her own look whenever people asked if she really had the gift.

"No," said Polly finally.

"But you could sit down and play a little," asked Marta.

"Yeah."

"Or, maybe even play a whole piece or two if you had the music."

"Maybe. Or maybe not."

"For me..." Marta stopped and then started again. "My Nana used to say..." and then she stopped again, remembering her great-grandmother, an old, old woman who had lived out in a tiny little house that had once been a chicken coop behind her grandmother's house, not because she had been neglected or unloved, but because she was fiercely independent and didn't want to be under the feet of her children or grandchildren. Her face and hands had been covered with liver spots, and her skin every-where so wrinkled and crepey she sometimes joked with Marta and her brothers about using it to make an extra grandmother. "My Nana," said Marta, "my mother's grandmother, used to say that I had the eye." Unconsciously, as she said it she touched first her heart, and then her fore-head, just as Nana used to when she talked to her. Grandma and Mama had not approved of such talk, it was very old country, it filled the child's head with foolishness, so it had been done infrequently and in private.

"But she also said that not all eyes are wide open." She tried to take herself back to that time. Her great-grandmother had been a storybook kind of woman, the kind of grandmother every child should be issued at birth. Her kitchen, which had taken up most of the house, had usually smelled like cookies, and she was always delighted by a visit from her many great-grandchildren, to whom she had spoken as if they had great sense. But it had all been in Basque, and so much of Marta's Basque had faded because of disuse. "I think what she meant was—well, it's like you playing a little piano. Or, even more, it's like my brother playing a little piano. He's genuinely talented. But it didn't really pan out into anything. He's an accountant—he only plays at family parties for the kids. A lot of people have a little gift. Sometimes it seems like I do know things. Sometimes it seems like I don't."

"Oh." Polly was disappointed. "Then you couldn't...if you held something, could you tell anything about the person who owned it?"

Marta hesitated again, because it was another question to which there really was no simple yes or no answer. Yeah, she could do that sometimes. She could go into a strange room or house and pick out every single thing belonging to Mary Clare without hesitation. That gift had been handy several times when Mary Clare had been trying to break up with maniac lovers and had sent Marta in to cover her retreat. And sometimes she would touch something—a quilt or a picture at an art show, and she would be flooded with the feeling of the artist—the worry over her children, her joy in the work, her anxiety over the unpaid bills she was hoping this piece would pay for. But it didn't happen all the time. It didn't even happen half the time.

"I..." began Polly, and then all in a rush, "I had a friend when I was a little girl. She moved away. I've thought about her for years. It... the thing is, I think maybe my dad—you know—got to her as well. We were very close. She spent a lot of time at my house—overnights, things like that. He treated her very much the same way that he treated me—courting her like she was a grown woman—taking us out for special dinners and buying us treats. I was even jealous sometimes. I've been thinking about it a lot lately, she's really been on my mind. I don't know why. I'd like to talk to her. I hope he didn't touch her—I really do! I hope that's what she'll tell me. But, if he did... I don't know, maybe we can help each other."

"Are you thinking of a court case?" asked Marta, for there had been several such cases in the media within the last year.

"Maybe." Polly shrugged. "I don't know. I think it's more that I keep seeing stories in the paper about parents who claim they were falsely accused. My father denies the whole thing. He's even hooked up with those people—you know, the False Memory Syndrome people. My mother denies the whole thing. I guess I would just like to talk to someone else who was there, who knows it happened." She had something, a piece of jewelry, in her hand, and she held it up for Marta's inspection. "This was hers. My father bought them for us. Nancy Kate sent me hers to keep after she moved away."

'This' was a heart shaped locket, not a cheap child's locket, but a lovely and expensive piece a woman could wear. The initials NK were entwined on the front.

"It's lovely," said Marta. She reached out to take the locket in her hand.

She thought at first there was something that had gone bad in the dumpster, something the boys had thrown out that caused the awful smell of decay. But there was no explanation for the dark. For the cold. And the awful feeling of loneliness, of a child frightened and lonely beyond all human endurance.

She's dead, she thought to herself as she crumpled down to her knees. She's been dead a long time.

Far away, she could hear Polly asking, "Are you okay? Are you okay?" but Marta could not answer. With a wrench, she pulled herself back from the edge of the black void on which she was teetering, dropping the locket on the sidewalk. The moment it left her hand, her head began to clear.

"Yeah, yeah," she said, holding up her hand to stave off Polly's concern. "Sometimes it's like that—you know, I get kind of lightheaded." There was no way she was going to tell Polly that she thought her friend had been buried long ago in a shallow grave. That was the kind of information you didn't give out unless you were damn sure, and she was not sure. In fact, her conviction had all but faded in the thirty seconds since she had dropped the locket. Still, she did not stoop to pick it up.

"Did you see anything?" Polly asked anxiously. "Could you tell...?" She bent over and retrieved the locket without taking her eyes off Marta's face.

"Yeah, I...no, I... I really need to get back to work, Polly." She needed to be alone to think about the feelings and images that had crowded into her mind.

"Oh," said Polly, a world of disappointment in the one word.

"It's not always clear cut," Marta said, attempting to soften the blow, and at the same time clear the way for more disappointment. "I need to process—but it hardly ever happens..."

"Oh." A different oh, the voice of someone accepting the baffling ways of a psychic.

Oh, god, thought Marta, why couldn't I have perfect pitch or be able to run the four minute mile instead of this, this thing?

"Well, can I leave the locket with you?"

Reluctantly, Marta agreed. Anything to get her out of there. She stuck her hand into one of her mismatched gloves before taking the locket again, and quickly dropped it into the pocket of her jacket.

"See you at group tonight," said Polly.

"Yeah, sure." Anything you say, just get out of here.

"Did you get laid?" asked Louann, who was sitting with her feet up on the Womminsight phone shrine, eating egg rolls from upstairs.

Marta looked at her blankly, unable to even make an attempt at banter. Louann, who was not known for great sensitivity in anything but phone sex, continued blithely.

"So why didn't you tell me you were interested in DJ's ex?" she asked, scarfing down half a roll. Having the deli above them was just a bit too easy—come payday they often both owed their souls to the company store.

"What are you talking about?" Marta's head had begun to pound. She took off her coat, and went into the bathroom to sort through the tampons and over the counter medications they kept there. Thank god for Advil. She popped four.

"You know—Polly, DJ?" Louann held up her fingers and made a fucking motion Marta had not seen since high school. She wished she had not seen it now.

"What?" she asked again.

"DJ! The woman at the bar! You know—Mr. Rough Trade?"

"And Polly?" asked Marta stupidly, looking at the stairs as if one or the other was going to suddenly appear.

"Dur!" said Louann, who had little patience for any conversation that didn't move right along, particular if she were not getting paid for it. "They were together for fucking ever—until DJ hooked up with this new chickie."

Marta sat down in the bad chair, still having trouble comprehending. If Polly were DJ's ex, didn't that...did that...then that meant that she was the one who had been sending those hate-filled articles to Karen.

EIGHT

Mary Clare, who played first cello in the gay and lesbian orchestra, had practice that night, so Marta dropped her off and took the truck up Colfax to the building where the group she had privately begun to think of as "The Crazies" was meeting.

Things were already in full swing by the time she walked in.

"I stayed home from work for two years to care for that child. I was his mother!" The woman who was speaking was looking, not at any of the rest of them, but straight at the wall, as if it would help her gain some semblance of control. Tears were running regularly down her cheeks and dripping onto her cotton sweater. "I am his mother—more than she ever was! Which was fine—that was how we planned things. And now she's making me go to court just so I can visit once a week!"

"At least court is an option," Polly said who was sitting by the door. "At least you've got some kind of legal agreement to fall back on."

"That's not the point," said the first woman in an angry tone. "Yeah, we can go to court, and I might even win. But, for her to make me do it! You know, sometimes you can think to yourself, okay, it's not that she hates me, it just didn't work out, I have issues, she has issues, neither one of us is a bad person. You can kind of comfort yourself that way." The five women in the room nodded—they had all tried this litany before. "But to force me to take her to court—I can't lie to myself about that. She might as well be wearing a big T-shirt that says, 'Fuck you bitch!' on it!"

The facilitator said the things there were to say—the ex was angry and hurt and was striking out like a little child. Another woman said court was going to be horrible and draining, and the first woman should be aware of needing extra support and help during this time.

"How's it going with your little girl, Polly?" asked the facilitator. Polly sighed, and then laughed.

"DJ can be such as asshole," she said.

"Well," said one of the other women, "it's nice to know some things never change." Everyone laughed, and some of the tight tension went out of the room.

"Oh, but this is classic," said Polly. "Okay, she's been punishing me for months now. Fuck me—if I'm too fucked up to have sex with her, then I'm just too fucked up to see Lexy. Six years with the kid—well, that doesn't count at all, she's the mother, and she's got a new little wifey-poo and they're going to be a family now and so I can just drop dead. It's like she's got this little wife spot in her mind, and anybody can fill it if they do the right things. Like—check this out—she's even got the people at CAP to move Karen into my old shift—she actually has Karen taking Lexy around to visit the PWAs I used to visit!"

"That's sick," said one of the other women.

"That's DJ. So, she calls me up a couple of weeks ago, and she's changed her tune, maybe I should get to see Lexy once a week. At the time she chooses, on her terms, at her house. But, because she's so considerate, she'll make sure she and Karen aren't there to get in my face with their happiness. So she goes on and on about how considerate she is, but what finally comes out in the wash is she and Karen want to take two-stepping lessons! She just doesn't want to pay a baby sitter!"

"So did you call her on it?" asked the facilitator.

"No. I really want to see Lexy." Polly held up her hands—what can you do? "I don't want to let her push me around. But she's the one with the power."

"Feeling angry?" asked the facilitator.

"Pow!" Polly shot her index finger at the opposite wall, and then blew away the smoke. "I feel like Hothead Paisan. I wanted to take DJ's head off when I figured out what her bullshit was on this one." She shrugged her shoulders like someone trying on a new jacket. "Angry— it's a little weird. A little scary." Marta did not share her vision of shooting up the bar—Polly could damn well make up her own sick fantasies without stealing hers.

Marta shared little, mostly nodding when other women spoke. Afterwards, when they walked into the parking lot, Polly called, "Hey! Can I have a ride?"

Marta nodded her head without speaking. Her feelings about the woman were a tangled mess—onions and pineapple and anchovies on the same pizza. What Polly was doing to Karen was just one bare step above stalking. So, how was she supposed to treat Polly? There was a spark of something between them that, under other circumstances, she might have labeled romantic interest. Hell, she just liked the woman, she empathized with her situation. So what if she had sent the clippings? she told herself. It wasn't any of her business. Karen's real problem was not a vengeful ex-lover—it was having become involved with a woman like DJ while so far from home. And, frankly, there was another part of Marta that admired Polly for being able to strike out, instead of just carving herself with her sorrow.

"Do you want to go out for coffee, since I have wheels? I think Delafield's is open again." Marta felt quite pleased with herself—it was the first invitation she had issued in over six months. Maybe Mary Clare was right—maybe this group thing was helping.

But Polly grimaced, and put her hand up to her cheek. "I can't. All I want to do is get home and take another pain killer and lie in bed and watch TV. I should have taken one a couple of hours ago, but they really knock me on my butt—I wouldn't have been able to come."

"The bus must have been a drag."

"Yeah. I was supposed to borrow my brother's car, but we had a tiff and he backed out."

"Oh, he doesn't approve of obsessive lesbians? We need an anagram."

"D.O.P.E.S. I don't know what it can stand for, but it's perfect. Women too dumb to know when it's over. Jim doesn't approve of anything I am or do. He was put on earth to disapprove of me." She must have sensed Marta's disappointment behind the banter, because she added, "Do you want to come in and watch *Star Trek*?"

Marta knew from looking at the paper earlier that she had already seen the episode playing in the late night spot. But it was a good one, and Rikker did not fall in love, which was always a plus. Polly climbed into the cab, and as they drove they talked about the fire that the skinheads had set and where to get the best shoes second hand and whether or not the new management at Delafield's was going to keep the cute tables. At a light, Polly showed Marta a wallet photo of Lexy, and turned down a ticket to Mary Clare's winter concert because she didn't like classical music. No one spoke of incest or ex-lovers.

Polly's apartment was a tiny studio, which Marta guessed was what you could afford on a disability check. If you sat on the futon in the main room you could reach not only the little black and white TV, but the bookshelf and the desk and practically into the bathroom. The rooms were decorated mostly with artwork Polly had obviously done herself. One piece was close enough for Marta to examine from where she was sitting. It consisted of three rows of photographs, mounted with black paper corners, as if in an old fashioned photograph album. The photos were of Polly's father and a young boy whom she assumed to be her brother. Jim and Dad fishing. Jim and Dad dressed up for church. Jim—much older— and Dad pointing to the new patio, trowels in hand. A cement mixer and a very young Polly with her back to the camera, kneeling by the freshly poured forms were in the background of that one. There were little comments written underneath the photos, just as Marta's Nana used to do in her photo album. 'They were sure biting that day!' was written under the fishing photo. Driven into the wood, through the photos, were rows and rows of tiny wire nails, laid out neatly, as with a ruler. Their heads were painted red. Across the bottom of the frame were hanging guy things—fishing lures, a hammer, a trowel. The piece was labeled "Like father, like son." Marta turned her head away. That was enough primal therapy artwork for her, thank you. If she had to look at shit like that, she wanted to be paid forty dollars an hour.

She scanned the rest of the room. It did not look as if Polly had come out well in the divorce with DJ at all. The few furnishings were second hand, and there was an air over the whole place of someone living close to the bone. Marta had done that enough times herself to know.

Polly went into the bathroom to pop the pills, and Marta took the opportunity to scope out the kitchen. The cupboards, the refrigerator, the freezer were all bare. Marta's little stores of Ramen noodles and canned chili, furnished by Mary Clare, looked positively opulent in comparison. There was, however, some evidence there had been food within memory—a sink piled high with dirty dishes.

She didn't want to be caught snooping, so she made sure she was in the main room by the time Polly came out of the bathroom. Her turn. She proceeded to casually snoop while she peed and washed her hands—a small medicine cabinet as sparsely stocked as the kitchen cupboards. Generic toothpaste. Generic lube. Marta shivered, remembered Polly's comment about her father. A bar of soap that should have been thrown away.

She rejoined Polly and sat beside her on the futon—there wasn't much of a choice. She was surprised when Polly moved close beside her. She had not touched another woman since Teri had left her. This did not mean just she had not made love to another woman. She had not touched another woman, except to dance. The only person whom she might have permitted to penetrate her pain was Mary Clare, and she and Mary Clare did not have a touching relationship. She was startled by her reaction. She did not feel, as in a romantic novel, a rush of passion that overpowered all. What she wanted to do was cry. She wanted to curl up in Polly's lap and weep.

But weeping was not what Polly had in mind. She leaned full back against Marta, curling her head against her shoulder. And then, before Marta knew quite how, they were kissing. Kissing was not bad. It was, in fact, kind of sweet and comforting. But then Polly's hand slipped down Marta's shoulder to her breast, and to Marta's dismay, she responded with a flicker of arousal. Dismay for a number of reasons. Dismay because excitement was vulnerability. If Polly, if anyone could excite her, then perhaps one day Polly could hurt her. Without even being emotionally involved—cast that to the wind— she could hurt her. One time of mean-ingless sex and Marta would be hurt, for she knew that when she reached that place where you suddenly have to throw back your head and give it all up what would enter her head would not be bells or stars, but Teri. Oh, yes, she could probably struggle not to reach that place, but what would be the point? That would be work.

The other part of the dismay came from something quite different. She had spent almost six months in a state close to hibernation, mourning the loss of Teri. She had come as close to suicide as is possible without actually using the knife. She had expected she would never feel attraction to another woman again. Her sexuality would be a gift to be left upon Teri's alter, and Teri's rejection of it would somehow make it more fine and pure. To feel turned on to Polly—what did that make of the last six months? Didn't it make a mockery of something fine? Didn't it make her seem just another foolish dyke, instead of the heroine of a sad ballad?

She needed to get out of this embrace. She needed to explain her vulnerability to Polly. Dykes would get pissed about all kinds of excuses—they hated it when you just wanted to be friends, or weren't in that kind of space or wanted to be courted, but they were suckers for vulnerability. Marta began to gently extract herself.

Then, suddenly, it was no longer necessary. Or rather, suddenly the quality of what was happening changed. Polly was still kissing her, but it was no longer as if she had initiated the kiss out of desire, or was performing the act out of pleasure. It was as if—well, it was the way Marta had always imagined having sex with Data, the android from *Star Trek*, would be like. There would always be that quality of knowing you were with a machine—finely tuned to take care of your every desire, but his mind solving problems in another part of the galaxy as he touched you.

Marta pushed tentatively, and Polly released immediately. At first she had clung passionately as if from desire—now she sat more as if she were being paid, and was eager to do a good job. There was a vacant look in her eyes, and Marta realized, for the first time, she was seeing the disassociation she had read about in the book that Mary Clare had given her.

"Polly," she said tentatively, and Polly turned towards her name the way Marta's old blind retriever used to, not quite sure of the direction, tentatively wagging his tail in case it was going to be something good and not a bath or medicine. "Polly," she said, and then stopped, not sure of what to say next. Polly sat as if on point. "Polly," Marta said a third time, "I don't think this is a good idea. I don't think this is a good idea at all."

A quiver ran through Polly, a gesture Marta could not at first identify. Then she realized that it was a sign of relief. She stood for a moment, unsure of what to do. Did Polly need to be de-disassociated, the way a diver is brought back from the depths? She had no idea how to go about that. Or would it happen naturally if she simply left?

"Polly," she said again, and then "I think I'd better go."

"That's fine," said Polly graciously, and the way she said it made

Marta's skin crawl. It was as if all the little-girl desire or need to please was spilling out into that one sentence. She shrugged herself back into her coat, shivering. What kind of person would want to have sex with someone in that state? It would be like fucking one of the Stepford Wives, or one of the mannequins at Disneyland.

NINE

The next day was one of those mornings when the phones did not stop ringing. Marta spoke to women who wished to have the cards confirm their wedding plans, and who wanted advice on new jobs. She gave readings to women wondering whether abortion or adoption was the right choice this time. She barely had time to snatch a few minutes in the bathroom, or to fill her cup from the bottle of apple juice with which Louann had stocked the refrigerator in her payday flush. It had been almost two weeks since Karen had called. It was time to give up on a call back. Marta remembered the way Karen had refused to meet her eye at the bar. She had reached out a tentative hand with the phone call, and then slammed the door tightly back on her own prison.

Mary Clare showed up about five and Marta smiled. She had paid her tab at the deli—now that she was clean again, Mary Clare could be sent upstairs for chicken and potato salad, and they could eat in the truck. Calls were dying down now that husbands and boyfriends were getting home from work.

"Hey," she said, but Mary Clare plowed right over the top of her without even a greeting.

"Have you seen the paper?" she asked Marta shortly. Louann, with whom she usually took a few minutes to flirt, she ignored completely.

"No," answered Marta. It had been a rhetorical question because Mary Clare knew she hadn't read anything but *Reader's Digest*—a gift subscription from her grandmother every Christmas—for months, and *that* only because the "Drama in Real Life" section gave her an excuse to cry.

"Look at this." Mary Clare flipped the paper open on the Women's Psychic table, and pointed to a story on the fourth page.

Marta scanned it quickly. Body, police, child, weapon—what the hell was Mary Clare showing her this for? She knew that a murder in Denver, or in this case, Aurora, was not rare, but she liked to pretend that it wasn't an everyday thing, that she and Mary Clare were still living in their hometown. She turned quizzically to Mary Clare.

"So?" she asked, and then, with dismay, "Oh, this isn't one of those

57

touch-the-weapon-and-find-the-killer things, is it? You haven't told anybody that I can do that, have you? Because I *can't* and even if I *could* I wouldn't want to and..."

"No, no, no!" Mary Clare jerked the paper out from underneath the elbow of Louann, who was trying to see what all the fuss was about herself, and sent her sprawling. Only then, when she did not even look Louann's way, let alone apologize, did Marta realize how truly agitated she was.

"Police arrested King at the scene of the crime. King! King! Don't you realize who that is? That's Polly, Marta! That's Polly who they've arrested for murder!"

"What?" Marta pulled the paper back. The phone sex line rang, and sulkily Louann picked herself up and answered it. Okay, there was the reason she had missed the significance of the story—the *Rocky Mountain News* had the sometimes confusing policy of using last names only after the first line of their news stories. Marta was not even sure if she had ever been told Polly's last name, and her casual glance had not caught the one reference to her first.

"Jesus!" she said to Mary Clare, as she reread the first paragraph of the story. "They really think that *Polly* slashed somebody? Oh, God..." Now that she had Polly clear, Marta was horrified to realize that she also knew, or at least knew of some of the other characters. Alexandra Lewis, the nine-year-old girl who was taken from the scene of the crime, drugged, but unharmed—that had to be Lexy. The house belonged to her mother, Dorothy Jane Lewis—of course, that must be DJ's name before she had butched it down. The police responded to a 911 call made from the house, but it was too late. And the woman who was killed...

Marta turned to Mary Clare, her face twisted with horror. "Oh, my god," she said. "Oh, my god, she did it. She killed Karen, just like she told her she would."

"Get your coat," said Mary Clare shortly. "I want to talk to her—I want to find out what this is about."

***

"Look," said Polly. Then for a long time she said nothing. Finally, she asked for a cigarette. Much to Marta's amazement, Mary Clare, who had not smoked since she was in high school, produced a whole pack of Camels. Marta glanced quickly around the visiting room, which was packed. They were not supposed to give "the prisoner" anything—that had been right on the little card they had filled out, and the guards had made Mary Clare check her backpack in one of the lockers in the waiting room. But cigarettes were being pretty much ignored. The air hung heavy with smoke. No one passed a full pack—they eked them over the table one at a time as if to say, 'Nothing here, no guns, no files, just another cancer stick.` Marta had a feeling some people wanted the touch of the tips of the fingers as much as anything else. You were allowed to have contact only twice—a hug when you came, a hug when you left. Polly had hung back when they brought her out, dressed in the brown uniform that looked like hospital scrubs, but Mary Clare had grabbed her and held her fiercely until the guard cleared his throat. Good old Mary Clare.

Both women lit up. "I have no idea what happened," Polly said, when there was an inch of ash dangling off the end of her cigarette. "The last thing I remember was Marta leaving. Then the next thing was I woke up...." She drifted off, looking at the ash. Mary Clare pushed a foil ashtray over her way. "Oh, yes!" Polly seemed to recall herself with difficulty. "I woke up, and there was blood all over my hands, and all over my sweater. So I thought, so, great, another bad dream. Especially when I looked around and saw that it was our—DJ's house. So, I'm thinking, okay, who did I *kill* this time and all of a sudden the police are there. And at first I still don't realize that it's not a dream, I'm like, okay, new twist, we'll play along with this one. I can see Karen there, she's all covered with blood, and it's nothing new—I've killed Karen in my dreams tons of times. But then they brought Lexy out on a stretcher, and that was what made me realize that it wasn't a dream at all. Because I never hurt Lexy in my dreams. Never." She had come to the end of the cigarette, and without being asked Mary Clare stuck two more into the corner of her mouth and lit them with what appeared to be a brand new lighter. She handed one to Polly as if she were the romantic lead in an old pre-Surgeon General movie. Mary Clare would have looked good in black and white.

"You don't remember anything?" Marta asked, puzzled. "Do you think someone slipped you some drugs, or...?" It was the only explanation she could think of that would put Polly at the scene of the crime without knowing what had happened.

"No." Polly shook her head. "First of all—no one would have had to give me drugs. I was zonked on those pain killers. Also, you know I can't work. I'm going through extreme disassociation. When I began to remember the incest, I started getting really fragmented. I've had blackouts before."

"How'd you get to DJ's?" asked Marta quickly. The newspaper article had not mentioned this in the story, but it was more than curiosity which made her ask. She didn't want to hear where this conversation of fragmentation and amnesia might be leading.

Polly spread her hands. "Your guess is just as good as mine."

"What's brought on blackouts before?" asked Mary Clare.

"Sometimes dealing with my father," Polly answered, blowing a long stream of smoke out over their heads, "and sometimes," and here she was very careful not to look at Marta, "sex."

"But, you haven't been having sex, right?" Mary Clare asked.

"Because of that."

There was a long silence. Polly looked at Marta, and Marta looked at the wall. Come on, Polly, don't do this to me! She had behaved with honor, she had stopped it before it started—she wasn't going to be the one to confess.

"Marta stopped by after group," said Polly, waggling her fingers for another cigarette. "We..."

Mary Clare turned towards Marta with such a look of horror that she had to look away. Christ, she was going to get her butt chewed big time.

"We didn't have sex," she said quickly. "There was one kiss. One."

Polly shrugged. "I had sex," she said.

"How do you know, if you don't remember?" asked Marta, feeling rather frantic from the daggers Mary Clare was shooting. She didn't really want to debate with Polly over what had or had not taken place—their visit was timed, and they had only a few minutes left, according to the clock on the wall. But neither could she allow such a warped version of something this important to be told.

"One—I was all covered with KY Jelly. Two—I had a couple of fresh scratches on my thighs." She ticked these things off with no apparent emotion, as if she were making a shopping list, but Marta noticed her glancing down at her hands as if checking for a hangnail.

"Not me," was the only thing she had time to say again, before the bell that signaled the end of this shift of visitors rang. Mary Clare gave Polly another hug, but Marta held back. She'd give Mary Clare the facts in the car. Surely she would understand.

But Mary Clare did not want to hear the facts. She didn't even wait till they were out of the building to attack.

"I can't believe, I *can not* believe you had sex with that woman!" Anger tended to increase Mary Clare's speed, and so Marta was practically running to keep up with her as she headed out to her truck. Other visitors, heading into the jail against the wind, did not even bother to look, though Mary Clare had all but shouted the words.

"I didn't have sex with her!"

"You use KY Jelly!"

"Who the hell doesn't use KY Jelly, Mary Clare! You use it yourself! I'm not eighteen anymore—I don't lube up as well as I used to! Polly had lube in her bathroom—I saw it myself when I went to pee! But I didn't have sex with her! She kissed me and I said no! That's what I'm trying to tell you—I was incredibly responsible about *not* having sex with her!"

"Oh, and you're supposed to get congratulations for that? Like it was some big, responsible thing you did, to pull back? What the fuck were you doing, kissing on that woman to begin with? You knew how fucked up she was!"

"She started it!" Marta protested, aware that she was sounding like a whiny first grader, but not willing to take the rap. "She started it and I stopped it—and I didn't have to! She was totally ready to go all the way! Now, I'm sorry, but I don't feel like this was me being abusive. I don't think…"

"Oh you don't think, you don't think!" Mary Clare was on a roll. Spit was not exactly flying from her mouth, but the effect was the same. Her hysteria was catching—suddenly Marta found herself yelling as well.

"Fuck you, Mary Clare! Just go fuck yourself!"

"I do fuck myself! I fuck myself all the time! And I don't just do it because I can't get a date, I do it because I'd rather do myself than get into a bad situation! And it sounds to me like you'd better learn to do the same thing, or it's going to be Teri all over again!"

Marta could feel the angry blood rushing to her face. If they had been closer to home, she would have jumped out of the truck. Instead, they sat in icy and angry silence until Mary Clare pulled up in front of her house, idling the truck in the middle of the street so there was no question at all of her coming up.

"I have to go to King Soopers," Mary Clare announced nastily. "Because some of us never go."

"I never asked you…"

"Oh, you didn't have to ask! What was I supposed to do if your mother called? "Oh, we think she's dead, Aunt Elaina. At least her apartment smells that way. Oh, no, not over anything important. Just some woman who treated her bad from the first day they met."

"Fuck you," Marta mumbled after she had slammed the door of the cab. "And fuck Polly, too." She had let herself be taken to the jail hoping that Polly would have some kind of rational explanation. She had wanted to hear that Polly had just wandered into DJ's house on a legitimate errand, or that she had been set up and the police were just gay bashing. She had wanted to hear anything at all but what Polly had said—that it had been just as the paper had reported it—she had been found at the scene of the crime, holding the knife, covered with blood and no recall of the previous three hours. Marta shuddered, knowing Mary Clare had yelled at her because she, too, must have a sick, hopeless feeling in her stomach. What were they to do here? She had never before known anyone accused of murder. Hell, she had never even had a friend arrested for anything more serious than an unpaid traffic violations, though the Echevarrias were always being called into small claims for turning back their odometers. And Polly was not a close friend. It would be easy to just wash her hands of her—surely sisterhood did not include condoning murder, no matter how badly Polly had been treated.

Marta looked down the street at Mary Clare's tail lights. Mary Clare was the one she wanted to talk this out with—how silly they were to have fought. She shrugged. She and Mary Clare could never stay angry with one another long. She would be around soon to apologize, if not tonight, then tomorrow. And it was cold out.

Marta crossed the street carefully, watching for the ice that had refused to melt during the spring-like weather. It would snow again soon and another layer would be packed down. Denver side streets were five to ten inches higher during a bad winter than they were during the summer.

If she had been paying more attention, had not been so upset, she would have noticed the two skinheads crossing from the other direction, and would have altered her path to avoid them. As it was, they passed within a few feet.

"Mmmph!" It was one of the male skinheads, the one to whom she and May Clare referred as The Big Dog, for he seemed to be loosely in control, and certainly top in the pecking order. He made a sound of disgust, and spit in front of her. "Goddamn place is crawling with dykes."

"So move to Lakewood," suggested Marta. "Better yet, move to Nebraska. Or here's an idea—move to the North Pole. I hear they're actively recruiting young men with futures as bright as yours." The retort popped out of her mouth just ahead of the thought that it might be smarter, this one time, to keep her mouth shut. She was not afraid of the boys when they were alone—she was bigger than most of them and felt she could hold her own with one if push came to shove and there were no weapons. She had not a hope against two, however. She looked up at her building and was relieved to see lights in the windows of Janie and Renee, her second story neighbors. The Big Dog followed her glance.

"Mow! Mow!" Gravy, waiting at the back door as usual, called from between the houses. What was the hold up here? There was cat food to be scarfed and furniture to be shredded.

"Me-ooow!" said the Big Dog to his friend, cutting the sound off into a gurgle, making a slashing motion to his throat.

A car pulled around the corner and into a space in front of the house, and five or six of the young Queer Nation girls who lived in the basement and confronted the hell out of everyone piled out. They had probably been heading for the alley, or maybe Salad had hogged up all the spaces again. The skinheads knew when it was time to make tracks.

Trembling, Marta walked up onto the lawn and picked up Gravy in her arms.

***

It took Mary Clare about fifteen minutes to decide that she had been somewhat unfair, and another ten to change unfair to a real butthead. She had been driving aimlessly—she always drove when she was upset. She had ended up in Colorado Springs so many times after a fight that she had a favorite restaurant there, with waitresses who recognized her. She turned her truck to head back towards Marta's house.

Though, just like Marta and Polly, she had caught the window of sun the day before, it seemed to her that she could not remember a day on which it had not snowed for months, just as it seemed it had always gotten dark at five in the evening. Detroit Street was hard packed with ice and snow, as all of Denver's side streets are every winter, all winter long despite long and bitter letters to the editors of both daily papers criticizing the mayor and city council members. Because of this, she chose to drive up to the end of the block, where she could pull into a space, instead of attempting to parallel.

The sidewalks on the block were mostly shoveled, but when Mary Clare got out of the truck she saw ahead of her that the skinhead girl had fallen on the one walk which had not been cleared. A torn bag and scattered groceries were thrown up on the snowy lawn. She must have gone down just the moment before.

"Oh, are you okay?" asked Mary Clare with real concern, bending down to put her hand on the girl's shoulder. Denver was not such a big city that the people in Capital Hill had acquired the New York habit of looking the other way and walking faster when a neighbor was hurt, particularly when one was a dyke who had grown up in a small town.

"I...wow..." the girl shook her head as if to clear it, and then began moving her arms and legs in that gingerly, testing way people use after a fall. "Boy, I'm going to have a bruise." Tentatively she felt her hip. Her jeans were soaked, and through a tear in the knee Mary Clare could see she was not wearing long underwear, as she herself had been doing for three months. Everything the girl wore seemed inadequate to the bitter cold—the cheap knit gloves, the jeans jacket, the sneakers. She had no hood or cap. Mary Clare, who was bundled inside her ugly down jacket over a thick sweatshirt and could still feel the chill, shivered.

"My groceries," said the girl, looking at the food thrown about in the snow with a totally bewildered air, as if she were a child who had been taught to do a routine task, but had not the ability to deal with deviation. "My bag," she added, for the paper bag had ripped not just down the side, but across the bottom.

"It's okay," Mary Clare soothed. She opened her day pack, took out the plastic King Soopers bag in which she had packed her lunch that morning and began loading the scattered groceries into it, not bothering to take out the apple core or the empty juice box. Mary Clare was good about favors, but you had to take them as they came. She was interested to see that the skinheads did not, as would have been her first two guesses, survive solely on the vilest of junk food; nor did they appear to be meat and potatoes kind of guys. The latter, however, might not have been because of choice, but lack of money and cooking skills. All the groceries were of the cheap and easy variety. Mary Clare had not known even Ramen noodles came with a black and white generic label.

"Let me." The girl seized the sack from her with a brusqueness meant to mask embarrassment.

"I always hate it at the store when they ask you to choose paper or plastic," said Mary Clare. "Don't you? I feel like I'm having to make a huge decision, like I'm really going to cause some impact, only neither choice is any good. I have the canvas bags, but I never remember to bring them."

The girl looked up at her curiously, as if she were speaking in a foreign tongue. She scrambled in the snow for the two last cans of soup before she spoke. "It don't matter. In a few years we'll all be dead—it don't matter if you put another plastic bag in the land fill." The street light hit her full in the face, and Mary Clare had to stop herself from raising her hands to her own face, wondering if the harsh light highlighted every blemish and pock mark on her skin, too. She noticed that several of the girl's front teeth were out of line—a sign of childhood poverty in a nation that wore braces.

"Why…" she began finally, wanting to know what brought about this fatalistic attitude, and wanting to know, further, if their demise was so close at hand, what the point was in buying noodles and chicken pot pies.

"Hey!" said a voice unpleasantly close to her face, "Are you bothering her?" It was the Big Dog.

Carefully, Mary Clare stood up, absurdly remembering the instructions posted on the trails up in the Jeffco open space; the ones telling you what to do when you encountered a mountain lion. The first point was to appear as large as possible.

"Hi," she said pleasantly to the boy, who was dressed in a long pea jacket. That was the second recommendation on the park's sign—try to convince the lion you are not prey.

"Are you bothering her?" he demanded again, as if she had not spoken.

Mary Clare had the sometimes unfortunate habit of becoming dry and witty in times of attack, and, much to her dismay, she felt an uncontrollable change of mode. "Why, yes," she answered, "I was getting out of my car, and I looked down the street and said to myself—There's a woman who's fallen down. Why don't I run down and try to help her? That's sure to annoy the hell out of her." She stood on her tip toes, and spread her arms out wide, gestures that did not particularly go with her scathing reply, but were recommended tactics for appearing bigger than you really were. Mountain lions preferred small prey.

"My woman," said the boy, coming close and tapping her chest for emphasis, "doesn't need help from dykes."

"Oh, damn," said Mary Clare. "And I was just about to go down on her. Well, I'll just have to cruise around the block and see if I can find another victim. We're like vampires, you know, if we can't suck a straight girl once a night we die."

There was no telling where the exchange would have gone from there, for at that moment a new voice split the cool night air.

"Mary Clare!" the words boomed down three stories from Marta's bedroom window, "Are you okay? Do you need some help?"

"I'm just being harassed by the skinheads," Mary Clare screamed back, and every dyke in the building who had not been brought to her window by the first part of the exchange responded immediately. So suddenly G-hey! and Salad, half dressed, were at the door of the third floor balcony, and Janie and Renee, the rugby players, were silhouetted in the second, while the whole Queer Nation crowd downstairs was spilling out onto the snow. Marta had pulled her own head in, but all over the building and the one next door dykes' windows were lit up and women were hanging out, eager to join in the fray. For the second time that evening, the Big Dog was forced into retreat.

"Don't you bother my woman again," he said in a threatening voice. He grabbed the girl's arm in a way that was probably meant to look protective, but looked only hasty. She almost spilled the groceries again.

"If she's your woman, get her a coat," said Mary Clare. "Who the hell would let somebody they cared about go out in the snow to get him groceries dressed like that?"

At that moment Marta burst on the scene at a run. She was dressed even more inadequately than the girl, wearing only a T-shirt and slippers with her jeans. For a moment Mary Clare thought that, like the cavalry, she was going to barrel right into the Big Dog and take him down. What she did instead was to pull herself up short in front of him and ask, as if they had all simply met at a party without altercation, "Do you have a cigarette I can bum?"

This apparently was the last straw—worse than any of Mary Clare's remarks because there was no quick and ugly retort. The Big Dog sputtered, and plunged into the street, dragging the girl with him. Halfway across he turned to yell back at them. "You fucking dykes are fucking nuts!" he screamed, but it was a poor exit line, made even weaker by the laughter with which the women in the windows greeted it.

"Well, you don't need a Betazoid to tell you that," shouted G-hey! and one of the Queer Nation girls added, "Captain, I'm sensing great hostility!"

"What was *that*?" asked Mary Clare as they headed for the back door.

"Well, sometimes the best defense is allowing plenty of room for retreat. I saw it on Oprah. And I figured that you'd probably fired him up with your witty remarks. Am I right?"

Mary Clare refused to admit to this. She followed Marta up the stairs. *Star Trek* was playing—with the sound on. It was a favorite—the one where everyone gets space drunk and Tasha Yar has her way with Data.

It was obvious to Mary Clare and Marta that Tasha was a dyke, but if the network was going to keep her in the closet it was much better she have sex with Data, the android, than Rikker, whom they loathed. Data was just a more advanced version of a vibrator.

"Oh," said Mary Clare, "is this the one where Tasha fucks Data?"

"Yeah." They watched in silence for a moment. Or rather, Mary Clare watched and Marta listened as she finished up the mountain of dishes she had been working on for almost an hour, and through three complete changes of water. She'd had no idea she owned so many dishes. There was something about the huge, gleaming pile that made her hungry, for the first time in a long while.

"Did I ever tell you Tasha Yar looks just like an old lover of mine?" asked Mary Clare.

"Oh?"

"Yeah. Woman who treated me real bad. I had the hardest time getting over this woman. And then remember when Tasha was killed and came back as the evil Romulan? Evil. Evil to the core. Associating my ex with that character really helped move this thing with her on down the road."

"This could be a service," Marta said. "I think it might be very helpful to me to see Teri as a Feringie." They looked at each other, and then they both began to laugh, for Teri had smooth butch good looks of which she was very aware, and the Feringie were loathsome. Nothing would offend Teri more.

Mary Clare wiped her eyes. "Look," Mary Clare said, "I'm sorry I yelled at you. It was very upsetting to me to see Polly in jail."

"Yeah." Marta wiped her hands on a dishtowel, suddenly apprehensive Mary Clare would say something self-righteous about the sparkling kitchen. "I didn't know you were so pissed about me being depressed, though."

"Oh, not pissed, exactly. Tired of it, though. I get to be tired of it— you know?"

"I guess. I'm pretty tired of it myself."

"I'm sorry I got so pissed about the sex thing. I guess I just...well, it was kind of like being hit in the face, you know? Like I'm going through all this stuff about my sexuality, and it's really hard. And one of the hardest things is women act like they're really listening or they really understand and then after they're done listening, they want to fuck. Like, we're done with this week's session, you've had your cry, let's do it, baby."

"And I knew Polly was an incest survivor, so I should have known better, huh?" said Marta. "But that's not fair! Yeah, I've known for years about what happened to you. But you never wanted to talk about it. You never brought it up. And now all of a sudden it's really central to your life, and you expect me to know everything you know, even though you're telling me the most intimate things at a fucking White Spot with a stranger there like some kind of buffer—like you wanted to have feelings, but you wanted to make sure I didn't have any feelings back. I mean, how do you think it felt to hear you wished your brother had raped me? I would have liked to have had a few feelings there."

"Yeah," said Mary Clare, and then, "If you're on a roll you ought to change those cat boxes next."

"Don't try to push my envelope," Marta replied. "I did not have sex with that woman." She was not willing to let the point slide, not in light of what had happened afterward.

"Well, somebody did."

"That's way twisted." Marta shuddered, trying not to fixate on the sickening feeling which must accompany being unable to remember how or with whom you'd had sex. "Do you think…" Marta began, and then fell silent, for she didn't want to ask if Mary Clare thought Polly actually had killed poor, frightened Karen. And Mary Clare, who surely must have known exactly what the question was going to be, did not ask her to finish.

TEN

Mary Clare two-stepped the way that some women meditated, so Marta was not surprised to find herself out at Ms C's the next evening. That was just Mary Clare processing.

What did surprise Marta, however, was to see DJ leaning over the rail surrounding the dance floor. She noticed her about halfway through the dance lesson. "Look at that," she said, throwing Mary Clare completely off balance as she jerked her head around.

"You're fucking me up," Mary Clare complained. "I never should have let you lead." She had done so only because there were a lot of cross-unders in the dance—Stickup—and it was hard for her to get her arms smoothly above Marta's head.

"No, but look," Marta persisted as she twirled. "Polly's ex is here. I'll tell you, the bar is the last place I'd be if my girlfriend had just been killed."

"Grief is weird," said Mary Clare in her therapist's voice. "There's no telling what it will make you do."

What it made DJ do, Marta observed about an hour later, was drink. She was putting away a beer every time the waitress came around. Marta, who had stationed herself on the rail not far from her, watched her covertly. She had thought, perhaps, DJ had come out so she would be surrounded by supportive friends. But no one, so far, had approached her with condolences. Oh, people knew. There was back buzz and subtle indicating with nods of the head. Everyone knew. But no one, apparently, was enough of a buddy to stand DJ to a drink. Which actually made sense—both Karen and Polly had complained about the way she had isolated them, about her jealousy. Now she was paying her own price. On impulse, Marta moved up beside her.

"I'm... I was so sorry to hear about Karen," she said. If she had consumed as many beers as DJ had she would have been able to answer only blearily. But DJ fixed her with a clear, piercing look.

"How did you know Karen?" she asked in a voice laced with belligerence and, belatedly, Marta remembered Karen had known no one, had no friends at all.

"I only knew her slightly," she said hurriedly. Somehow she knew the truth—that Karen had been lonely and frightened and unhappy and came to her for help—would not go down well right at this moment.

"We met at..." she quickly dug through the information Karen had given her. Hadn't Polly said that Karen had volunteered at the Capital Hill Aids Project, had in fact edged her out of the project? "We met at CAP. We both worked there—we would see each other occasionally."

She stopped, hoping the half truth would keep DJ from beating the shit out of her in a fit of retroactive jealousy. DJ gave her another long look, and then sighed, and with a sudden flash of insight Marta knew she had been dismissed, not because DJ necessarily believed her or her story, but because she just couldn't see her as any kind of threat. Marta was both relieved and offended.

"She must have been fucking around on me," was the next thing DJ said.

"Karen? No!" Of this Marta was sure—Karen had been far too frightened of DJ to even talk to another woman behind her back. "I mean, you're DJ, right? Her girlfriend? You're all she ever talked about." She felt as if the lie were somehow honoring Karen's memory. Karen might have been foolishly idealistic, but she had not been disloyal—of that Marta was certain.

There was a long silence. DJ looked into her beer, as if within it were the answers to all questions of fidelity.

"It wasn't a stranger," she said finally. "The police said there was no sign of a struggle. She let her in. It was someone she knew. She was having an affair. I worked late once a week. She must have been seeing someone the whole time. That was why she drugged the kid. It went bad." She spoke matter of factly, as if it were standard fare for dykes to leave a trail of knifed ex-lovers behind them. Perhaps in her world it was. "Bitch," she added, and suddenly Marta knew why she was in the bar. Not because she had hoped for company or consolation. She wasn't in mourning. She was pissed off.

She turned and gave Marta a long look of appraisal that both confirmed her guess and filled her with horror, for as clearly as if DJ had spoken, she could hear her listing her physical strengths and flaws—Nice tits, too tall, I don't like a woman to be taller than me, pretty hair if she did something with it...

"I thought they had arrested your ex-lover, Polly," said Marta hurriedly, more to break off the appraisal than anything else. "Wasn't she there?" She didn't want to push the Polly theory, but DJ's talk of clandestine lovers made no sense.

"Polly? Ha!" DJ waved a dismissive, contemptuous hand. "Polly was just at the wrong place at the wrong time. Polly wouldn't have the guts to kill anybody." Her tone made it clear that her respect for Polly would have been much higher if she had stabbed her rival to death. "Polly—" She stopped and shook her head as if to clear it. "Polly and I had the hottest sex there ever was." She spoke slowly, as if to impress the gravity of this upon Marta. "Polly and I—the earth moved for us. Our souls touched. When I went inside her I held her heart in my hand. That was what Polly and I had." She paused and regarded her beer again. "That was what Polly and I had," she finally repeated. "And do you know what she did with that? She walked away from it. She walked away from it! Everybody we knew—after two years tops they never went to bed together. Maybe once a month. Polly and I had been together six years, and we still fucked four or five times a week. And then one day she decided that she had incest issues and—poof—we were done. She didn't want me to touch her any more. She wouldn't *let* me. And she thought I was going to be okay with that—hell, she didn't care if I was okay with that, that was just the way it was going to be. Like I was going to wait around for six months or a year."

"Sometimes sex is really hard for women who are having flash-backs," Marta ventured.

"Oh, fuck that." DJ dismissed other women's difficulties with a deri-sive wave of her hand. "Roseanne Arnold does it, so everybody does it. It's all part of this inner child crap—everybody's dysfunctional."

"You don't think Polly was incested?" Marta was confused.

"No." DJ held up her bottle, signaling the waitress. "Her old man fucked her. That's obvious." Her tone had changed just a bit—for the first time Marta heard in it the touch of anything like compassion.

"Did Polly confront him about it?" asked Marta, partly because she was curious and partly because she wanted to know to what depth Polly had confided in DJ.

"Did Polly confront him?" DJ laughed. "Oh, yeah, not long after she started that group of hers. That's their thing, right? What a bunch of assholes." She shook her head.

"Why was that so stupid? What did he do?"

"What do you suppose? Denied it, for one thing. Had her thrown in the loony bin, for another. What did she think he would do—apologize?"

"How could he have her locked up?" Marta was confused.

"It's not that hard if you're the daddy."

"But she's over-age..."

"Polly has a record! She's been in and out of the nuthouse since she was a kid. All he had to do was take her to Denver General and claim she attacked him—which she might have, she flips out when she's upset. They have it all written down."

"What a pig!" Marta was outraged.

"No shit. But I got her out." DJ spoke with pride.

"You?" Marta could not conceal her astonishment.

"Yeah, me. What did you think, those flakes from her group did it? They probably held a healing circle for her."

"No, but after she left you I thought..."

"I left her." DJ held up an angry and serious finger. They were going to get this straight. "I left her. And, yeah, I got with Karen right away. I don't like to be alone. I need a woman in my house." She made this sound like something of which to be proud. "But Polly—I had touched Polly's soul. We had been through a lot together—I'll always be there for Polly."

Yeah, on your terms, thought Marta, remembering how DJ had tried to keep Polly away from Lexy until she needed a baby-sitter. "How did you get her released?"

"Twisted Daddy's tail. He's a dentist, has an office over in Cherry Creek. Lots of yuppies bring in their kids. I just went over there and told him Queer Nation had a whole squad of street kids who weren't busy right now and would jump at the chance of picketing his place for the price of a pizza. With signs calling him a baby fucker. Told him I'd already called that woman who used to be Miss America, she was ready to fly out and speak right there in the mall. On TV. Just scared him. He thought that if he had Polly locked up nobody would believe her. Maybe. But she was out that night." She signaled for another beer and turned away, signifying the conversation was over. Mary Clare was waving to Marta from the dance floor—a Mary-Chapin Carpenter song was on, and they never missed Mary-C.C.

"Well," said Marta, "I'm really sorry. I liked Karen. It must be so hard."

"Yeah." For the first time DJ showed something besides anger at the mention of Karen's name. She looked down into her bottle and swished the beer in a circle. "We're having a wake on Friday," she said. "If you were a friend of hers—well, you might want to come."

71

ELEVEN

The phone on the lavender desk began to ring, but Marta made no move to answer it, even though Louann was upstairs negotiating egg rolls with the boys. She was not in the mood to play out anybody's fantasy. After the one disastrous kiss with Polly, she did not care if she never had sex again in her whole life. And she was no good at pretending—she couldn't make it sound as if she were coming while laying out a hand of solitaire, like Louann could. Fuck Louann, anyway—she was always sticking her with the straight girls—she could just have the damn sex line.

Louann came pounding down the stairs after the third ring, throwing her a look that could have killed.

"Hot Women Talkline," Louann said into the phone, automatically falling into the slightly breathy voice that made even Marta, who was looking right at her ripped-up old sweats and greasy hair, think she was lounging naked on a bearskin, waiting to be phone fucked. "You're talking to a hot woman." Then she did something Marta had never seen her do before. Instead of saying, "Oh, that sounds so hot," or, "Oh, tell me all about it" while cleaning her nails or picking at the zits on her arms, she sat straight up and said, "What?" She looked over at Marta with an expression of total befuddlement and said, "It's for you."

Marta might have been insulted by her amazement, had she not been equally astonished. Their friends did not call either of them at work—really important messages came through Peter and Joe upstairs, who did not charge three dollars just to pick up the phone.

Louann handed her the receiver. "Hello?" she said very tentatively, thinking, like Louann, there must be a mistake.

"My name is Liz Smith," said the woman on the other end of the line. "I got your name from Polly."

"Did you know this is costing you three dollars a minute?" Marta blurted, unable to think of anything else. A three dollar a minute bill on her phone—if she still had one—would have put her into a tailspin that would have lasted until the next payday.

"I can afford it," said Liz Smith. "I'm a lawyer. Actually, I would

72

like to talk to you in person, but this was the only way Polly could think of to get hold of you during the day. Could you go out to the jail with me this evening?"

"Why?"

Liz Smith sighed. "It's a long story and, like you said, this is costing three dollars a minute. I can pay it, but that doesn't mean I want to. Could I just pick you up after work and tell you then?"

***

Though Marta had not recognized the voice or name, Liz Smith, a small blonde woman with freckles, turned out to be a woman she had seen around the lesbian community for years. They knew some of the same people and, in fact, Liz had played soccer with Mary Clare two years before.

Liz had also made a splash in the gay papers, a year or so earlier, when she had taken the leader of a right-wing Christian organization—a group that specialized in "deprogramming" lesbians and gays—to court for stalking her lover. Marta had been very impressed by this case. It made her more inclined to go along to the jail when, truthfully, all she wanted to do was go home and watch Captain Picard. Liz scored another point by asking immediately, "Have you eaten?" and then pulling into a sandwich shop, her wallet out, without waiting for an answer.

Liz obviously did not want to explain anything without Polly, and so while she drove and Marta ate her turkey and avocado sub, they talked about mutual friends, and Amendment Two and Linda Lane's new book. Only after they had passed through the security and Polly was brought in from the back of the building did Liz suddenly switch to business. Seeing your lawyer, apparently, was different than seeing friends. They did not go into the big room, but were ushered into a small room containing a tiny plastic table and attached yellow chairs that, in a sick way, reminded Marta of McDonald's. There was room for only two to sit, so Polly insisted on standing.

"Polly wants you to work with us," Liz said, and then stopped, as if that sentence explained everything.

"Doing what?" Liz did not answer, and Marta saw now why she had been reluctant to say anything in the car. Marta was there at Polly's insistence, and, though she had cooperated in the transportation, Liz wanted to make it quite clear whatever help Polly wanted was not her idea.

"Do you remember Nancy Kate's locket?" Polly asked hesitantly.

"Of course." Actually, she had almost succeeded in putting it out of her mind. It was sitting in a desk drawer at work, inside an envelope. Louann had been the one who had handled it.

"I want you to...I want you to ask around...I want you to see..." Polly stopped, leaving Marta no clearer as to what she was asking.

73

Liz spoke. "We are going to plead not guilty," she told Marta. Marta nodded. "Not guilty by reason of temporary insanity."

"Then you think you did it?" Marta blurted without thinking. The color drained out of Polly's face, and she cursed herself. Way to be supportive, Marta! Then again, if this was how they were going to play it, Polly was going to have to get used to much harder questions. Marta thought back to the last time they had been at group, when Polly had made the gun with her finger. Had she come out of depression so full speed into anger she had been unable to stop?

"This is the way we've decided to plead," Liz replied for her, carefully not answering the question. "We're going to build a defense very similar to battered wife defense. Have you ever read about that?"

"Yeah, that's where a woman who's been battered over a period of time might kill her husband even when he's not attacking her? Because she's so afraid of what he's going to do next?"

"Basically."

"But Polly—" Marta stopped herself, unable to say the words, 'Polly killed'. "But Karen…" she started again, "…wasn't a threat to Polly."

"Let me make another analogy," Liz said. "Do you know what post traumatic stress syndrome is?"

"Isn't that what you get if you were in Vietnam?" Marta asked.

"Yeah, sometimes. Sometimes incest survivors get it, too. It can cause disassociation, blackouts. You might do something you wouldn't normally do because you thought you were in another time and place. If you had been in Vietnam, a frightening noise might make you flash back, might make you attack in what you perceived as self defense."

"So someone having an incest flashback might defend herself as well?"

"Yes. And like a battered woman, she might do it at a time when the molester or whoever she perceived to be the molester, was not actually threatening her."

"But wasn't Karen drugged to the gills? Doesn't that establish premeditation?" This was actually not the only hole that Marta could see in what sounded to her like a very iffy defense, but it was the most immediate.

"We're working on it," said Liz smoothly.

"What we…what I want you to do," Polly broke in, "is to find Nancy Kate. The more I think about it, the more sure I am that my father must have sexually abused her as well as me. My whole family—well, except for my brother—denies it even happened. My dad has set me up with a background of "mental illness." I've been locked up repeatedly—he belongs to that damn group—so no one is going to believe me on the stand."

"Another victim would be a big help." Liz nodded.

Marta spread her hands. "But why me? There's lots of people who do this kind of thing. I mean, find people. For a living." She remembered the feeling of death she had gotten from the locket—how, now that Polly was counting on her friend to turn up and support her on the stand, did she tell her that she thought she had been laid in a lonely grave years before?

"Because...because you should have seen your face when you held her locket. Because I could tell that you really felt something. I don't want a stranger—you have the feel." Marta stared at her across the table. Had Polly heard a word of what she had been saying that day? Had she heard that it flashed off and on at random and really, for the most part, annoyed more than enlightened? Had she heard any of that? Or had the only thing that stuck in her mind been the way Marta had sunk down to the pavement with her head between her knees?

Liz leaned back in her chair, detaching herself from the whole transaction again.

"I'll pay you," Polly said.

"That's not it!" Marta said, embarrassed that Polly even would think that it was. But, then, was the real reason any better—that she wanted to sit in her apartment with the lights off, mourning a woman who had treated her badly?

"But I will," said Polly. "I don't have much money—Liz is donating her services because it's an incest case." Liz looked embarrassed, as if she would rather this had not come out. "But my brother gave me fifty dollars. I know it's not much, but I would give to you." Actually, fifty dollars looked pretty damn good—it would buy two sacks of the expensive kibble Five-Cents' delicate bladder kept all the cats on. But it seemed cold to take it from poor Polly sitting there in her prison scrubs.

"No, look I'll..."

"We will pay you the money," said Liz. "Find the woman."

"Can I ask you a couple questions?" asked Marta hesitantly.

"I'm going to the bathroom," said Liz abruptly, gesturing the guard through the mesh reinforced window in the door. No lesbian psychics for her, thank you.

"I talked to DJ at the bar last night." Marta repeated the conversation. Too late it occurred to her Polly might wonder about her connection with DJ. She had not yet mentioned knowing Karen, and this hardly seemed the time. She decided to forge ahead, hoping the lapse would not be noticed. "Is that true? Did she really go to your dad?"

"It's true," Polly said. "DJ was always there for me after I left. What you have to understand was, it was within real narrow limits."

"Such as?"

"OK." Polly smoothed down the brown scrub pants. They were starting to look as if they needed a wash, and Marta wondered for a moment how laundry was handled in the jail. Did you get a new outfit

75

once a week? And what if you were a messy eater? "DJ—I'm kind of beginning to understand this better through my own therapy—DJ was raised in a very neglectful family. The outer trappings of caring are very important to her. I'll give you an example. When we first got together, I had to be at work an hour before she did. I didn't have a car—I'd been taking the bus. She didn't like that. Me standing out at the bus stop at 6:00 a.m. when my girlfriend had a car—it was trashy, it meant she wasn't taking care of me. So she would get up in the morning early to take me to work. Only she hated to get up, so it was always this huge ordeal—she'd be bitching and grouching—she was mean in the morning—and I'd be holding my breath trying not to say the wrong thing, and it was a horrible way to start the day. But she insisted on doing it, because it looked good. You see, getting me out of the hospital was like that—it looked good. She got to be butch, she got to do a little confrontation, she got to show I still needed her to take care of me. It was a good show. She saw nothing contradictory about doing that and then in the next breath denying me access to Alexandra. In fact, this whole thing about Lexy is all part of the same attitude. I won't say she doesn't care about Lexy in her own little twisted way—it's just her caring is all part of the same pattern—what's important are the trappings. She's one of these people who freaks if the kid is dirty, but it doesn't go a lot beyond that. She might never talk to her or find out her feelings or anything else. If she would be honest, she would be just as happy if Lexy was with me. I was Lexy's mommy for six years, for Christ's sake! She was totally my responsibility. DJ doesn't even know where to buy her clothes or how to braid her hair."

"You don't even have a job," Marta said bluntly. "How could you have custody of a kid?"

"Well, obviously I couldn't right now. But things were getting better for me financially—I'm getting some guilt money from my dad—he's calling it a loan—and I hope I'll be able to work soon. But what I'm getting at is the reason DJ blocks me from Lexy is an ex doesn't fit into her little happy family scene. It wouldn't look right, it wouldn't look caring if she were to give Lexy up. It doesn't look right for me to even spend time with Lexy, except in that stupid baby-sitting role. DJ wanted Karen to come in and fill the mommy role, and she was very unhappy when that didn't happen."

"Hmm." Marta folded her hands over her eyes for a moment. "DJ thinks Karen was cheating on her, that it was another lover who did her in. She thinks you were just in the wrong place at the wrong time."

"Oh?" For the first time Polly brightened a moment, then she shook her head.

"I can't imagine it. I mean…when I looked at Karen I saw this younger version of myself. DJ mesmerized her, just the same as she mesmerized me. I never looked at another woman the whole time I was with her—never once. But she accused me of it all the time. I think it was some kind of power thing—she wanted me to be really aware there was a big potential for violence if 'her woman' stepped out on her."

"Hmm." A new idea occurred to Marta. "Was there...I mean, is there a possibility that DJ could have done it herself?" She recalled DJ's cool rage at the bar. "Could she have convinced herself Karen had cheated on her and freaked out?"

Polly did not answer quickly this time, and when she did answer, it was not helpful. "I don't know," she said, shaking her head. "I just don't know."

***

The ride home was not as friendly as the ride out had been. Liz was a criminal lawyer—she must be used to visiting clients in jail. Yet, no matter how hardened she was, the forty-five minutes in the private cell seemed to have taken just as much out of her as it had Marta.

"Are you sure," Marta asked tentatively after they had entered the freeway, "Polly did it? Couldn't she have been set up?" It was becoming quickly obvious to her she was the only person with any kind of doubt at all around the murder. And was it even doubt? Or was it just a fantasy that she wanted so badly to be true that she was convincing herself there was a bad feel to the whole thing?

Liz barely cut her eyes to the right.

"Well, we've decided to plead not guilty by reason of insanity."

"I know what you've decided to plead." Marta spoke sharply, angered by the polite little bit of fencing. "Don't talk lawyer talk to me, okay? Either tell Polly you can't work with me and don't call again, or be straight with me. Fifty bucks won't pay for half the time it will take me to find Nancy Kate's parents' address—I'm donating my time to a good cause just as much as you are."

Liz sighed, a heartfelt, from the gut sigh, but she did not apologize.

"Look," she said. "The drugs came from the house of an AIDS patient who was connected with the Capital Hill Aids Project. He had been saving them in case he decided on suicide. The cops also found a copy of a Hemlock Society pamphlet belonging to him. Don't you get it? He was one of the men Polly used to visit when she was with CAP."

"Karen could have picked those up," Marta said stubbornly. "She took over Polly's visits."

"Yeah. She could have. You want to tell the court why, and why she drugged herself and the kid? Make it convincing."

Marta was silent.

"That wasn't all. There was a big stack of newspaper clippings in Karen's drawer. All stories about the first girlfriend popping the second."

Oh, shit, Marta thought. She opened her mouth, but Liz cut her off.

77

"And they had Polly's fingerprints all over them."

"Only Polly's?" asked Marta, hoping her voice didn't sound as shaky as she felt.

"Actually, no. Everybody's. Karen's, of course. DJ's. I think the kid's, too. Some they couldn't identify. But they picked up a couple of good prints belonging to Polly."

And probably mine, thought Marta. This was the time to come clean about Karen. But if she did that, what would Liz do? She wasn't happy about having her on board to begin with—if Marta mentioned her one meeting with Karen, would Liz consider her contaminated? Would she retrieve Polly's fifty dollars and tell Marta to mind her own business?

She couldn't chance it. She kept her mouth shut.

Nothing else was said. Marta was thinking about Nancy Kate, and who knows what Liz was thinking. Maybe that she was going to lose this one. She followed Marta's terse directions and pulled up to the curb.

"Look," she said, taking a checkbook out of her briefcase. "I'm going to write you a check. Okay? That's important. Because it's not Polly who is hiring you. I'm hiring you. Get it?"

"But Polly..."

"No." Liz shook her head. "We have to do it this way. Understand? Because I'm her lawyer. I can't be forced to testify against her. If I hire you, you're protected under that cloak as well. You can't be forced to testify, either."

"What in the world do you think I'm going to find out?" Marta protested.

Liz was silent for a moment. "I saw your face when Polly was talking about that friend of hers. You think she's dead, don't you?"

"Yeah." What Marta had been reluctant to say to Polly she could say easily to Liz. After all, it was not her life on the line.

"What if you find out that's true?" asked Liz.

"Well, then..." Marta floundered, not sure where she was leading.

"What if you find out she was killed?" asked Liz. "What if she was killed, and nobody knows who did it? What if it's an open case? What if," she leaned close to Marta, "someone quite small could have done it. Say, another child?"

Marta leaned back in her seat, as far from her as she could get. "I..." she said, trying to organize this new version of Polly's history, in which Liz all but accused her of committing not one murder, but two.

"I never felt anything like that around Polly," she was finally able to protest. "I'm sure she was telling the truth..."

"She was telling you what she remembered," said Liz. "And just you remember—I'm the one who hired you."

TWELVE

The one good thing about being depressed, thought Marta, was that her friends were so eager to see her back into mainstream they were willing to indulge her every little whim. Mary Clare had been delighted to hear that Marta wanted to attend a wake, happy to drive to Aurora.

They found the house without any trouble, a two story on a block of ranch houses. They rang the bell and waited. There were still Christmas lights strung up under the eaves of the house, and someone had turned them on, which gave the whole scene a rather garish and inappropriate note. When no one answered, they rang again, and then Mary Clare, who was not known for her patience, tried the door.

"It's open," they heard someone yell from the back of the house.

The house in which first Polly and then Karen had lived with DJ was decorated rather impersonally. There was nothing about it that spoke to Marta of Karen. Part of that, no doubt, was the emptiness of the front room.

"Did they just move?" asked Mary Clare, looking around at the freshly painted walls and new carpet. Then, "Oh!" It took Marta a second to catch up with her. Then it hit her. Of course the room had been done over. This was where Karen had been killed. There must have been blood everywhere. DJ must have moved fast—had the painters waiting the moment the detectives took down the yellow tape. Rush job. She guessed the painters came out right away if there had been a murder. Something to tell the other guys at work.

"Let's get out of here," she whispered to Mary Clare out of the side of her mouth. "It gives me the creeps." It sounded as if the real party was taking place in the kitchen. No one had even looked around the corner. Only Polly's fifty dollars had made her come, and now she was sorry.

"I'm not wasting this," said Mary Clare. "I'm going to snoop." Without further ado she headed down the hall that went off to the right. Marta hesitated. Really, it was more than the fifty dollars, but she had not yet said the rest of it aloud to herself. The real reason she had dragged Mary Clare out to the suburbs had nothing to do with money at all. It was just that this thing with Polly was the first thing about which she had cared in months. For half a year she had been consumed with her own pain. Fall had turned to winter, a new president had been elected, the people of Colorado had voted in a hate amendment, Picard had indulged in an affair, and none of it had mattered. Women had called her for advice on marriages and divorces and abortions and revenge, and she had remained untouched by their stories.

Then Karen had come along, and she had done nothing for her. Oh, it was very fine and well to say there had been nothing she could have done. She had offered advice and Karen had ignored it, just as Marta herself had ignored the advice of her own friends. It was fine to talk about free choice and grown women, but when the smoke all cleared there were three things left. One, she had known there was something wrong. Two, she had done nothing. Three, Karen was dead.

There was nothing she could do to change any of these things. But there was Polly. And Polly was not yet beyond help.

The party was in the kitchen, centered around a keg of beer. Marta wondered if the women were really friends, or just drinking buddies who had showed up to see the crime scene. Too bad for them DJ had already painted the walls. There were platters of cold cuts and cheese sitting on the table, but no one was eating yet. DJ, holding court in the middle of the crowd, looked over at Marta without interest or recognition. She had already popped back more than few.

Off to the side was a little girl who could only have been Lexy. She had her hair pulled back with a headband, just as she did in the photo Polly had showed Marta, but there the similarity ended. This little girl was pale and gaunt. She looked as if she had neither eaten nor slept in days. Marta looked from her to her mother indignantly. What was she doing there to begin with? And, if DJ had decided it was appropriate for a child to be at a wake, why in the world wasn't she paying some attention to her, instead of acting like she was the bride at a shower?

"And so he said..." Though Marta heard only the punch line of the joke being told, it was enough to tell her Lexy shouldn't be in the room. She shot her another glance—she was leaning against the counter in a strangely apathetic way, as if she was tired, but unable to think of bed.

"Com'ere." Mary Clare suddenly materialized at her elbow.

"I want to..."

"No, you gotta see this." Mary Clare took her firmly by the elbow and led her upstairs. "Look at this."

The bedroom door had probably been closed tightly at one time, but now it was ajar. Mary Clare nudged it with her toe. "Check it out," she said.

The bedroom, apparently, was femme domain. It was decorated in mauve, with dried flower wreaths on the walls. On the dresser sat a mirrored tray covered with glass perfume bottles. Somehow Marta could not reconcile this room with Karen. Suddenly she knew that DJ had paid to have the room decorated for a generic femme, a woman who would receive her in the canopy bed wearing the lingerie she had laid out. She wondered if this room had been the same when Polly had lived here, and suspected it had.

But what Mary Clare was nudging her to look at was the wall. Marta caught her breath. There were five black and white nudes of Karen hanging in a cluster there.

"God, she was gorgeous," Mary Clare said. "Do you suppose DJ took the pictures herself?"

Marta shook her head. "Uh uh. Those weren't done by an amateur. She paid a lot of money for these babies."

"I'm surprised she allowed another woman to see Karen with her clothes off."

"Maybe she had a man do it." Marta shrugged. "Maybe she killed him and ate him when he was done."

There was a small movement behind them, and they both jumped guiltily. Marta instinctively looked around for a weapon—if DJ went into berserker mode and decided to beat them to death for looking at her dead girlfriend, she wanted to be prepared.

But it was not DJ, or any of the half drunk women she had seen in the kitchen. It was the little girl Polly had called her daughter.

Marta felt her face burning, as though she had been caught doing something inappropriate and lewd, though surely the child had seen the photos before—after all, it was her house. Or had this door been kept locked all the time?

"Hello," said Mary Clare, and the little girl nodded gravely, but in a jerky fashion that reinforced Marta's impression of too little sleep and food.

"We're friend's of Polly's." Marta looked hastily out in the hall to see if any of DJ's friends were there to hear this, but the upstairs was empty.

The child considered this for a moment. Then she said. "Mommy used to have pictures like that of Polly, but Polly wouldn't let her put them on the wall."

"I'm not sure how comfortable I'd be with pictures like that of myself on the wall, either," said Mary Clare.

Lexy considered her carefully. "I don't think Mommy would want your picture on the wall," she said finally.

"I'll bet not." Mary Clare laughed in that short way that meant she didn't really think it was funny. "Your mom likes...." she hesitated over the word femme, and Lexy went on like a robot programmed to fill in the blank.

"Pretty women. My mom says ugly women are a waste of space." There was something wrong here, Marta realized. She was not around children much, but she knew from Christmas visits with her brother's families that Lexy was old enough to have some social sense. She seemed to just be playing things back like a tape recorder, without any concept of audience reaction. Marta looked closer at her drawn little face. Her pupils were pin points. Was it possible the kid was zonked on drugs? Mary Clare said nothing. Her feelings had been hurt, and when your feelings have been hurt by a ten year-old it's best to remain silent.

Tentatively Marta picked up the ball. It's what we came here for, she argued to herself, but still, there seemed something not quite right about questioning a drugged up fourth grader. She compromised by starting slowly. "Polly said to say hi to you if we saw you. She was worried about how you were feeling."

Again the long consideration. When Lexy answered, it seemed not to do with Marta's statement at all. "Mommy said she was never going to be with a woman who told her no again." It took Marta a moment to realize this was related to the photographs Polly would not allow to be displayed on the wall, and by then Lexy was talking again in that slow, drugged out way. "Polly killed Karen?" she was saying, as if someone had said it to her, but, like her mother, she couldn't quite believe it. "Polly killed Karen?"

"The police think so. What do you think?" Another long pause. "Polly used to live here. She lived here for a long time. She took me to school the first day of kindergarten."

"You miss her," said Mary Clare, her therapist side winning out over her hurt feeling. "It must have been hard for you when she moved out."

Lexy turned her head slowly from Marta to Mary Clare. "Polly's in jail," she said and then, "Mama wouldn't let Polly take me camping anymore. She said Karen was our new family now. Karen's dead now." Because of the monotone, it was hard to tell how she felt about that.

"When my brother died," said Mary Clare, still trying to work up some empathy, "I was so glad. I knew I wasn't supposed to say I was glad, but, oh, I was happy he wasn't going to be around anymore. You're not always sad when someone dies."

The other reactions had been slow. This one was startling both in it's rapidity and it's vehemence.

"No," said Lexy. "No, I'm not glad. No, no, no!" She was not yet screaming, but it was obvious that was coming next.

Oh, Jesus, thought Marta, that was just what they needed, a scene with the kid and their whole cover blown.

"Get out of here!" she said to Mary Clare. They'd worry later about hurt feelings. Lexy's screams changed to dry sobs.

"Come here." What Marta wanted to do was pick the little girl up and

82

cuddle her, but she was afraid that would be too much coming from a stranger. Lexy needed her mother to hold her, but her mother was downstairs telling off-color jokes. The best Marta could do was hold out her hand and lead the little girl into her bedroom. The room was small—just big enough for a desk with a computer and printer, a set of bookshelves, a single bed and a rocking chair.

"How about a story?" Marta said, spotting a couple of old favorites. Just as she had known the bedroom had not been put together by Karen, she knew that Polly had filled this shelf for Lexy—had bought *Winnie-the-Pooh* and *The Borrowers* and *Mrs. Piggle-Wiggle*, because DJ had not known what books to get for a child. "You lie down in bed," she said, "and I'll read you a story before you go to sleep."

Lexy seemed relieved that someone had taken charge. She started to crawl under the covers, and then stopped.

"My mama says I'm not supposed to sleep in my clothes," she said woodenly. Obviously, this had been hammered home hard, and just as obviously she was totally incapable of changing herself. Marta located a long nightgown under the pillow on her bed. "Let me help you," she said, in case Lexy needed to save face. Quickly she undressed her and dropped the nightgown over her head. Lexy was as passive as a small child.

There was a knock on the door, just as Lexy was sliding under the covers. In the hall, on the floor, was a glass of milk and a plate with a two sandwiches and a pile of cookies on it. There was no one in sight, but Marta knew Mary Clare must have brought them. She was the only other person in the house who would have noticed Lexy's wane, unfed look.

"Here's a snack for us while we read," said Marta, setting the plate on the bedside table. She did not want to read to this little girl—she wanted to take her home. Or, if not to her home at least to Mary Clare's. She picked out a volume of *Winnie-the-Pooh* and turned back towards the bed.

"Barney," said Lexy. She had reached first for the cookies. Marta bit back a reproach. At least she was eating *something*.

"What?"

"I want the Barney book."

Marta turned back to the bookshelf, looking for a cover showing an ugly purple dinosaur. Lexy seemed a little old for such things, but it was only natural that she would revert. Instead, what she found was a slender volume by Judith Voist, pushed back between two larger books.

"*The Tenth Good Thing About Barney*," she read. "Is this what you want?"

Lexy nodded. She had found the milk. She was drinking long and hard, as if she had been dry all day.

"My cat Barney died today..." read Marta. Jeeze, what was this? She read the first page, and when she looked up Lexy had gone to sleep, still holding a cookie in her hand. Marta eased it back onto the plate, just in case there was a no eating in bed rule.

Let's get out of here!" Mary Clare hissed from the door, keeping a leery eye on Lexy.

"Yeah." Marta was more than glad to oblige. Her only regret was leaving the little girl in the bed.

They did not go by the kitchen, from which was now coming bursts of song, but left the plate on the floor of the pristine front room.

"Thank you so much for that professional touch, counselor," Marta said as they cruised back through Aurora. "I wouldn't have been able to handle that one myself. What in the world made you tell her about Joey?"

"Fuck you," said Mary Clare. "At least you didn't get told you were wasting space on earth."

"She just said her mother wouldn't want to date you. You don't do butch on butch yourself, hotshot."

"Well." Mary Clare pouted a further moment. "I didn't mean to set her off. I thought she might be feeling guilty because she wasn't crying over Karen. What do you think that kid was on?"

"I think she was tranked to the gills. I think it's a damn good thing for us she was, too, because otherwise she would have brought the house down. Did you say anything to her mom?"

"Her Mom was three sheets to the wind by the time I got downstairs. She must have already known the kid was upset—I assume she wasn't getting that caliber of drugs by herself."

"I guess not." Marta was silent for a moment. Then she said, "I wonder why it's so important we *not know* she was glad Karen was dead?

84

THIRTEEN

If she'd had her choice, Marta would have gone out to the suburbs and talked with Polly's mother the next day. If either of Polly's parents had kept in touch with Nancy Kate's family after they moved, Polly's mother was more likely to be the one—sending a card at Christmas or birthdays. That was the way chores were traditionally divided in American families, especially those of Polly's parents' generation.

But, Mary Clare was teaching some kind of all-day seminar for which she was reluctantly wearing a power suit and heels, and she was not disposed towards favors when she had on pantyhose. Mary Clare in a dress was much less believable than most queens—hose and purse did not soften her in any way.

So, because Lakewood on the bus was a chore Marta could not manage, and because Cherry Creek was within walking distance, she went to Polly's father's office first.

"Mr. King?" She had not intended to say the name that way, as if were a question. She had meant to say it firm and assertive, perhaps with just a tiny touch of scorn, so the man knew she knew what he had done to his daughter. But, when she had made that plan, she had pictured a different man than the one coming out the door of the dentist's office. The man she had planned on confronting, wresting a bit of information from, was seedier than this man. He would have his hair slicked back, a pock-marked face and a nervous, weasely way of glancing from side to side and licking his lips. All right, perhaps not, for she was a big girl, she knew that the fathers who did these things did not always wear it on their chests like a scarlet letter.

But she had no place in her mind at all for the man who stopped at her query. This man was tall and dignified looking, but dignity with a generous smile. He looked the way Santa Claus would look forty pounds lighter, twenty years younger and employed by corporate America. Silver hair that still held traces of Polly's red. Could she have been mistaken? Could there have been one last patient in the office? No, she had seen the nurse leave for lunch. And the man had turned his head towards her question.

"Yes?" he said, smiling, unsuspicious, and Marta felt herself stuttering. Everything she had planned, all the questions about Polly and Nancy Kate, gone.

"I'm a friend of your daughter," she said finally.

His face immediately became a mask of sadness, though even pulling his mouth down did not erase the smile lines around his eyes.

"Polly?" he said, and then answered himself. "Of course, Polly. What other daughter do I have? How can I help you?" His face became stern. "You really are her friend? You're not from a newspaper? You have to understand, I can't say anything against my own child, no matter what it seems she might have done."

"I am a friend," Marta replied. "And I'm looking for another friend of hers. An old friend." Was it her imagination, or had a quick shadow passed over his twinkling blue eyes?

"Who?" he asked.

"Nancy Kate Collins. You remember her, don't you?" She watched his face carefully, but all she saw was a pursing of lips, the gesture of a man trying to remember.

"Nancy Kate," he said, musingly. "Nancy Kate! Of course! You say you're in touch with her? I'd love to see little Nancy Kate again. Of course," he laughed ruefully at himself, "I guess she's not so little anymore, is she? She must be as big as my Polly. They grow up when you're not looking, don't they?" He laughed again.

"I'm looking for her," said Marta. "I haven't found her. I thought maybe you could help me." She hadn't, of course, really thought that. If everything Polly said was true, there would be no reason in the world for him to direct Marta to Nancy Kate, every reason for him to hide anything he knew. What she had really wanted was just to see him, to confront him with her knowledge, and to see how he responded. But now she caught herself wondering if he might not, after all, take the address of Nancy Kate's parents out of his wallet, if he might not direct her right to them, because he had nothing to hide. What would a talk with Nancy Kate tell her, anyway? That Polly's father had been a good friend who had never behaved in anything but a fatherly way? That Polly had been given to stories even as a child? That Polly was crazy, or a little liar? Jesus, what was she doing, suddenly doubting everything that Polly had told her, just because her father had a smoother facade than she had anticipated? She could not read the man at all—he must be well used to blocking.

He was speaking again.

"I can't help you there, I'm afraid," he said in a voice laced with regret. "I'd like to, but I lost track of the family when they moved."

"Maybe your wife…"

"My wife isn't well. I hope you won't bother her with this, she's having enough stress coping with the idea of Polly being in prison." It was the first time that he had broken in, the first time that his speech had been anything but measured. As if the hurried way that he replied had jump-started her brain, Marta suddenly wondered why he had not asked her motive for locating Nancy Kate. Didn't he wonder why, with his daughter in jail for murder, they were trying to find a friend she had not seen for over twenty years? Or, did he already know why?

"Maybe just a phone call," Marta pushed. But if she were hoping he would snap, she was disappointed.

"I think you'll be wasting your time." He smiled and shrugged, indicating that it certainly was her time to waste.

Marta did not know what she would have said next. Perhaps just thank you. Perhaps she would have just walked away. But speculation was useless, for at that moment the door that said Chet King, D.D.S. opened once again and a girl walked out. This time, Marta did not have to struggle for category. She was nicely dressed in very grown-up clothes, she was wearing make up and heels, but there was no way she could have been a day over eighteen. At the very most. There was a tag that said "Receptionist" pinned to her sweater.

"Let me help you with that," said Polly's father, taking her coat from her hands. He held the collar while she slipped it on, and then gently pulled her long, strawberry blonde hair loose. His manner was no more than polite. Marta's own father had done the same for her many times, and, if anything, had shown more warmth. Again Marta felt the doubt welling up inside her. Then, as the girl turned to continue down the hall, she caught a little flash of gold resting in the hollow of her throat. A locket. Identical, except for the initial, to the one Polly said her father had given Nancy Kate.

"Don't you want to know why we're trying to find Nancy Kate?" Marta asked. Her voice had changed, she was no longer tentative, but hard. She was burning with an anger so intense she could actually feel the heat rising off her. How dare he! The bastard—how dare he put on the act of the caring father, and how could she have fallen for it so easily?

He looked at her with mild surprise, as if their conversation had ended, or as if, perhaps, he had simply forgotten that she was there.

"Why?" he said obligingly. "Why do you want to find Polly's little friend?"

"Because," she said, through clenched teeth, "Polly wants to find out if you raped her, too."

The girl gasped, and a look of distaste passed over the face of Polly's father, as if she had said not something horrible but ill mannered, as if she had talked about shit or garbage at the supper table.

"I'm sorry you believe that," he said gently, though this time the gentleness was edged with just a slight touch of impatience. He patted the girl on the shoulder, apologizing for subjecting her to anything so distasteful. "You have to understand—if you know Polly, you know that she is..." he struggled over the world. "Different. All right, she is disturbed. As a child, she would come home from her preschool and tell us dreadful stories about the things that went on there. We changed two schools before we realized nothing bad was going on at school, that there was no hitting or withholding snacks, that the teachers were not monsters. We only found out when the people from the social services came to our house. She had been telling her teachers stories about us—just as horrible and just as untrue! We made her sleep in the bathtub, she had told them, we beat her and didn't feed her. They only had to look around to see that none of it was true. But we could never understand why she did it, why she continued to do it! We tried to get help for her, but it never changed. The only thing we could do was warn her teachers, her friends' parents, that she was a—liar isn't the right word, because there didn't seem to be any malice behind it. She was horrified when the social worker came to her house, and she wept for her old teachers when she changed schools. We could only warn them that she felt persecuted, and tell them we were hearing the same kind of stories about them they were hearing about us. You must know that about her, if you really are friends." He leaned suddenly towards her, as if he were going to tell her a secret the receptionist was just too young to hear.

"She has a history of mental illness," he said softly. "She has been institutionalized before. It is well documented."

And Marta did not even have to ask who, faced with this man or Polly, a jury would believe. She knew that they would believe him.

***

The receptionist's name was Jennifer. She was not a high school girl, which was too bad, because that might have been a nice little lever for blackmail right there. Probably mommy and daddy wouldn't have been happy at all about their daughter getting popped by the dentist for class credit. But she was over age, if just barely. Under the cloak of Liz's visiting privileges, Marta found this out from Polly, who had heard it from her mother at Thanksgiving. She had taken the bus back to the jail after her the confrontation with Polly's father. She was not sure why. Perhaps it was because she was using her feelings as a kind of crude barometer, and wanted to see if Polly still read "Not guilty."

"He started doing receptionists about the same time he stopped doing me," said Polly. "My mother is clueless. They're all just such nice girls."

"I've never understood the thing with young women and older guys," said Marta thoughtfully. "How does he carry it off?"

"Think about it," said Polly. "He's a dentist—we're talking big bucks. We're talking going out for a nice dinner every single time you go out, we're talking nice presents a boyfriend your own age can't afford and

88

a good salary for being a receptionist with no experience, just out of high school. Plus, my dad can be charming. I told you he treated me as if I were his lover. That's part of what fucks me up so much—it felt good to be treated special. It felt good to be taken out to lunch and the movies and to have him bring me presents and tell me how pretty I was. It fucks with everybody's perception of what an incest victim is—she's this little girl who is beaten and abused, not somebody Daddy treated like a princess. But, I can see how you might be impressed if you were just out of high school. And he wasn't your daddy."

Marta said nothing. There was nothing to say. She relit the cigarette she had put out a few minutes before. Visiting the jail was deadly—all there was to do was smoke, and if she didn't watch it she'd soon be back to the pack a day she struggled so hard to get off five years before. At least, now that Liz had put her on the list, she could meet with Polly in one of the private cubicles, and according to her own schedule.

"Anyway, he's always keeping some young thing, and it never seems to be against her will. The only thing is, he's got a bad habit of trading last year's model in for the new model, and that's caused a little furor in the old office a couple of times. Even though every one of them knows she's replacing an old girlfriend, she doesn't think the same thing is going to happen to her."

"How do you know so much about it?" Marta asked, more idly than curiously. Through the window in the door she was watching one of the small dramas going on in the restricted visit room—a black woman whose face was crumpling with grief over something her male visitor was telling her. Was he leaving her for another woman? Had her mother died? Had the court taken her child? Separated by the glass, there was no body language between them to help Marta guess.

"Well, I was in for some dental work a while back when the old girl-friend came back and made a scene with new girlfriend."

"You let him work on your teeth?" This snapped Marta around so quickly the words flew out without any thought, and a moment later she wished she could recall them, for she could see she had offended Polly. "I mean, I just would think ..." she trailed off, not wanting to come right out and say, 'I'd think, at the very least, if you didn't shoot the bastard, you'd at least stay away from him!' The thought of Polly allowing her father to put his hands in her mouth made Marta squirm.

"It's so fucking easy for you," said Polly angrily, and Marta cringed, because she knew it was easy. She knew it was easy because Mary Clare had lectured her about it just the night before. She had talked about how the victim had to be the one who took control, about how she had to be the one to decide whether to cut things off with her abuser or continue some kind of relationship, whether to confront or forgive or neither or both.

"I know, I know, I know, I'm sorry, I'm sorry," Marta said hastily, wishing she could just lie on her back and expose her throat like a dog. It seemed as if scolding was the only kind of interaction she'd had with anyone in days.

"Well," said Polly. She stopped and looked away. "I needed two root canals" she said after a moment, still angry. "Do you know how much that costs? I get less than four hundred dollars a month disability. To pay for everything."

"I know," said Marta again, and again, "I'm sorry. I wasn't thinking. I just opened my mouth and it came out." They both lit another cigarette, looking in opposite directions. It would be a good time to leave, thought Marta, and then she thought, no, that would just add insult to injury. Confront me, and I'll just walk away, because you're in jail, and I'm not. In silence they smoked their cigarettes almost identically halfway down, and then Marta spoke. "Does DJ give Lexy drugs routinely?"

"Damn!" Polly slammed her hand down on the counter hard enough to draw the attention of the guard in the hall. She frowned in their direction, and both Marta and Polly put on uneasy false smiles, trying to show things were okay, that they were talking about rents going up or Clinton in the White House, that no one was going to erupt into violence. "Is she doing it again? God, that pisses me off! And that woman says I'm unfit to spend time with her child!"

You're in prison charged with murder, thought Marta, but instead she said, "This is a habit, then?"

"It was at one time." Polly spread her hands helplessly. "I had thought—I had hoped I had gotten her away from it. I should have known she'd go right back to it as soon as I wasn't there to deal with Lexy anymore."

"Is something wrong with Lexy?"

"No!" Polly was emphatic, hitting the counter again, though this time in a controlled way that did not draw attention. "There is nothing at all wrong with Lexy. There never has been! That was all in DJ's head! That fucking…" she made a visible effort to calm herself and started again. "DJ was never much for the motherhood thing. You noticed that?" Marta nodded. "DJ never should have had children. She's way too self-centered. The pregnancy was an accident—a typical DJ thing. She had a girlfriend who was thinking maybe she was bisexual. The girlfriend was paying way too much attention to some man. So what did DJ do? She went out and fucked this guy herself—put everybody in a twist—killed things between him and the girlfriend, and then threw the girlfriend out. Or so I pieced together. She tells the story a little differently—she's the heroine. But anyway, even though she got back at everyone else, she ended up pregnant. She should have had an abortion, or put the baby up for adoption. But I've told you how concerned she is about how things look to

90

other people—I think probably she was afraid if she did either one the ex would be laughing behind her back—you know, yeah, maybe she screwed me, but look what happened to her in the end. So I suspect she acted like this was part of the plan, she was just delighted. Only, in the end, there was a baby to deal with. And as far as she's concerned, every single normal kid thing Lexy has done from the moment she was born has been to annoy her. She had Lexy on Ritilan when I first met them. You give Ritilan to kids who are uncontrollably hyper—Lexy was just a normally active little girl who wanted some attention from her mother. DJ is not the type who wants to arrange her schedule to fit a child's needs."

"How could she get Ritilan for a normal child?" asked Marta.

Polly threw up her hands. "Some doctors are willing to do anything to turn a buck. And DJ's persistent. She used to drug Lexy like she was a bad dog whenever she had company coming—it took me a while to figure out why she was always so placid. Was it at the wake that she was doped up?" Marta nodded. She had mentioned the wake to Polly, but had not gone into any of the ugly details. What was the point? This drugging thing, though, that was important. "That's typical. If we're not drugged, we might have feelings. If we have feelings, Mommy might have to deal with the kid instead of doing her own thing." Marta nodded again. It certainly seemed to fit in with what she had seen at the wake. "But I stopped the drugs after I moved in. DJ was fine with it, as long as I was willing to be in charge of Lexy. She liked the wife and daughter scene—as long as she came first, of course." Polly shook her head, as if marveling at her ability to have put up with this for so long. Then her expression changed from one of anger to one of tenderness. "I didn't mind," she said. "I love Lexy. I loved doing things with her. One summer I was unemployed, and we spent Lexy's whole vacation just hanging out together. It was the best summer of my life." She looked at her hands in her lap. "I worry about Lexy now that I'm not there."

And, thought Marta though she saw no sense in saying it aloud, you have good reason to worry about Lexy.

She gestured through the window, and as the guard came to open the door, she wondered about this tenderness. Liz was working on the assumption Polly had drugged Karen and Lexy, but would Polly have done that to a child she loved so much? Could Marta have been right in her original suggestion? Could Karen have drugged Lexy? Could she have been pushed to suicide and, either accidentally, or on purpose, decided to take the little girl with her? And, if Polly had gone to the house for some reason and discovered Lexy unconscious, could that have raised a killing rage in her?

She didn't know. She only had a little of the shine, and all it would reveal to her was a feeling Polly was not guilty. The barometer was holding steady.

"I'd like to talk to Lexy," she said slowly, partly because it was true, and partly because she wanted to see Polly's reaction. Jesus, she didn't even believe her own feelings, how could she expect anyone else to believe them?

Polly looked a little alarmed. "Do you have to do? I mean, that poor kid, she's been through so much..."

"The police have already talked to her, I'm sure. Don't you think?"

Polly looked startled, as if she had not thought of this before. "I guess. But why would they? She was drugged, she was asleep when Karen was killed." Marta noticed that she talked about the event in the third person, like someone who had heard about what had happened, rather than someone who had been there.

"She might have known something about how she was drugged, don't you think?" asked Marta.

"Liz said that she didn't," said Polly. "And she claims that she never saw anyone but Karen that night."

"Oh!" said Marta. For the first time, it occurred to her that Liz, as Polly's lawyer, had access to all kinds of information that she did not. Would she be willing to share it? Probably not, she had made it clear that she was hiring Marta solely on Polly's whim.

"If I wanted to get DJ to let me talk to Lexy alone, how would I do it?"

"Offer to baby-sit," Polly said promptly. "Saturday night. DJ hates to stay home Saturday night. But how is that going to help with Nancy Kate?"

"It's just a feeling I have," said Marta vaguely. She was embarrassed by the way Polly accepted the cosmic brush off, and knew it wouldn't fly with either Liz or Mary Clare. "But we're going out to see your mom tomorrow—maybe she can set us on the trail. You don't remember where they moved?"

Polly shook her head. "No. I was only a kid then."

FOURTEEN

The directions Polly had given Marta were not very good, which she found a little strange. One would think directions to a childhood home would come automatically. But then, Polly's memory was patchy. Just how patchy she was discussing with Mary Clare.

"This guy says another mile or two down the road," said Mary Clare, who had climbed out from behind the wheel for the second time to ask directions to supplement Polly's.

"Do you think," Marta asked, thinking back to Liz's what-ifs "she could have done it herself?" Too late, she realized she might be treading on confidential ground. Well, that was too bad—if she was Liz's employee, then Mary Clare was her assistant.

"What?" asked Mary Clare crossly—she didn't like being lost. In Mary Clare's mind the perfect trip consisted of getting in the car, driving the car, and getting there. There was no stopping for gas, food, sights, side trips or particularly directions. Mary Clare was very like Marta's father in this way.

"Have you been listening at all?" asked Marta. She was cross herself, but her crossness had to do with facing Polly's mother rather than admitting she was lost. Don't call, Polly had said. She won't make a date with you—she'll say she's going out. But she never really does go out. Just go by in the afternoon. She'll be there.

"No," said Mary Clare, "I haven't been listening. I think we're just going to the store. I think that you've found a fantastic Safeway in Lakewood. I can hardly wait to see the produce."

They drove in a prickly silence for a few minutes. The problem was that this was the suburbs, where all rules of street layout were temporarily suspended, as if they had entered another dimension. Streets looped and dead-ended and curved back upon themselves. Mary Clare was obviously thinking longingly of Capital Hill, where everything was laid out in blocks as if with a ruler.

"Is that what you think?" Mary Clare asked finally. "Polly killed that other little girl?"

Marta sighed, and experimented with rolling her window down. Nope, the sun was shining, but it was still too damn cold. "I don't know," she said. "I do think her friend—Nancy Kate—is dead. Oh, Mary Clare, if you could have felt what I felt! I think she's dead, and she's been dead a long time, and it wasn't a natural death. Liz, Polly's own lawyer thinks she killed Karen, and Polly can't even tell her she didn't. Her memory is like Swiss cheese—she remembers some things, she doesn't remember others, she remembers some things symbolically, she disassociates—she's not what you'd call a reliable witness in a courtroom, that's for sure!"

"Memory loss is very common in incest cases. You know that! It doesn't make her a killer!"

"I'm not saying that it makes her a killer. I'm saying it might cover up the fact she's a killer." What, Marta wondered, would make a woman a killer? Would she have killed Teri's girlfriend if given the chance, if pushed just a tiny bit more? She was afraid to look at the answer to that one. "Mary Clare. I know Polly is the victim here. I am not saying she is a bad person. What I *am* saying is she is tremendously fucked up."

"Oh, that's pretty judgmental—" began Mary Clare hotly.

"No, it's not! Fucked-up-ness is a universal condition. It's like being wet. You can be wet because it rained on you, or because someone threw water on you, or because you fell in the river, but when it comes right down to it, wet is wet and fucked up is fucked up. It's not about laying blame right now—I couldn't be more sympathetic to the things that have happened to Polly—God, I couldn't be more sympathetic to the things that happened to *you*! But this isn't about blaming—it's about what happened."

"I thought you wanted to help Polly," said Mary Clare accusingly.

"I thought I wanted to help Polly, too." Marta sighed. "I don't know what helping Polly is any more. I don't know if looking into her background is going to help her or hurt her. But she paid me to look for Nancy Kate."

"And what if it turns out this kid was killed—she didn't move away at all? Are you going to go to the DA and suggest they try to hang that on Polly, too?"

"Luckily, Liz Smith solved that problem for me. I don't think I'm allowed to go to the DA." She was actually a bit unclear on this. Hopefully, it would never come up. She did not know why she was trying to convince Mary Clare that Polly could be guilty of murder—it had to do with convincing herself of Polly's innocence. "Pull into the 7-Eleven."

Mary Clare obeyed, crossing two lanes of traffic without so much as a backwards glance. Marta, who had driven with Mary Clare for years and was convinced she was guarded by a special traffic angel—there was no other explanation for the fact they had not been killed years ago—did not even flinch. She took a handful of change out of the ashtray, and a few moments later they were both settled back with Big Gulps. a bag of chips between them.

"Did I tell you what G-hey! and I decided the other night?" asked Mary Clare after a long pull on her Coke.

"I dread to ask."

"There are only two reasons to be fucked up."

"Which are?"

"Your family and chemical imbalance." Marta opened her mouth, shut it, opened and shut it again, and then opened and shut it a third time.

"See," said Mary Clare, delighted with herself, "You can't come up with an example that doesn't fit."

"It's pretty encompassing," Marta admitted, tossing back a handful of Doritos. "But I think you should add Vietnam."

Mary Clare considered. "Maybe," she said. "I'll discuss it with G-hey! before we submit it to the American Psychiatric Association."

"You can't discuss it with G-hey!. She doesn't know what Vietnam is."

"You're right." Mary Clare took another long swallow. "But here's another theory—caffeine cures all ills."

"Cures or creates," said Marta, draining her Diet Pepsi.

"Well. All I know is that I'm a new woman. Now, what are you trying to say about Polly and this other little girl?"

"Polly said her father treated her like an adult, like his lover. Now, how would an adult react if her lover became involved with, started courting someone else?"

"Well, *I* never handle it well," said Mary Clare, turning the key in the ignition. "I've been known to break a tail light or two. But I've never killed anyone." She backed them straight out into traffic with only a token glance over her shoulder.

"Well, imagine that rage in a child, especially with all the other things that were going on. By that time she knew on some level what her father was doing to her wasn't right—she had all kinds of feelings of anger and fear and self hate."

"Oh, yeah," said Mary Clare, "you always blame yourself."

"Would you have been jealous if Joey had a girlfriend?" asked Marta curiously.

"Joey had girlfriends," said Mary Clare grimly. "It never slowed him down as far as I was concerned. He dated nice Catholic girls who wouldn't put out. Actually, I don't think it would have made a difference if they had. Joey's thing wasn't sex—Joey's thing was power. Joey was a typical rapist—he just did it over and over to the same person instead of preying on strangers."

"Oh." They drove in silence for a moment, Marta wondering if she had overstepped herself by bringing up Mary Clare's brother. But, damn it, Mary Clare was the one who had said she didn't want to have it treated with shame anymore, as if it were something she had done that no one could even bear to talk about.

"But," said Mary Clare finally, "to get back to Polly. Her father began fucking her at a much earlier age than Joey started fucking me. And he had a very different style. Yeah, I can see how she might have been very jealous if he started paying attention to another little girl. Incidentally—what age are we talking about here?"

Marta threw up her hands. "This is unclear. Polly thinks she was in fourth grade when Nancy Kate moved—or disappeared. She also thinks Nancy Kate was a little older than she was—at least she can never remember them being in the same classroom at school."

"So how easy would it be for a ten year old to kill another child— maybe one who was older? And to keep it concealed?"

"I don't know. Maybe very easy. Remember, when Polly was a child there was a lot of open country out here." Even now the area in which they were driving had occasional pastures and fields. "They went out walking, they got mad, they fought, Polly picked up a bottle or a rock and hit Nancy Kate over the head. Kids see that kind of shit on Westerns all the time—they think people can survive having a bottle broken over their heads—no problem! She wouldn't even have had to kill Nancy Kate outright. If she had incapacitated her, if she got scared and ran and didn't tell anyone, a cold night could have finished her off."

"And the body?" asked Mary Clare doubtfully. "A little girl is missing, and there isn't a search? This may have been farm land, but it wasn't the Everglades. A little kid without a car couldn't have hidden a body."

"She didn't have to! Preadolescent girls are murdered all the time! The police aren't going expect a playmate—they're going to expect a pervert. Polly kills Nancy Kate and runs—blocks it out. Nancy Kate's body is found, but the police never identify a killer. The family moves away—it's too hard to stay here and look at the field where she was found. Polly's mom and dad don't talk about it, because it upsets her— maybe because Dad suspects. Gradually Polly forgets about it—she's already done that with a large part of her life because of the incest. Nancy Kate simply moved away. We have only Polly's word for it." She paused for a moment, trying the story on for size the way another woman might have tried on a jacket. Did it fit? Could it have happened that way?

"This is it," said Mary Clare, jerking to a stop in front of an older split-level. The neighborhood was reminiscent of the one in which DJ lived, except that it was thirty years older. You had to look twice, here, to see that all the houses had once been the same—their uniformity was broken with add-ons and sheds and trees and basketball hoops.

There was a grapevine wreath on the door of the house, and within it two geese smirked and held a welcome sign. Marta's grandmother had kept geese off and on for years when Marta was a child. She had been nipped and had stepped in goose shit many times. Only a city girl would put geese on her door.

"Yes?" The woman who answered the door did not look much like Polly. She did not have her fair hair or skin. She was also much thinner. Not by ten or fifteen pounds, but by twenty-five or thirty pounds. The bones in her face showed sharply, directly below the skin, without any padding at all. It was in her face, when she turned her head sideways, that you got the only glimpse of Polly, in the high cheekbones and pointed chin.

"We're friends of Polly's," Mary Clare, at her most charming, said when the woman cracked the door, still on its chain. It was a cautious gesture which seemed strange in the suburb. Even in Capital Hill, Marta had no second thoughts about opening to a knock during daylight.

"Polly?" A strange vague expression crossed the woman's face, and for a moment Marta wondered if they were going to have to remind her of who Polly was.

Mary Clare did remind her. "Your daughter, Polly," she said, her voice losing a little of its charm. Mary Clare needed another Coke.

"Oh, Polly's not here," said the woman, as if Polly had just stepped out to go to the store.

"No. Polly's in jail for murder. We know. That's why we're here."

Maybe it was the ugly bluntness of the statement that made the woman open the door.

"We wanted to ask you some questions," said Mary Clare, and since she seemed to be handling the interrogation, Marta looked around the room. From what she could see, the house was kept as neat and clean as a museum. The decor added to the museum feeling. The exhibit might have been called, "Folk art from around the world." Not the tiny molas or paper cuttings that Marta's friends could afford to hang on their walls. This was folk art with money behind it. In the front hall stood a carved wooden statue—African, Marta guessed—that stood at least ten feet tall. Antique quilts covered two walls of the next room, and in among all the books and functional things were little statues of wood and clay, pottery, silver jewelry, fetishes and gourds with screw tops mounted on their necks. Somebody—Marta suspected Daddy—was a collector.

"Nancy Kate Collins," said Polly's mother. Mary Clare must have asked the question while Marta had been playing cash register in her mind—the quilts cost this much, the statue that much and, any way you added it up, there had been more spent in these two rooms than Marta had forked over in rent for the last two years. "I haven't thought of Nancy Kate in years. She and Polly were such good friends when they were little girls. Nancy Kate loved Polly from the time she was a baby. I remember when I first came home from the hospital, and Judith Collins came over to visit with Nancy Kate. She wasn't more than two years old herself, but she was so excited! Most little children are jealous of babies, but not Nancy Kate. She loved Polly from the first moment—I think she would have been happy if we'd just gone away and left them totally alone. She wanted to hold Polly and feed her and even change her diaper." She drifted off, looking out the front window as if soon Nancy Kate would be coming up the walk. Her dark hair was in a ponytail, just as Polly's had been in the jail. But hers was perky and held high on the back of her head with a bright red scrunchy that matched her baggy cotton sweater. She was dressed nicely and carefully for a woman Polly claimed rarely went out. Heavy silver jewelry in her ears and around her wrists.

"Did Nancy Kate move away?" asked Marta abruptly. She held her breath, waiting for Polly's mother to say in surprise, 'Why, no, didn't you know? It was a terrible tragedy, but Nancy Kate was killed. They never found the murderer.'

"Oh, yes," said Polly's mother, as she stared out the window. "I thought Polly would never stop crying. She acted like her heart was broken."

No. How could it be—another dead end? Marta asked again, thinking perhaps somehow there had been a mistake. "And Nancy Kate moved with them? Nancy Kate went along?" Polly's mother turned and looked at her for the first time.

"Nancy Kate was a little girl," she said. "Nancy Kate wasn't any more than twelve years old. Of course she went with her family—how could she do anything else?" She paused for a moment, and Marta tried to regroup herself. There must have been other questions she had wanted to ask, but she could not think of what they had been. She had been certain that Nancy Kate had been killed. Everything had been based on the picture that had swept through her head when Polly had handed her the locket—the cold lifeless hand dropping open, and the locket falling out and landing on the ground. "Polly wanted to go and visit Nancy Kate, but it was long drive, and I wasn't well…" Polly's mother trailed off, and then started again. "And Chet thought that she ought to make new friends. He didn't see any point in her hanging on to something long distance, someone she could see only once or twice a year at the most. Maybe if we'd been special friends with her parents, it would have been worth the drive. But we weren't. They were good neighbors, they were wonderful neighbors, but they weren't special friends." She was silent again and Marta wondered suddenly if this woman had ever had any special friends.

"Did you ever hear from Nancy Kate's family?" Marta asked, because she could think of nothing else to ask.

"Christmas cards," said Polly's mother vaguely. She cleared her throat, as if to say more, but what came out was, "Is Polly all right? Have you seen her?"

"You haven't seen her yet?" It was not what Marta had meant to say, but it was what leapt out. How could she not have been to see her own daughter in jail?

Polly's mother flushed. "I haven't been well."

There was a sudden whimpering sound, and a small, black cocker spaniel appeared from the back of the house. Her weight, and the grey around her jaws said that she was an old girl, but she moved with all the liveliness of a puppy, sliding ten feet on the hardwood floor to reach them.

"Is it time to go out, Missy?" the woman asked, with something like relief in her voice.

"Here, let me," said Mary Clare, and she was off like a shot, following the dog through the house. Polly's mother made a little squeak of protest, but she was much too late. All she could do was follow Mary Clare. Marta trailed behind. The kitchen had much the same folk theme as the foyer and the living room—great copper colanders and pottery bowls and carved wooden measuring spoons hanging from the walls. On the huge old table, which looked as if it had been liberated from the kitchen of an Amish farmer, was a huge mess of metallic cloth, thread, feathers, beads—a treasure trove that would have made any child with an eye for collage catch her breath with delight. Marta smelled a hot glue gun.

"What are you making?" she asked curiously, forgetting, for a moment, her mission. Mary Clare was fussing with the back door.

"Oh, just some dolls." Polly's mother's voice did not change, but her face lit up. "Here, let me show you." The doll was two inches of glitzy fabric adorned with a button for a face and a feather head dress. It looked like a fetish for a drag queen. It was quite wonderful.

"Do you sell these?" Marta asked, turning it over, and noticing that there was a pin on the back, so it could be worn on a lapel.

"Yes..." she trailed off and then restarted again. "For Second Chance. They have a gift shop. It's good to help other people," she said. "I like to do what I can."

Marta was not familiar with the name. She supposed it was a charity, maybe part of Junior League. Before she could ask, Mary Clare spoke.

"Is Missy supposed to go in the dog pen?" she asked, looking out the back window.

"Oh, no," said Polly's mother, and for the first time she laughed. "I don't know what Chet was thinking," she said. She joined Mary Clare at the window, and Marta tagged along behind. The back yard was nice in an impersonal kind of way. You knew immediately someone was hired to come in once a week during the summer and mow and edge the lawn.

There were no borders of roses or pansies, no vegetable plot or compost heap, no fruit trees—nothing that would be a bother. There were evergreens—no leaves to rake—and a row of poplars probably put in when the house was first built. They were starting to die now. There was a plain cement slab for a patio, upon which sat a picnic table that needed to be refinished. Marta could tell by the way the table stood that the patio was a bit tilted—probably an amateur job. Her Cheecha had liked to putter, and she had come to recognize the enthusiastic homemade touch.

The fence was tall and well maintained—a privacy fence. The snow had been trampled by the dog, and then frozen and defecated upon. The dog run was a pen in the back corner with a concrete floor, the kind of thing in which people kept hunting dogs for whom they had no time the rest of the year. It was not the type of habitat one would normally associate with a small dog.

"I don't know what Chet was thinking," Polly's mother repeated. "He got such a bee in his bonnet—he worked on that thing like a maniac—after work until it was too dark to see. He gets like that—once he has a new project, that's the last we see of him for a while. He's very handy, but he's so single minded! His car broke down just as he started this project, and he wouldn't even take the time to take it into the shop until he was done. He had to use mine." She gestured to a Buick sedan, at least twenty years old, parked on a gravel patch beside the pen. A gate in the back of the fence was designed to roll away to provide off the street parking. Marta suspected this was necessary because Polly's mother's car might sit for days, months at a time.

"And poor Jim! His dad decides to remodel the whole back yard, and there he is! He hadn't planned to spend his spring break pouring cement, but..." She trailed off, and then began again.

"Of course I wasn't going to put Missy in it! She's never set a foot in it, and neither did Sissy!" For an awful moment Marta thought she was using a nickname for sister—then she realized they were not talking about Polly, but another dog, who had presumably long since gone to dog heaven.

"This isn't a Bette Davis thriller," she scolded herself—no one kept little girls penned in the backyard. It was much more subtle than that—that's why he was able to keep doing it so long.

As if to prove false Polly's mother's words, Missy suddenly abandoned a squirrel on the fence and ran over to the pen. The gate was ajar, and she walked inside and lay down on the concrete. It was probably, thought Marta, the only place in the yard that was dry and soaking up the afternoon sun, for the patio was shaded by the house this time of day.

"Oh, no," said Polly's mother in a vexed tone, "she mustn't go in there!" She pulled open the door and called sharply, but the little dog ignored her.

"Do you want me to go and get her?" asked Mary Clare. Polly's mother looked at the sandals on her feet, and then at the snow.

"Yes—if you would. It's just that…someone, a neighbor, a teenager, backed into the fence there. We haven't had it repaired yet—I'm afraid she'll wiggle out of the pen and get into the alley."

Mary Clare set off stoically, picking her way carefully across the fouled snow.

"Polly," Marta said to the woman, and then she stopped, unsure of what to say next. The woman had not once protested her daughter's innocence or offered a theory of frame-up. In a way it was as if it was Polly and not Nancy Kate who had been dead for twenty years. In a way, thought Marta, she had been.

Mary Clare came back inside, carrying the dog under her arm as if she were a football. "You were right," said Mary Clare, setting her on the floor with an oomph. "She could get out back there. But I locked the gate of the dog run—she'll be fine in the rest of the yard. Somebody must have been backing up pretty hard to have done a number like that. "

Marta opened her mouth. She was going to tell the story about the time one of the skinheads had gotten drunk and jumped the curb and taken out the neighbors' brick porch, and had then driven the car away. But Mary Clare did not pause. "So," she said, without changing her tone whatsoever, "you know your husband raped your daughter for years when she was a child." It wasn't a question. Marta drew her breath in sharply, and looked at Polly's mother. She would have predicted a number of responses. Denial, indignation, anger—what she would not have predicted was the same vague calmness the woman had showed all along.

"Oh, no," she said, as if they had delivered the mail to the wrong address, "Polly's father was a very gentle man. Polly's father would never hurt anyone." She walked across the kitchen, clucking to the little dog, who was putting pawprints on her clean kitchen floor.

"You don't have to be…" began Mary Clare indignantly.

"No." The woman cut in for the first time. "Polly's father would never hurt her. Polly's father took very good care of her. He's always taken good care of all of us." Her gaze swept around the tidy kitchen, and came to rest on the mirror hanging on the wall. She made a little gesture that Marta did not recognize—only after she drew herself up and looked in the mirror sideways did Marta realize the painfully thin woman was sucking in her stomach.

There was no more to say. Even if there had been more to say, Marta was not sure that it could be said, for Mary Clare was still puffed up with indignation. Marta grabbed her shoulder and headed her towards the front door. Polly's mother did not look up as they left the room. She was gluing a tiny bead onto one of the dolls.

"What did you hope to find out by confronting that woman about

Polly's father?" Marta hissed, as they passed the big bookshelves again.

"Find out?" Mary Clare looked at her as if she were crazy. "I didn't hope to "find out"."

"Then why do it? What was the point?" Marta could see immediately that she had pissed off Mary Clare.

"The point was..." she began hotly. "Oh, damn it, that kind of woman just pisses me off so much! The point was she obviously knew her husband was fucking her daughter. She knew it! Only everybody pretends she didn't—poor mommy has her own problems, and so no one can expect her to protect her child, and in fact we'll lie about what happened to avoid hurting her feelings. That's such bullshit!"

"Why are you so sure she knew what was happening?"

"Did you see the way she reacted? No upset, no freak out—she had that reaction planned. And what did she say? Not even "That didn't happen" but "He wouldn't hurt her." Not he wouldn't fuck her—he wouldn't hurt her. In that family the agreement was as long as it was done gently it was okay. As far as I'm concerned, she's just as guilty as he is. That's why I said something. She thinks she can just hide in her house with her dolls and pretend the whole thing didn't happen. And she can't."

There was a small sound behind them, and Marta whirled around, blushing already. But it was not Polly's mother. Standing on the stairs was a man, tall and redheaded, older than Mary Clare. A man with the same high cheekbones as Polly. A man, in fact, who looked enough like Polly to be her brother. Oh.

"Hi," he said to Mary Clare, who had her chin jutted out belligerently. "You're friends of Polly's?"

It was Marta who nodded.

"I'm Polly's brother," he said.

"Jim," said Marta.

"Yeah, Jim," he said, showing no surprise that she knew his name. "I'm one of those adult children you read about—you know, the kind that come back to live in their parent's house when they've lost their jobs?"

Neither of the women replied.

"I couldn't help but overhear what you were saying about my mother," he said. "You know, you're judging her kind of harshly."

"No," said Mary Clare, willing to take this battle right down to the mat. "She knew."

"She did know," said Jim. Marta had been expecting him to say, 'Oh, no, Polly lied, or My father would never hurt her.' All she could do was close her mouth around her rebuke. "Or, maybe, it wasn't that she really didn't know as much as she worked very hard not to know. There's a difference, you know."

"Not to the child," said Mary Clare shortly.

"No, but you have to understand what was happening with my

mother. My parents are both Catholics. From the old school. Birth control is unthinkable to my father. He planned on having just as big a family as his parents did. I'm ten years older than Polly. My mother miscarried six times between Polly and me. Three times after. And then my father left her alone."

"You mean she was using Polly as a kind of birth control?" Marta felt sick.

"Not that clear. Not that easy." Jim sat down on the steps. "I don't think she ever really imagined in her mind what was happening between Polly and my father. How could she? She could never have allowed it to happen if she did. But, as long as she could keep it out of her mind..." He did not finish the sentence.

"You think Polly killed this woman?" asked Mary Clare bluntly. Mary Clare was not a big one for pulling her punches.

"Oh, yeah," he said "absolutely."

It was not the answer Marta had expected, and she could tell by the look on Mary Clare's face she was equally shocked. Surely there was one person in Polly's family who believed in her innocence?

"What?" said Mary Clare, as if there had been a misunderstanding.

"Yeah, I think she killed her. She thinks she killed her. But I don't think she should be doing hard time for it. After what my dad did to her— he should be the one up on the stand."

Marta and Mary Clare looked at one another. This was the first member of Polly's family to back up her reality.

"So you believe that your dad incested her?"

"Oh, yeah, everything she says is true. I'm sure of it." Marta looked away from Polly's brother, and then back. It was quite disarming to look at him—Polly, but not quite. Even their speech pattern was much the same. "I was only a kid when it was happening, but even I could tell something was wrong. None of my friend's dads treated their daughters like my dad treated Polly. He acted like she was his girlfriend—he was always taking her out on little—well, you couldn't call them anything but dates. Out for dinner, out shopping, out for the weekend. I was jealous for a long time—Polly and I didn't get along, believe me. Before Polly was born, my dad used to spend a lot of time with me—camping and fishing trips every weekend. It wasn't until Polly told me what he'd been doing the whole time that I realized I'd been lucky he ignored me."

"He didn't try anything with you at all?" Mary Clare asked curiously.

Jim shrugged. "Maybe he didn't like little boys."

"Yeah," said Marta, and nothing else, because there was nothing else to say.

He sighed. "Poor Pol. She's going to get screwed. This is going to be a big lesbian revenge trial—the *National Enquirer* will probably pick it up! I hope her lawyer has enough sense to bring up the incest and the blackouts—that's the only thing that might get her off. Although it might get her some time in the loony bin, too, and I don't know if that wouldn't be worse than jail."

"We came here to look for one of Polly's old friends," said Marta. "Nancy Kate Collins. Do you remember her?"

"Why in the world are you looking for her?" Jim was the first member of Polly's family to react in a way that Marta found normal at all. "They must have moved twenty years ago."

"Do you know where?" She didn't feel good about letting Jim in on Liz's plans. In fact, she was getting a kind of creepy feeling off Jim. The house, probably. The whole place gave her the willies.

Jim shrugged. "Someplace in Nebraska, I think. To be with some grandparents who were ill?" He said it as if it were a question. "It was a long time ago. I was only..."

"About twenty, actually," said Mary Clare. "So you should remember it pretty well."

"I was away at school by then," Jim said. "Anything I knew about it I heard second hand. And I didn't spend a lot of time chatting up Polly when I was home—I didn't have time for a kid." He shook his head ruefully. "If I'd known what was happening, maybe I could have gotten her away from here, and she wouldn't be in jail now." He shook his head again. "I'll always blame myself for that."

Marta glanced quickly over at Mary Clare. For all the sighing and expressions of regret, there was a strong air of performance about the whole thing. Was she just inventing this because of the general creepy air that she had already noticed? No, Mary Clare was rolling her eyes back in her head, too.

"Why are you so convinced she did it?" Mary Clare asked the question Marta was thinking.

"You mean besides the evidence? You mean besides the fact she was splattered with blood and holding a knife? You mean besides the fact she was absolutely obsessed with that DJ woman? Well, this isn't the first time our Polly has cut somebody up, you know."

The rest of it might have been a performance, but Marta had no doubt that this one part, at least, was absolutely true. Jim was still hanging his head, but there was a tone of glee in his voice he could barely disguise. He might think he had worked things out with his sister, and even Polly might think they were now friends, but at this moment he sounded like the jealous older brother of their childhood.

"What are you talking about?" asked Mary Clare. Marta wished she had kept quiet. He wanted them to ask—what might he have been provoked to say if they hadn't responded?

The mask of concern was replaced by a mask of remorse. "Boy, I thought for sure she would have told you. I guess if she hasn't, she wants to keep it quiet. I'd better not say anymore."

"Probably not," said Marta shortly. "Do you think your mom got any letters from the Collins family after they moved? Maybe a Christmas card?"

Jim slapped on a thoughtful face. "Maybe. I can look."

"We'd appreciate it." Marta realized that she had not left her address or number with Polly's mother—it had seemed futile. She opened her day pack—among the clutter was the empty envelope in which her telephone bill had arrived. She handed it to Jim. She was eager to leave. Out of Polly's whole family, the person she had found most likable was Polly's father, which made her a bit sick to her stomach.

Mary Clare, instead of heading out the way they had come in, pulled her little truck around the corner and into the alley.

"What are you doing?" Marta asked.

"I want to show you something," Mary Clare replied. She parked the truck halfway down the ally, behind the tall privacy fence that surrounded Polly's parents' yard. The alley was bordered by two rows of identical fences, but they could tell this was the right one because a span of boards on the end had been crushed in at the bottom by a car. "Come here." There were two gates in the fence, the car gate, and a standard gate for foot traffic. Mary Clare pushed against the latter. To Marta's surprise—everything about the King house seemed so tightly shut and closed—it opened immediately.

"I popped the latch when I was back here," said Mary Clare, catching the look. "I wanted you to see this."

The car which had crumpled the wooden fence had hit hard enough to cause damage to the dog run as well. One corner post, in fact, had been hit with enough force so it had lifted a chunk of concrete out of the ground. This crumpling was what had concerned Polly's mother—in one place the wire fence of the run in front of the broken boards had folded in and left a gap that even a fat old cocker spaniel could easily squeeze through. But this was not what Mary Clare was interested in.

"Look at this," she said, pointing to the cement base of the dog run. Marta had to squat down to see. She looked nervously over her shoulder, hoping Missy wouldn't need to go out again soon.

"Polly's locket," she said. She reached out a hand as if to pluck it free, but the little heart was stuck fast. It was tarnished from the weather, but otherwise it was identical to the one Polly's father had given Nancy Kate. Except, of course, the initial was a P. "March of '67," said Marta, reading the date scratched into the wet cement. "Didn't you say Polly was about my age?"

"About," Mary Clare agreed. "So that makes her about ten when she did this."

"Which is about when she thinks her dad stopped incesting her. So could this have been some kind of ritual around that? Getting rid of the token, marking the date?"

"Maybe. But I'll tell you what." Mary Clare stood and brushed her hands together. "If both of those people in there hadn't said that little girl moved, I'd guess she was right under that cement."

***

They were both silent on the drive back home. Mary Clare gave an audible sigh of relief when they crossed Santa Fe.

"Delafield's?" she asked.

"Yeah," replied Marta, who hadn't had a piece of cheesecake in a *really* long time.

"So what did you think of her family?" asked Marta. "Do you think any of them had anything to do with it? They're all kind of nasty." The new owners had not kept the cute Formica tables, which she thought a huge loss.

Mary Clare was silent, which was strange. Marta looked over at her. "Do you?" she asked again.

"Okay," said Mary Clare. "You want to know the truth? I think Polly did it. I think she did it, and I think she was probably sane when she did it. Okay? You wanted the truth, and that's the truth. I think you're wasting your time. *And*, I think you should stay the hell away from that therapy group. Bad call on my part, I apologize, and you should run like a fucking bunny."

"You think that Polly killed Karen because of the group?" asked Marta. She was confused. Up until this moment, she had been operating on the premise that Mary Clare shared her conviction of Polly's innocence. If she was not, what in the world was she doing visiting Polly in prison and schlepping Marta out to her parents' house?

"Yes." Mary Clare was agitated, one step away from a scene. She whipped out a pack of cigarettes, the ones from the prison. Or a new pack, half smoked, which was going to be something to worry about later. She lit two and handed one to Marta. "Yes. I do. I think she got all worked up in a frenzy and went over there and slashed that woman. Didn't you say you had talked about that? Didn't you say that nobody in that group had any control?"

"Mary Clare, nobody in that group has the ability to plan anything like this! All we can do is sit around and cry!" Even as she said this Marta was uneasily aware that she was skirting the truth. Or perhaps, just not telling the whole truth—that while they were a mess, she could see Mary Clare's point. Suppose she had decided to ride on one of her twisted little fantasies of blowing Teri and the young one away? What better time to act than right after a session of serious obsessing? "If you don't believe that Polly is innocent, what the hell was that all about—taking her shampoo and books? You're doing that for someone you think is a killer? Jesus, Mary Clare, I've seen you blow off women totally because you didn't like the way they voted in the primaries! You're going to be buddies with someone who you think is a murderer? What is it going to be—some kind of prison romance or something? Wow, that'd be safe, wouldn't it?" Oooh, that last thought had popped up clear out of the dark. Mary Clare was going to take her head off.

But, maybe because the look on her face told Mary Clare how surprised she herself was to hear those words, or maybe just because Mary Clare was a compassionate woman, she chose to ignore them and cut to the chase.

"I did that...I took you there...I took you there because, damnit, Marta, I thought maybe you could tell me no! Because I thought maybe you could be the one who could find something..."

"Why? Why would you think that? You know how I am!" She held up both hands and wordlessly opened and closed them rapidly, signaling off and on, off and on.

"I know, I know!" Between deep draws on her cigarette, Mary Clare was gesturing broadly with in it a way that promised disaster. Too late, Marta wondered if they were in a smoking section, or if Delafield's even had a smoking section. "Off and on! But that's such bullshit, Marta! That's just because you...I mean, if you..."

"What are you saying to me?" asked Marta incredulously, gesturing with her own cigarette. Might as well be busted for a sheep as a lamb. "Are you trying to tell me that this stuff flashes erratically because I don't *try*?"

"Yes!" Burst out Mary Clare. "Yes! Or, no. I mean, you have this gift, and you spend all your time watching TV in the dark, or in a basement giving drug and alcohol counseling to women who are too wacked out to go to a therapist. Hell, I could do that! I could do that better than you do!"

"Then do it better!" Marta tried to squeeze in another sentence or two, but Mary Clare was on a tear, and it was going to take something serious to stop her.

"You have a gift, you *always* have had a gift, ever since you were a little kid, and you dick around with it!"

"It's off and on!" said Marta, as Mary Clare stopped for a breath.

"It's off and on because you dick around with it! Just because you have a talent doesn't mean you don't have to work at it! Do you think Martina Navratilova got where she is just by having a gift? Do you think Marge Piercy..."

"It's off and on!" Marta shouted.

There was one of those total silences that happen only in public places, when you suddenly realize everyone else has stopped talking to listen to you. Marta stole a quick look over her shoulder. Called that one right, every single dyke there, including the waitresses, were frankly staring. They were the best entertainment since the last poetry reading. Better.

"Have you noticed," she hissed to Mary Clare between her teeth, "that ever since you stopped having sex, all you want to do is have public scenes with me?"

Mary Clare, who was so agitated that she had not even noticed the silence, gave a startled look around. Two dozen pairs of eyes stared back.

Marta slapped a five on the table. "I am going to go wait in the truck," she said.

Luckily, Mary Clare recognized this as an exit line, for it was far too chilly to be waiting.

"Hey, baby," said one of the men coming out of the Shamrock Bar next door. "Are you feeling good? Because you sure are looking good!"

"That's what I love about Broadway," said Mary Clare as she climbed behind the wheel. "No matter how unattractive I'm feeling, I can always get a date down here. Now, first of all..."

"No, it's my turn to be first of all! If you can believe that Polly can't remember anything about her childhood, how come you can't believe that I don't have any control about what I know?"

"But if you tried..."

"And if Polly tried, if any of those women in your group tried—"

"It's totally different! That's suppression of a very traumatic event."

"And you think this is not traumatic?" Marta made a gesture that encompassed her whole body, her whole self. "You think it isn't traumatic having this, this..." she struggled for a word, and then settled for slamming the back of her wrist up against her forehead, making the same blinking motion with her hand. "This *thing*? This fucking eye? It's like seeing everything under a strobe light! Flash—Nancy Kate is dead! Flash—Joey's fucking Mary Clare! Flash—Grandma just had a stroke! And not even important things—hey, Grandma doesn't like the channel the TV is on, even though she can't talk, she doesn't like it, and how am I going to get Mom to change it when she doesn't even want to talk about that stuff, when she thinks the second biggest failure of her whole life, right behind me being a lesbian, is that she ever let Nana fill my head with that old world crap..."

"You knew that Joey was fucking me?"

Marta stopped short and blinked. The words had just seemed to roll out—she had to go back over them to see what she had said. "Yes," she said slowly. "When I was about ten." She put her hand back up to her forehead and made the blinking eye again. "Flash," she said.

"What did you do?" asked Mary Clare, already sounding cold and remote before she had even answered.

What could she tell Mary Clare?

"I cried," Marta said. "I cried and cried. Because I was frightened. Because, even though I didn't know what he was doing, I knew he was hurting you. Because I knew, Mary Clare I..." She stopped and struggled for the words.

"Because what?" asked Mary Clare, remote.

"Because I knew that your parents knew, and they weren't going to do anything to stop it, and I knew that meant I couldn't do anything either."

Mary Clare turned on the engine of the truck. Her admirer from the bar had wandered over by the door—she pulled away so fast that Marta feared he might have lost a hand. She looked back over her shoulder—no, he was tipping his hat to some other dyke. He was never going to score if he didn't change his territory.

"So," said Mary Clare, a final, definite word that said this was going to be another of the things about which they were not going to speak. "Yes, I think she did it. Unless you tell me something else, what else can I think? You told me she sent Karen those articles—God, they were just one step away from one of those ransom notes cut out of the newspaper." She mimed scissors with her right hand, and Marta had a clear flash of the type of letter to which she refereed. She guessed computer printouts had made them obsolete. "She hated the woman—she made no bones about that."

"Polly was the one who left DJ," Marta reminded her.

"Oh, what difference does that make?" asked Mary Clare scornfully. "I've left women and then called and wept and begged them to take me back. Maybe it's good for your self respect to be the one who leaves, but that's all. It doesn't mean that you've accepted that it's over or that you want her to pick up someone else the *very same day!*"

Marta was silent, for she knew that what Mary Clare was saying was true. She herself had left Teri twice before she had ultimately been left, and the pain she felt in each case was indistinguishable. Besides, even if Polly had been reconciled to leaving, it was quite another thing to find out that, instead of mourning, your ex had taken a new lover into the house within a week.

Mary Clare parked the truck back behind Marta's house and they headed inside.

"So she had the motive." Mary Clare was now ticking off the list on her fingers. "She had access to the drugs, she was right fucking *there* with the murder weapon. She was covered with blood, Marta! What else do you want? Unless you know something else," she added hopefully.

"I don't know anything else. Don't you think that I wish I did? But I still don't think that she did it."

"Based on what?"

"Based on a feeling, okay? I don't think that she did it because I like her, all right?"

"Oh, that's going to go over well in court!"

"I don't intend to take it to court! And do you think it would go over any better if I could tell the judge, 'Hey, my psychic power told me that somebody else did it'? 'I saw it with my third eye?' I'm usually right about how people are—you know that."

Mary Clare, who clearly did not want to back down, mumbled, "Well, at least it would give us somewhere to start."

"We already have somewhere to start, Mary Clare." Marta held up her own hands and began listing. "One, what the hell was she doing over at DJ's to begin with? When I left her, she was settling down for an evening at home."

"She was disassociating when you left her," reminded Mary Clare.

"Yeah, but that's not like sleep walking, is it? Why didn't she just disassociate to bed, instead of going out in the cold? And how did she get there? She doesn't have a car."

"Well, you just can't predict what she might have done if she disassociated," said Mary Clare with a frown. "There are women in my group who have all kinds of weird shit happen to them when they have flashbacks—they hear voices, they feel compelled to go outside. It's a reach, but it's sure not impossible. She disassociated, she got angry, she fixated on Karen, that's all she wrote. Didn't she talk about Karen in your little session?"

"Yes, but—"

"Well, there you are!"

"Mary Clare, I said I wanted to pull Teri's head off like she was a roasting chicken in that group, and I don't think it's going to happen!"

Mary Clare looked at her for a long moment. "That's the advantage to being tall," she said finally. "If I was going to pull anybody's head off, I'd have to stand on a chair."

"That'd spoil the effect, all right," agreed Marta. "Okay, let's say she could have done it in some kind of fugue state. Then, still, how did she get over there?"

"She took a cab, she took the bus, she hitchhiked," Mary Clare waved that off. "She got there the same way you get places."

"Yeah. And I don't have the money to call a cab, and neither did she. And there's no way a woman who's been raped is going to hitchhike. I'm sorry, but I just don't believe it."

Mary Clare nodded her head, conceding. "Yeah, and she's little, like me. That makes you cautious. So she took the bus."

"Jesus, I hope not! And they're going to plead crime of passion? Maybe the jury is going to accept flashback, maybe they're going to accept delayed trauma, but nobody is going to accept that Polly left her own apartment in the freezing cold, waited for a bus, caught the bus, had the right change and then forty-five minutes later hacked some woman to death without being aware of what she was doing!"

Mary Clare had a horrified expression on her face, which Marta realized had been sparked by her description of the crime. She must have been pushing that part out of her mind, just as Marta herself had been doing. But, wasn't that exactly what had happened? And didn't they need to keep it in mind? Marta wasn't even sure that, when push came to shove, she could gouge out an assailant's eyes, as she had been taught in the self defense class to which Mary Clare had dragged her last summer. She was positive she could not stab someone who had been drugged. Repeatedly. Could Polly have done so?

"And," Marta continued, pressing on while Mary Clare was maintaining her shocked silence, "What about Lexy? Surely Polly wouldn't have done that while Lexy was there. It must have been awful."

"Yeah," agreed Mary Clare. "Actually, I've been meaning to ask you not to pull off anyone's head while I'm around. That sounds bad enough."

"Unless it was Teri," said Marta thoughtfully.

"Oh, I'd buy a ticket to see that. But, remember, Lexy was drugged, too."

"And that's been bothering me, too. Would Polly have drugged Lexy? That was dangerous."

"She was confused," began Mary Clare doubtfully.

"No," argued Marta, "we can't have it both ways. I mean, the way it looks now is that it was done by someone who carried out a pretty cold and calculated plan and then at the last minute turned into a berserker."

"Jury isn't going to buy that," agreed Mary Clare. "She's screwed."

Marta got up and went over to the window. She opened it and hung out. It was so cold that it made her eyes water immediately, but still she held the pose, surveying her little winter domain. Caught-With-Baloney jumped up on her back and looked out over her head. Across the street, four of the skinheads were coming out of their apartment. One looked up, saw her and shot her the finger.

"Close the window," begged Mary Clare. Marta pulled herself back in and straightened slowly, so that Baloney slid down her back and landed on the floor."

"What if..." she said slowly, turning so she faced the room again, "Okay, who cares how she got there. What if when she got there someone else was already there..."

"What?" scoffed Mary Clare. "Sitting around and popping pills with Karen. What was it, a suicide pact? Where's the other body?"

"Okay, okay, that won't work. But what about this? What if Karen was trying to commit suicide, and for some reason Polly arrived after she passed out?"

"That doesn't help much," said Mary Clare, shaking her head. "Okay, it explains the drugs, but Karen didn't stab herself. What did Polly do—just seize the moment? And why bother—didn't the coroner say she had ingested enough stuff to kill her anyway? If Polly wandered into a suicide attempt, why not just let Karen die? Easier, less mess and didn't implicate her."

"Except," argued Marta, "that Lexy was drugged, too. Maybe that sent Polly off the deep end. I mean, Karen could have just fed Lexy a pill or two so she wouldn't wake up and find her. But Polly didn't know that. Maybe she walked in, thought Lexy was dead and that pushed her over the edge. There was Karen, there was the knife, she freaked."

"Which still means that she killed her," pointed out Mary Clare. "I mean, I guess Liz could argue that Polly thought Karen was already dead, and was just venting on the body."

"Ick," said Marta.

"Uh huh. I personally think that mutilation would be a little difficult, unless you were raised to it. I think probably even cannibals tell their kids not to eat Grandma or the baby."

They sat still for a while, both thinking. Mary Clare wandered over to the TV and turned it on. A blurry picture of the bridge of the Starship Enterprise filled the screen. An alien being was arguing with Picard.

"Uh oh," said Mary Clare. "He's ugly. Gotta be bad."

They watched in silence until the commercial break.

"Commercials during *Star Trek* should have to be theme," said Mary Clare. "You know, Data should have to feel like chicken tonight."

Marta was not thinking about *Star Trek*.

"What if," she said slowly, "there was a third person. Okay, forget the drugs for a minute. What if there was a third person who ultimately stabbed Karen, but left Polly there to take the blame?"

Mary Clare looked at her over the heads of Gravy and Five-Cents, who had both taken the opportunity for a little lap time.

"What if *Lexy* stabbed Karen?" she suggested. "For that matter, what if Lexy drugged Karen? She was in the house, she hated Karen, and she's sure ready to freak about something."

Marta recoiled. "Oh, my god, I don't want to find that out! That's horrible!"

"It's not any more horrible than thinking that Polly hit Nancy Kate over the head with a Coke bottle twenty years ago! And, at least if Lexy did it, they'd take her out of that house and get her some help."

"They'd institutionalize her," said Marta. "Help..." she spread her hands, bonking Baloney, who didn't want to be left out in case there was petting, on the head. "Sorry," she said to him, scratching his ears by way of apology. "I don't know how much help kids get in institutions."

"What was the feel that you got off her?" asked Mary Clare, who apparently was going to allow feels within certain perimeters.

"Weird. Blocked. The drugs, I guess." She lapsed back into silence as the show returned.

"I see someone is going to get walked in on in the holodeck again," commented Mary Clare. "That's the most unrealistic part of this whole show. You know that everybody would be fucking in the holodeck all the time—they'd have to have a time lock on it. There'd have to be a whole program on Tasha Yar in leather."

"I wish we had a holodeck," said Marta, as she watched Deanna Troi recreate an incident in the past of her patient. "I would pull Teri's head off. And I'd find out what went on over at that house Sunday night."

"How?"

"Oh, I'd recreate the scene. Tell it everything we know and see what it came up with."

"You know," said Mary Clare thoughtfully, "I'll bet we could do that anyway. I mean, we could at least go over and talk to the kid."

"I'm one jump ahead of you." Marta could not help sounding smug—being one jump ahead of Mary Clare did not happen often. "I know how to get invited back to that house."

"Cool!" said Mary Clare without asking for details. She was not always gracious about being a jump behind. "What do you suppose Polly's brother meant about her cutting somebody up?"

"I don't know," said Marta, looking at her watch. "Let's go out to the jail and find out."

***

"I should have known that visit was too good to be true," Polly said in a disgusted tone. "I thought it was kind of nice that my brother visited—you know, it was good to get support from *somebody* in my family. Nobody's been out, nobody's talked about bail."

Marta said nothing. If she had been in jail for any reason at all she would have expected both her parents and all three of her brothers to fly into Denver within forty-eight hours—and they would. God, she was lucky!

"I mean, he acted like a dick, but he always does. He used to torment the hell out of me when I was a kid—he was so jealous! Of course, everything he did only made it worse, because I was a little tattle-tale, and Dad always took my side. But I thought things would get better between Jim and I once I told him what had really been going on."

"He talked about that," said Marta. "He actually sounded fairly sympathetic."

"He was a creep," said Mary Clare, handing cigarettes around to all. The woman sitting on the other side of Polly looked longingly, and she passed one out to her as well. Marta could have asked for a lawyer's cell, but she had wanted Mary Clare to come with her, and that meant the common room. It also meant using Polly's one "family visit," which just meant that it was the one visit during the week when she could see up to three people at one time. Marta did not feel guilty about using it. She didn't think there was a chance in the world that Mommy and Daddy and Jim were going to come out and see "Poor Pol" together.

"Yeah," said Polly in a tone that held more than a trace of bitterness. "He is a creep. But he's been the only one in my family who's given me any support at all. He's never tried to make me think I was hallucinating or I was crazy. I gotta give him credit for that."

"Yeah," said Marta, thinking of Mary Clare's family.

"But it's not easy to change that family stuff, you know? Now he just has a superior air, 'There's our Polly, time in the loony bin, picks bad women, can't ever quite get it together.' " She imitated him perfectly, and Marta looked away. "He's Mr. Yes/No—'Here I am, Sis, you can count on me all the way, brought you cookies and money, but aren't you a dumbshit to get into this situation? I mean, I mean, I think it's Dad's fault and all, but aren't you just stupid, and haven't you always been?' "

There was a long silence.

"So, what's the story on the cutting?" Marta finally pressed.

"It was a long time ago," said Polly. "It wasn't that I forgot it. It was just a long time ago—I didn't see how it could be important. I was in junior high, for god's sake! Think of the stuff you did in junior high—does any of it relate to your life now?"

"What did you do?" asked Marta.

"I cut up a woman's face." Polly shrugged. "That sounds more effective than it actually was. I doubt she even had to have stitches."

"Who?" asked Marta.

"One of my dad's chippies. The first one, as far as I know." She shrugged again. "Look, I was jealous. I had been the apple of his eye for ten years—I had been his girlfriend, his lover. All of a sudden, I wasn't anymore. It was like he dumped me flat without any kind of explanation."

"I would have thought..." said Marta tentatively, knowing she was no doubt about to say something wrong, "you would have been relieved..."

"It's not that clear cut," said Polly shortly. "By the time you're ten—most kids don't even know about sex. Just because I was having sex didn't mean I knew what was right or normal. For all I knew all my friends were having sex with their fathers. Even the way he got me to keep it a secret was confusing. It was 'special'—not a bad secret, just special and it might make other people like my mom and my brother jealous. Then we'd have to stop doing 'special' things like going out and trips. It was 'private'—it wasn't bad, it was just poor manners to tell anyone I was Daddy's favorite. Why do you think I was telling my teachers all those lies when I was little? I needed them to know that something wasn't right, but I wasn't even sure what it was myself. And I certainly didn't want another woman to take my place. You don't understand how this was—one day my father's schedule revolved around me, and the next he didn't have the time of day for me."

Marta looked away, remembering the feeling that had hit her in the pit of her stomach when she called Teri and her new girlfriend had answered. So how did you handle that if you were a *child* and laying on the couch for six months and watching *Star Trek* in the dark was not an option?

"So?"

"So, I went in to have my teeth cleaned. And he had a new receptionist. Just a kid. And she was wearing a locket just like mine. And she had a bowl of candy on her desk. Denver mints—my kind, the special kind he used to bring me. He wasn't an innovative kind of guy. So I lost it. I had an Exacto knife in my book bag—I had been using it for a project at school. I don't remember planning to do it. All I remember was realizing she was his new girlfriend, and then I was up on the desk, right in her face and the blood was flying."

She told the story in a rather removed way, as if it had nothing much to do with her.

"So what happened?"

"Oh," Polly shrugged again. "That was the first time he had me locked up."

The bell rang. Their shift was over. There were new wives and pimps waiting for their forty-five minutes. Mary Clare passed a final cigarette to Polly and the woman beside her. Marta asked a final question.

"The girls who worked for your dad—would there be anyone who knows where to find them now?"

"Sure," said Polly. "Talk to Gwen. His nurse. She's everybody's mommy. She'd know."

FIFTEEN

"I'll be at Ms. C's if you need me," DJ said over her shoulder on her way out the door. It better be pretty damn good, was the message implied. DJ was not the kind of mommy who wanted to be called about the sniffles. Marta watched her clip across the walk in her black cowboy boots, careful to avoid the patches of snow. She was wearing a matching leather jacket and cowboy hat—she looked like a woman who was going to paint the town red.

"So," said Marta, closing the door and looking down at Lexy. Polly had been right on the money about the baby-sitting—Marta had hardly been able to get out the words—Polly's friend, what can I do in your time of grief, do you need a break?—before DJ had been eagerly agreeing. But, now that she was here, what did she do to gain this child's confidence? According to the police report, which Liz had shared with great reluctance, making it obvious that she thought Marta was stepping outside her boundaries, the detective who interviewed Lexy had found out nothing of importance. She'd had a milkshake after dinner, she didn't notice anything strange about it, she'd gone to sleep and woke up in the hospital and that was it. There was a little note on the bottom of the report saying the police had on tape the 911 call that Lexy had made, even though she claimed not to remember it.

But it also said that Lexy had ultimately dissolved into hysterics, at which point DJ had terminated the interview. Maybe there was something there, maybe not. Even if there was nothing, Marta wanted to hear it for herself.

"Do you want to make some cookies?" she asked hopefully. Making cookies had been one of her very favorite childhood lures. In childhood, whenever her mother had wanted to tell Marta something that was going to cause a stink—that she was going to have to wear her patent leather shoes to church or let Grandma cut her hair into a pixie cut—she softened the news by letting her mix up a batch of cookies first. She did the same thing with Marta's father and martinis.

"Okay." Lexy shrugged lethargically. She followed Marta into the

116

kitchen placidly, but showed no excitement, not even when Marta pulled the chocolate chips out of her grocery bag.

"Do you want to measure? Do you want to put the egg in?" Marta asked.

"Okay." Again Lexy responded as if it were a job and not a treat. Marta watched her slowly stir, a worried little frown between her eyes. She didn't think that Lexy was drugged up this time—her eyes were clear, and she wasn't talking in the same slow monotone. But there was still something wrong.

"Do you want to taste the dough?" she asked. "It's my favorite part. Sometimes I don't even bother to make the cookies."

"Okay," said Lexy, with a heavy sigh. As she dutifully licked the spoon, glancing once or twice longingly in the direction of her bedroom, Marta suddenly realized what the problem was. Lexy was depressed! She was responding to all of Marta's suggestions just as Marta herself had been responding to Mary Clare for the past six months, with that same resigned air of doing what was good for her, no matter how much it hurt.

"Lexy," she asked carefully, "do you feel bad?"

Lexy stopped licking the spoon and looked at her warily.

"Do you feel..." Marta struggled a minute to put own her feelings into order. "Do you feel kind of heavy all the time? Like it's too hard to move? Or sleepy—like the best thing to do would be to stay in bed all the time?"

Slowly, Lexy nodded her head. Clearly, she was afraid that there was some kind of trick involved here.

"My mom says it's just faking," she said in a voice that was barely above a whisper.

Fuck your mom, thought Marta fiercely, but she did not say the words. Instead she said, "Do you feel like you're going to cry a lot? Like really stupid things might make you cry?"

Lexy's answer to this was to burst into tears. This time Marta did not hesitate. She picked the little girl up and held her on her lap until the tears subsided.

"Do you want to lie down?" she asked. "I could read you a story." She had no idea what to say to this sad little waif. She knew what she had been through with her own depression. She had barely hung on with the support of friends—all Lexy had was a mother who thought she was a hypochondriac. Not for the first time, Marta wanted to pop DJ.

It was only after Lexy was undressed and under the covers that Marta remembered her trump card.

"Oh!" she said. "I brought you a note from Polly."

The note had been her idea, and she had been the one who had picked out the card with the little dancing cats on the front. They didn't sell cards in the commissary at the jail. But Polly had written the words. Marta watched Lexy's face as she read them. She had read the card herself after she had left the jail, testing the barometer again. Would Polly say "I'm sorry" and if so, what would it mean? But all Polly had written was, "I miss you. I love you. Hang on 'til we can be together again."

Lexy closed the card and looked up.

"My mom wouldn't like it if she knew you brought me this," she said slowly.

She'd shit a brick, Marta thought, but didn't say.

"You know what? I'm here to be your friend, not your mom's friend. 'Cause Polly told me that you're the one who needs a friend, and she can't be here right now."

This was pure improvisation, but Lexy listened with a little frown.

"My mom wouldn't like to find this card," was what she finally said.

"I'll take in home with me," said Marta, holding out her hand. The longing look Lexy gave as she handed it over made her add, "Anytime you want to hear it, you can call me and I'll read it to you. How long have you felt so bad?" she asked.

"A long time," Lexy said in a little, faraway voice. "Since Polly went away."

"I'm trying to help Polly," Marta said. "I don't think that she killed Karen. But she doesn't remember what happened, or why she was here at the house." She stopped, feeling that it was a little too soon to question Lexy outright. She wandered over to the bookshelf. The thin book Lexy had requested the night of the wake was pushed in crookedly, just as Marta had left it. She pulled it out.

"I'll read you a story," she said, sitting in the rocking chair beside the bed. Polly's touch again. " 'My cat Barney died today...' "

She was not prepared for the depth of emotion that would be evoked by the simple story about a child's questions of the afterlife. Both she and Lexy were in tears by the end of the book. They sat quietly for a moment, looking in different directions.

"Do you think that's true," Lexy asked finally. "That Karen will become part of the ground?"

"Oh, yeah." Marta, who had been raised as a good Catholic girl, had all kinds of questions about the afterlife. She could not accept the Catholic concept of heaven and hell, especially when she and her friends were casually condemned without even a review of their lives, but neither could she believe, like the Navajo, that people wandered unhappily as ghosts after death. The actual changing of the body, however, she had down pat. "Yeah," she said, "I think that's just what will happen. My grandfather always said he wanted to be buried in his garden when he died—I liked that idea. I liked thinking he would be part of the flowers and the raspberry bushes and the grapes."

There was another silence. Lexy looked out the window, and Marta tried to keep herself from reliving the awful thing that had happened inside the house.

"Do you think she went to heaven?" asked Lexy, not saying Karen's name. Which was surely the walk-in for which Marta had been waiting. Yet she wanted to answer the question with the dignity it deserved.

"I think," she said finally, "when someone dies, their soul goes to live in the hearts of the people who loved them. Like, if you were to die, part of your soul would live in Polly's heart and part in your mother's." She felt a little funny about including DJ, but, then, she wasn't a mother. She had no idea of what the feelings were between Lexy and DJ, and not to have mentioned her seemed like throwing up her neglect in Lexy's face. "Yeah," said Lexy doubtfully, as if the clouds and harps and cans of tuna in the book were much more comforting.

"And Karen?" Marta prompted gently. "She'll live in your mother's heart?"

"Yeah," said Lexy in a voice even more hesitant, as if she, like Marta, saw DJ's relationship with Karen as more like usury, a way to get back at Polly than anything else.

"Do you think," said Lexy, after another moment of silence, "when someone is killed, their ghost hangs out in that place? You know, until the killer is caught?"

Whoa, this one was out of left field. This one must be coming from the kids at school, because it certainly wasn't coming from the gentle children's book she'd read. Marta's first impulse was to comfort—no, of course not, that's all nonsense, you have nothing to worry about, her bloody ghost is not going to hang around your house wailing for justice. But she stopped herself. For the sake of Polly, she needed to know what had happened that night, and this might be the lever.

"No," she said finally, slowly, because even to get the information she wasn't willing to plant a nightmare in the child. "I think once you die you're beyond that. I don't believe in ghosts. What I do believe in…" and here she paused again, because this was something she had never before voiced, "what I do believe is that the people who are left behind when someone is killed can be very upset and angry, and they can create something like a ghost." Lexy looked doubtful.

"What I mean is," Marta struggled for words. "What I mean is— when someone is killed, generally the people who loved that person are very upset. They're angry, they're sad, they're scared and upset. If you're around them, you feel all those feelings, even if nobody is talking about them. I think when people who are alive get stuck with bad feelings they can't resolve, that's what creates what we call a ghost. That's why they say ghosts hang around where there are unsolved murders—it's those bad and sad feelings."

She looked at Lexy, wondering if the explanation had been too abstract. Large tears were leaking from beneath the girl's closed lids, and gently Marta pulled her over to hold her against her chest.

"Is there anything you should tell me about the night Karen died?" It was difficult to understand the little girl's words through her choking sobs, so finally Marta stopped questioning her and just held her, gently stroking the back of her head. "Now," she said, when the sobs finally died down, "tell me what happened."

"Karen," said the child, and then hiccuped and sighed deeply.

"On the night she was killed," Marta prompted. "What happened on the night she was killed?"

"I don't know!" Lexy cried despairingly. "I don't know what happened!" She was silent once again, and Marta thought back to things written in the police report Liz had showed her.

"The police," she said slowly, an idea beginning to form in her head, "think Polly killed Karen. They think she had been sending her magazine articles, stories from the paper to scare her for quite a while."

"No," said Lexy, a sad but firm little denial, and suddenly Marta saw how it must have been.

"You sent those articles to Karen yourself, didn't you?" she asked, careful to keep her voice factual rather than judgmental. "And that's why they've been able to pick up Polly's fingerprints on them. She must have looked at your magazines and newspapers at your house when she came to visit." Lexy was a kid from the computer generation—that must have been how she had generated the envelopes. Her fingerprints could have easily been obliterated by the dozens of postal employees who had handled it. Jesus, and she'd never even asked Polly about the clippings!

"I just wanted her to go away," said Lexy in a voice that was still not far from tears. "I wanted her to go away! I wanted her to leave so Polly could come home!" She burst into a fresh storm of tears. "I needed Polly to come home," she sobbed. "She wasn't going to come home while Karen was there! My mom acted like…she thought that…"

She acted, Marta thought grimly, like Polly and Karen were inter-changeable. And perhaps to her they had been. But Polly had functioned as Lexy's mother for most of her life—a girl of twenty-two who had not signed on for a child could not possibly have taken Polly's place.

"I wanted her to leave," Lexy said. "I thought maybe she would leave if she was frightened. She wasn't happy. I thought maybe if she was scared she would go away. But she didn't. And then I wanted to die." She leaned her face against Marta's chest, and Marta's heart ached for the despair in her voice.

"*You* wanted to die?" Marta asked, the question making her voice rise. This was not what she had expected.

"Yes. It was no good. Nothing was good."

Marta's heart went out to her, remembering her own journey into darkness over the past six months. How could it have been borne without Mary Clare? How could it have been borne if she had been eight and not thirty-five?

"So you took the pills," she prompted slowly, "You took the pills from Roger's house." Because it was not just Karen and Polly who had visited the AIDS patients—both of the women had taken Lexy with them

120

as well. And Lexy was an overly bright child who not only would have no trouble understanding the pamphlet put out by the Hemlock Society, but who, as well, had grown up around a mother who drugged her regularly. Suicide must not have seemed far-fetched to her.

"And I made a milkshake," said Lexy in a far away voice, as if she were settling in to tell Marta a bedtime story. "Because I don't like to swallow pills. I used Chunky Monkey ice cream—it has nuts and stuff in it."

"It disguised it," said Marta. Lexy nodded. "But how did Karen get the pills inside her?"

"I couldn't drink it all. I made too much. I thought it would be enough if I drank half. But before I went to sleep I had to get up and go to the bathroom. And when I did..."

"What?" prompted Marta.

"Karen. She drank it. I didn't think she would. She was on a diet. But she drank all the rest. Her head was down on the table."

Karen, Marta remembered from the autopsy, had ingested far more of the drug than Lexy, which was what had led the police to believe, whatever else had happened, there was no intent to kill the child. Perhaps, if Lexy had just dumped everything into the blender, the pills had not been evenly distributed, but had settled down to the bottom, where Karen had thought they were just nuts and bits of chocolate.

"Why didn't the police find the dirty glasses?"

"She'd put everything in the dishwasher, and it was running. I didn't want my mom to find out!" Her soft little voice rose with anxiety. "She's so mad at me all the time! She said if Karen left it would be my fault, and to stop being such a baby. So I thought I'd just go back to bed. But then..." she paused and hung her head down.

"You were okay with suicide, but it didn't seem right to kill someone else? Was that it?"

"Yes." Lexy let out a gusty sigh of relief, happy she had not been forced to say the words. She leaned back against Marta's chest, as if now things were over and settled, and finally she could rest. There were tears in Marta's eyes, and at the moment she hated DJ, a woman she hardly knew, with a passion. She had been disgusted with the manner in which she treated Polly and Karen, but, my god, what kind of woman didn't even notice that her fourth grade daughter was seriously suicidal? What kind of selfishness was that? Just the same kind that Teri always showed you, flashed a little voice in her head, there and gone so quickly there was no chance to reply.

"So, what did you do then?"

"I called Polly. She said she'd be there right away, but she sounded funny, and I was afraid, so I called the ambulance, too." Lexy's tired little voice interrupted her indignant thoughts. Okay, that explained both why

Polly was at DJ's to begin with and the 911 call. But what had happened afterwards? Who had wielded the fatal knife?

"And then?" Marta prompted. Lexy shrugged. "I went back to bed. I hoped they would only find Karen. But when I woke up, I was in the hospital. They said Polly killed her with a knife! And I was afraid to say anything to my mom!"

"I know," Marta soothed. "We know now." She sat quietly, rocking the little girl on her lap and wondering if an attempted suicide were reason enough for the social services people to intervene, and, if it were, if a foster home would be better or worse for this child.

SIXTEEN

Gravy was waiting for Marta on the back steps when she got home from work the next day. She was exhausted. DJ had stayed out so late that she had finally fallen asleep on the couch. She had hardly been able to be civil to the woman—she hoped DJ had written it off as the hour. She didn't want her alienated just yet.

Of course, this would be the week she pulled a Sunday shift. Gloria was of the opinion that one person could cover the phones on Sunday, and Louann would not back Marta up in telling her this was not true. She was afraid of being forced to work every Sunday or, even worse, having to share her hours with a new employee who might not be as easy to top as Marta.

Gravy began to tell Marta a little tale of woe that included hours outside in the freezing cold and nothing to eat for days. Marta bent down to look closely at his white ruff. "You have fish stuck to your fur," she told him. "Aren't you ashamed of lying to me?" Gravy closed his eyes and looked the other way. Marta really did have poor manners.

There was one letter in Marta's mailbox. She tore the envelope open as she trudged up the stairs, Gravy galloping ahead of her. Inside, they could hear Five-Cents calling anxiously to him.

Inside the envelope was a Christmas card. Marta stood by the door and looked at the cover. It showed, far off on a hill, the wise men, and farther yet the star. Inside, there was a verse from the Bible, and underneath a signature Marta did not recognize, and which did nothing to explain to her why she was getting a Christmas card in February. There was a typed letter folded inside the card. Marta unfolded it, absentmindedly pushing the cats' dish with one toe in an effort to fool them into thinking that she was adding new food. Gravy gave her a disgusted look, and went to sit by the sink. He knew where the food was kept, and he wasn't interested in eating nibbies that had been sitting in the dish all day.

There was a little yellow sticky stuck to the inside of the letter. It read, "I found this in our Christmas stuff." There was no salutation. It was signed, "Jim". Oh, of course, he had said he would look to see if he could find the Collins' address.

There was a terrible commotion at the bottom of the stairs, as if

123

someone were trying to come through the bottom door without opening it. The door slammed open and then quickly shut, and Mary Clare was calling Marta's name.

Marta dashed out onto the landing, scattering cats left and right. At the bottom of the stairs Mary Clare, who was so bundled up that she looked no more than six years old, was holding up another woman, whose face was covered with blood.

"Here," Mary Clare said, her face lighting with relief as Marta came running down the stairs, trailed by Gravy and Baloney. She thrust the young woman at Marta. She was not much bigger than Mary Clare, so it was easy to haul her up the stairs. She was not unconscious, as Marta had thought at first, but she had been beaten up fairly badly. Marta caught sight of a bloody nose and a cut lip before the young woman hid her face in her shoulder. She was wearing a jeans jacket, and underneath it a thin sweater that must have done no more to cut out the cold than a plastic bag. Her bare hands and her face were freezing cold to the touch. The blood on her face was frozen.

"Put some water on," Marta said over her shoulder, as she half carried the girl to the couch. She pulled the red and white afghan her Nana had knit off the rocking chair and tucked it around the girl, then went into the bedroom to get the comforter. The girl had, besides the beginning of an impressive shiner, terrible acne. Marta looked at her closely. Where had she seen that before? She tucked the comforter around her, then stormed into the kitchen.

"You brought," she hissed at Mary Clare through her teeth, softly, so the sound would not carry into the next room, "that skinhead girl into my house!"

Mary Clare was looking for coffee or tea, and of course there was neither. "What was I supposed to do with her?" she asked. "Pretend I didn't see her? I'm going to go ask G-hey! if she has any tea."

Marta caught at her sleeve. Bringing G-hey! onto the scene was only going to complicate things. G-hey! saw things as they ought to be, not as they were, and could not comprehend discussions concerning fear and repercussion.

"What if her boyfriend comes looking for her?" Marta asked. "I don't want him looking in my apartment!"

"I'll take her to my place as soon as she warms up," said Mary Clare. "Marta, she was sitting out there in the bushes, in the dark, in the cold. Waiting for one of us."

"Waiting for you!"

"Okay, waiting for me." She started to say something else, but stopped herself, and Marta knew they were thinking the same thing, of the desperation that had made the girl wait in the freezing cold for a stranger who might not even show. This was a woman with no resources at all.

G-hey! did have tea and honey, with which they laced it liberally. Mary Clare, who had been knocked around a lot while growing up, did not consider any of the bangs and cuts a danger—what she was worried about was hypothermia. She suggested a warm bath, but the girl shrank visibly from the suggestion. The three of them—for of course G-hey! had trailed them back into the apartment—rolled their eyes at one another. Another straight girl afraid of losing her virtue to the dykes. Were these women insane? So instead they gave her another mug of tea, and put G-hey!'s hot water bottle on her stomach, and Marta's on her feet. The girl had pulled the comforter up around her head like a hood, and she peered out at them with frightened eyes, rather like the Closet Kitty. Without consulting one another, Marta and Mary Clare went back into the kitchen. It was too weird to stand beside someone who obviously, at least on some level, feared you. G-hey!, who was oblivious, turned on the TV and settled on the end of the couch.

"What's this?" Mary Clare asked, picking the letter up off the kitchen counter. Mary Clare considered anything that was open fair game.

"Oh," said Marta, "It came in the mail today."

Mary Clare gave her a look. "It's Sunday, girlfriend."

Marta shrugged. "It was in my box." She looked at the letter over Mary Clare's shoulder. It was one of those Xeroxed Christmas newsletters.

Hello, friends, it began. *It hardly seems like it can be Christmas again already, does it? Jerry swears he was just taking the lights down last week. (Of course, that's not so far from the truth—I think they actually did stay up until February. You all know our Mr. Procrastination!)*

The boys have both been involved in basketball this year. As if getting ready for Christmas wasn't enough to make us scurry, someone (it must have been a man, right?) scheduled tournaments for both the junior high and high school teams the second week in December. Talk about chaotic! But we don't mind—it's a pleasure to chauffeur such hard working players. A wonderful thing about moving to a smaller school has been both boys, and all the players, in fact, get more time on the court. Are you envious, all you big league players?

The same small town spirit is evident on the drill team as well. You don't have to be a model to get out and march (though, of course we think our girls would have made the grade anywhere!) All you have to do is have the spirit and the uniform and a mom who'll drive you in to practice at seven a.m. every morning. Let me tell you—after all those early morning runs, we'd better make state this year!

The store has been doing well, and Jerry is still loving and hating being his own boss. He had a terrible cold last month that should have kept him in bed, but no, he was right there selling snow blowers and rock salt every day. A town without a hardware store is like a day without sunshine! His dad would be proud of him carrying on the tradition. I offered to keep the home fires burning, but he didn't think the ranchers would feel comfortable buying their nails and rabbit chow from a woman. Haven't they ever heard of women's lib out here? (No.)

Jerry's mom has been staying with us since his dad passed away. She has been wonderful—I never would have gotten those darn drill team uniforms put together without her! The kids love having Grandma right on hand to spoil them.

All in all, we're doing as well as can be expected—life goes on in spite of our loss. Thanks to all of you who sent a card or letter.

It was signed, *Judith Collins and family.*

"Nancy Kate's mom," said Mary Clare. "So they really did move. Guess we don't have to go tear up that dog run after all."

"No," said Marta. She picked up the card. There was a feeling of sadness in it as heavy as the jolt of terror she had gotten off the locket. There was something not right here, but before she could define it, Mary Clare peered into the next room.

"She's falling asleep—do you have any warm clothes I can put her in before I take her home?"

Marta threw up her hands. "She can stay here."

"No, you're right, it would be foolish. She can stay at my place for the night, and then I'll hook her up with a battered women's shelter tomorrow. If she doesn't go right back to him. They do sometimes."

Mary Clare persuaded the skinhead girl to put on a pair of Marta's ripped sweats over her jeans, and a light jacket Marta dug out from under the bed over her own. Teri had left the jacket, and it had been gathering dust for almost half a year.

"Pull up the hood," said Mary Clare, and she did not have to say to any of the three of them that this was for disguise as much as warmth. "You," she said to G-hey!, "keep your mouth shut. I don't care how you think it should be—we're going to get the shit kicked out of us if those guys find out we're here. If you tell, it will be *your fault!*" Trying to be diplomatic around G-hey! was a waste of time.

The girl pulled the hood up over her head. Marta did not have any extra gloves. She handed the girl her own pair, a Christmas present from her family. She had a job and a place to live, and Mary Clare and her family to fall back on, and three pairs of warm socks left after she gave the girl one pair. She was rich.

G-hey!, apparently deciding to make it a night, wandered into the kitchen and picked up the letter.

"I didn't know they had computers that long ago," she said to Marta. "What?"

"Well, this was printed on a dot-matrix. Typewriters didn't work on a dot-matrix, did they? I thought they had a daisy-wheel."

"Someday," said Marta, "I will take you to the museum and show you a manual typewriter. Now give me that." She looked at the letter closely. G-hey! was right about both things—it was printed on a dot matrix, and they hadn't had home computers back in '69. G-hey!'s parents probably hadn't even met in '69.

She put the letter back down, regretting handling it. Suppose…oh, god, here she was, back to the set up theory again. But, somebody had obviously tampered with the letter. Who? Jim? Polly's father? Her mother? What was being concealed? She wondered if the address—box number, really—at the top of the page was real. Well, that could easily be tested. She glanced at her watch. The day seemed to have gone on forever, but it was really just a little past six. She realized that she had not had the chance to tell Mary Clare anything she had learned from Lexy. Or Liz, either.

"I'm going to go use your phone," she said to G-hey!, who had settled back in front of the TV with Five-cents in her lap. Five-cents was telling G-hey! about Marta's failings.

"Did she really?" G-hey! was murmuring. "That's terrible! Of course you should have more tuna."

G-hey!'s little apartment looked so nice that Marta felt a bit embarrassed about her own place. It smelled good, too. G-hey! was a big one for using a crock pot. Something was bubbling on the counter.

It took two tries to get the right Collins. The first number that the long distance operator gave her belonged to a cousin. She gave Marta both the number of Fred and Judith Collins' home and the hardware store without even asking who she was. It was Sunday night, so Marta tried the home number first.

"Collins residence." A woman, older, from the sound of her voice, answered.

"May I speak with Mrs. Collins?" Marta asked. She could have just asked for Nancy Kate. Maybe she had stayed at home, and was working side by side with Mom and Dad. Nah, too much coincidence. She'd start with her mother, and hopefully get a few more numbers. She hoped Nancy Kate wasn't estranged from her family.

"This is she."

"My name is Marta Goicochea. I'm calling for Polly King. Do you remember her, Mrs. Collins?"

"Yes." The woman on the other end sounded a little leery. Well, that was normal. Nobody really wants a blast from the past—there were way too many ways for it to get ugly. Wasn't this a perfect example? No one in the Collins family was going to say thank you to Polly when they learned why she wanted to contact Nancy Kate, particularly if her suspicions about her father were true.

"Polly would like to get in contact with your daughter, Nancy Kate," said Marta. No way was she spilling the whole can of beans over the phone. "Do you know how she could get in touch with her?"

There was a long, strange silence, then a scuffling sound, as if the phone had been dropped. There were voices in the background. "Hello? Hello?" said Marta, wondering if they had been somehow cut off.

"Hello, who is this?" Now a man was on the line.

"Well, this is Marta Goicochea." Marta repeated herself, wondering what was going on. This was not what she had expected. "I'm just trying to get hold of your daughter, Nancy Kate. I have the right number, don't I? I mean, you're her parents, aren't you?"

"Yes. Yes. You say you're a friend of hers?"

"No. Actually, I've never met her. I'm trying to get in touch with her for a friend of mine, a woman named Polly King. She was friends with Nancy Kate when she was little, when you lived in Lakewood."

There was another long pause, though this time someone covered the mouth of the phone. Marta could practically see the dollars and cents piling up on G-hey!'s phone bill. She lifted the lid of G-hey's crock pot. Lentil stew.

Finally, the man came back on the line. "Excuse us," he said. "My wife thought that you said that you knew Nancy Kate now. She was confused. It upset her."

"No," said Marta slowly. What in the world was all the fuss about? Whatever it was, she had the feeling that finding Nancy Kate was not going to be just one easy phone call. "I wanted to find her and talk to her. I'm not from a collection agency," she added hastily.

"No. I understand that."

"So, can you tell me how to reach Nancy Kate?"

"No." A long pause. "Nancy Kate is dead. She's been dead almost thirty years."

There was a sudden burst of frantic conversation in the background—high pitched and rapid, and for a moment Marta thought that she had lost him.

"Wait! Wait!" she cried. "Don't get off the line! Are you still there?"

"Yes. But if this is for some kind of article on missing children, we don't want to have any part of it. We've been through enough, we can't keep hanging on—not after thirty years!" He sounded close to despair, and suddenly Marta understood the words she had heard in the background. "She's not dead!" Nancy Kate's mother had said. "We don't know that! We don't know that she's dead!"

"No," Marta said, trying frantically to think. She had not laid any plans for this twist—Polly's mother and brother, along with the Christmas letter, had convinced her that the sickening feeling of Nancy Kate in the ground had been some kind of random flashback. It happened, though not usually with such intensity. It had never occurred to her that Nancy Kate could have been killed after she and her family moved.

"She's dead," she said without thinking, picturing again Nancy Kate's locket dropping from her cold, lifeless hand.

"What?"

"No, no I mean….Mr. Collins, you're going to have to trust me. I don't want to write about your daughter, or hurt you in any way. I didn't even know she was dead. But, could you tell me what happened? Polly King is in jail here for a murder that I don't believe she committed. I think the killer might be the same man who killed Nancy Kate." She dared not mention the name of Chet King—it might queer the pitch totally if Nancy Kate's father felt compelled to defend their good neighbor. Men who abducted and killed children were always drifters and wanderers—not people you knew, not the father of your child's best friend. Or, had that changed? Via Oprah and Rickie Lake was America finally learning that fathers and uncles and next door neighbors were far more dangerous than drifters?

Another pause. Marta opened her mouth to plead, and then shut it again. They lived less than five hours away. If he said no, she would get Mary Clare to drive her there, so that she could try in person. Five hours. She hit herself in the forehead. Of course! Five hours was nothing. Polly's father could have easily driven there and back in a day. But why? If he was able to stop raping his daughter, why was he not able to leave Nancy Kate alone after they moved? Or, had it happened the other way? Had he killed Nancy Kate, accidentally or on purpose, and then quit with Polly, frightened by what had happened?

"She disappeared," Mr. Collins said suddenly, abruptly. "Soon after we moved. We thought we were getting away from the city, the crime. All the kids walked to school. She was in sixth grade! She disappeared after school one day. We searched and searched—they had blood hounds, and search and rescue teams and the Boy Scouts, and the state troopers. They never found anything. One little girl thought she saw her getting into a car."

"What kind of car?" asked Marta, thinking of the old Buick that had sat inside the Kings' yard while Polly's father had frantically worked on the dog run.

"She didn't know. She was a very little girl—a first grader who had been kept after school. In the end the sheriff decided that she had been making it up in order to feel important—she was prone to that."

So now what? What did she tell this man, who must now be in his fifties and sounded close to tears over a child he had not seen for twenty-five years?

"Thank-you," she said. "I'll call you if we catch the man."

She stood for a moment with her hand on the phone, and then went back into her own apartment to look for the card Liz had given her, on which she had written her home number.

"Salad's mom got a big screen TV," said G-hey!. "She wants to sell her old TV. Seventy-five bucks. In great shape. You want to go in on it?"

"What's wrong with that TV?" asked Marta.

"You mean besides the fact that you can't tell Data from Deanna Troi until they talk? Nothing, I guess."

"I'll think about it," said Marta. "What are you cooking?"

"Lentil and lamb stew. Help yourself. Bring me a bowl, too."

Liz had her answering machine on, but she picked up after Marta gave her name.

"Oh, screening?" asked Marta.

"It's the curse of the nineties," said Liz. "What do you want?"

"Nancy Kate is dead," said Marta. "I talked to her parents."

"Oh, shit!" said Liz. "Damnit, you had to go and find that out, didn't you?"

"No, no, it's okay. Polly couldn't have done it. She disappeared after she moved to Nebraska."

"Thank God for small favors, at least. Good, it'll never even come up."

"No! We want it to come up! It was her dad. Don't you see? And if he killed Nancy Kate, don't you think there's a good chance that he set Polly up? He doesn't have an alibi for the time of the murder—you told me that yourself."

"He doesn't need an alibi, because he's not a suspect."

"But if the police found Nancy Kate's body! Don't you think that would throw a new light on Polly's case?"

"If you mean, do I think they would start investigating him as a suspect, the answer is no."

There was a short pause. Marta could hear laughter in the background.

"But I would like to get him if he killed the kid," Liz finally said thoughtfully. "And if he was convicted, that could make Polly's case stronger. I can't bring in what he did, but I would bring in anything she saw. The jury would eat up trauma if she'd witnessed a murder as a child. Do you think she witnessed it?"

"I don't know if she actually saw it," said Marta. "But I think she knew about it." She told Liz about the date that had been scratched in the dog run.

"Do you have some concrete evidence that it was her dad?" Liz asked. "Or did this just come to you in a vision?"

"I saw it in a burning bush," said Marta crossly. "What do you think—just because you don't approve of the way I make my living I can't put two and two together? I have…"

"I don't want to hear what you have…" Liz interrupted. "I want to hear what he has. Is there any kind of physical evidence at all that will tie him to the death?"

"What—do you mean do I think he has her panties hidden up in her bedroom after all these years? How the hell should I know that? It's been twenty-five years! Dig up the dog run! That's where she's buried."

"I can't get that run dug up on psychic say so! I'd have to get a court order!"

"So get a court order!"

"So call me back when you get some evidence!"

It took great restraint not to slam the phone down. Sullenly, in short sentences that gave the story without embellishment, Marta repeated to Liz what Lexy had told her the night before.

"Do you think she's telling the truth?" asked Liz. "She's not lying to get her mom out of jail, is she?"

"I don't think so. I had to pry it out of her."

"Good work," Liz said in a voice that sounded rather reluctant to Marta.

"Don't worry," said Marta. "There were no trances involved. I need the light of the full moon for that."

Liz laughed. "Sorry," she said. "It's just that I can't go into the court room and tell the judge we got the evidence by using ESP and then expect anyone to take us seriously. It'll be bad enough if we have to put a kid on the stand."

"Oh, god," said Marta. "Try to avoid that. That'd send Polly right over the edge."

They said good-by. Marta got into G-hey!'s cupboard and pulled out two hand-thrown bowls. She filled them both to the brim with lentil stew and carried them back to her own apartment. G-hey! was putting a pan of cornbread into her oven.

"You had a mix in your cupboard," she explained to Marta, who tried to look as if she had known this all along. "You had a brownie mix, too. It looks like the Borg are back."

Marta sat down on the end of the couch. "How much did you say Salad's mother wanted for that TV?" she asked, trying to adjust the antenna Mary Clare had made from a coat hanger and foil.

"Seventy-five bucks. But I'll bet she'd give it to me for fifty. She likes me. She thinks I'm a good influence on Salad."

"Hmm," said Marta, looking at G-hey!'s shaved head and piercings. Not what *her* mother would call a good influence. But G-hey! was smart and kind and a hard worker and a loyal friend. Good for Salad's mother.

Marta was suddenly starving. She dug into the stew. G-hey! pulled the cornbread and the brownies out of the oven, pulling the sleeves of her sweatshirt down over her hands to use as hotpads. She dropped a hot, crumbling piece of corn bread into both bowls.

"This is possibly the best food I have ever had in my life," Marta told her. "You're going to make some lucky gal a great wife."

"No," said G-hey! "I won't do floors."

Marta picked up her bowl and went back across the hall. She looked at Nancy Kate's parents' number, which she had left on a pad beside G-hey!'s phone. She hesitated a moment, and then picked up the phone again.

"Collins' residence." This time, Nancy Kate's father answered the phone. She blessed her luck.

"Mr. Collins, it's me, Marta Goicochea again. I needed to ask you a couple more questions."

"Look," he said softly, obviously trying to convey the impression that it was just a routine phone call, nothing to worry about, "I can't do this. I can't help you. We went through that a long time ago."

"Just a couple of questions!" Frantically, Marta tried to think of a way to keep him on the phone. "I don't want to harass you, but it's really important." Suddenly, it came to her. Frank Collins was past hearing promises that Nancy Kate might be alive. The only promise he wanted was, yes, she was dead.

"Mr. Collins," she said, "wouldn't you like to know for sure? Wouldn't you like to bring Nancy Kate home and bury her?"

There was a short pause. "I can't talk here," was what he finally said. "Call me tomorrow at the store." He gave the number.

"Just one thing. Did you put out a poster of Nancy Kate? Did you keep any of them?"

"I don't think so. Maybe the..." he caught himself. Didn't want to say 'Police', thought Marta. "Call me tomorrow at work."

SEVENTEEN

The next day, Louann took off from work early, so Marta walked home. It could have been a miserable experience. It was snowing. Only lightly, true, but there was a bitter wind that blew the hard little flakes back into her face and down the neck of her jacket.

But Marta was far too preoccupied even to notice the weather. She was going to have to get her phone hooked up again. Surely she was past the stage of calling Teri. And Gloria was going to chew her butt six ways to Sunday when the phone bill told her that Marta had spent fifteen minutes during prime time talking long distance to Nebraska to a non-paying customer.

Well, that wasn't going to happen till the first of the month. What was on her mind now was the conversation with Nancy Kate's father, and the fax that she had carefully rolled up and was carrying in her coat sleeve.

At her door, she called and called for Gravy, who had insisted on going out that morning against all advice, but he was nowhere to be seen.

She heard noises in her apartment before she reached the top of the stairs. Normally, this would not have been alarming. Mary Clare had a key to her apartment. G-hey! had a key to her apartment, and in return for phone use, (oh, damn, another long distance bill) Marta would sometimes find her on the couch when she got home from work, watching reruns of *Roseanne* and *Designing Women*. Teri had a key, but...well, the point was just because she heard noises didn't necessarily mean the skinheads had broken in and trashed the place because she had given refuge to their woman.

Still, Marta opened the door cautiously. There was a strange, unfamiliar smell in the apartment—it took her a moment to recognize it as ammonia. She pushed the door open cautiously, banging it into three full trash bags sitting on the floor. Her kitchen was sparkling. The cupboards had been scrubbed—no more dribbles of food and dishwater.

In the living room Five-Cents, Gravy and Baloney were all in a row on the couch, watching with interest as a woman on her hands and knees vacuumed around the floor boards and in the corners with a tiny little vacuum. Marta did not own a vacuum at all, let alone a tiny little one for corners.

She stood in the door way for a minute, watching. She was sure she didn't know this woman, and yet there was a disconcerting air of familiarity about her.

The woman flipped off the vacuum and stood.

"Oh," she said, giving a little jump of surprise. "I didn't hear you come in." It was the skinhead girl who had huddled so pitifully on her couch the evening before. In spite of the bruises and cuts on her face, she looked much better than she had then. There was an air about her of having been scrubbed down and cleaned up.

"I didn't hear you come in," she said again, and then looked over at the cats as if wondering if they had heard Marta come in. All three looked at Marta as if they had never seen her before.

"This looks great," said Marta. A good five or six hours works had been put in the apartment. It looked like a whole new home. She looked around at the prints and hangings on her walls and thought with surprise, 'Hey, I've got some great stuff!'

"Mary Clare," the girl said, unplugging the vacuum, "said she'd pay me to clean your house. Mary Clare said it was a real pig sty. She sure was right."

There was not a lot to say to this, but luckily Marta did not have to respond. The girl continued chattering.

"Mary Clare," the girl said, "said if I had some money she'd help me find an apartment. Mary Clare said if I had an apartment, then I could get a job?" She raised her tone at the end of this last statement, making it into a question. Mary Clare had obviously overnight acquired the status of a prophet, but just as obviously some things—like an apartment of one's own and a job—seemed too farfetched to accept without questioning.

"What were you doing for money before?" Marta asked.

The girl shrugged. "Didn't need money," she said. "Billy had money." She hard a sharp, hard edged accent Marta could not place.

"Well," said Marta, looking around, "you could certainly get a cleaning job. You did a great job here." The girl looked totally blank, and she expanded a little. "Cleaning houses? For other people? Lots of people pay to have this done once a week."

The girl looked around with a frown on her face, and it didn't take a Betazoid to read her mind.

"They're not usually this dirty. I've been pretty depressed—I haven't taken care of things."

"Mary Clare said," the girl agreed. She carried the basket of cleaning things to the head of the stairs. Watching her, Marta realized what had given her the confused air of recognition. It was because the girl was totally dressed in a combination of her own and Mary Clare's clothing.

"My name is Marta."

"Karleve," said the girl.

Though Marta had not heard the door at the bottom of the stairs open or close, suddenly all three of the cats were alert. There was a knock obviously for the sake of form only, for without a pause Mary Clare let herself in. She was dragging behind her a huge tote of clean laundry.

"Hello," said Mary Clare brightly, and then, "Hello. Hello. Hello," to the cats. "Hello!" she called to the direction of the closet. "There's more in the car," she said to the girl. "Could you get it?" Obediently, the girl started down the stairs, taking one of the bags of trash with her.

"What am I, now?" Marta asked, in a tone that was not quite cross, "the Salvation Army training ground?"

"Well, I'm sorry, but it started becoming obvious I was going to have to give her money one way or another and I don't have a woodpile, so she couldn't split any kindling for me."

"I thought you were going to try to get her into a battered women's shelter."

"I called. And I called. And I called. There is no space anywhere. Besides, how are you ever going to feel any better if you're living in a pig sty?"

"I've already heard that from your protégé, thank you."

Mary Clare frowned. "Yeah, the social skills definitely need to be worked on."

"At least you got her cleaned up. What is her name? I couldn't catch it."

"Caroleve." Mary Clare pronounced it carefully, as if it were two separate words, like her own name. "I had her write it down."

The door of the apartment opened, and the girl wrestled in another huge tote, this one containing clothes and towels and even Marta's bedroom curtains. Her own jeans were on top of the load. Without a word, she opened the door and went back down the stairs with another trash bag. She had the hood of Teri's jacket pulled up around her face.

"We have already discussed Jews, queers and the mud races," said Mary Clare. "For the time being, we have agreed to disagree, although she has grudgingly admitted that I'm 'really nice for a queer' and could probably 'get a guy whenever I wanted one'. That last was no doubt intended to be a compliment."

"No doubt," Marta agreed. "This is not a stray, is it?"

Mary Clare shrugged. "I might need a new project, now that you're cleaned up." Then they said nothing, thinking of the early years when their houses were always open to any dyke in trouble, anyone who had run away, or been evicted, or who was crazy, or between jobs, or just traveling lesbian style. From her experience with strays, Marta had gotten good at picking out the ones who had actual potential— who really only did need a little helping hand and would clean up and fly straight and turn into friends. In Marta's opinion, this girl was not in the high success category, and Mary Clare knew that as well as she did.

The girl came back up the stairs a third time. Gravy walked over to the door and began to nag. "Oh, all right, you big baby," Marta said. "But you're not going to like it out there." She put her hand on the knob.

"No," the girl said sharply. "Don't let your cat out. Billy'll kill your cat."

Marta felt as if the bottom of her stomach had dropped out, and this feeling was the only thing that kept her from screaming at Mary Clare, 'Look what you fucking did by bringing this Nazi white trash into my house, look what you did!' She could feel the blood drain out of her face as she pictured Gravy, who had lived with her for eight years, starting out as a wretched, beaten-up little kitten whom the vet had given only a fifty percent chance of survival, in pieces on her back doorstep. She thought she was going to throw up, so great was her rage and terror. She swayed, and Mary Clare reached for her arm. Savagely she shook her off.

"Uh uh, no," the girl said vehemently, interpreting the gesture correctly. "Not causa me being here. He didn't know that—I was real careful last night and today both. You can't see a thing that happens in the alley—I never saw either one a you unless you come out in the street. He's already pissed off at you causa the way you both talked to him last week. Said he'd catch your cat and cut off his tail and send him back without it. Kill him. Just hadn't caught him yet."

But he would, Marta thought. Gravy was a friendly cat, not leery of strangers, and besides, his stomach ruled his mind. A can of tuna sealed a friendship with anyone. Gravy, who was used to be let in and out upon demand, began to howl.

"Fuck," said Mary Clare. "Knock it off," she said to Gravy. Gravy retreated sullenly to the couch. Mary Clare took G-hey's key off the hook and went out the door. Caroleve picked up another bag of trash and started downstairs.

"No," said Marta.

"I was real careful..."

"I don't care," said Marta. "I don't want to chance it. I don't want those assholes knocking on my door."

Mary Clare came back from next door, trailed by G-hey!. "I called a locksmith," she said. "I'm going to feel a lot bet if you and G-hey! have better locks on your doors."

There was little to do but take the situation with good grace. Marta hung up her coat and put on water for tea, since G-hey! had not yet reclaimed her box of Red Zinger. Mary Clare sat down on the couch and began comforting Gravy. G-hey!, seeing that Marta was unwrapping the leftover brownies and cornbread, went back into her apartment and returned with a big Tupperware container full of lentil stew. Caroleve picked her clean clothes off the top of the laundry and went into the bathroom to change.

"What's this?" G-hey! asked Marta, picking up the rolled paper that she had placed on the counter. Without waiting for an answer, she smoothed it out and looked at the photograph. "Who's she?"

Mary Clare came into the kitchen to get in on the news.

"Hey!" she said, reading over G-hey!'s shoulder. "That's Nancy Kate! How'd you get this?"

"Her dad faxed it to me this morning. He didn't have a copy, but the local cops had one on file."

Mary Clare did not ask when she had called Nancy Kate's father or why she wanted the poster or any of the questions Marta herself would have asked. "Where in the world can you receive a fax?" is what she asked.

"At Kinko's," said Marta haughtily. "Anybody can receive a fax at Kinko's."

"I'll keep that in mind." She looked again at the paper G-hey! was holding. It showed a photo of a young girl. Marta had been surprised to see just how young. She had forgotten that somewhere in the chase. She had long, dark hair, parted in the middle. There was nothing in the picture or the accompanying information—height, weight, last seen—to distinguish her from dozens of other girls Marta had seen on milk cartons. Except for the date.

"I don't get it," said Mary Clare. "I thought the letter last night..."

Belatedly, Marta remembered that, because of the commotion surrounding Caroleve, Mary Clare was about two days behind. Hurriedly she filled her in on not only the phone calls to Nebraska, but the conversation with Lexy, as well.

"Oh," said Mary Clare. "I guess that changes things a little, doesn't it?"

"I guess," Marta agreed, though she was not sure it changed things in a way that would matter to Polly.

"You sure stirred that up with a big stick," said Mary Clare rather admiringly. Mary Clare liked stirring.

"So you're on my side now?" asked Marta. "You don't think she did it?"

"Let's say you've planted a real kernel of doubt. That's all that you need to do. The jury can't convict if there's doubt."

Marta grimaced. She did not want to merely cast doubt. She wanted to know. Not even as much for Polly's sake as her own. What if she was wrong, what if Polly was guilty? What if she were acquitted on evidence Marta had unearthed and then went out and killed again? Marta didn't want to live with that.

"So now what?" asked Mary Clare. "Who are you going to stir now?"

"You know who I'd like to stir?" Marta replied. "I'd like to stir her dad. I mean, he's the bad guy—we've known that all along. Polly had work on her teeth the same day Karen was killed. Do you think he could have—oh, I don't know. Drugged her? Suggested something to her while she was under? Suggested violence?"

"Why would he do that?" asked Mary Clare.

"Well, we already know he was trying to discredit her. Remember, he had her thrown in the loony bin? He didn't want anybody to believe what she said about the incest. And what if he killed Nancy Kate and Polly was starting to remember? He sure as hell wouldn't want anybody to believe that! I've had some pretty weird experiences when my wisdom teeth were pulled. My oral surgeon said I swore like a sailor when I was under."

"Me too," said Mary Clare. "I was convinced that my oral surgeon kept a peacock in her office for the longest time after I had my wisdom teeth removed."

"She does," said G-hey! unexpectedly.

"What?"

"We go to the same oral surgeon," said G-hey! "You were the one who recommended her to me. Except the peacock isn't in the office—it's outside in a little plaza. You can see it sometimes when you're sitting in the chair."

Marta and Mary Clare looked at one another.

"Proves that point," said Mary Clare. "Made me think I hadn't seen something when I really had. How are you going to stir Daddy?"

"I don't know. I think the best way to stir him would be to get at his girlfriend. Don't you think? He wasn't home the night Karen was murdered."

"How do you know that?"

"Liz told me. The police went to his house after they found Polly—her folks' address was the only one she could remember. He wasn't home, and Mommy said he hadn't been home all evening."

"Oh, let me!" said G-hey! unexpectedly, looking up from the poster.

"Let you do what?" asked Marta.

"Let me stir the girlfriend! You and Mary Clare have been doing everything by yourself and not even asking me to help."

"That's because you have no connection with the real world," said Mary Clare bluntly. "We're afraid if you question anyone you'll come back with a sob story about how society is at fault."

"Fuck you," said G-hey! so sweetly that it sounded like an endearment. "I'll bet you money that Salad and I can get more out of her than you and Marta can. Because we're closer to her age. And I've fucked guys, and you haven't."

"I've fucked guys," said Mary Clare.

"Yeah, but you didn't do it on purpose. And wasn't I right about the dot matrix? That's what made you call, wasn't it?" she asked Marta. "You would have just accepted that letter otherwise."

"She's right," said Marta. "And there's another little mystery—who planted that letter in the card? Mom or Daddy or Jim? He sent it, but any of the three of them could have gone down to the basement and put it in."

"Fine," said Mary Clare to G-hey! without consulting Marta. "I'll bet you tickets to see Holly Near that you can't find out shit from this girl, let alone what Daddy was doing that night. Plus, you have to do it in a way that won't fuck things up for Marta when she has to go talk to her."

"Holly Near tickets!" said G-hey! scornfully. "Who wants to go see that old doll?"

"Youth today should be taught respect," said Mary Clare. "Now you're going to the concert with us whether you win or lose. And I'm going to sit next to you and explain all the songs."

The tea and the lentils were both steaming. Everyone loaded a plate. Marta took one to Caroleve, who had slipped out of the bathroom and was sitting on the couch watching TV.

"You don get a very good picture," she said to Marta when she handed her the food.

"My friend Salad's mother wants to sell me her old TV," said G-hey!. "Do you want to go in on it? If Marta goes in, we'd only have to pay about fifteen bucks apiece."

"Caroleve isn't going to live here," said Marta, wishing she were close enough to G-hey! to give her a big pinch. "She's going to get her own apartment." She tried to sound polite, but firm.

"Janie and Renee are going to…" G-hey! squawked to a stop with a reproachful look at Mary Clare who *was* close enough to give her a big pinch.

"Why didn't you have them send the fax to Liz," asked Mary Clare hastily. "I'll bet she's got a fax machine."

"Liz is afraid that I'm going to go into a trance and locate Jimmy Hoffa's body," replied Marta. "The less contact, the better for us all." She did not want to tell the real reason, which was that Liz must remain totally removed from what she was willing to do to have Polly's father apprehended. She was not even sure she was going to tell Mary Clare, and she was certainly not going to tell G-hey! and Caroleve.

"You have your assignments," she said instead.

"G-hey! has an assignment," said Mary Clare, sulking.

"You have one, too. Find me a dyke cop. I know he did it! I know he did! Liz needs hard evidence to get that dog run dug up. I want to set this fucker up and we're going to need inside help to do it."

EIGHTEEN

Marta stayed home from work the next day. Luckily, she had filled in for Char several times while she had the flu—she groused and fussed, but in the end she agreed to cover her shift.

She let herself into G-hey's' apartment as soon as she left for work. She called Mary Clare, who had been able to find a dyke cop in only two degrees of separation. Then she called the Nebraska number that had been given to her by Nancy Kate's father. She called Gwen, Polly's father's nurse, at home and then made several local calls. She was lucky. Everyone was at home. Everyone agreed.

The phone rang as soon as she put it down.

"Hello?"

It was G-hey!, sounding very smug. "Have you got your information?" she asked. "Because I've got mine. Did I beat you?"

"No," said Marta. "But, if it's good I'll tell Mary Clare that you did."

"Cool. Here it is—Daddy was with his girlfriend that night. They had dinner out and went to a late movie and fucked. She didn't say that last part—I just assumed."

"How'd you find out that much?"

"I can talk to anybody who has braces," said G-hey! smugly. "Has braces, had braces, is going to have braces. Anybody. All I had to do was wander in, talk about braces and then wonder if Dr. King was the man for me—wasn't he implicated in a murder?"

"She was anxious to defend him, huh?"

"Big time. Didn't even care what it looked like. Said she was an old family friend and it was her birthday. Bullshit."

"Bullshit" agreed Marta. "Good job." Not that she believed it. Lovers were notorious liars. But jilted lovers were notoriously bitter. Polly's father was going to get stirred big time.

***

"Hi." Marta was being her most charming, hoping the girl would not recognize her immediately from their brief encounter outside Polly's father's office. She didn't think she would. She had tied her hair back with a scarf, and slapped on her sunglasses. More important, the girl had never really looked at her—she had been merely an annoyance, something standing in the way of a romantic lunch.

The girl looked up from her yogurt, suspicious, but not afraid. There were other people around. The park behind Cherry Creek Mall was a safe place to have lunch in the sun. According to Gwen, the dental hygienist, she had lunch there every nice day, unless Polly's father took her out. Again, according to Gwen, she had been a somewhat inept receptionist for almost nine months, which meant it was about time for a trade in. Gwen, who had been reluctant at first to speak when Marta called her at home, had turned into a mine of information about a third of the way through the conversation. She had not been easy in her mind about what was happening between her boss and his receptionists for a long time, Marta had suspected, and her call was the perfect opportunity to vent without taking action herself. Of course, Marta did not tell her the truth, did not tell her she was stalking a murderer. She told her instead that she was a friend of Jennifer, the receptionist, and just wanted her to see the light about this jerk before it was too late.

"Hi." Jennifer turned back to her book, signifying the end of the exchange.

"You're Jennifer, right? My name is Marta Goicochea. I'm here because of Polly?" She made the last sentence into a question. She was not sure if the girl knew about Polly's incarceration. She might not even know her lover had children.

But the girl did know. She gave a little start. "Oh!" she said, gathering up her things, "Dr. Chet said I shouldn't talk to you." This, more than her perfect skin or her slender legs spoke of her youth. She said 'Dr. Chet' not as if she were trying to cover up their relationship, but as if it were what she always called her lover.

Marta put her hand on her wrist. "He's wrong. You should talk to me. You should talk to me before he hurts you really bad."

"I know that daughter of his tells those dirty lies about him, but you just don't understand at all. I know him, I know he couldn't...I beg your pardon?" She had rushed ahead so quickly into her indignant defense it took her a moment to hear what Marta was saying. "What are you talking about? Dr. Chet would never hurt me." She smiled smugly, and Marta's heart went out to her youth, and that absolute security that comes only with naivete.

"You know he has a wife," Marta said.

"He's going to divorce her," the girl said. "He's going to marry me. It hasn't been a real marriage for a long time, anyway."

It hasn't been a real marriage since he started fucking his daughter, thought Marta, but she did not say it. The girl was absolutely closed down against hearing that truth. You could not hear that about a man you hoped to marry. But, Marta hoped, there were other truths the girl *could* hear.

"No," Marta said, "he's not going to marry you. He's going to use you up and throw you away as soon as the new crop graduates from high school."

"I'm not supposed to talk to you," the girl said sharply, but her pride made her retort. "He's going to marry me. He loves me. There's no reason for him to break up with me. I give him everything he wants. Everything."

"There was no reason for him to dump me, either." Marta had heard the voice of the woman who spoke behind her only over the phone, but she fit the picture that had formed in her mind while they talked. Like Jennifer she was small, and looked younger than her age, which was probably still early twenties. There was another woman standing behind her, and the three of them, in fact, looked enough alike to be sisters. It was not just their strawberry blonde hair and their size, it was the way all three of them—without ever having met before—dressed. They were all wearing dresses—expensive, nice—all wearing shoes with a little heel. They could have gone to a garden party together. Marta saw this recognition register in all three sets of eyes. The two older women took it in with a touch of sadness and anger—the younger one with fear.

"He didn't have any reason to dump me," the woman repeated, sitting beside Jennifer on the bench. "He told me he loved me, just like he told you. He told me he'd marry me—he'd been faithful to his wife for years because of the children, but I was too much of an angel to resist. That he'd just settled down, waiting to die, and then I had come along and given him back his life and his youth. That it wasn't really cheating on his wife, because she had rejected him years ago, she wasn't a woman to him. That I made the sun rise and the moon set."

Jennifer opened her mouth, but was unable to come out with a sound. She didn't need to. Everyone there knew she was hearing words, phrases, she had thought Polly's father had said to her alone.

"And then," the woman leaned forward and placed a light hand on the other's arm, "one day he told me we were through. No warning, we were through. He was so sad about it, but he was going to do the right thing, he was going back to his wife, and I didn't have a job anymore, because it would break his heart if he had to see me in the office every day without being able to have me. But he didn't go back to his wife. I kept in contact with his nurse—he just replaced me with somebody new. Somebody younger. Somebody like you."

The third woman—Marta was not sure if she were two or three receptionists ago—had not said a word. Now she came closer, and held up her hand. She opened her fist—she was holding a chain, and from it dangled a gold locket. Jennifer made a little choking sound, and automatically her hand flew up to her neck, where a delicate gold chain disappeared beneath her collar.

"Yeah," said the first woman. She dipped her hand into her purse and came out with another locket. This one looked as if she had smashed it with a hammer in rage, but they could tell it had once been identical. "Not exactly an innovative kind of guy, huh? He probably has an account with the jeweler, he probably gets them made up by the gross."

"Trips to Victoria's Secret at noon," said the second woman, speaking for the first time. "'You'd look beautiful in anything, darling, but I like the black lace. Wear it back to the office. I'll be thinking of you all afternoon.'"

"'You don't have to be anything but my little girl. I'll take care of you. You'll always be my little girl. Darling. Angel. I owe my life to you—I had given up on life before I met you.'" The third woman completed the words.

Jennifer gave a little cry, and again Marta's heart went out to her. It would be so easy to stop the other women. But they were too close now, and hearing the truth was the only way that she would ever tell the truth.

"He used you, Jennifer," she said. "He used you just the way he used them. Worse. He was going to throw you away, but he was going to make you perjure yourself for him, first. He was going to use you for an alibi." She was not yet confident enough to say aloud, "He killed Karen, set his own daughter up for murder," but more than ever she was sure that was what had happened. Sure enough to involve not just herself, but Mary Clare, in something illegal. The girl was crying by now, but she did not say a word.

"Hey. Hey, are you the woman I'm supposed to talk to?" Marta pulled back in confusion. Damn this kid—who the hell was she? She was interrupting just when Jennifer was about to break! Marta waved her hand—you're confused, take yourself somewhere else—but the girl persisted. "I'm supposed to talk to you about the job, right?" She had come up the bike path, and was wearing neon rollerblades, and a lycra shorts and halter outfit to match. People did that in Denver, seized a sunny winter day as if it were spring. Her strawberry blonde hair was pulled back in a ponytail. "The old lady at the doctor's office, the nurse, she called me up and sent me over here. To talk about the job?"

Oh, thought Marta. She had misjudged Gwen. She *was* willing to act on her own.

"What job?" Jennifer, breathed the two words between lips that were hardly parted at all.

"The job over at the doctor's office. My dentist." The girl smiled, showing a mouthful of braces. "After I get these off, of course. Hey, I know you, don't I? You're the receptionist there now. Dr. Chet said you're going to college or something, huh? So don't worry—I can't work full time until after graduation." She did not have to say graduation meant high school.

Perhaps, if she had been faced only with her predecessors, Jennifer would have been able to keep her composure. But a replacement was too much.

"That bastard!" she said, covering her eyes, her tears with her fingers. You got the idea she might never have used the word aloud before. She broke into sobs, and then visibly tried to compose herself. If there had been another way, Marta would have chosen it. She had not wanted to humiliate the girl as well as crush her dreams. But Polly was in jail. That's what was important."He wasn't ever with you that night, was he?" she asked, leaning close. "He told the police he was, but he asked you to lie for him, didn't he?"

"Yes. Yes! He said he had been driving by himself, thinking about us, thinking about the best way to ask his wife for a divorce without her taking him for everything. He said he was sure his daughter would try to bring him into it somehow, she was crazy, she always tried to blame him for whatever she did. That ever since she had made up this..." she choked, and Marta knew that suddenly, in the light of information she had just been given, she had just realized that maybe Dr. Chet's daughter had not been lying. She made a little retching noise.

While the iron was hot, Marta reached down and took her by the hand. "Come on," she said to her, and the others as well. "I'll bet he's back from lunch." To the girl on skates she said, "Thanks. You can go home. There's not going to be a job."

She walked them slowly across the street. None of them spoke. In the office she said to Gwen, who was eating a sack lunch at the desk, "He's not going to be seeing anyone this afternoon." Gwen nodded. There was a moment of hesitation on her face, as if she regretted what she had helped Marta do, but it lasted only a second. They sat down in the nicely matched chairs of the outer office and waited. Jennifer wept quietly into a handkerchief.

"Is there a back door?" Marta asked Gwen, who was on the phone quietly canceling appointments.

"There is," she said. "But it's locked." She dialed the next number without looking up.

They had not been seated more than ten minutes when the door was flung open and Polly's father came into the room, emulating that good-natured, center-of-attention bustle that some men have."We've got a busy afternoon, girls," he called before he saw them.

That's the truth, thought Marta, and then bit her lip to keep from giggling. What if this didn't work out? What if Jennifer lost her fire?

She needn't have worried.

"You lied to me!" Jennifer shouted, her voice high and wavering and very, very young. "You lied to me! You said you were going to marry me and you're going to fire me instead!"

Startled, he glanced around the room, and then back at the door, against which Marta was leaning, her arms crossed. He looked quickly at the door that led back into the office, but it was closed. And locked as well, Marta was willing to bet. Gwen must have decided she was going to lose her job either way. She was going to help take him down first.

"We'll talk about this later." He tried to cut Jennifer off with a twinkle, but she had been pushed too far. If she had only broken down in front of Marta, she might have backed off. But she had been humiliated in front of his old lovers, and anger was the only way to come back from that place.

"No, we won't! You lied to me! And you made me lie for you! I defended you ! I told people you were with me that night!"

Again, he glanced around the room, this time with the frantic eye of a caged animal. One of the other two women, the older, caught his eye and raised her hand. "Hi, Daddy," she said. "What goes around comes around, doesn't it?"

He pulled himself together, visibly, but well. "I'm sure we can all…" he began.

"Yeah," said Marta slowly. "There goes the alibi you set up, just in case. And without that, everything else is going to be pretty easy to prove, isn't it, Mr. King?"

"Yeah! If you wanted me to lie about where you were, then you must have been with your daughter that night!" shrilled Jennifer, close to hysterics. "Why else would you make me lie!"

He ignored the girl and smiled instead at Marta, gently, fatherly. "I understand how upset you are. You care for Polly. But this, this…" he waved a hand to indicate that it was too ridiculous to name. "Polly has been suffering from delusions for years. That's a well documented fact. When you have a child like Polly, well," he gave a rueful little laugh, "you prepare yourself for the worst. Polly has always blamed me for her problems. I thought it probable that she might try to pull me into this mess. And, well…" He spread his hands, to show chagrin, still trying the twinkle, the nice-guy-who-never-fucked-his-daughter act. "I admit—setting up an alibi was wrong. What can I say? I know how Polly works."

"That's what you want everybody to think, isn't it, Mr. King? That Polly's crazy?" Marta moved away from the door as she spoke. He wasn't going anywhere. "As long as everybody thinks Polly is just crazy, then nobody will take any of her accusations seriously. She can't destroy your business or your reputation. Just another accusation by crazy Polly. Because she had finally remembered, hadn't she?"

He looked at her with sad eyes that said she was misguided, but could not be blamed. He had played this role for a long time. He was very good. "Tell me," he said, "do you really think that it is in anyone's best interests that Polly be allowed to run free?" He did not even address her accusation, as if it were beneath him even to notice it. "What if it's a child next time? It was only luck that the police arrived before she got to the little girl. Maybe they can help her this time—surely no jury will send her to prison with her background." The only thing that spoiled his calm was the way that he kept his head turned away from the three other women in the room.

"She remembered where the body was," said Marta softly. "She finally remembered something that was going to put you behind bars."

He looked at his watch. "I'm sorry, but I've given you all the time I can." He stood, and started for the door. And then stopped. In his path stood the three women. He was a large man, and they were all petite women, all dressed similarly in pretty floral prints and heels. One would not have thought they would detour a man his size. But the way they were standing, all three with their arms crossed and their feet apart, said more clearly than words he would not be able to just push them aside, and he was not yet ready to fight.

"She remembered Nancy Kate," said Marta, as if there had been no interruption. "She had been worried all along about Nancy Kate, about her little friend. She was afraid that her daddy had raped her as well. But Nancy Kate's family had moved away. She'd been saved. But Polly still wanted to find her. She showed me something that belonged to her, thinking maybe I could help. And the first thing I felt was that Nancy Kate was dead, she had been dead a long time."

Again that feeling of the frightened little girl, lonely in her unmarked grave, swept through her, and she felt her eyes fill with tears. "She'd been dead a long time," she repeated. "At first I wondered how that could be. Nancy Kate had moved away, and Polly had never seen her again. How could Polly have something Nancy Kate had worn after she was dead? Especially since Polly didn't know Nancy Kate was dead, had been dead for over *twenty* years. At first I thought maybe Polly had confused the two things, she had translated 'died' into 'moved.' She was just a little girl— she had suppressed so many of the terrible things you had done to her it wasn't really a stretch to consider her rewriting this incident. But everybody agreed Nancy Kate's family had moved. Your wife agreed, your son agreed. Your wife, in fact, had received a Christmas card from Nancy Kate's mother the year after they moved. Your son Jim brought it over to me."

A look of annoyance and surprise crossed his face, which surprised her. She had assumed that he had been the one who had tampered with the Christmas letter. Had it been his wife or son covering for him? No time for that now.

"The letter made it sound as if everything was fine in their new home. But I called Nancy Kate's parents. Nancy Kate had disappeared within a month after they moved." Marta paused for a moment, remembering how, after almost twenty-five years, the woman's voice had caught over the phone when she spoke of her daughter. "Maybe there had been another letter—maybe you got home in time to get the one that told about Nancy Kate disappearing. But you knew, didn't you? Because you killed her. Nancy Kate moved far, far away, too far for Polly to visit. But you had a car, a four or five hour drive was nothing to you. You needed to see Nancy Kate, because you were afraid she was going to tell. Polly was right there where you could continue to manipulate her into silence, but something Nancy Kate said or did must have made you think that once she was away from you she might tell what you had been doing to the two of them. And you couldn't let that happen."

Marta paused for breath.

"A fantasy…" said Mr. King. He was losing his crisp, grandfatherly edge. Casually, he slid over to the door that led into the examination room and tried the knob. Locked. He looked at the other door.

"Don't even think about it," said the woman who had spoken before. "I want to hear the rest of this story."

Marta took a deep breath and faced him again.

"So you drove to Nancy Kate's new town, and you went to her new school, and she got in the car with you. Maybe you threatened her, maybe you tricked her. Maybe in spite of it all she still thought she was safe with you because you weren't a stranger, you were her friend's father. Then you drove out to the country, and you killed her. Probably with your bare hands. It's easy to kill a child, isn't it? You don't need a weapon."

She looked at his large hands, as did the three women by the door.

"This is the most ridiculous thing I have every heard! Are you under the impression you can just make some sort of wild accusation like this and anyone will take it seriously?" He had seated himself in the chair and was leaning back, his arms crossed, trying for an amused look on his face. But his forehead was beaded up with sweat.

"It's not a wild accusation, Mr. King. And not everybody has to believe it. Only the police have to believe it. And they will believe it, Mr. King. Because we know where the body is. Did you know we came over to your house the other day, Mr. King? Your neighbor had backed into your dog run and knocked the posts down. But your wife said it didn't matter—there had never been a dog in the run anyway. She told us how you'd decided to make the run one day and you'd been all in a frenzy about it—you worked late at night, and you didn't even try to fix your car, which you'd told her wouldn't run.

"Nancy Kate was in the trunk of the car, wasn't she? That's what the frenzy was about. You probably had her wrapped in plastic, or packed in dry ice, but you knew sooner or later she would smell. That was why it was so important to pour the cement, and why it didn't matter the dog had never used the run."

Something happened suddenly, something that Marta knew only she could feel. Up until that moment, Polly's father, for all his calm posturing, had squirmed like a worm on a hook. Suddenly, though, she felt from him a great rush of relief. She had said something that convinced him he was off the hook. What had it been? Doggedly, she continued. "And that was why Polly had something Nancy Kate had worn on her body after she was dead, after she had begun to decay. Nancy Kate didn't give it to Polly."

It was awkward to talk about the locket without naming it, but she had to do it. She could not put it into the heads of any of the women. "Polly remembered that wrong. Polly *found* it—she found it out in the grass by the dog pen. It must have fallen off Nancy Kate's body when you moved it from the car to the grave. Later she thought Nancy Kate had sent it to her in the mail—it protected her from what she must have suspected about you already. Because even at the time, even as her poor little mind was protecting her from the idea you had murdered her friend, she did something that showed on some level that she knew exactly where Nancy Kate was. She took something *identical* of her *own*, and she pushed it into the wet cement you had poured over Nancy Kate. And she took a stick and wrote a date."

"All kids write in cement. She wrote the day that it was poured." He had become suddenly nonchalant, almost bored.

"No, she didn't, even though I'll bet you told her that story over and over as she got older. That way—if she did learn of Nancy Kate's death, if she did start to remember—she would think the cement had been poured and hard by the time Nancy Kate died. No—Nancy Kate disappeared in May, the same time that Jim had a school break. Your wife told us that he helped you with the run. But Polly scratched in a March date, two months earlier than the day you poured the cement. I asked Nancy Kate's father how old she was, and he told me her birthday. That was the date in the cement—a date in March, when the ground still would have been frozen. You couldn't have buried her then. Polly was creating a tombstone for her friend.

"She remembered all that while she was under gas for her root canals, didn't she? You knew she remembered before she knew. But you knew that she was close to it, she'd remember sooner or later. You didn't want to kill her. I don't think it was because you had any compassion for her— your own daughter. You had already put her through so much that killing her seems rather insignificant in comparison. I think what stopped you was you were afraid that you would be suspected. Everyone knew Polly had repeatedly accused you of incest. I think that if the information about your girlfriends was made public, your wife might finally collaborate— certainly your son would. If Polly was murdered they would go public with what they knew, and that would point the finger right at you. No, you wanted to make it appear Polly was crazy. Then, even if she did remember what had happened to Nancy Kate, no one would believe her. Probably it wasn't your neighbor at all who hit your fence—you did that yourself in order to have an excuse to tear down the dog pen and move Nancy Kate's body. But it was going to take time—especially with the ground frozen.

"So you went to Polly's house the night Karen was killed. Polly'd had dental work earlier in the day. You'd given her pills for the pain—her mouth was sensitive, and the pain killers you'd given her were stronger than a normal dosage. By the time you got there she was doped up enough so she couldn't fight you when you raped her. And because she couldn't fight, she did what she had always done, ever since she had been a little girl. She disassociated. You wouldn't go away, so she went away. I don't know what you intended to do originally, but when Lexy called, you saw the perfect way to set her up. When she woke up, she was in DJ's house, covered with blood, and Karen was dead."

She looked at her watch. He was getting ready to bolt—she could sense it. If only Mary Clare had done what she was supposed to do!

As if reading her mind he said suddenly, "I don't have to stand here and listen to this in my own office. You can either leave on your own, or I'll have the police remove you." He looked back towards the reception's area, but it was closed and locked as well. "Fine," he said. "I'll call from my car." With a move too sudden to anticipate, he went for the door, pushing one of the women so hard that she went down to her knee.

"You lied to me! You used me!" Jennifer ran down the hall after him, wailing. Marta and the two other women looked at one another, grinning. It was always good to see an old adversary getting his own, and Jennifer could not be causing a bigger scene if they had paid her. Marta heard at least one child's voice in the hall say, "Dr. Chet?"

"Thanks," she said to the other women. They were both standing open mouthed—she had given them much the same story she had given Gwen. They hadn't been expecting an accusation of murder.

"I wouldn't have missed it for the world," said the second. "I would have paid money to bring that bastard down."

But bringing him down was not enough. Now, if only Mary Clare and the Nebraska sheriff had done what they had promised...

They had. Marta saw the squad car the minute she stepped out the door. Dr. Chet had not gotten even the length of the block before he had been pulled over. She looked at the cops. Marta had seen the woman—small, black, hair up under her hat—at the bar before, but didn't know her name. Trying to look as if she was just one of the crowd, she glanced at his tail lights. Bingo—the right one was shattered. One quick thrust with a screwdriver in and out. That was an Echevarria trademark if she ever saw one. Across the street, in front of the library, she saw Mary Clare herself, pretending she was a patron. She was even carrying a bag of books. She caught Marta's eye, but did not wink or nod. Instead, she began to walk the other way. After a moment, Marta followed her.

She had parked in back of the library.

"Great work," Marta said, sliding into the truck. "Where'd you put the locket?"

"In the glove compartment. You realize, don't you, that we just committed a felony?"

"Not if we don't get caught."

"And what if he didn't do it? What if we set up an innocent man?"

"If he didn't do it, then they won't find the body. They won't convict on the locket alone." Now, if only the Nebraska sheriff had done what he said he would do over the phone—flooded the Denver PD with the old posters of Nancy Kate, updated to say they had been tipped to a Denver man owning a dog-run. Nancy Kate's father had given her the sheriff's name and number almost reluctantly, still afraid of stirring up old memories. Marta hadn't had much information to give the man in exchange for the fliers. Luckily for her he was an old friend of the Collins family and the unsolved death of a child had never set well with him. After listening to her story, minus all references to her 'shine', he had promised to fax the fliers to the right desks immediately. The request from Polly's father had helped.

"Do you think they got a copy of the poster?" she asked, turning around in her seat.

"Of course they got it. I Xeroxed that one you had and handed it to Janet myself. I saw it in the car when I walked by. Quit making a spectacle of yourself."

"Chill out! Nobody's looking at us. Nobody is even looking at them!"

"I don't like being anywhere around a felony. It's an Echevarria thing, okay? Call us paranoid, but we believe that whenever you see a cop it's just best to turn around and go the other way."

"Who was the cop?"

"I don't even want to tell you. I called in a favor, okay? You're lucky we found someone who was willing to hang around for a tail light violation. You're lucky we found somebody who'd listen at all."

"Janet? Is that her name? How'd you know her?"

"I don't want to talk about it," said Mary Clare. "Let me put it this way—she's an honest woman, and she has no idea exactly what we did. And I hope you never said the word locket in front of those other people."

"Never," said Marta, crossing her heart. "Let's go."

Mary Clare started to pull out of the lot.

"Wait a minute!" said Marta. "Oh, damn, I forgot about that silly girl." They looked down the street. There was Jennifer, standing on the sidewalk and weeping loudly, totally oblivious to the stares of the crowd that was rapidly forming to ogle what was obviously becoming more than just a routine arrest. For the first time, Marta thought there was some advantage to depression. At least she had done all her mourning at home, rather than making a public spectacle of herself.

NINETEEN

Marta did not get home until after it was dark. Gravy did not greet her at the door—she had been keeping him inside, much to his disgust. But as she paused by the mailbox, there was a cat-like rustling in the shrubs. Marta glanced behind her, cursing G-hey!. Goddamnit, she had told her not to let the cats out! But it was not a big black and white cat that stepped out of the shadows. It was a man.

At first, she thought it was the Big Dog.

"You get the fuck away from me!" She said it loud and firm, looking around for a weapon. Quickly, she rang all the doorbells and laced her fingers through her keys. "Get out of here right now before I have the cops on your tail!"

The man—boy, really—held up his hands. It was not the Big Dog, but one of his minions, a boy so newly arrived and low on the totem that he did not even have a nickname among the dykes yet.

"Don't wanna hurt ya," he said, his voice flat with an accent that Marta could not place, yet seemed somehow familiar. "Just wanna give you somethin'." He put his hand in his coat pocket, and Marta fumbled for the door knob behind her, even though she knew it was locked. Oh, Jesus, he had a gun, this fucking crazy was going to shoot her and the Coloradans for Family Values were probably going to back him up, get a lawyer who would say *this* is what happens when you let queers live with normal people, can anyone blame him? She hit the buzzers again, but with little hope—she had seen no lights on her way in.

"To hell with this!" she said suddenly, springing forward. Maybe he did have a gun, but he was a fool to think she'd wait for him to draw it. She slammed him full in the chest with both hands, pushing him back into the garbage cans. He hit them with a clatter, and then careened off the porch into the snow. He laid on his back without moving for a moment, obvious flabbergasted. It was not until Marta leaped off the porch and landed beside him, drawing her foot back for a disabling kick, that he protested.

"Knock it off, you crazy bitch! I said I didn't wanna hurt you! I just

152

wanna to give you this!" "This," which he had finally wrested from his pocket, was a wad of money. Marta looked at it, and then at him. She allowed him to rise, slowly, keeping his distance and with his hands out of his pockets.

"Why do you want to give me money?" she asked, waiting for the kicker. She should have just rushed inside and called the police while he was down, but she had been too busy channeling Tasha Yar to think of that. Now that her blood was up she wanted to gut her own kill.

"Not for you," he said sullenly. "For Karleve."

"I don't..." Marta began automatically, but he began talking right over the top of her.

"I know she come here. It's okay, I didn't tell nobody else. Billy don't know." Again, he held out the money. Marta could see that the wad was mostly ones. She had the feeling it was every cent that he owned.

"Why..."

"He shouldn't've hit her like that. Okay? He shouldn't've hit her. He said it was okay for her to come and stay for a while, and she didn't have to do it with any of them. He shouldn't have hit her for talking to your woman and saying no to him." He had moved a bit as he was talking, and now the porch light was shining on his face, showing her what she should have realized to begin with.

"You're Caroleve's brother, aren't you? And she's not my woman, she's my cousin," she added automatically.

The skinhead boy looked startled, as if the idea of lesbians having cousins was totally outside his world of possibility.

"Anyway," he said finally. "I know she come here. I couldn't keep her over there—Billy would a pounded on her a lot more, 'cept he ran outta cigarettes." For the first time he smiled, pleased with himself. His eye teeth were far out of line with his others, bespeaking poverty as Caroleve's had. "I hid 'em," he said proudly. "I knew he'd want one soon—have to go out and get some." He moved off the lawn and back up to the porch, where he was masked by the shadows.

"You stood there and watched him beat on your sister and didn't do anything but hide his cigarettes?" Marta felt a little pang of guilt—she had not told her brothers how wonderful they were, how much she loved them in months. She remembered how they had defended her, not just from Joey, but from countless other bullies. They were all getting cards tomorrow.

"I gotta live there," he said, explanation, not apology. "Or you gonna take me in, too?"

Marta put out her hand without speaking. They both knew what the answer to that would be.

"Why don't you get out of there?" she asked, after the money had changed hands.

153

"Cause I think he's right. Think he's right about the niggers and the Jews and the queers...." Funny, for two minutes he had become a person to her, someone's brother. And she had been a person, too, someone's cousin, the woman who had taken his sister in. Now, as he spoke, he became just another skinhead again and she just another queer.

"Karleve alright?" he asked, suddenly a brother again. The quick changes were making Marta sick to her stomach. She did not want to see the quick glimpses of caring peeking out between his prejudices—it seemed to make the life he had chosen even more horrible. She had assumed the skinheads were all just too dumb to know any better, that they were like sharks—programmed by birth to live a certain kind of life. Speaking to Caroleve's brother was like realizing a Great White had free will and just preferred to go on slashing.

"She's alright," she answered. "But she's not here. You've got to believe that. Don't come back here. You'll screw us all."

He nodded, and turned to leave. Over his shoulder he said, "Billy's mad. Mad at your wo....cousin, especially. She better watch out."

Inside her apartment, Marta grabbed G-hey!'s spare key off the hook where she kept it, ignoring the sad tales of kitty neglect. G-hey! had something cooking in her crock pot again—the smell overwhelmed her cozy little apartment and aroused feelings in Marta that she had thought were dead. Cooking. Yes. It might be nice to cook something.

She dialed Mary Clare's number, but there was no answer. Mary Clare was working or at practice or anywhere. Maybe on her way over. Mary Clare would be careful, she told herself. She always was. That was a lie—Mary Clare was always too interested it what was happening to watch her back, but it was a lie that Marta needed to tell herself in order to keep calm. Mary Clare was probably on her way over, and she'd be careful even before she was warned, and probably the Big Dog was just blowing steam—angry that Caroleve had escaped. The brother wasn't going to tell—he would have to admit his own part if he did.

Back in her own apartment, she sat down on the couch, absentmindedly petting Baloney. The urge to cook had disappeared. She lay down on the couch, thinking she would check on Captain Picard and Data. It had been a long and hard day. She had felt positively triumphant when the dyke cop had put the handcuffs on Polly's father. The only twist was that Marta had been left with the weeping Jennifer, who obviously could not get herself anywhere—not home, where she lived with her parents, not down to the police station, where someone might be interested in the story of the set-up alibi. Finally Gwen, who probably wanted to go home and think about being unemployed herself, stepped in and pulled the girl together through a combination of hot coffee and grandmotherly scolding.

So, considering the emotional roller coaster she had been riding, it was not surprising that she fell asleep on the couch before she even turned on the TV. What was surprising came two hours later, when she sat bolt upright out of a sound sleep for no reason at all. The cats, who had been tucked all around her like hot water bottles, scattered. There was no sound, no movement to indicate what had woken her. The apartment was dark. She lay still, listening to the crunching that meant Gravy had seized the moment for a little snack. Then she was up off the couch and fumbling in the dark for the door, and the words, 'Mary Clare, Mary Clare, Mary Clare' were pounding through her head as if being played on a drum.

On her way down the stairs she beat a hasty tattoo on G-hey!'s door, and also on the door of Janie and Renee, but she did not stay long enough to see if anyone was home, for the pounding in her head was becoming more frantic.

She did not go automatically in the front of the building, which was where she would have usually looked for trouble. She could not have said later what sent her to the back parking spaces, any more than she could have said what had woken her. But there was Mary Clare's truck, which certainly had not been parked in the space when she'd come in.

Mary Clare herself was nowhere to be seen. The only sounds were the normal sounds of the city—ambulance sirens and traffic and neighbors calling to one another. Marta almost turned to run to the street. Then the light in the cab of the truck came on. Only for a second, as if perhaps someone were lying on the seat of the truck, and pushing the door open for a fraction of a second with the movement of his feet. On and off. On and off again.

At that moment Marta had a revelation, and it had nothing to do with Mary Clare, or the skinheads or anything about being afraid or a victim again. It had to do with realizing she had run outside in her stocking feet, and was now standing in ice water. She had read about berserkers—those Celts who went into a killing rage and surged ahead in face of all adversaries—in spite of, in some cases, actually having received a death blow— propelled forward by rage like a chicken running with its head cut off.

It did not work quite that way for her. Certainly the rage was there— white hot like a coal fire—pictures of Teri, her cousin Joey, Mary Clare's complacent parents. Pictures of Polly's father, and DJ. Pictures of the Big Dog across the street, about whom Caroleve had said, "He'll kill your cat." But it was not these pictures that sent her over the edge.

What sent her over the edge was the realization that some asshole, some predator of women had caused her to be standing in ice water in her stocking feet, that now she would be sick with a cold on top of being depressed, and she just didn't fucking know if she could live through the two things together.

That was what was on her mind when she opened the door of the truck with one hand and grabbed Mary Clare's snow shovel out of the back of the truck with the other, bringing it down of the shaved head of the man pinning Mary Clare beneath him.

***

The cop who was the white and female half of the team sent in response to Janie and Renee's call was obviously family. Marta could have picked her out at fifty paces, even if it hadn't so happened that they had met before. She nodded at Marta before turning to Mary Clare—cop stuff before socializing. What the hell was her name? Marta tried to maneuver herself into a position from where she could read her name tag without being too obvious.

With a show of concern, the cop asked Mary Clare if she would like her to call someone from the Rape Crisis project.

"My brother raped me every single day from the time I was twelve to the time I was fifteen," said Mary Clare brusquely. "I'm not going to be too bothered about some guy who didn't even get it in."

The dyke cop—oh yeah, Alison, it came to Marta in a flash—didn't even bat an eye. She heard this kind of stuff all the time. "Nobody can fuck us up like our families, can they?"

"Probably he won't even be off the street, will he?" Mary Clare asked, looking over at the cop car. Everything was made more menacing by the flashing blue light on top—even the other women from the building, standing in the snow with their heavy coats on, looked sinister. After the cops had arrived, Marta had run back upstairs and changed her socks and put on her coat and boots, but she was still chilled to the bone.

"He threatened to kill my cat, too. And he beat up a woman who was living with them." Marta volunteered. She wondered if she should introduce Mary Clare now that she had remembered the name, but the moment was long past.

Alison—Kaine, was it?—rubbed her nose with her pencil.

"Assault, attempted rape—who knows how much time he'll get? Who knows what his record is like? Lots of judges don't like skinheads."

"Lots of judges don't like dykes, either," said Mary Clare. G-hey! had brought out big mugs of coffee for all three of them, and she took a long pull on hers. The cop shrugged.

"I don't know. But nothing's going to happen unless you press charges. And the gals from rape crisis don't care if he got it in or not—all they care about is that he tried."

They went around about that for a while. Mary Clare's obvious inclination was to blow the whole thing off—she didn't like the police even when they were on her side—and she didn't believe that there was ever any justice around rape. Marta had beaten the Big Dog fairly badly—it had taken both Renee and G-hey! to pull her off—and they could hear him in the car trying to tell the dyke officer's partner that she was the one

156

who should be arrested. It was obviously hard for him to plead with a black man—the word 'nigger' was never said aloud, but everyone listening could hear its promise hanging in the air. His aggression kind of forced Mary Clare's hand. And maybe he would be off the streets for a couple of days. So she signed, and Alison told Marta to take care and pressed her hand in a way that said she certainly remembered Marta. Then they took the Big Dog away and everyone went gratefully back inside where it was warm. Marta saw Caroleve's brother in the crowd, but did not wave.

"Let's order a pizza," said Mary Clare. "I need to do a little stress eating."

Marta nodded, and dealt with the phone call and explaining where the door was, which was just a power issue by the phone guy because the delivery guy knew where it was.

"Did that dyke cop know you?" asked Mary Clare as they were watching the clock, hoping the delivery would take longer than thirty minutes so they could get it free. "She acted like she knew you."

"Yeah. Barely. Remember that women in my Thursday group who committed suicide last year?"

"Yeah." Mary Clare had on her not-quite-with-the-program expression, so Marta expanded.

"Remember? The vibrator in the tub?* Come on, you went to the wake with me."

"Oh!" Light bulb. "Yeah, I met this really cute leathergirl there!"

"I'm glad we have our priorities straight," said Marta dryly. "While you were chatting up the leathergirls, I was crying all over this Alison woman. And then I ran into her at Tam's when I went to get some stuff I'd lent her. Only I didn't know she was a cop until tonight."

"Oh." Mary Clare blew Alison off, bored. "There was a reason I came over," she said. "Liz called. I guess you gave her my number?"

"And G-hey's. Is Polly out?" Marta sat up straighter and gently booted Gravy to the floor.

"Well, G-hey must not be home. And no. That's why she called. They haven't charged her father with Karen's murder."

"But..but the whole point is...he must have set Polly up. He must have! Why else would he have lied."

"They don't care, Marta." Mary Clare shook her head. "There's nothing else to link him with the murder. Polly is still their suspect."

"Then they've let him go?" Marta felt the biting cold that had engulfed her outside seep back into her bones. She had thought that all she would have needed to do was point the police in the right direction. It would have been enough for any cop on *Hill Street Blues*.

Give My Secrets Back, New Victoria Publishers, 1995

"No." Mary Clare shook her head. "They're still holding him. Liz went to town with the DA—they're out in Lakewood with a backhoe right now, digging up that dog run. Well, probably tomorrow—I'll bet nobody's working overtime. There's not a statue of limitations on murder—if Nancy Kate is really buried beneath it they'll charge him."

"She is," said Marta positively. "I know she is. And when they find her, surely they'll consider him a suspect. Don't you think? Why else would he go out of his way to set up an alibi?"

"Because he was fucking a thirteen-year-old," Mary Clare replied. "At least, that's what Liz says. He was covering up statutory rape—not murder. He was cheating on his receptionist with some kid—that's why he got her to lie for him."

"Damn!" Marta slammed her hand down onto the counter, causing all the cats to look at her with mild surprise. They were back to square one. Which meant, once again, she was wondering if they were chasing around after shadows, because she didn't want Polly to have been the one who had stabbed another woman to death.

***

Louann ran Marta out to the prison after work the next day, where she evoked her working-for-the-lawyer status to get a private cubical.

Polly, when told of the scene with her father, covered her face with her hands.

"He killed her," she said between her fingers. "The son-of-bitch killed her, didn't he?"

"I think so," said Marta. She tried to delicately adjust her fine tuning wires—how was the barometer reading today? Still not guilty, she decided. "But they haven't found a body. Liz got the DA involved, and the cops took out the dog run. But they didn't find a body." The one sentence did nothing towards expressing what Marta was feeling. She had been so sure!

"If only I could remember!" Polly rubbed at her eyes and then took her hands away. She looked wretched. Her eyes were bloodshot and her hair was limp and greasy, as if she had been washing it with dish soap. "I remember him pouring the cement," she said in a low voice, more to herself than Marta. "And I remember pushing the locket into it. I remember making handprints—all four of us did that, and we wrote our names."

Marta stifled a sigh. There had been nothing like that in the cement floor of the dog run. Polly was mixing up her memories again. "Did he ever pour cement again?" she asked without much hope.

Polly shook her head. "He didn't go much for home improvement." It was time to say what she had come to say.

"So, since we know now that Nancy Kate's dead, there's not really any reason..." she trailed off, stopped by the look of despair on Polly's face. For Marta, it had been almost like a game, a puzzle that had turned out to be just too hard to solve in the end, though she had given it a good go. She had almost forgotten that for Polly, they were bargaining with her life.

"Nancy Kate is dead," she said finally, hoping that perhaps Polly herself would say the words that would set her free. But Polly only stared at her with dazed, bloodshot eyes, as if she were her last hope. Perhaps she was.

"I'll look around some more," she said finally. "Ask some more questions." Like what? she said to herself. They had put all their eggs in one basket when they had persuaded the DA to dig up the dog run. She had been so sure that was where the body was hidden! Without it, she and Mary Clare had risked time in jail for nothing. She had no idea what the consequence was for planting evidence, and she did not want to find out.

"Okay," said Polly placidly. You had to be watching closely to see the shiver of relief run through her body. She let the guard lead her from the room, clutching the paperback novel that Marta had been allowed, after much scrutiny, to give her. The jail, where prisoners were held before trial, was not like the state prison. There was no library, no jobs or classes. What there was, according to Polly, was lots of playing cards and doing each other's hair. The book was precious. The book, thought Marta bitterly, was probably the best thing she was going to be able to do for Polly. And, she thought, glancing at the clock on the wall, she had just missed her bus as well. Well, she couldn't wait here—they'd be wanting the room soon. She stood to exit.

"Fucking dyke," said someone almost in her ear. Marta was thirty-five-years-old—she'd been out almost twenty years. It wasn't the first time she'd been called a name, and certainly not the most inventive name she'd been called. If she had been on the street, she might not even have turned. But she wasn't on the street, and her blood seemed to run cold in her veins just from the sound of the man's voice. She glanced quickly sideways, and froze.

It was the Big Dog. Dressed in the prison brown, cleaner than she had seen him before. A long row of stitches down the side of his face where she had opened it up with the snow shovel, bruises everywhere from her fists and her feet. She couldn't help a small smile of satisfaction when she saw that.

"You're not going to be smiling much longer, bitch!" He was with a group of men who were being ushered into the visitors' room. None of them were even looking his way. They were eager to visit, wary of having their privileges revoked just because some asshole who didn't know the drill was having a tantrum. Marta glanced up and down the hall quickly—where was the guard who was supposed to be escorting them? Oh, over breaking up a hug that had turned into tongue kissing.

"They burn women like you where I come from!" He was so angry that spittle was flying from his mouth.

"And they arrest men like you where I come from," Marta could not help retorting. "That's why I'm walking out of here and you're not."

"I'm going to cut your cat open and nail his guts to your door," he snarled at her, coming far too close. "I'm not just going fuck your girlfriend with my dick, I'm going to fuck her with my knife…"

"That's enough!" The man who stepped in between them did not hit the Big Dog in the head with the butt of his rifle, the way they did in the movies, but Marta could tell that he wanted to. To hell with prison reform—she wished he could do it as well. She wished he could kill him.

"I'll see you," said the Big Dog over his shoulder as the guard muscled him down the hall. Marta stood and watched, her hand over her mouth. She felt sick to her stomach. She was going to have to move, she thought, because he was going to be out soon, and she had no doubt that he would come after her, or Mary Clare or Gravy the moment they popped the door. She wished Renee and G-hey! had not pulled her off him as he'd lay there in the snow, where she had dumped him after that first blow. She wished they had let her kick him to death.

TWENTY

Mary Clare showed up around eight o'clock the next night without warning, carrying a King Sooper's bag beneath her arm.

"Let's go dancing," she said. She was wearing her best jeans and a very butch black t-shirt with the sleeves rolled twice.

Obediently Marta rose and picked up her jacket, but this was not quite what Mary Clare had in mind.

"Hey! Kaixo Neska! Chica!" she chided. "Let's like get you all duded up so you can knock the bad girls' eyes out! And no talking about depressing stuff—that's the rule."

Marta thought that the bad girls' eyes were pretty safe, but still she allowed herself to be cajoled into the shower, washing her hair with the new cherry-smelling shampoo that had been in Mary Clare's bag.

"I smell like a pastry," she complained, pulling on the pants and blouse Mary Clare had picked from her closet.

"You smell like you're alive," said Mary Clare, fussing with her hair. "You can't go around forever smelling like an open grave. You might like it, but the rest of us don't." She left Marta with the blow drier, and went to retrieve a pair of earrings from beneath her dresser. Marta had some really great jewelry, but her earring rack had fallen off the wall some three months before and there, except for the ones that Closet-Kitty had picked up and hidden in a safe place, they had remained.

Fixing Marta up took about an hour, and then they had to stop at 7-eleven to use the cash machine, so it was close to ten when they reached the bar. It was cold when they stepped outside the car. Mary Clare had left her parka at home and was shivering in her leather jacket. Let us be fashionable or die. She gave Marta a critical once-over before they went inside, making sure she hadn't changed shirts or rearranged jewelry on the way over. She opened her mouth, obviously to suggest Marta stash her jacket as well, but Marta stopped her with a look. No way. Mary Clare contented herself with reaching up and pushing a strand of hair behind Marta's ear.

The sound system was blaring—even outside the door they could hear the strains of 'Black Velvet,' the all time fuck song. You got out on the floor with the woman you were taking home on this one, or you didn't get out at all. Marta shuddered, and half turned towards the car, but Mary Clare had the keys, and she was halfway to the bar and already taking her jacket off. There were a lot of women out for a week night. Everybody was tired of the weather, needed a change, Marta guessed. She ran a perfunctory eye over the crowd on the dance floor—nobody she knew. Oh, Louann, who was two-stepping her way into some stranger's panties. She caught Marta's eye, but looked away blankly, which meant they were not to know her tonight, she was busy.

"What do you want?" asked Mary Clare over her shoulder, pulling a twenty out of her wallet. "Coke?" She named Marta's usual.

"Oh, I must have been a good girl to deserve this." The voice, projected from beside Marta but aimed at Mary Clare, was all too familiar. Marta would recognize that voice on her deathbed. Mary Clare had been with a lot of women, and a lot of them had been bad, but no one had torn her heart out the way that Delores Morales had, and no one so many times.

"Looking hot as ever," Delores purred at Mary Clare in a husky, take-me-home-and-fuck-me voice, ignoring Marta as she always did. Mary Clare stood with her mouth open, oblivious to the bartender hovering in front of her in annoyance. Marta wanted to throw her coat over Mary Clare's head and lead her out of the bar as if she were a horse in a burning barn, but she knew it was too late already. Mary Clare had never once run from Delores when she was hunting—incest issues or no incest issues—and Delores was hunting tonight. She was sending out the signals so strong that to the right and left of them women were turning and looking around in confusion, as if they almost smelled a fire.

"It's our song," said Delores, holding out a hand to Mary Clare. She wasn't wearing a dress—Delores was the kind of woman who would never overdress on a weekday. But Marta knew that she had stood in front of a mirror for hours achieving the casual black jeans, black boots, pink nails look. She tossed her head as she closed in on Mary Clare, flashing her earrings like a fishing lure.

Mary Clare took her hand with all the placidity of a big mouthed bass. Her look was excitement over resignation—you could tell she already knew what was going to happen, and saw no point or benefit in resisting. Ground-moving sex, and then an equally ground-moving jerk around. Marta put her hand out to catch her sleeve as Delores led her away, but Mary Clare brushed it off gently. Not as if disputing Marta's right to interfere, but more like a brave soul who knows that she is doomed, whose last wish is to take no one down with her.

Marta watched them meld into one on the dance floor. The twenty was still on the bar, the bartender tapping her foot. God damn Mary Clare!

thought Marta. In a snit, she ordered a margarita, that being the most expensive drink she could think of. Not that Mary Clare would notice the drink, or even that she had pocketed the change. Marta took her drink to the pool room, not wanting to watch Delores setting Mary Clare up for a fool for the—what was it, tenth time? She was surprised to see that one of the pool players was Alison Kaine, the cop who had taken the Big Dog off to jail.

"Oh, hi!" Alison sounded delighted to see her when she turned from her shot. Perhaps Mary Clare's clean-up had not been in vain. Marta had downed the drink as if she were marathoning, and she could already feel its signals racing from her empty stomach to her brain. Why was it that the sexual part was always the first to give in? One drink, and she could feel the desolving of the careful barriers that had stood her so well against Polly.

"Hi!" she said, reaching up to touch her hair. Damnit—everybody who'd ever read any pop psychology knew that was about flirting. Get out of Dodge, screamed the few brain cells that had not been hit in the first deluge of liquor. Oh, have another! said the majority.

"Let me buy you a drink," said Alison, signaling to the bartender before Marta could say yes or no. It was her shot—she left money on the bar. Marta watched her flub a bank shot.

"Aren't I an awful player?" she said to Marta, picking up her new beer. Marta sipped her margarita. The first glass had disappeared so swiftly beneath the hands of the bartender that it was possible to pretend it hadn't happened at all.

"Yeah," said Marta sincerely, already so well lubed that she had forgotten how to respond to rhetorical questions.

Alison, luckily, appeared to have knocked back a few herself. She laughed. "My—" she started, and then stopped. "My friends," she said finally. "Always give me a break. There's usually no one here on week nights."

"It's the weather," said Marta. "Everybody has cabin fever. Let me show you how to take this one." She took the cue from Alison's hand. Alison really must be a bad player—nobody but a complete novice would have chosen such a warped cue. Marta exchanged cues, catching a disgruntled look in the eye of Alison's opponent, a real butch girl in a black cowboy hat. Hustling Alison or setting her up, Marta bet.

"You can't just come in and start playing in the middle of the game," Cowboy Hat objected when Marta bent over the table.

"We're playing doubles now," said Marta, banking the shot. "Perfect! Yes! Pick a partner." She resisted the urge to clear the table—it seemed like poor manners.

Cowboy Hat was not at all happy, but her girlfriend was delighted. There was an obvious inner struggle—be an asshole or accept it graciously?—before she chose the latter.

"Fine," she said, motioning to the girlfriend. "Your shot, Darlin'."

They did not win. Alison was already too far behind for that. But Cowboy Hat had to fight for it. Alison, inspired by Marta and another beer, even sunk a few herself. Marta had another drink as well, switching to straight tequila. If she kept on drinking margaritas she'd be in the bathroom all night long—you had to down so much superfluous liquid to get to the booze.

They shook hands with the winners and then leaned back against the bar with their drinks. Alison turned to Marta, and for a moment she was sure that she was going to bring up the Big Dog. That mustn't happen. Mary Clare might have been carried off by Delores Morales, but the rules were still in effect: No Polly. No Caroleve. No skinheads.

To cut Alison off, Marta stood and offered her hand. "Dance?" she said, nodding towards the floor. She had not checked the music before issuing the invitation, so she was relieved to hear Randy Travis singing a love song about all the things he knew. Very danceable. They walked together onto the floor. Mary Clare and Delores were still moving as one. When they passed, Marta could hear Delores murmuring to Mary Clare in Spanish, a language she neither spoke nor understood, but melted beneath. Marta would actually have to kill Delores to keep Mary Clare from going home with her tonight. It didn't seem like a bad idea.

Alison led. No surprise—all the butch girls wanted to lead, even if it was beyond them. She was also a very good dancer, which *was* something of a surprise, though Marta couldn't have said why. She was not as tall as Marta— few women were—but she was close. Being the same size as her partner put a whole new spin on dancing that Marta had forgotten. She let Alison twirl her around and around, following as if they were long-time partners, right from Randy Travis into Patty Loveless.

"You're a good dancer," Marta said without opening her eyes. "This is nice." They danced a song or two in silence.

"Your friend is waving to you," said Alison as she guided them across the back wall, tiled with mirrors.

Marta opened her eyes—dancing with them closed was a rare luxury in which only a following partner could indulge. Sure enough, there was Mary Clare, waving at her with her keys dangling from one hand—a longtime signal that meant find a ride home, I'm getting laid. If looks could kill, Mary Clare would have toppled right over the bar rail. But Mary Clare was in one-night love, and she had planned her escape well. She'd be in the truck with the motor running before Marta could fight her way across the dance floor. She gave Mary Clare the finger, to let her know she had seen the signal and just what she thought of it. Who the hell was she going to get to take her home? Louann liked to make out in her truck with her conquests—she wasn't going to take the idea of a third wheel graciously. If she was even still here.

Marta looked around. "Damn it all!" she said aloud.

"What's the matter?" asked Alison without missing a beat. On the sound system the first step was now the two-step.

"My goddamn ride just left to go screw her ex. I'm going to have to take the bus home." This was not really a discomfort—the Colfax bus ran every half hour until some ungodly time of the morning, and it took Marta within a block of her house, but it was the principle of the thing. That, and knowing that she was going to be picking pieces of Delores Morales out of Mary Clare's life for the next month.

"Oh, I can give you a ride home," said Alison, swinging her around the hardwood floor just as the singer suggested. "You live in Capital Hill near me, don't you?" Oh, right, Marta remembered, she had been there.

They did not speak any more. They danced, Marta with her eyes closed. Even when they left, Marta sat with her eyes closed in the the the car, the alcohol enabling her to shut out all the things that had been troubling her for the past six months, and the more immediate problems of the past week as well.

"Do you want to come up and have a cup of coffee at my place?" asked Alison, instead of inquiring for Marta's address. There was an almost buried part of Marta that suggested this would be a very bad choice indeed, but José Cuervo was speaking for Marta tonight, and José was a lover as well as a dancer.

"Yes," she said, and did not demur when Alison laid a hand on her thigh, nor when she pulled her close and kissed her once they were in the front hall just off the living room in Alison's apartment. Teri had been left at the front door. Marta's mind was filled only with the passion of the kiss. Alison kissed just the way she liked it—lots of small nibbles and only a hint of tongue. She tilted her head back as Alison breathed warm and moist on her neck, following the line down to her collar bone. Alison nuzzled her shirt aside and kissed the hollows at the base and sides of her neck. Except for the noises she could not control, Marta was completely passive. So much of her mind was engaged in blocking memories that she could do nothing else. A part of her did wonder if this passivity would make Alison back off in boredom, or if she would carry through in spite of it. Either way, there was nothing she could do to change it.

Marta often went about with a kind of cloak about her, an almost unconscious block against the minds of strangers. A kind of psychic equivalent to wearing a Walkman on the bus, it was particularly essential when she visited any place like the bar, where women were quarreling and flirting and spilling more of their lives than perhaps they should under the influence of José's friends Jim and Jack. Polly had been way too live a wire to block, but Alison did not seem to be spewing raw emotion. Marta tried to turn up the white noise.

Then, experimentally, she brought her hand up across Alison's t-shirt to her breast. She loved butch girls with big tits—it seemed a particularly delightful oxymoron. She was surprised at the depth of passion released in herself by that one small movement.

Suddenly she was breathing in short, quick gasps, stolen between the moments when Alison's mouth lay hot against her own.

She moved her hand from Alison's breast to her throat, her fingers splayed, her palm pressed against her wind pipe. She was not into the leather scene—her experiences of domination and bondage came third hand through the adventures of Mary Clare. But holding her hand thus, in this possession of power, never failed in make her jeans wet.

Alison must have felt the same. Suddenly her touch was more sure. Marta was standing backed against the wall with one knee bent, and Alison straddled her leg, clutching it between her thighs.

Marta could feel the sudden rush of heat rising off her cunt through the two layers of denim. She hadn't felt a woman rub against her fully clothed for years—somehow that was a step that had been deleted during adult dating. It brought back a deluge of memories that had nothing to do with Teri. High school—the first tentative touch with the captain of the field hockey team. She felt herself begin to sink down the wall as if melting. She did not loosen her grip on Alison's throat. She wanted her right on top of her. She wanted to be taken right there on the floor of the living room, her pants around her ankles.

Alison was above her now, holding her weight on one hand as she unbuttoned Marta's shirt with the other.

Marta moved her hand from Alison's throat over her shoulder, sliding it down the length of her back to her ass. She pulled Alison closer, grinding her right up against her hip. She wanted this woman as she had not wanted another woman for a year, wanted her every way imaginable, wanted everything she had ever heard Louann describe over the phone.

She reached up between them to pull at her fly. Love those button-down jeans. Now she had one hand down the front of Alison's pants, the tips of her fingers just touching her cunt where it was so wet and open. No room to move, no room to go inside her, but it was enough just to feel the heat rising off her like a flame. She wanted to be inside that fire.

The phone, sitting on the end table somewhere above Marta's head, began to ring. They both ignored it. The answering machine kicked on, and between kisses that had grown frenzied, Marta heard Alison's voice asking the caller to leave a message.

"Oh!" Another woman's voice came on the line. "I can be such an asshole sometimes! I'm really—"

Alison jerked her hand off Marta's shoulder and groped the table top. With a click, the machine was silenced.

Marta hardly noticed. She still had her hand in Alison's pants, and she had no idea what the next move would be. It really didn't matter. She was more excited by this one touch than she had been during whole affairs with other women. She wanted to possess this woman—to get inside her head, feel her fantasies and give them back to her.

Alison had torn open the front of her blouse—buttons flying—and Marta could feel the heat increase between them.

Suddenly, without warning, Marta smelled smoke. She opened her eyes, and for a moment she panicked. They seemed about to be enveloped by a wall of fire that had sprung up from nowhere.

Then, an instant later, she realized that this fire burnt in a place where it could not harm her. Be careful what you ask for—you might get it. Alison's passion and fantasy fire had slipped into her own mind with the same ease that Alison's tongue had slipped into her mouth. The fire dimmed and become background. It could have been a bonfire, but Marta knew that it was not...

It was the fire caused by the explosion of a car. She could see the sleek lines of a Jag beneath the flames. The occupant had been escaping, and she had almost made it. It was only the last tight turn of the alley before she reached the wharf that had betrayed her. She was lucky to have escaped alive. Her hands and knees—torn beneath her gloves and pants—were bleeding from the leap she had made to the pavement.

With a shock she realized the woman was her. This was Alison's fantasy!

She rose painfully to her knees, shielding her eyes against the flames with one hand.

Alison's mind had dressed her in denim and leather, down to her gloves and cowgirl boots. There was no question who the bad girl was in this scene. She was Jezzabella, named for a devil, queen of the underworld. In her mind's eye, Marta could see that she had also been given a haircut—shaggy, wild, slutty. She still had her own earrings—Alison and Mary Clare must have similar tastes.

In the alley, Jezzabella fought to rise from her knees. Her enemy had been stalking her for months—the only one to keep up the chase when all the others had given up. This stalker had talked to old friends and family in her quest—had come close to capturing her at least twice before. Jezzabella had smelled the stalker's scent on her car and in her apartment. But somehow it was as if they were allies rather than antagonists. She struggled to gain her feet, but the blast had left her shaken.

The stalker walked between Jezzabella and the fire, careful, measured steps. A cop. It was over now. Jezzabella almost held up her wrists for the cuffs. She had played a good game, but it was over—the running, the hiding. At least she had played against a partner with her own skill. How dreadful if she had been brought down on a traffic violation or a license check!

Jezzabella licked her lips, looking up at the woman who stood in front of her, legs braced two feet apart, hands on her hips, a revolver in one hand and her nightstick in the other. A heat was rising off her that made the fire at her back seem dim. This cop had finally cornered her prey after weeks of elusion. She was not going to be content with a mere collar.

Jezzabella felt a new surge of hope. Was there a possibility of escape? Could she use the fact that this woman, who had been trailing her for weeks, wanted her? Why not? And there was something that drew her to this woman. She wanted to know what it was like to taste a woman who was her equal.

She made a motion as if to place a gloved, bleeding hand upon the cop's thigh, but the cop brought her nightstick up quickly and pushed it away. "I'm in charge," she said, talking deep in her throat. She brought the stick up beneath Jezzabella's chin and tilted her face to look at her.

If she had not been on her knees in an alley, Jezzabella would have taken her out for that act. But her gun—she flicked her eyes briefly to the side—was out of immediate reach beneath a dumpster. Had the cop seen her slide it over, the first thing she had done when she dove from the car? She thought not. If she could play along, perhaps she could retrieve it.

The cop was looking towards her own car...

The fantasy faded. But it didn't matter—Marta's body had taken over the challenge of their duel, expressed in the movement of their bodies together in real time.

But then as Alison's lips touched hers the images flowed back. She couldn't have stopped it if she had wanted to. Inside another woman's fantasy the action did not stop merely because Marta lost touch with it.

Jezzabella was still on her knees, her face pressed into the cop's shirt, her hands clutching the fabric of the uniform pants. The cop bent down over her... The night stick was looped on her wrist, hanging free. She snapped open a switchblade knife—fantasies meant you could accessorize however you wanted—*and with a movement at once deft and powerful, split the crotch of the criminal queen's leather pants.*

Jezzabella turned her head to the side. Now her left cheek was grinding into the cop's belt buckle, but she was able to see. In the low window of one of the warehouses that lined the alley, they were reflected through a shimmering overlay of flame. The light of the fire shone off the dull grey metal of the cop's gun, just as it shone off Jezzabella's gun, waiting for her beneath the dumpster. She watched in the window-mirrors as the cop snapped the knife shut and shoved it in her pocket with one hand.

She had to concentrate, try and keep her mind on the gun, to remember that this was just a way to trap the cop into letting her guard down. She could not lose herself in the desire that she had felt so long for this woman, the desire that she had carried from the first moment she had spotted the cop on her tail.

Without thinking, the criminal spread her knees in anticipation, as she caught the swift glimpse of a smile on the cop's lips reflected in the windows. Well, why should she have to fight—pretend that she didn't want it? She did want it. Just because she was willing to kill this woman in order to escape didn't make that desire any less urgent. Her cunt was hot, totally exposed, totally open.

Carefully, with a combination of delicacy and power, the cop lowered herself into a squat in front of her. Better angle. Now they were face to face as she pushed the nightstick up inside her. It went in easily—she was dripping wet. Jezzabella's cheek was marked with the pattern of the cop's belt buckle.

Jezzabella tried to keep the image of her own gun in her mind. She would make this woman pay! But she fixed upon it with difficulty. The cop was fucking her cunt with a need, and she was responding the same way. With hunger.

Jezzabella rarely gave herself to another woman. It could only happen with a woman who was strong enough to take her, and there were few who were willing to do what it took.

Now she gave up all gestures of resistance. It was not because of the gun still in the woman's hand. Death did not frighten her. It was because of the will of the woman dominating her...

Gone...Again Marta lost Alison's fantasy, but the excitement was bringing her to a quick climax that she could not suppress. In her own mind she saw the ball of fire that the car had become, and she held the image as she panted for release. She wanted to go up in those same flames.

Jezzabella was moaning and the cop laughed with a wicked delight. "That's right," she said, her voice low and nasty. "Tell me how much you like getting fucked."

She felt the wall of flame pass over her, an explosion that seemed to come from both her body and her mind.

Through smoke threatening to block the images out, she could see the cop panting with the same excitement while holding her by the shoulders so that she would not collapse on the bricks beneath them. The nightstick fell to the ground.

Marta started as Jezzabella heard the sound. So *that's* what Alison was using all this time!

Then it was Marta herself who seemed to take control of the fantasy. It was in her own mind now...

Jezzabella had no time to think—she had only the one second of inattentiveness in the cop she needed as she grasped the stick which had been inside her and struck the cop's wrist. The gun went clattering to the pavement. Jezzabella kicked it against a wall as she dove for her own gun. She was still trembling with aftershocks, but she was in control once again. She peered around the side of the dumpster. The cop was writhing in pain as she scrambled for cover.

Jezzabella took aim and then lowered her gun. She was near the wharf and could always find shelter there. She could disappear before the cop called for back-up. She would spare her. They might meet again some other night. Bent over, she took off running without looking back...

***

Marta came to herself with a little start. She and Alison were in the bedroom, but she had no recollection of how that had happened, nor did she know how her shoes and boots had ended up on the floor. Alison was lying beside her on her back, a contented just-fucked smile on her face, snoring gently.

Wow! That was one hell of a fantasy, thought Marta. Who'da thought? She carefully crawled out of the bed without jarring it and went back into the living room, picking up the trail of clothing she had left behind her. She had never had anything quite like that happen to her. She wondered if they had actually acted out the fantasy. No, she didn't see any props.

In an effort to keep her own mind blank, she must have just served as a kind of viewing screen for one of Alison's fantasies. Scary! But very hot. That woman's fantasy had opened parts of herself that she hadn't wanted to look at, had disassociated from for a long time. Too long. She saw power in a new way—that she had it with this woman as an equal and that they could face a great deal more together. She wanted to find out. She wanted to do it again.

At home she always slept with a white noise machine to shut out the sounds of the city. Here the pipes were creaking, and there was the sound of a siren in the distance. She would never be able to sleep with the strange noises, and she was exhausted. She was close to home, and used to walking the streets of Capital Hill late at night, so she left Alison a note with her phone number and let herself out, locking the door behind her.

***

The next morning G-hey! knocked on the door.

"Let's go down to China Brown's place and have breakfast," she said. Salad was going through a period of working as a fry cook at Denny's, which just about ruled her out as a breakfast companion. "Do you want to call Mary Clare?"

"Mary Clare went home with Delores Morales last night," said Marta grimly. She did not need to elaborate. G-hey! had watched a few episodes of the Delores and Mary Clare show herself.

"Couldn't you stop her?" asked G-hey!, distracted somewhat from

170

her concern by scratching Five-Cents' tattered old head. Her rusty purr filled the kitchen.

"Not without a gun. And I probably would have needed to take them both." She said nothing about her own little tryst. That could remain in the Need to Know category until she saw how it panned out. It had been hot, and she'd left her phone number. She'd see if Alison called, she told herself, trying not to overlay it with a glimmer of hope. It had felt good to her, it had seemed to feel good to Alison, but she'd see. No sense getting her hopes dashed. Still, there was a swing to her walk as she followed G-hey! outside.

The Milky Way Cafe, run by China Brown, had been around in one form or another as long as Marta could remember. It's latest and most stable incarnation was an old warehouse, and word was that China owned this building and the nomadic period had came to an end. Everybody came to China Brown's place. All of Marta's friends hit it at least once a week—it was laid-back and gay friendly, and while eating real food that had never seen the inside of a microwave, you could also read the alternative papers and find out where Monkey Siren was playing for the next three weeks.

They had not even made it through one cup of coffee—seated beneath a sculpture of a full sized tiger jumping through a hoop that made Marta rather uneasy—when through the door who should walk but Mary Clare, with a copy of the *Rocky Mountain News* folded beneath her arm. Mary Clare would not subscribe to the *News* because of a long standing disagreement with their editorial policies, but she could not keep from buying it at 7-Eleven because its comics were so much better than the *Post*'s. She spotted them and came over.

"I thought you'd be here," she said with a self-satisfied smile. Marta examined her critically. She seemed neither heart broken or madly in love, which were usually the only two choices after a night with Delores Morales. In fact, Mary Clare seldom surfaced for at least three days after she and Delores did their thing. What had gone down?

"And I thought you didn't take the *News*," said G-hey! critically.

"They don't know I take it, and I always lecture their phone salesmen. Me buying a copy once a week at 7-Eleven isn't going to make them or break them. If you want to put them out of business, then you'd better get Joslin's and Foley's to stop putting in full page ads."

"What happened?" blurted Marta, who wanted to hear about the power of Delores far more than the power of a boycott. "You seem…" she lifted her hands, rejecting both "normal" and "unscathed" but unable to come up with a better word.

"I didn't spend the night with Delores," replied Mary Clare in a pleased voice, gesturing for coffee. It always took forever to get served at the Milky Way.

"How did *that* happen?" asked Marta in astonishment. Mary Clare could avoid Delores, and if she was not blindsided she could resist Delores, but never once had Alison heard of her actually escaping from Delores after she had been captured.

"Oh, through absolutely no action of my own." Mary Clare never tried to pretend that free will or common sense existed where Delores was concerned—there was no point. She was in a wonderful mood, as chipper as a woman who had been spared by the Governor's call just before they pulled the switch. "Her girlfriend came by while we were in the parking lot. They had a huge fight. Isn't that great? I was able to escape while they were still going at it."

She unfurled her paper with a self satisfied air. Delores was busy with someone else, she had escaped, God was in his heaven and all was right in the world.

"That must have been a hell of a fight," said G-hey!.

"Oh, it was," Mary Clare assured her. "I would have stayed to watch if I hadn't been afraid of getting sucked in. The girlfriend tried to pop me one."

"Mary Clare!" cried Marta, as if this were something to which she had agreed. "Are you all right?"

"Can I change places with you?" Mary Clare asked G-hey!. "I don't like the way that tiger is looking at me. Oh, sure, I'm fine." She tilted her head back and showed them a little bruise on her cheekbone. "She barely caught me. Knocked me on my butt in the snow, though." Even this, told through the miracle of not getting caught up again in the Delores saga, was related cheerfully. Mary Clare had rather a gift for being on the edge of bar fights. She was forever being thrown out of places when truly all she had been doing was trying to keep from being trampled.

"Why didn't you come inside and get me?" Marta asked, though her evening had turned out so much more interesting. Mary Clare could not be allowed to think that this leaving thing was going to be tolerated.

"Oh, honey, I couldn't." Mary Clare was apologetic but unrepentant. "There was only a small window of escape—I had to seize it or be seized."

Since Marta having a one night stand with anyone was preferable to Mary Clare having a one night with Delores, she dropped it. The waitress arrived, and Mary Clare ordered a Santa Fe Breakfast without looking at the menu.

"Where's Monkey Siren playing this week?" she asked G-hey!, who had picked up all the fliers on the way in. "Did Louann take you home?" she said to Marta, who could not answer before she went on. "Oh! Look! There's that nice cop who was over the other night." She waved. "Sure, now I remember her at the wake. That must have been her girlfriend that I chatted up—she was that cutie who got so drunk and caused a scene."

Another little wave, this one much more flirtatious.

Marta lifted her head casually, as if her whole intestinal tract did not feel as if had been suddenly and violently turned inside out. She looked across the room where Mary Clare was pointing. The north side of the building was fronted with a row of big warehouse windows that had to be opened and closed with a pole. Twelve circular stained glass pieces—the signs of the zodiac—hung across their top, reflecting bits of rainbow light here and there in the room.

In the front booth, just sitting down, was Alison Kaine. Alison was wearing sunglasses, carrying herself a little stiffly as if she didn't want to jar her head, as if somebody had done a little too much partying the night before.

And her girlfriend, who Marta now remembered chatting up Mary Clare at the wake as well. She was one of the women who had been in and out of Tam's apartment the following night. She was tall, but not so tall as Marta, with dark curly hair. A good height for a woman. Pretty. Prettier than Marta. Probably didn't struggle with her weight as Marta did, either. The girlfriend leaned across the table and spoke to Alison, placing her hand on her arm. Marta didn't have to hear the girlfriend's voice to know that it had been the voice on the answering machine.

Alison, despite the fragile way in which she was carrying herself, glowed as she bent forward to reply. New love was happening. You only had to have experienced it even once to see the sparks fly. Or perhaps, thought Marta, trying to keep from betraying herself with any change of breathing, not new love at all. Perhaps what they were all seeing now, so publicly at China Brown's was the tail end of a lovers' quarrel. Perhaps they were seeing the part where the apologies had been made and vows renewed and both women had resolved to forget about anything rash that had been said or done the night before in the heat of anger...

"This plate is really hot," said the waitress, sliding Marta's burrito down in front of her with a practiced move. Like all of the waitresses at the Milky Way, her outfit—some kind of fifties house dress over a black lace body suit and obviously nothing else—seemed to have been picked to entertain. At any other time Marta would have enjoyed her grunge/punk/garage sale look, but at the moment she felt as if she could not breathe. She took a sip of water—the Milky Way did not serve diet soda.

Mary Clare was not only babbling—still celebrating her narrow escape from destiny, but she had begun to pick at Marta's food as well. Normally, this would have been fine, but not now. She could not deal with anything at all now. All she could do, perhaps if she moved quickly and was lucky, was get herself into the bathroom where she could freak out in private. There wasn't a great deal of face to be saved—it was therefore that much more important.

"I have to go to the bathroom," she said brusquely, leaving Mary Clare and G-hey! to compare notes on the singles' ads in *Westword*.

Behind the door, she stood cautiously by the sinks, the same way you stand by the door of the bathroom when recovering from stomach flu. Not quite ready to lose it, but not quite ready to be more than a dash away, either. Damn it all! What had she been thinking? Oh, yeah, she hadn't really allowed herself to think that this might be more than a one night stand, but she also had never allowed herself to think that it might be something even less than a one night stand, a blow at a woman who wasn't even there! She splashed a double handful of cold water on her face, feeling the steam rise almost immediately. Thank god, thank god in heaven she hadn't told G-hey! Thank god that she had not raised any hopes but her own.

The door of the bathroom opened, and she fumbled for a paper towel. The Milky Way, of course, didn't have anything so fancy as a dispenser, but made do with a roll sitting on the edge of the middle sink. It escaped Marta's hands and leapt to the floor, rolling out ten squares as it traveled. The woman who had entered picked it up. She straightened, her hand outstretched, her eyes meeting Marta's for the first time.

It was Alison Kaine.

For a dreadful moment Marta thought that she had come into the bathroom to catch her alone, to beg her to keep their secret. Then she realized, more awful still, that Alison had come into the bathroom to pee, that, her head in a cloud, she had no more seen Marta in the restaurant than Mary Clare had seen her in the bar the night before.

"Oh," she said. To her credit, she did not try to pretend nothing had happened, or that they were just old friends. She just stood and looked uncomfortable, not quite edging towards the door.

Except for the occasional moment when Mary Clare pushed her too far, Marta did not do public scenes. It had been quite a bone of contention between her and Teri, who had loved them. She nodded at Alison with cold civility, meaning to push pass her without words.

At the last moment, however, she halted. "If you're going to use another woman to hurt your girlfriend, then you'd better have the decency to tell her that up-front. Because I want to know in advance if I'm going to be a one night stand or a weapon." She could not resist adding, "Same might be asked about your nightstick." She swept through the door with a gesture that would have done Vivian Leigh proud.

TWENTY-ONE

The rest of the day was not much better. It snowed. The warm weather seemed like a trick of the imagination. Had there really had been sun and clear days at the flea market—had Louann really come into work in ripped up shorts one day? It seemed like a thing of the dim, dim past. What was real was grey, snowy days and freezing cold. Work was drudgery—Marta predicted bad relationships and disaster to women who hung up quickly.

It was group night. She borrowed Mary Clare's truck, though she didn't really want to go. Her mood had become as black and cold as the weather, as if the whole city was but a backdrop for her life. The shivering people on the street, picked up by Mary Clare's headlights near the bus stops and convenience stores, were like earnest extras in a tragedy that had played on so long it had turned into a farce. Group was farcical as well. Everyone wanted to talk about Polly, but no one did. It was a relief when the facilitator called time.

The drive home was dangerous. Marta braked carefully and far ahead at all lights, and still she slid a few feet into the intersection at Colfax and Broadway. A city bus swerved to avoid her and blared its horn. She took a terse sip from the can of Diet Pepsi she held tightly clenched between her legs. She should have stayed home. But the weather had worsened dramatically while her group met—while they spoke of broken hearts and renewing life, careful not to speak of Polly for fear they might have to name their own craziness—a front as terrible as Teri's anger had blown in over the mountains and was now raging over the city. Marta had not seen anything like it since the big blizzard of '87, when people had abandoned their cars in the middle of the streets and roped themselves together to walk home. She should have called Mary Clare, whom she had left sitting on her couch, covered with cats as she critiqued *Star Trek: The Next Generation.* No doubt she was worried. But she was almost home now. Just a few more careful blocks on back streets.

She decided not to try parking in back of the house—the alley was treacherous when it was slick, and they had a better chance of shoveling Mary Clare out in the morning if she were in the front. The snow was coming down so thick by the time she turned the corner that she could not scan the whole block. She had to creep along, looking for a parking place house by house. She could see light in some of the houses. The windows of the apartment where the skinheads lived were blazing.

There it was—finally. A space big enough to pull into—no way was she going to parallel. She began to turn her wheel.

Then, from out of the storm like a vision, a figure appeared in front of her. It was so abrupt, so unexpected that at first she thought it was a flashback of the encounter at the jail. But no, there he was in real life, the Big Dog stepping out off the curb in front of her, wrapped in his long peacoat, his head bare to the elements. Marta froze, her foot still on the gas. What in the world was he doing on the street? She had assumed he would be in the jail for at least several more days—she hadn't imagined his friends being affluent enough to raise bail. But then, anything could have happened. There was always a shortage of space at the jail, always one set of prisoners being released to make way for another. Battering husbands were deemed low risk. Some of them went back home and killed their wives, and then the officials were apologetic and talked about new bond funding. It didn't matter why. He was out.

He turned, caught in her headlights, and he must have recognized Mary Clare's little red truck, because suddenly his face burst open with rage, and he reached out a gloved fist to pound on her hood.

That was his undoing. Marta had begun to brake, gently pumping, but the angry gesture caught her off guard. It brought him dangerously close to her bumper, and she pulled sharply to the left. The hood slid sideways beneath his hand, and suddenly he was sliding sideways as well, his face changing from anger to fear in just a second. She slammed the brakes on, but it did no good—there was a sickening thump, as if she had driven too fast over a speed bump.

Later, all the right people said the accident was not her fault. The police tested the Big Dog's blood alcohol high enough to explain why he was wandering around in the storm when he should have been bundled in by the heater. His buddies said he had gone out for cigarettes, and since they were in about the same state of inebriation, this had made sense to them. The were too drunk to think about looking for him when he didn't come back. Both newspapers ran feature articles on victims of the storm, street people who had been frozen in drifts and couples caught in their cars on country roads, as well as babies born at home or in restaurants because the ambulances couldn't get around to all the accidents fast enough. They made much of the efforts that Marta and the other women had taken to save the dead man. There was even a photo of G-hey! in both papers, showing how she had popped up her dome tent inside the downstairs apartment and then slit the floor so they could ease it over his unconscious body to protect it from the storm. Mary Clare, who had worked with Outward Bound in her younger days, had quite a long quote about first aide and the decision not to try to move the boy up the three flights of stairs, bleeding and broken as he was. Being Mary Clare, she made sure the gay angle came out, and both papers printed philosophical little editorials on the irony of a bunch of dykes out in the snow trying in vain to save the life of a man who had tormented them. Would that have changed his mind? wondered the writer from the *Post*. Would he have been touched by it if he had lived?

The local and then the national gay presses picked up the gay angle and there were reprints of the story for several months. The gay papers were split half and half—some saying this kind of compassion was good for the cause, others scornfully insisting queers made themselves victims and they should have left him to die alone in the street.

But they were the only ones who blamed Marta for anything. The police, who finally came in the morning, long after the Big Dog's lifeblood had ebbed away onto Marta's sleeping bag and Janie's comforter, didn't even give her a ticket.

But then, the police didn't know everything.

TWENTY-TWO

Louann and Gloria were both solicitous when Marta called in sick to work the next day, explaining what had happened in a few terse sentences, and Mary Clare not only took her out to the jail, but out to lunch first as well. She sat in the waiting room, reading her new copy of *Lesbian Connection* while Marta talked to Polly. She could not come in, because they had already used up Polly's weekly family visit.

Polly looked worse than she had the day before, and Marta did not tell her that she, too, had killed someone. What comfort would that be, when Marta was walking around free? Marta took a quick look at the iron door as it swung shut behind her. The police had not even blinked when she explained that she had backed up again over the body of the Big Dog after he'd gone beneath the truck, accepting that she had panicked and done the first thing that came into her mind. But would she be here locked in with Polly if the police knew she had sat in Mary Clare's truck for almost an hour, until the cold became too much to bear, before she gotten out and even looked at the skinhead laying in the street? Mary Clare knew—she had used the windshield brush from her car to sweep the snow off him as she sent Marta for blankets and bandages, but she had not said a word. Not then, not later. It was G-hey! who had said innocently, after the paramedics had zipped him up and loaded him on the gurney. "Well, I guess he won't be bothering you or Gravy anymore." Then they had shared one guilty look.

"My dad," said Polly, and then she didn't say any more. She waved her hand vaguely to indicate it all. For the first time Marta saw that, though Polly had accepted Liz's suggestion for a plea, she herself had not believed, had hoped she had not done this thing, had not splattered another woman's blood all over her ex's walls. Now there was no hope. Marta had killed a man and Polly had killed a woman, and they both had to live or die with the knowledge. The only difference, thought Marta savagely, was that the man she had killed deserved to die. The man she killed was a rapist and a hate monger and, if he had lived, would certainly

178

have one day hurt her, or Mary Clare or Gravy or Baloney. But she knew, really, the important difference was that Polly was going to spend a good part of her life in prison, and she was going to go free without a night in jail.

"Do you have your keys?" she asked Polly brusquely, as if this were her fault. "I want to go over to your place." She did not know why— perhaps just because she had done every single other thing she could think to do.

"Liz says the police have already been there," said Polly dully. "They didn't find anything."

"Well, it won't hurt to try." Marta did not mention anything at all about being an inside player. She did not want to put any hope into Polly's head, when truthfully she feared there was none.

Getting the keys turned out to be a problem. They were not, as she assumed, in an envelope with her effects, though that envelope was brought out. Finally, Polly wrote a note to her landlady, who lived in the building.

"Bring in the mail, too," said Polly as Marta was leaving.

The sun was shining outside as if there had been no storm, as if, in fact, it had never snowed in Denver. There were huge piles of snow by the side of the road, but for the most part the main roads were clear, running with rivers of melt-off.

"How about a movie?" said Mary Clare to Marta.

The idea of spending two hours in the dark, away from all thoughts of prison and death was too tempting to resist. The Tivoli was playing a couple of thriller killers, but that seemed a bit too close to home, so they went instead to the dollar movies, where they sat for the third time through *Fried Green Tomatoes*.

It was only after Mary Clare dropped Marta off that the full implication of the last twenty-four hours hit her. She had killed a man, and Polly was in jail. She was walking free, and Polly was locked up for a crime she did not commit. Damnit, she knew Polly hadn't done it! She knew it as firmly as she had ever known anything, and her conviction wasn't worth the breath it would take to tell it. So what happened now? Did Polly just go to trial, and hope she drew a jury would could accept hearing about incest and its aftermath? Even if she was acquitted, the stigma was going to follow her the rest of her days.

Without quite knowing why, Marta found herself putting on her jacket.

***

The landlady was an older woman in jeans, who frowned as she looked at the note Polly had written.

"I read about it in the paper," she said to Marta. "Is it true?" She clucked her tongue and shook her head. "She seemed like such a nice, quiet girl. Hardly made any noise. A few visitors." She peered hopefully at Marta, obviously hoping for a good gossip. It wasn't everyday one of her tenants was arrested for murder.

"Who visited?" asked Marta, not because she cared, but because she was learning that there was a certain etiquette to a murder investigation. They told you a little, and you told them a little and everybody was happy.

"Men," said the woman. "At night." She looked meaningfully at Marta over the top of her glasses just to make sure she got the meaning of that. Marta sighed. Men, right. This was the kind of woman who would automatically call any dyke with a short haircut 'Sir.'

"I wish I'd stopped her that evening," the landlady continued, as she rummaged for the spare keys. "Maybe..." again she trailed off.

"You saw her?" Marta asked.

"A couple of times, late that night. She went in and out, and in and back out again. Must have decided to change her coat. Slammed the door. That was what made me look. Wasn't like her to be going out so late." She threw her hands up. "Here's her apartment keys, but I can't find a spare for the mailbox. I'm not sure I have it."

Polly's little apartment stank with a heavy air of abandonment. Marta stood aimlessly in the doorway for a moment before moving inside. What was it she was looking for? She had no idea.

There was something a little askew about the room. The police had been here, Marta realized. Looking for what? They had Polly, they had the knife, they had the letters. Maybe a diary? Maybe signs of the drug they thought Polly had given Lexy and Karen? Maybe nothing, maybe just another step of a job well done. Maybe she was wasting her time as well.

The feel of abandonment was giving her a little shiver. She reached over and turned on the radio for company. It was turned to a classical station, which was strange, for she remembered Polly turning down her invitation to Mary Clare's concert. Was this the clue for which she was looking? True, it was not something she could pick up and carry into the police, but was it the first sign she was right? Had there really been someone there with Polly after she had left her that last night—someone who had turned the radio to play classical music? Or had one of the cops liked Bach?

She sat heavily down in the one straight-backed chair—Polly must move it into the bathroom when she unfolded the futon—and tried to think. What was it she hoped to accomplish by being here? Already, she could feel the depression she had been fighting all day puddling up around her. The apartment was not a happy place. It was the place of a woman who had been too long alone, fighting demons no one else could see. Marta looked at Polly's artwork on the wall, remembering how she had turned away from their pain the week before. Like the first, the second was a collage. It had for a background an amateur but still recognizable charcoal sketch of Polly's father. In the foreground was a paper doll of a little girl with pigtails, dressed in sensible little girl panties and undershirt. A nail had been driven between her legs to hold her to the picture of the man. Over in the corner was a Xerox of the locket that had belonged to Nancy Kate. It was repeated over and over—locket upon locket threatened to crowd out of the corner and overwhelm the other images. Marta sat down again. It was all very interesting from a psychological point of view—hell, she had read dissertations done on less—but in the end, was there anything beyond occupational therapy?

She sighed again. There was nothing for her here. She was grabbing at straws. She did not know what to look for, and if she lingered much longer without a goal she was afraid the whole atmosphere of despair would bring back her own depression, and this she could not afford.

The kitchen was a little L off the main room, and she decided that she would get herself a glass of water before she left.

She recoiled as she walked around the corner. Jesus, what a smell! Polly's sink looked just as it had the night she had come inside—only now, nearly two weeks later, all the little orts of food that had been stuck to the plates and backed up in the stopper had begun to rot. A good time to get out.

She had her hand on the knob before she stopped, ashamed, remembering how Mary Clare had hired the girl to scrub her cupboards and vacuum her floor. If Polly was released, what kind of homecoming would it be to return to that smell? And if she wasn't…well, Marta decided not to think along those lines.

There was dish soap. It was the cheap kind from the flea market, the kind that never quite sudsed and left a slick scum if you didn't rinse well. Marta looked at the scummy, slimly water in which the dishes were soaking and shuddered. This, she thought, called for a change in music and maybe the Diet Pepsi she had carried over in her coat pocket. She flicked the knob on the radio, and tuned right into the middle of Tanya Tucker on KYGO, putting on her walking shoes. She used a pair of tongs to pull the plug in the sink—the water rushed down the drain with a sickening slurp that left her with a basket full of rotted food. Turning her head, and breathing through her mouth, she searched for the garbage. Under the sink, a cardboard box lined with a white plastic bag, both from King Soopers. Had the police sorted through the scraps and ends? She doubted it. She bent to pick up the box, and when she pulled her head back she hit it sharply on the shelf above the sink. At almost the same time, she heard a key scraping in the door.

For a moment, she did not move. Things became confused in her head—perhaps it was the blow—and for an instant she thought she was back in her own apartment, and it was the Big Dog, out of his grave, searching for her sweet cats. So she did not do any of the things you are supposed to do to show a burglar you are not prey. She did not raise her voice and shout before he ever got the door open, to convince him to try another place today. She did not look for another exit. She just stood there as if frozen in place, expecting the door to open upon the scarred face and shaved head.

"Hi!" The man at the door was obviously as surprised as she—she got the idea it was only at the last moment he had been able to substitute the greeting for "Shit!" or "Damn!"

"Hi!…" What was he doing here? "…Jim." Because there had been such a space between the two words that they had seemed unrelated, Marta tried again. "Hi, Jim." She felt compelled to explain her presence. The drainer was still in her hand. "I was just cleaning up Polly's kitchen—I don't want her to get salmonella when she comes home." It sounded lame. But, on the other hand, why did she need an excuse at all? Polly had given her permission to come. What was he doing here himself?

"Oh," he said. "I came to pick up Polly's mail." Indeed, he was carrying a handful of envelopes. Most looked like bills or offers for discounts on carpet cleaning or car tune-ups. He walked past her and into the kitchen. "Why are you bothering?" he asked. "Polly's screwed—she's not going to be coming back here. She can't keep up the rent from prison." He had seemed friendly at his own house—now he was curt. Maybe he thought he had spilled too much personal shit. Some guys were like that—they punished you if they said anything personal. Or maybe this was the real Jim, and it had been the facade that had set her on edge at his mother's. Either way, the very words irritated Marta. She could not help but think again of her own brothers whom she knew would never talk about her with that air of resignation. Polly was lucky that her own family could not be on the jury.

"Well," she said, trying to make the words sound as if they were not coming through gritted teeth, "even if that's true, somebody's going to have to come in here and deal with things eventually. You or your mom— you're going to have to pack things up."

Jim snorted. "The landlady can do that at the end of the month. She can box it up or throw it out. Do you think that I want something like *that* at my house?" He pointed to the collages.

Marta had thought the same thing herself, but it sounded much harsher coming from Jim. She wanted to smack him. She tried to hide her feelings by turning away and starting the dishes.

"Well," he said. "I'm starving." He brushed past Marta in the small space, leaving her with an unpleasant tingle, and opened the door of the avocado colored refrigerator. From the freezer he pulled a pizza carry-out box. He removed a slice and stuck it into the built-in microwave. "No napkins, I suppose? Paper towels? No? Ah, that's our Polly, living the good life." He twisted the dial, and the oven began to hum. He walked past Marta again and into the other room.

Marta felt a huge anger rising in her chest—the kind of anger that goes beyond the actual incident, the kind of anger that, when you explain later to your friends the reason you went off on a screaming rampage they say, "And?" as if you surely must have left out some key piece of information. She could not have broken down what it was that was tripping her trigger. If pressed to explain, the best she could have done would have been to rave about women being thrown away. This was so clearly the attitude of Polly's brother—as Polly herself had mimed for them at the prison—'Poor Pol, so fucked up.' Innocence had never entered this man's head; the best he had in the way of loyalty seemed to be to say, well, of course she did it, but it wasn't her fault.

The sink was full of clean water, the disgusting dishes now stacked neatly by the side. Marta picked up the garbage box. Taking it out to the dumpster would give her a little time to cool off. She walked back through the other room and opened the door to the hall, then put down the box while she shrugged on her coat.

"Where are you going?" Jim asked sharply, and his very tone pissed her off again.

"I'm going to go talk to Polly's lawyer," she said, because it was the only thing she could think to say that carried a tone of rebuke without coming right out and calling him a pig. "*I* think she's innocent. I'm going to prove it. How did she get over there that night? Somebody took her—there was somebody here. And I'm going to take her artwork home with me and save it for her." Smoke that, you asshole. She looked over at the wall as she spoke, and noticed that there was an empty space in the middle of the first collage. One of the photos had fallen—no, been torn, she could see the scraps around the nails—down. She gave Jim a disgusted look. Polly was in jail, and he was worried about an unflattering photo. What an asshole. She opened the door to the hall and left without another word. Polly's keys were in her pocket.

The dumpster was out back and around the side, so that, though she had gone down the hall to the door, she actually ended up right outside Polly's window. The shades were drawn, but through the closed windows she could hear the tail end of the Trisha Yearwood song that had been playing as she stormed out. She had not bothered zipping her coat, and it was chilly, but nothing like it had been two days before. The weather was obviously getting ready to do the Denver Thing—after the debilitating snowstorm they would now have a few days of balmy weather that would melt the snow down into a dreadful ice pack and delude the natives into thinking spring was on the way. Then, another blizzard. The flea market was going to be packed this weekend.

The heavy metal lid of the dumpster was closed, and she had to put down the box and step on a wheel in order to hoist it open with both hands. There was a cement ramp leading up the side so that residents who weren't quite so tall or strong could get an edge. There was a security light directly over the dumpster, and as Marta shoved up the top, she had rather too good a view of last night's leftovers and last week's newspapers, which set her off on another inner tirade. She *recycled*. She couldn't even afford to get the newspaper every day, but she got the Sunday edition for the TV guide, and she recycled it faithfully, along with her glass and plastic shampoo bottles. What was wrong with these people— had the whole world gone mad? She jumped down off of the dumpster, almost turning an ankle, and picked up the box. She glanced inside it.

You can tell a lot about people from their trash. Everybody knows that. Archaeologists have built a science on it. One of the richest places to start an excavation is a midden. Detectives can find divorce material in your garbage, and cops can estimate your last meal.

What Polly's trash showed Marta was mostly something she already knew—that Polly was living close to the bone. The first evidence, of course, was the fact she was using a box for her garbage, instead of a plastic barrel costing five dollars. Then there were the things that were not in the box—no individual containers for juice or soda or apple sauce or cheese or yogurt—all those little modern conveniences in which single people with paying jobs can indulge. There had been one plastic cottage cheese container, but it was a large one, and it was sitting in the sink waiting to be washed out and reused. Mary Clare called those kind of containers Lesbian Tupperware.

What was in Polly's trash were a couple of generic wrappers. Ramen noodles, and beans and rice, and a lot of tissues. She didn't blame the police for not bagging and labeling. She grabbed the two handles on the bag and picked it up.

Again, the smell was what hit her and again she thought at first it was just something bad in the dumpster. Not until she realized she was graying out, sinking to her knees did she know the smell for what it was— the foretaste of something much worse. Pictures were spinning through her head on fast-forward—she could not identify the people or the place. Then suddenly, with a jerk, one frame separated itself in her mind and showed itself in all its ugliness. Nancy Kate. She had never had a face before, but now that part of her was filled in from the leaflet and Marta was able to look full upon her as she lay on the ground with her head turned to the side. She looked older than twelve. She had developed early, Polly's mother had said.

She didn't look as if she were sleeping. She was dead, and she looked dead. And if there had been any hope at all in Marta's mind, the dirt that lay across her chest and arms was enough to crush it. She lay within a hole that was boxed on four sides by wood—a concrete pouring form. To the'

184

right of her was a slab of cement that had already been poured and hardened, and in the corner of that slab was a hand print....

Marta came to with a start. Old building on a not-so-great street, smell of trash in the dumpster—she must have dropped the bag. Thank God. What the hell had set that off? Something Nancy Kate owned in the trash? No, Nancy Kate couldn't have seen anything she had seen. Something belonging to Polly's father? Gingerly, without touching the bag, she tipped the box over on its side. She picked up a stick to sort through it. Tissues, wrappers, nothing out of the ordinary.

Using the stick, she picked up the bag. As she lifted it, she noticed that there was something stuck to the bottom. Another tissue? She lifted the bag towards the light.

It was a condom. Used. Marta reached her hand towards it, and then drew it out again without touching anything. Watching *Hill Street Blues* had taught her that much. She had been right! She had been right all along! Polly's father had been there the night of the murder! He had fucked her and set her up. Marta didn't care what his alibi was! He'd gotten one woman to lie for him—why not two?

She needed to find a phone. She needed to call Liz. G-hey!'s phone was probably just as good as any—she doubted if Liz would be able to put any wheels into motion until morning. But Liz would know what buttons to push.

But what if the condom wasn't good enough? What if sperm was like milk—it went bad after a couple of days—and this was beyond the limit for testing? Or, said a cynical little voice inside, what if Polly has a street life she doesn't remember? What if she hooks on the side and has no clue? Or, worse than all of those, what if it was Daddy's sperm, and the police just didn't care? Who was going to arrest a man for having sex with his adult, apparently consenting daughter when they were thinking about a murder?

Tell me where the body is, Liz had said. Get me some evidence! What was she going to say when Marta called to offer her a used condom and a boatload of theories? Tell me where the body is!

She turned from the dumpster, still holding the bag on the stick. Oh, God. And I cleaned out the sink. Did I flush anything down the drain? And there was that damn Jim inside, destroying more evidence. He had changed Marta's radio station without so much as a by-your-leave. The piece now playing was something light and classical she recognized—by sound only, not by name or composer—from Mary Clare's winter concert. For a moment an old memory threatened to intrude—the feeling of leaning against Teri's arm as they sat in the pew of the church where the concert had been held, feeling nothing but contentment. The terrible aloneness and abandonment she had been feeling for half a year threatened to rise in her throat, like breakfast the first day back to work after the flu. For the first time in six months, she clenched her teeth and held it down. It could not be the most important thing now. *It could not.*

She looked around her. There was no one else on the street. It was cold, and they weren't near Colfax, two factors that cut way down on street people. Prowlers and the skinheads both lost some of their zeal when they had to put on mittens and a hat. This wasn't smart—she should wait until she was locked inside her own apartment. But she couldn't bring herself to wait. Not this close. Hesitantly, she reached out her hand to touch the condom.

Pictures too fast again. Dark, but lights from the city, from the neighbors in the background. Not the country. Nancy Kate, bruises around her neck, buried to the waist and then another shovelful of dirt landing plop on her face, right on the eye that was still open and that just didn't seem right…He had known her since she was a little girl and wouldn't ever have thought of her the way he thought of his sister if it hadn't been for Dad. She had been packed in dry ice, but that hadn't been enough. There were places the flies were crawling and there was the goddamn dog…go away…Sissy pulling on Nancy Kate's hand like she could get her to play…why had he done this…Wasn't Polly enough?…that he had to go and do this…Go away…Sissy pulling on something that glittered and then snapped in the light…It was too hard to see and Dad was saying, "Don't just stand there…Do you think I'm the only one who'll go to jail?…You're in it now and it just isn't worth it for a little piece of trash like this…

Marta vomited. She could not help herself. Over and over she retched, bringing up her dinner and lunch as well. The missing picture from the collage floated across her mind. The patio. The dog run. He had put them in at the same time. Oh, god, and he'd brought his son into it. And what had she done? She had just bragged to him that she had found evidence; she had let him know that she was going to look again at the artwork which pointed so clearly in the right direction that he had hurriedly removed a photo—Daddy and Polly and Jim by the patio—while she was in the kitchen.

She had dropped the bag down between the dumpster and the ramp. She would retrieve it as soon as she stopped throwing up. Was she done yet? No, better yet she would get the hell out of here and come back with the cavalry, because what if he didn't realize she was bluffing and came after her? She thought she really was done now, and put one hand on the side of the building to pull herself up.

And looked up into his eyes.

He hit her when she was only halfway to her feet.

The very first thing she thought, as she was crumpling to her knees, and then down flat on her face, was, "I didn't know Polly played softball." But Polly must play softball, because he had hit her with a bat, and he had come from Polly's apartment. Polly didn't look like much of a softball player. What position did she play? What had DJ thought about her playing? Or had she just given up on the game while they were together—another way of being isolated and dependent? There seemed a whole myriad of questions concerning Polly and softball that could serve to occupy her—could keep her from thinking about the fact that Polly's brother had hit her with a bat, he was hitting her again and again. The last thing in her mind before she blacked out was to wonder, so intensely she may even have said the words aloud, whether Polly would be interested in playing on the over-thirty team with them this year.

***

Mary Clare was itchy. No, that wasn't right. It was not Mary Clare who could not settle down to a book or the TV, who was getting up every few minutes to take care of non-existent needs or simply pace. It was Caroleve, but her restlessness was rubbing off on Mary Clare. She had meant to devote this evening to practice, but she had not been able to play all the way through even one piece.

"What is the problem?" she asked Caroleve finally, crossly, as she put down her bow. The apartment was not big—there was not room for both her and her cello in the bedroom, and they had a concert next week. "Can't you sit down?"

"Yeah, sure," said Caroleve, and then was up again the next minute, peering out the window. "Marta got a phone?" she asked, though she knew she didn't. "Maybe you could call her, see what she's doing?"

This situation must change, thought Mary Clare grimly. She didn't need a teen-age roommate at her age—and a non-paying one at that. Another week—that was it. By then Caroleve's paycheck from Taco Bell should arrive—she had been working two days now—and surely it would be enough to put some money down for an apartment. She did a quick calculation in her head. Yeah—not enough for anything big, but a studio. Mary Clare had lived in studios herself for years, and Caroleve could eat at work until the next check came in. Or, she could go back to the skin-heads. At the moment Mary Clare did not care which.

"No," she answered the question shortly, "Marta doesn't have a phone. Why don't you take a walk?"

"Yeah, sure," said Caroleve, but she did not look around for Teri's jacket. "Didn't her friend have a phone? You could call her?"

Mary Clare shrugged and picked up her phone, which had accompanied her on every move since she had fled to Denver. It was so old it still had a rotary dial that made a little chinking noise as it spun itself back into place.

"Anything special you want me to say to her?" she asked politely as G-hey!'s phone began to ring. Caroleve shrugged.

But G-hey! was not home, and the phone rang and rang. Now Mary Clare was antsy as well.

"Why did you want to talk to Marta?" she asked, thinking to herself there could be a million reasons G-hey! had not answered the phone, and Marta was probably just sitting in the dark watching TV. So why did she now feel so damn on edge herself?

Caroleve shrugged. "I dunno. You think she killed Billy on purpose?"

Mary Clare was not ready for this sudden switch of topics. This time she shrugged.

"She thinks she did," said Caroleve. "You think she's at home?"

Mary Clare stood up. "Let's go see."

TWENTY-THREE

Later, in the retelling, Marta would say the first thing she was aware of upon regaining consciousness was the terrible pounding in her head. This was not true. The first thing she was really aware of was the smell, the feel of rotten things around her face. For one terrible moment she panicked, remembering the smell that had preceded her vision of Nancy Kate. Was she, too, lying in an open grave dug by one of Polly's relatives? Would a shovelful of dirt be thrown down upon her face at any moment? It would be a joke—wouldn't it—if Jim had taken her back to his father's house, if he was planning on sealing her into the hole the coroner had opened? He could even repour the dog run—a solicitous act from a supportive son—he and his folks would need to pull together now that crazy Polly was in jail.

For a moment Marta panicked, screaming and clawing against the loose earth beneath her. Then she realized she was not lying in the ground, but upon a mound of garbage—rotten food and empty bags and newspapers and clumping cat litter and an old foam pad. She was not in a grave—she was in the dumpster.

This was also when she realized she was not really conscious. At least, not in the sense she usually thought of the word. Her mind seemed to be working, but in an airy, disjointed way. She remembered her thoughts about Polly and softball, and for a moment was almost swept away by them again, for they seemed just as important as figuring how she was going to get out of the dumpster.

But, what clued her into her limitations, more than the erratic working of her thoughts, was the fact that, though she had thought she was screaming and clawing, in reality nothing had happened. It had been like one of those early morning dreams—the kind where you dream you're up, you've done the shower, the clothes, the carton of yogurt, only to be blasted by the alarm again as you're walking down the dream stairs to catch the bus. She knew where she was, she knew what had happened, but she seemed to have no control over her voice or body. She could not even turn her head so her face was not lying in one of Polly's neighbors table scraps. Fish.

With one eye—the other was down in the trash—she stared up at the light over the dumpster. She had been right. She had been right all along, and the only thing she had missed was which man. She should have clued in when Jim got the pizza out of the freezer. Both the freezer and refrigerator had been bare the night she had come home with Polly—she remembered that all too clearly. Polly had no money—she couldn't have ordered out after Marta left, even if her mouth had not been hurting her. The only way Jim could have known to look in the freezer so confidently was if he had brought the food in himself. That explained the neighbor who had heard the door slam, and then seen Polly go in and out several times. Polly and Jim looked a great deal alike—bundled up for the cold and through a window the neighbor had mistaken two people going outside for one person going out several times. Jim had come over again…Marta's heart turned away from the thought. Yet wasn't this exactly what Polly's artwork had been trying to tell her?

She drifted here for a moment, wondering how Jim had gotten her into the dumpster. Lucky for him there was a ramp. With an effort, she recalled herself to the problem. The answer was so obvious! What had Polly's father done before Polly? He had molested his first child. Both Marta and Polly had taken Jim's word this had not happened, that his jealousy and tormenting had only been a normal reaction—the big brother against the baby, the favorite. But it had been more than that. Of course Jim was jealous—Jim was jealous of Polly the same way Polly had been jealous of her father's receptionist, the same way any favorite is jealous when suddenly replaced by someone younger and prettier. Up until Polly came along, there had been camping trips and outings and presents. The twisted secret they had hidden had been no different for Jim than Polly. "It would have been better," Polly had said, "if he had been brutal. Then I would have known I was the victim." She had finally realized it. But had her brother? Did he ever know that the reason he hated Polly was because she had replaced him as Daddy's lover?

He had Polly's keys. Polly hadn't even known where her own keys were—they had not taken them off her at the prison. She had told Marta to ask the landlady about the mailbox. But the key-ring Jim had held in his hand had Polly's mailbox key on it. He did not have a duplicate set. He had Polly's original set.

What becomes of the children victimized by incest? They become angry like Mary Clare. They become crippled like Polly. They become protective of their own children, or they become crusaders. Or, thought Marta, did they sometimes become incesters as well? Did some of them react like battered children, growing up to beat their own sons and daughters? Had Jim taken out his vengeance on Polly's body? She had never mentioned it, but Polly *didn't remember everything.* Could it be that both her brother and her father had incested her, but she had only yet remembered the one? Why not? Marta remembered her describing the zombie-like state she went into when she was sexual—hell, she had seen it herself! She had left Polly's house and Jim had come afterward, knowing she would be taking a pain killer and that it would knock her out. He brings a pizza, and turns on the classical music to wait. He touches her. She disassociates. He rapes her, using a condom to cover up the evidence. The KY Jelly? Maybe a touch he had learned from Daddy. Or maybe he liked to fuck with her head that much, liked knowing the next day she was wondering what had happened.

The scenario rushed ahead in Marta's mind like a movie shot by Tarantino—all jumbled together and out of sequence so that suddenly, in the middle of it all, Marta saw the first collage that she had looked at on Polly's wall. Jim and Dad fishing. Jim and Dad laying the new patio. *Jim and Dad laying the new patio.* That was it, that was where the body was! The hand prints—she had seen them in the photo! Just as suddenly, her mind shifted back to the main plot. Lexy on the phone. Lexy had said Polly sounded funny, but Marta had put it down to the fact they were both drugged. But that was not it at all. Jim had answered the phone and talked to the little girl. His speech pattern was remarkably similar to Polly's, his voice in the high range for a man. Up to this point it might have just been for a fuck. Marta suppressed a shudder. Who knows how long he had been playing this little game? Polly fought against her memories, not realizing she lost a night whenever her brother came over, kindly bringing her a pizza because she was too poor to go out.

But the phone had rung, and Lexy had blurted out what she had done. Had there been any compassion in the man at that point? Had he driven Polly over to DJ's with the hope of saving Lexy and Karen's life? Or had he begun planning the moment he hung up the phone? A good way to get back at Polly, a good way to get back at Daddy. Again.

Marta felt a wave of illness that cut through the pain. Karen had not even been a victim of jealousy—she had merely been a pawn, picked randomly except for the phone call. She could have wept for the sense-lessness of it all. Except there was no time to weep—her mind—suddenly free of all distraction—was brusquely sweeping her forward to complete the movie. Jim driving to DJ's house, Polly beside him like a big blow up doll with a key in her hand. Had he planned it in the car? Or had he just seized the moment—the knife, his rival, and the drugged woman he did not know?

He didn't know Lexy had managed to make a second phone call—this one to 911. How surprised he must have been to hear the sirens! Had he slipped out the back door? Or, even worse, stayed hidden in the house, pumped with excitement as he listened to Polly's arrest? The police had probably not done much of a search, not after finding Polly with the murder weapon. Why had he taken Polly's keys? And why had he come tonight?

Because Polly had told him what Marta was planning on doing. Of course, she had said he was coming. And when she told him, he remembered he had left the condom. No doubt, if this was a regular thing, he usually took them with him—he would not want to raise Polly's suspicions. But something in the routine of that night had thrown him off. And what had Marta done? Bragged to him that she was going to solve the case, told him her theories. Everything but name him.

So that was that. For a long moment it seemed to Marta that now that she had solved the puzzle, she could rest. It was over and done with—like some brain teaser that mattered only to her. She could close her one eye and settle down into the garbage and go to sleep. The mystery was solved.

But there was a little part of her, small and nagging, like Mary Clare talking to her about exercising or antidepressants, that would not allow this. You're in a dumpster, it said to her sternly, and when she tried to make it go away by saying, inside her head, that someone was sure to find her in the morning, bringing their trash out on the way to work, it became even more stern. You'll be dead by morning, was what it said.

Which, though it was indeed stern—did not seem, really, like much of an incentive. Maybe it was the blows to the head, or maybe it was just that she had hovered so near to death for so long that it no longer seemed like a threat, but an invitation. She had always heard dying from exposure was not really bad, that it was much like just lying down and going to sleep after a long, weary day. It even seemed fitting she be lying there amidst the garbage, after her conversation with Lexy. At least in the landfill she would turn back into dust—she wouldn't be around to haunt future generations like plastic six packs. She closed her eyes again, embracing the darkness. But there, again, was that one nagging little voice, and this time it did not bother with words or reasoning or anything civilized. This time it showed a picture in her head, and the picture was of the dumpster out in back of the skinhead's apartment building, filled with flames that lit up the sky.

Again she panicked, and screamed and shot to her feet and grabbed the side of the dumpster and vaulted over, and again it took place only in her mind. When she shook loose the wave, she was lying in the same position, face down. There was only one difference. The fingers of her right hand were moving. Really moving—not just dreaming they were moving.

Tentatively she made them into a fist, and that one controlled gesture jerked her back into a whole new level of consciousness. Now she could feel—along with the horrible pain in her head, her arm, her back the cold. She could hear the music playing inside the apartment—"Water Suite."

And she knew two things concretely. One was that the nagging voice was absolutely right—Jim had gone only for gasoline or lighter fluid. The story of the dumpster had been written up in the paper, as had the story of Marta and Billy the Big Dog. The police would assume his friends had torched her. Jim would go free, Polly would go to jail, and Marta would be dead.

The other thing she knew for certain was that she did not want to die this way.

* * *

When they got over to Marta's place, and Mary Clare began struggling with the new deadbolt on the back door, G-hey! jumped out of her parked car and came over to join her.

"It's about time somebody got here," she groused, tucking in her shirt. "My new key won't work, and we've been locked out for an hour." She didn't actually seem too upset—it was evident she and Salad had been using the time for a make-out session, though it was getting so cold Mary Clare wondered how they'd kept their mind on task. Obviously G-hey! must have rung Marta's bell—just as obviously Marta was not home. Just the same, Mary Clare went up the stairs, Caroleve following her, and struggled with that new deadbolt as well. So where was Marta, on foot, at this time of night? It had been so long since she had been anywhere but home in front of her TV that Mary Clare could not even begin to think where to look.

The cats had all been asleep in a heap on the couch, but the moment Caroleve entered the apartment they all jumped up as if they were one entity and began screaming at her. Even Closet-Kitty did not run for cover, but stood back a safe distance and meowed piercingly, while Gravy and Baloney got right up and slammed their heads into Caroleve's shins.

"What's going on?" asked Mary Clare. She had never seen the cats—or any cats—act this way before.

"Is Marta here?" Caroleve asked, although it was obvious Marta was not there. She seemed just as agitated as the cats, and before Mary Clare could even respond she asked again, "Is Marta here?"

"What's wrong with you?" Mary Clare shouted over the noise of the cats. She pulled Caroleve by the arm back through the door and out onto the landing. Halfway down the stairs the cats screaming abruptly ceased. "What's wrong with you?" she asked Caroleve again.

"My head." Caroleve held her hands over her ears as if she were trying to drown something out. "It hurts there's noise in it I can't stop thinking about Marta is she here I think I'm going to puke." The words were all run together like one big sentence. She stumbled down the stairs. Mary Clare stayed where she was. What was going on, and where was Marta? Wherever she was, she was in trouble.

193

Mary Clare had not one single touch of the sporadic gift Marta called "the shine." She could not pick up anything from Marta, even if it was piggybacked by pain or fear. This had been proved time and time again. Sometimes Marta had been pissed when she hadn't known she was needed in an emergency, as if Mary Clare were behaving like a stubborn child.

But what about Caroleve? Did she also have a touch of the shine? Was it possible what was filling Caroleve's head was something meant to be sent to Mary Clare? And where was Marta? She was on foot, it was cold, she hadn't been out of her apartment, except to go to work, for months. Where was she? Frantically Mary Clare cast back in her mind.

And remembered the ride home from the jail, when Marta had talked about Polly's keys.

Caroleve was bent over in the yard, retching, but not bringing anything up. Mary Clare caught her by the sleeve as she dashed across the yard, and propelled her roughly into the passenger side of the truck. She did not bother to talk. They must not be too late.

***

There was nothing Marta could do. She could not move or cry out because of the way he had beaten her. She could not climb out of the dumpster herself. She could not even stand. She was not enough of a psychic that she could project a holographic image into one of the apartments not more than twenty feet away, the way that people in *Time/Life* books could. She only had enough of the shine to be able to answer the phone before the first ring, and that was a party trick. She thought again of Mary Clare, calling to her inside her mind, but she knew that, too, was useless.

Her hand had been moving back and forth, without any direction at all from her mind, over the garbage and her own body. Now it had found something cold and hard. Oh, it was the can of Diet Pepsi she had put in the pocket of her coat before going out to brave the world. She worked it out of her pocket, because when you are going to be burnt to death within the next five or ten minutes, one mindless task is just as good as another. She looked up again at the light. If she could throw, she could knock the light out. She had, for over twenty years, been a shortstop of some prowess—she could knock that sucker right down with the can on the first try. Then, maybe when Jim came back, he wouldn't be able to see her. He might think she had escaped or been rescued. He might not, then, set the fire.

It was not a great plan. It depended on a great many ifs. It also depended on her being able to pitch a can straight up in the air while lying flat on her face. She might as well count on Wonder Woman or Karen's ghost.

She stared up again at the light. It was not one of those heavy bulbs that are made for outside sockets. It must have been replaced recently, probably by a tenant who had pulled a bulb out of her own reading lamp, not realizing you couldn't just do that with an uncovered outside light. The minute it began to snow or rain again that sucker was going to crack.

Marta and her brothers had, one boring summer, gone through a stage of cracking all the exposed bulbs in their house by shooting them with water pistols. She could not remember the rest of the rules to this game. It had not lasted long at any rate. Her mother had discovered them in the act, and there had been hell to pay.

Now Marta found that her hand was shaking up the can of soda, as if it had some plan of its own. What could it be? Without thought she shook the soda back and forth, up and down, with the same vigor she used to put into setting a trap for one of her brothers. Shake up the can right before the ball game ended and everyone came running in for drinks, put it in the front of the fridge and step back to watch the fireworks. It didn't matter which one you got—everybody laughed every time and they all got in trouble and had to scrub the walls.

Now her hand was propping the can up beside her. Now popping the top. The soda sprayed up. She grabbed the can and held it aloft. The soda shot straight into the air. She watched it land on the bulb in huge spurts and gobs.

And then it popped.

Nothing huge or explosive. Just a soft little pop, and suddenly she was plunged into total darkness.

It seemed that surely now she would be allowed to sink back into unconsciousness, but her hand was still scrabbling about in the trash. She realized it was trying to pull something over her, to cover her. The thing it had chosen was the foam pad. With a tremendous effort she tried to direct her mind to help in this process. She was not sure why, but her hand had been right so far, and she certainly was not about to buck it now. It was the last thing she remembered before drifting back into unconsciousness.

She was brought back from a dream in which Karen and Polly and the Big Dog and even her dead cousin Joey had all made cameo appearances, by the sound of a man swearing. She was almost afraid to open her one eye for fear the moonlight would glitter off it and give it away, but finally she cracked it just the tiniest bit. A man stood silhouetted above her, only a slightly darker splotch against the dark sky. She could only see a bit of him, because of the pad she had pulled over her head. By his string of curses, she could tell that he could not see her at all. She lay motionless, hardly breathing, as he stared down into the pit, cursing softly, calling her names she had never before heard off the freeway.

"Go away," she thought, and then, carefully, she thought nothing, just in case he had a little of the shine, too, and the very feel of her desperation might give her away. Instead she thought of Mary Clare, and G-hey! and the trip the three of them had taken down to New Mexico in the days before Teri and Salad. She was not here at all.

There was a strange, spraying sound, and her heart sank. He was going to torch it after all; he was going to chance she was still lying down in the bottom, that the light was just a fluke. She thought of all the lesbians who had been burned as witches, back when the religious right still torched queers outright instead of trying to fence them in with the law. She'd read that most of them were killed by the smoke—you were unconscious by the time the flames started eating away at you. She supposed it wouldn't work that way with gasoline—she would be melted down by the flames while she was still alive and conscious.

She wanted to cry, but something, some little part of her that believed rescue was still possible, kept her quiet. If she wept, he would know for certain she was there. Still, one tear ran down her cheek.

There was a huge thump, followed by a great pain in her arm, and she realized he had jumped down into the dumpster to see if she was still there, one foot landing on her lifeless arm. She did not even twitch—perhaps he would think she was a bundle of last week's magazines. More cursing—then a tiny light. He had flicked on his lighter, holding it high above his head and away from the fluid.

"You stupid bitch," he said in a contemptuous tone, nudging her face with his foot. "You stupid, stupid bitch."

If he had just not done this last thing, she might have lain there, pretending to be already dead. In a way, she was ready to die. She had done what she could—she had fought the good fight and given it her all, and she was tired. But that one last remark moved her to anger beyond words. Perhaps she had been stupid to not realize he was the one. Perhaps she had been stupid to turn her back and allow him to hit her with a Louisville Slugger. But how dare, how dare he be contemptuous of her effort to save herself!

She did not think. Her one good hand shot out and grasped him by the ankle.

She did not expect his scream, and it was gratifying. It would, she supposed, be startling to have a corpse suddenly reach up out of her grave and lay her hand upon you, even if you were not a man with a tenuous grip on sanity. For the first time, it occurred to her that, as well as setting Polly up for the murder of Karen, he had also been the one who had exposed the old murder of Nancy Kate. She had thought the letter had been retyped to cover something up, but really, he had retyped it to contain just enough hints. He had known what his father had done. He had helped as his father had shoveled the dirt over the body of Nancy Kate. Had his father even taken him along on that dreadful trip? Another little secret between the boys?

She might never know. He was screaming horribly, kicking frantically at her head as if she were something out of *The Night of the Living Dead*, just a step away from pulling him down and having a snack. She hadn't realized she had such strength in that one good arm, and she held on grimly.

Then he dropped the lighter.

There was a sudden flash. She supposed the whole bin was lit up and, if she had opened her eyes, she might have been able to read the headlines on the papers which should have been recycled. She closed them instead, praying to a god in whom she had not believed for years, for a quick death while holding onto Jim's ankle like the grim reaper himself. If she was going to go, so was he.

There was a horrible screeching sound that seemed to come from quite close to her head, although it was hard to tell, screened as it was through the throbbing and Jim's screams. The screeching was followed by a crash that rocked the dumpster. Or maybe not. By this time it was possible, Marta thought, that she was hallucinating. Like Joan of Arc, perhaps she would see angels coming to take her home. That would not be a bad way to go. It seemed totally reasonable that her particular angel would have the voice of Mary Clare, although it would have been nice if Mary Clare was not screaming. It also, she thought looking up through the flames, would have been nice if Mary Clare had thought to don some kind of outfit a little more suitable to an angel. Instead, there she was, teetering on the edge of the dumpster in that butt-ugly rust colored jacket she had gotten from the flea market. Marta felt a little offended, the way you might feel if your prom date had not bothered to change out of her mechanic's overalls.

As if to add insult to injury, Mary Clare was not beckoning her gently to the side of Jesus—Marta had been a determined agnostic for years, but she always back-slid in an automatic way in dangerous situations—but was screaming down into the dumpster in a horrible and harsh voice. Not just Marta's name, but a string of profanity that rivaled anything Jim had come out with earlier. Mary Clare, decided Marta, for all her good qualities on earth, made a damn poor angel. Marta shut her eyes, hoping to call up a more peaceful vision, and so she missed the sight of Mary Clare hoisting her fire extinguisher above her head and letting loose a storm of foam.

TWENTY-FOUR

The food in the hospital was not good, so the first thing that they did after Marta was released from her two day observation—a broken arm, burns, a concussion and bruises for days—was to go out for Chinese food.

"You saved my life," Marta said to Mary Clare, not for the first time.

"Caroleve and those cats saved your life," Mary Clare replied. "Zzzz!" She shook her hand, showing Caroleve vibrating like a wire.

"No," said Marta. "You saved my life," and neither of them needed to say the rest—that it had been Mary Clare who had fed her and clothed her and not given up on her when she had been all but dead to the world, just as neither needed to say that now that time was over.

"Is Jim in jail?" asked Marta, not because she hadn't seen the papers, but because she wanted to hear it again, wanted to know that she was safe.

"Locked up behind bars," replied Mary Clare, helping herself to the lo mein. "Maybe he and Daddy can share a cell. They've got some catching up to do." Marta shuddered, and they talked about the cats, and G-hey! and the art work down at Delafield's.

Then, because Mary Clare wanted to dance, they went to Ms C's. It would not have occurred to Mary Clare that Marta might want to go home and rest, any more than it would have occurred to her that it might be awkward to pick up Polly on the way. Dancing was all—meditation, and healer and renewal of life. Mary Clare might have believed in Jesus if he had two-stepped. And it was only kind to bring along Polly, who had been through hell.

Marta had no intention of dancing, but at least it was a way to keep a distance from Polly. She had no idea what to say to her. How could one even comment on the betrayal she must have felt when she was told how her brother had set her up? Or, perhaps, she had not felt outrage at all. Perhaps she had been betrayed so often by the family who should have protected her that now she felt nothing.

Everyone they knew was at the bar. G-hey! and her girlfriend, Salad, carpooling with the Queer Nation girls who lived in the basement. Louann, bandbox fresh, courting some new honey with whom she was doing a hot talk scene right on the dance floor. Liz, who was wearing leather and dancing with the black dyke cop who had arrested Polly's father. Marta didn't recognize her for a moment—her hair was done in perfect shoulder length cornrows that she must have had pinned up beneath her hat while on duty. Alison Kaine, though Marta looked quickly the other way, seemed to be without her pretty girlfriend. Janie and Renee, who were hanging out with some of Marta's old friends, the ones she had cut off for months. Janie and Renee waved, and the women with them waved, giving big smiles as if Marta had been away in a sanitarium.

Mary Clare didn't even have a chance to check her jacket before someone snatched her onto the floor. Marta left Polly hanging over the cruise rail, watching the couples circle to k.d.lang, and went to get Cokes at the bar. When she got back, Liz was talking to Polly.

"Social services came out and picked up Lexy," Polly said abruptly. Marta did not ask how this had happened, knowing Mary Clare must have made the phone call she should have made.

"Foster home?" she asked Liz.

Liz shrugged. "At least some investigation." They were all three silent, each one thinking about the little girl who had been cast adrift by circumstances that started years before her birth. If Polly's father had treated her as a daughter instead of a lover...if DJ's parents had not abused her...Marta thought suddenly of the bones the police had recovered from beneath the King's patio. A girl of about twelve, with an infant carried almost to term. That was why it had been necessary to kill Nancy Kate. That was why she was going to tell.

Mary Clare surfaced in front of them, and stuck her hand out to Marta. Mary-Chapin Carpenter was singing her new song, the one where she talked about counting her good friends on one hand, and it was bad luck to miss Mary-C.C.

Mary Clare was on a roll—she spun them around and around, gently because of Marta's arm. They passed Alison and the other cop and Mary Clare smiled. The black cop gave Mary Clare a big grin and thumbs up.

"How do you know her?" asked Marta. "How'd you get her to wait for him?" And then suddenly, so obvious she wondered why she was only seeing it now, "She's in your incest survivor's group, isn't she? That's why she was willing to listen!" Mary Clare, who had a nice voice, sang along with Mary-C. and pretended not to hear.

They passed Louann and G-hey!, both in clinches. Then, as they whirled by the mirrored back wall, Marta's heart caught.

"That Teri is such a shitty dancer," said Mary Clare in a pleasant voice, as if commenting on the weather. "Always has been." She covered up Marta's misstep and pulled her close into a back turn. Marta followed automatically, her eyes fixed on Teri, who was not really dancing at all, but bumping and grinding against her new girlfriend as she kissed her. "I hate that shit," said Mary Clare conversationally. "I hated it when she did it with you, and I hate it with this new one—she acts like she's going to piss all over her any minute to mark her territory. You're lucky she didn't tattoo, 'Mine! Mine!' on your forehead."

"Let's go," Marta said, "I want..."

"Marta," Mary Clare, without breaking stride, took her hand off Marta's back and placed it on her face. "That girl is named Mindy. Teri has a new girlfriend, and the girlfriend has a name. Look at that kid's eyes."

"No, let's just..."

"Look at her eyes."

Reluctantly, Marta turned her head. The girlfriend was blonde and tiny and pretty like a Barbie doll—all the things Marta had not been. But her blue eyes, gazing out over Teri's shoulder as Teri kissed her neck—in them Marta read the same feeling of despair, of being trapped, that she had read in Karen's. I love her, but she can be so mean, so cold, I can't do anything right. The same despair Marta herself had felt with Teri between those brief moments of passion.

Mary Clare spun them around to the other side of the floor, while Mary-Chapin Carpenter, as if speaking to Marta alone, sung of the foolishness and futility of standing knee deep in a river, yet dying of thirst.

Another couple brushed their shoulders, and Marta turned to see Liz leading Polly, both paying more attention to their conversation than the music.

"Do you think Liz is interested in Polly?" Mary Clare asked.

"I don't know. Stranger things have happened."

"Speaking of which, how's Caroleve been working out as a substitute?"

"Louann says great. She's good on the housewife line—she still thinks the dykes are too weird to work with. But she's getting better. Now when she blurts out something offensive she usually realizes it ten minutes later." They looked at each other and shrugged. As Mary Clare said, there was no need to ever read fiction—everything happened all by itself.

The song ended, and Mary Clare took Marta by the hand to jostle their way off the floor. Their friends were all standing together in a group, laughing. Louann saw them coming and spoke, and the group opened up to include them. Teri and her girlfriend walked past, close enough to touch, but Marta did not look back over her shoulder.

Kate Allen lives in Denver. She has only recently installed a cat door and is horrified anew each time one of her four cats brings her a bird. When not dealing with dead bodies or removing rocks from her back yard, she visits the Mile High Flea Market and searches for a two-stepping partner. *I Knew You Would Call* is her third mystery with New Victoria Publishers. Her goal in life is one day to be able to quit at least one of her two day jobs with which she supports the expensive hobby of writing.

Other Mysteries From New Victoria

TELL ME WHAT YOU LIKE by Kate Allen—Alison Kaine, lesbian cop, enters the world of leather-dykes after a woman is brutally murdered at a Denver bar. She's fascinated, yet wary of her attraction to one of the suspects, a dominatrix named Stacy. In this fast-paced, yet slyly humorous novel, Allen confronts the sensitive issues of S & M, queer-bashers and women-identified sex workers. $9.95

GIVE MY SECRETS BACK by Kate Allen—Second in the Alison Kaine series. A well known author of steamy lesbian romances has just moved back to Denver when she is found dead in her bathtub, electrocuted by a vibrator. Alison investigates. $9.95

IF LOOKS COULD KILL by Frances Lucas—Diana Mendoza, a Latina lesbian lawyer is a scriptwriter for a hot new TV show featuring a woman detective.While on location in LA she meets blonde actress Lauren Lytch. When Lauren is accused of murdering her husband, Diana rushes to her defense. An entertaining mystery featuring a scriptwriter who finds herself in the middle of a plot she didn't create. $9.95

MURDER IS MATERIAL by Karen Saum—This third in the Brigid Donovan series *(Murder is Relative* and *Murder is Germane)* finds Brigid investigating the fiery death of a self-styled Buddhist guru and the kidnapping of the young woman with whom he lived, searching for clues from Maine to Nova Scotia. There, lured by the seductive Suzanne, she is involved in a tangled web of money, madness and murder. $9.95

NUN IN THE CLOSET by Joanna Michaels—Anne Hollis, the owner of a women's bar is charged with manslaughter in the death of a nun. Insisting she's innocent, Anne appeals to probation officer Callie Sinclair for help. The case grows more complex and puzzling when another nun is murdered, and Callie discovers that sex and money are involved. $9.95

EVERYWHERE HOUSE by Jane Meyerding—The brutal stabbing of a philosophy professor implicates Barb, an angry member of an ultra-radical lesbian collective, the Furies. Terry Barber begins her own investigation, uncovering Barb's secret identity, a sinister religious cult, and growing political and personal struggles within her lesbian collective, Everywhere House. $9.95

THE KALI CONNECTION by Claudia McKay—Lynn, an investigative reporter suspects the connection of a mysterious cult with possible drug trafficking. Her attraction to Marta, a charming and earnest devotee challenges Lynn's skepticism and sparks her desire. Then Marta disappears. Lynn travels to Nepal to find some answers. $9.95

DEATHS OF JOCASTA by J.M. Redmann—What was the body of a woman doing in the basement of the Cort Clinic? Could Dr. Cordelia James really have performed the incompetent abortion that killed her? Micky Knight has to answer these questions before the police and the news media find their own convenient solution. "Knight is witty, irreverent and very sexy." $9.95

DEATH BY THE RIVERSIDE by J.M. Redmann—Detective Micky Knight finds herself slugging through thugs and slogging through swamps in an attempt to expose a dangerous drug ring. The investigation turns personal when her own well-hidden past is exposed. Featuring fabulously sexual, all too fiercely independent lady dick. $9.95

More Fiction from New Victoria

LADY GOD by Lesa Luders—*A courageous and complex first novel about a daughter's relationship with a mother who is terrifying yet loving, destructive yet magical. In prose that is lyrical and haunting,* —Ursula Hegi. Landy flees the ghost of her disturbed mother and the mountains where she grew up. Slowly a friendship develops as out lesbian, Claire, helps Landy untangle her emerging sexuality. $9.95

ICED by Judith Alguire—The world of women's professional ice hockey. The story focuses on Alison Gutherie, now coach of the Toronto Teddies, and her growing interest in the talented but enigmatic former speed skater Molly Gavison. Through her well-drawn sympathetic characters Alguire tells the personal as well as professional stories of these women– their complex emotional relationships off the ice, and the fast-paced excitement of play and rivalry on the ice. $10.95

LESBOMANIA by Jorjet Harper with cartoons by Joan Hilty—Examine the scientific evidence that lesbonauts visited the Earth in prehistoric times. Cruise down the Nile with Ancient Egypt's lesbian Pharaoh, Hatshepsut! Lesbomania takes a humorous look at life within the lesbian community, its subculture, issues that divide us, romance sex, and coming out. $9.95

ALL THE WAYS HOME—Parenting and Children in the Lesbian and Gay Communities—A Collection of Short Fiction Includes well-known authors Beth Brant, Ruthann Robson, Jane Rule, Julie Blackwomon, Jameson Currier, as well as budding young authors writing about the experience of being part of lesbian and gay families. *"This is a powerful, inclusive collection, and oh so very real. We've been waiting a long time for a book like this."* —Irene Zahava
Hard cover $16.95, Paperback $10.95

EVERY WOMAN'S DREAM by Lesléa Newman—Lesbian life and love. As always, Newman brings a sharp yet playful style to these tales of sex, monogamy, fantasies, the future, and the possibility of lesbian motherhood. Who else can write about lesbian life through the story of a travelling sock? She's compassionate with her characters yet doesn't flinch from confronting hard issues faced by communities, gay and straight alike. *"Newman is a remarkable writer, and this collection highlights her ability to create fully realized characters and compelling narrative."* —Bay Area Reporter $9.95

SPARKS MIGHT FLY by Cris Newport—In this romantic first novel, Philippa Martin, a former child prodigy grown into an exceptional concert pianist, discovers that her music and her muse are gone—from her hands and from her heart—driven away by her lover Corinne's unfaithfulness. She returns home in shock and despair no longer able to play. To do so she must come to terms with the truth about her domineering grandfather, her long absent mother, and her tormenting ex-lover, all the while learning to love again in a whole new way. $9.95

FIRES OF AGGAR by Chris Anne Wolfe—Here, rich with action and romance, is the sequel so many readers have been waiting for! In this second epic of the Aggar sci-fi/fantasy series by Chris Anne Wolfe, Gwyn, a swashbuckling Royal Marshall and her bondpack of sandwolves go to aid and protect a Blue Sighted woman, the 'Dracoon' Llinolae, with the help of shadowmates Sparrow and Brit. After a daring rescue, Gwen and Llinolae combine forces to defend Llinolae's city against the brigand Terran clan.... *"genre fiction at its best "*—Women's Library Journal $10.95

SIX MYSTERIES BY SARAH DREHER

BAD COMPANY—a Stoner McTavish Mystery by SARAH DREHER—Stoner McTavish fans have been waiting (none too patiently) for her latest book, the sixth in the series. Stoner and Gwen investigate mysterious accidents, sabotage and menacing notes that threaten members of a feminist theater company. *"Sarah Dreher's endearing creation, Stoner McTavish, is on every list of beloved lesbian detectives."*
hardcover ISBN 0-934678-67-7 $19.95   paper ISBN 0-934678-66-9 $10.95

STONER McTAVISH—The first Stoner mystery introduces us to travel agent Stoner McTavish. On a trip to the Tetons, Stoner meets and falls in love with her dream lover, Gwen, whom she must rescue from danger and almost certain death.
ISBN 0-934678-06-5 $9.95

SOMETHING SHADY—Investigating the mysterious disappearance of a nurse at a suspicious rest home on the coast of Maine, Stoner finds herself trapped in the clutches of the evil psychiatrist Dr. Milicent Tunes. Can Gwen charge to the rescue before it's too late?   ISBN 0-934678-07-3 $8.95

GRAY MAGIC—After telling Gwen's grandmother that they are lovers, Stoner and Gwen go to Arizona to escape the fallout. But a peaceful vacation turns frightening when Stoner finds herself an unwitting combatant in a struggle between the Hopi spirits of Good and Evil.   ISBN 0-934678-11-1 $9.95

A CAPTIVE IN TIME—Stoner finds herself inexplicably transported to a town in Colorado Territory, time 1871. There she encounters Dot, the saloon keeper, Blue Mary, a local witch/healer, and an enigmatic teenage runaway named Billy.
ISBN 0-934678-22-7 $9.95

OTHERWORLD—All your favorite characters—business partner Marylou, eccentric Aunt Hermione, psychiatrist, Edith Kesselbaum, and of course, devoted lover, Gwen, on vacation at Disney World. Marylou is kidnapped and held hostage in an underground tunnel.   ISBN 0-934678-44-8 $10.95

Order From New Victoria.
PO Box 27   Norwich. VT. 05055 0027
1-800 326 5297